# JANE POLLER
# OATH
## OF
# REVENGE

VINCI

BOOKS

## By Jane Poller

Royal Oath

*Oath of Rebellion*
*Oath of Revenge*
*Oath of Redemption*

*For my children—skip the spicy scenes if you read it. Thanks for always brainstorming with me, offering plotting feedback, and being willing to bounce ideas off of. I couldn't ask for better kids, and I'm so proud of the little writers and artists that you're becoming. Keep chasing your dreams and never give up, even when things get difficult. Love you forever.*

Vinci Books

vinci-books.com

Published by Vinci Books Ltd in 2025

1

A CIP catalogue record for this book is available from the British Library.
Paperback ISBN: 9781036708016

## Trigger Warnings

This is an adult fairytale retelling, and definitely not for kids. There's a lot of blood and gore in part of this, along with some trauma from being a prisoner, several bloody fights, angry sex, etc. Also, there's monster peen shifted sex while in monster form. I'm warning you now, so don't come at me about beastiality because they're totally still themselves, just shifted. Please don't read it if this if these things trigger you.

# Preface

Scarlet was the most skilled Hunter in the mercenary guild, but a dying king and grieving queen changed her fate when they cursed the entire town. Now, she must break her curses or exact revenge. But when she reaches the cottage, it's not her grandmother she finds—it's a forbidden Growler, one of the very creatures she was hired to kill.

Wulfric remembers nothing of his life before becoming a Growler. As alpha, he leads his tribe with strength and wisdom, but a brutal attack by dissenters leaves him wounded and near death. Hoping the druid can save him, he instead is at a dreaded Hunter's mercy, one who just so happens to be his fated mate.

In a world of dark magic and fierce enemies, Scarlet and Wulfric are brought together by the gods themselves. Scarlet seeks vengeance, Wulfric is determined to reclaim his alpha position, and an evil queen with an army of daemons. As they face shared enemies and insurmountable odds, love may be the only thing that can help them survive the battle for the continent's future.

# Preface

PHOENIS

RIMEHOLD          HARTSGROVE

FERAL
FOREST

VIDELAND

DRIVE'S

DEMEREL                    BUSPARIA

GROMIERS

ALCOVALE

MYRRVANE

GLATHEN                    *CAPITOUS OF
                           DOPHIAS

# Prologue

The old woman's medallion glowed brighter with each minute she hesitated to answer the summons. She didn't want to face them again, not yet, not until she had fixed this. But there was no time for delay.

With a burst of energy that contradicted her age, she quickly tossed the special blend of herbs into the stone hearth along the wall of the one-room wooden cabin.

Purple and green flames flashed, and she closed her eyes as smoke billowed from the fireplace. Her mind spun, and she felt like she was falling. The magic pulled her apart, cell by cell, knitting her back together as she tumbled through the portal. A silent scream ripped from her throat as agony filled her. The burning flow of magic twisted and turned, offering no relief until she slammed into the floor, breathless and disoriented.

She lay there for gods knew how long, staring at the glowing medallion shape that matched her necklace on the door in front of her. She focused on her breathing and the glow, willing the pain to recede.

The magic listened, healing her by the time the light faded from the emblem on the door and her necklace stopped burning her skin. The sweet, citrus air that was only found in her homeland filled her nostrils as she slowly sat up.

Carvings as old as time itself adorned other doors like hers along the open-air corridor. She eased onto her feet and brushed her shaking hands down the white silk dress, thick stacks of golden bracelets jingling with the motion. The sight of the large, vibrant tree in the courtyard brought a pang of nostalgia. Birds swooped and played in the branches, but her gaze didn't stop to watch them.

There was an excessive amount of overgrowth. A quick glance down made her frown. Vines and weeds grew thick around the base of the tree. Her father never would've let this happen. The ache in her chest drew her gaze through the thick foliage to the corridor on the opposite side of the square building. That corridor housed only two doors, and she yearned to see the white and gold one restored and not this hacked and chipped, lifeless monstrosity. All life and magic had drained from it, just like her father.

Her chest burned with emotion as her gaze swung to the other door. Solid black, apart from the gold and red veins swirling along the surface as it vibrated and threatened to come off its hinges. Fear snaked down her spine and sent her down the hallway to the great room.

There was only one reason for a summons like this, and dread made her stomach twist as she went through the wide, tall marble archway.

The meeting room stretched the entire length of the building and it, too, was open to the elements. That used to be a good thing in this land of perpetual spring, where it never rained or snowed... but that was back when her father was alive.

Now, vines and ivy grew around the columns between the open windows, threatening to choke out all life. She paused in the doorway, the signs of decay and overgrowth driving her fear and anger into overdrive. Magic pulsed just under her skin, making her itch and want to expel it for relief from the raging emotions.

But she wouldn't—couldn't—do that.

If only her father and uncle had controlled their own emotions... They'd all be together, eating family dinners along the long, low table in the center of the room. Mother would sit at Father's right hand, and they'd both laugh with her brothers, sisters, cousins, aunts, and uncles.

Her gaze turned to the far end of the table where *that* uncle had always sat. No matter how clean, open, and airy the room was, the sun had never shone on his end of the table. Many in the family drew straws to see who would sit next to him. Someone always ran away in tears or tried to flip the table in anger before the end of the meal.

But Father had always diffused the situation with a laugh until that fateful day that she had tried to forget for hundreds of years. Tears pricked her eyes as birds flew in and out of the open arches. She focused on their movements, willing herself to calm. Stay rational, think logically, detach her emotions.

All wasn't lost like it had seemed all those years ago. The tree was still alive. Magic still flowed throughout the room, the gold pulsing occasionally over the floor and walls in ribbons so small one had to know they were there to see them.

A movement from the table drew her gaze. Almost

directly in the middle sat one of her sisters, arms crossed and frown in place as she stared into the bowl of fire in the center of the marble table.

The fire couldn't quite diminish the smell of ripe ambrosia on the vine, and she breathed deeply as nerves assailed her. This summons—the first in centuries—meant change was in the air. It made her nervous, but she strode to the table, tightening her control on her dread, fear, and anxiety.

Her sister looked up as she approached, and the frown turned to a small smile. Druexxa touched her right thumb to her forehead and pulled it away in a salute. "Well met, Fysica."

Fysica smiled at her lyrical voice, and the nostalgic memories of their childhood flooded her mind. Back when all was as it should be, their mother had tended the garden, singing in such a similar voice to Druexxa while their father played games with the boys.

Her limbs grew heavy at the peaceful memories long gone as she sat on a brightly decorated cushion. The pulsing golden veins in the table caught the light of the fire, casting the entire room in a warm glow. The white columns shimmered with gold between the vines as the light dipped below the horizon.

Druexxa's face eased with relief. "Thank the gods you're here too. It's been a long time."

"Too long," Fysica said, returning the gesture with her thumb to her forehead. "How many of us were summoned?"

Druexxa's frown returned, her tight curls full and rounded, perfectly framing her glowing face. They shared the same wide nose, high cheekbones, nearly white hair, and dark skin of their mother, Gaiana.

"Better yet, who summoned us?" Druexxa asked.

"I did," another voice echoed from across the doorway. They both turned to see their sister Honifery floating toward them, her light pink and white silk dress flowing behind her. "And it's just the three of us today."

Some of the tension in her shoulders relaxed. If they were the only three, perhaps things hadn't progressed quite as badly as she feared.

They greeted each other with thumbs to foreheads and soft murmurs as Honifery sat beside Fysica, her loose, long, blond curls flowing below her shoulders as she settled on the cushion.

"To what do we owe this meeting, Honifery? Is it time to act? Are we safe to meet like this?" Druexxa's lyrical voice asked. She uncrossed her arms to reveal golden veins glowing like intricate tattoos, bright against the dark skin as she sat her hands daintily on the table. Fysica breathed a sigh of relief to see both her sisters' magic flowing so strongly along their dark skin, the gold lines pulsing with life.

Honifery sighed, a wrinkle marring her smooth features. "We are safe if we keep this meeting short. I have distracted our uncle with a minor problem in the Deep at the moment," she said, pausing at the word uncle and clenching her teeth.

"Those who normally search for us have been recalled to Hells to stop the problem, so we're relatively safe," she said, pursing her lips and continuing. "Are your identities still intact?"

Fysica nodded, but Druexxa sighed and said, "There are four who know me like this, but they are my champions in the coming war. It was necessary to reveal my hand."

Silence met her pronouncement, and Honifery leaned

5

forward to whisper furiously, "You know how dangerous that is, Dru. If he finds us, you know what he'll do."

It wasn't a question. Fysica's arms pebbled at the thought of it.

Druexxa crossed her arms and wrinkled her nose, "I haven't forgotten what he did to Father."

"Or what he'll do to the rest of us!" Honifery whispered furiously.

Druexxa leaned forward and lowered her voice. "It's certain death, I know. These four are my champions. I have blessed them, and they will fight with us when the time comes."

Honifery leaned back, her chest heaving with emotions as she breathed. "You better hope so, because the war is coming faster than we thought."

"What do you mean?" Fysica asked.

Honifery turned to her. "Exactly that. My sources in the Deep say he's planning to open a route straight to Celawynn's surface. He wants to use it as a base to attack and destroy Paradise."

Fysica frowned as her stomach knotted. "He can't do that, can he? He's not strong enough."

Druexxa snorted. "We didn't think he was strong enough to take down Father either and look what happened there."

Honifery took Fysica's hand from the table, her touch instantly soothing. "No one knows you as Fysica?" she asked softly.

As a child, Honifery always protected her, but Fysica hadn't experienced any coddling in hundreds of years.

Her back stiffened as she shook her head. "No one, although I also may need to act in the coming months. Events are unfolding and will soon come to a head, events that will change the Asshole's hold on this part of the world."

Druexxa chuckled at the nickname for their uncle, but Honifery just wrinkled her nose in disgust and released her hand. She'd known her prim and proper eldest sister wouldn't like the term, which was why she'd used it.

"Why would you need to put yourself in danger like that?" Honifery sighed and rubbed her forehead, but Fysica twisted the silk of her dress and kept quiet.

Druexxa said softly, "She's not a child, Honi. If she needs to take action, she needs to take action."

Honifery sighed and her shoulders sagged. "I know. Why don't you tell us what's going on, then I'll share my news and plans," Honifery said, her genuine curiosity making some of Fysica's tension dissipate. Perhaps admitting the events of the past few weeks wouldn't disappoint them as much as she thought it would when she'd first received the summons.

Fysica waved a hand to the fire bowl on the table. The smoke changed to show a bedchamber. A woman kneeled beside the dead body of her husband, crying and wailing as she pounded on his chest. She kept the sound off for now, but they all could feel the emotions, Fysica more than the others.

Fysica swallowed past the lump in her throat to explain. "This is the queen and my protégé, Bella. She has been heavily influenced by the mirror, which held the trapped soul of Hanzel Crookilius, the wizard. On the floor is her dead husband, the former king. This happened only a week ago."

"Hanzel Crookilius? Why do I know that name?" Druexxa said, tapping a long, golden nail to her chin.

Fysica crossed her smooth, toned arms and said,

"Because he's the one who caused all the problems three hundred years ago. The last time I saw you. That was him. After he partnered with your Sea Witch, he slowly took over this continent and staged a coup that led to the dragons being nearly destroyed."

Druexxa's eyes narrowed, and her magic flared as a storm cloud gathered above her head. "She wasn't *my* Sea Witch. She made a deal with our uncle."

None of them needed to ask which uncle, as only one was obsessed with deals and contracts. Fysica nodded and waved her hand, a white and gold tea tray appearing on the table with them. She carefully poured three cups as she talked, keeping her tone friendly and even to calm her sister.

"I know, I'm sorry. I simply meant that she was on your side of the planet. Thank you for dealing with that problem, by the way. I saw the mermaid princess and her mate at the queen and king's wedding. Are they your champions?"

Druexxa nodded, her eyes narrowed until Fysica said, "You picked your champions well."

Druexxa relaxed as she took her tea, the cloud slowly dissolving into the air.

Honifery sipped hers silently, always watching and waiting, and then said, "Continue, Fysica. Tell me of your champion, the queen."

Fysica pointed her own golden nail at the bowl of fire, her hands and body now back to her normal, youthful, immortal self. Reluctantly, she said, "Watch."

The queen worked quickly at her vanity, tossing ingredients into a bowl. Then she sank to the floor and hovered her hand over the king's dead chest. The look of horror on Bella's face sent a twist of pain to Fysica's heart. She should've protected the girl better, blessed her with more magic, taught her more spells.

Fysica took a deep breath and watched as her heart broke all over again. Pain at failing the dear girl, frustration that she had to keep her identity a secret, and apprehension at telling her sisters of this whole mess made the hair on her arms stand up with barely contained magic.

Her foot bounced as they watched, and she fed her magic into the spell.

The king's shirt ripped open even as the queen cried and shook her head, tears pouring down her face as her mouth formed the spell to remove his heart. Still shaking her head, she stood, blood dripping from her hands, and put the heart into a bowl. She ground it with the pestle and added it to the potion.

In silence, they watched as she drank the potion, tears streaming down her face.

Honifery sighed. "Oh, dear."

Fysica simply nodded and held onto her magic, her lips pursed as the queen's body shook. She didn't want to watch this again, but she forced herself to stay in the moment. Poor Bella had survived it; watching was the least Fysica could do for failing her.

Energy and magic swirled under Bella's skin, making it ripple and move like a cat beneath a blanket. The queen's soundless scream sent a shiver up her spine, and her heart ached for her dear apprentice.

Her sisters would not be happy about this next part or Fysica's role in it. A pulse of magic shot from Bella's body, covering the room in an inky blackness.

"That's the curse that has infected thousands," Fysica said softly.

Another pulse of golden magic flashed in the room, then the queen's body shifted and morphed into a red-scaled horned monster. A row of horns spiked back from her temples and went down her back, growing bigger and bursting from her dress.

Honifery sat forward with a frown. "What is—"

"Dragon scales," Fysica interrupted. She had to explain, hopefully make them understand why she'd interfered. "Her human body couldn't handle the drakin king's magic. This was the only way she would've survived."

"Did you cast the spell?" Honifery's brows rose in surprise.

Fysica nodded as the queen in the fire image tried to scratch her back. Her hands shifted into claws as she held her head, digging into her skin and drawing blood before scales covered enough to protect her from herself.

Fysica's stomach twisted along with Bella's movements as she tried to escape her own body. She slammed into the vanity and the mirror wobbled. Fysica winced.

The light reflecting off the mirror caught the queen's dilated, reptilian eye, and she turned to it with a snarl. She grabbed both edges and threw it to the ground.

It shattered, and a burst of magic slammed out, throwing the queen against the vanity. She hit her head on the corner and sank to the ground.

But her spirit held onto the vanity, shaking and heaving. A black curl of smoke shot from the busted mirror on the floor to the drakin queen's body, and it began convulsing.

The pale blue spirit of the queen hovered over her body with a confused frown, even as the king's body turned to ash. Her eyes never left the convulsing body on the floor. It stilled, and Bella just stood there panting. Slowly, the drakin lumbered to its knees.

The queen's blue-tinted spirit backed up, yellow skirts swishing. Fysica waved her hand again to hear the sound, infusing double the magic into the spell. She simply hadn't been able to stomach hearing the screams again, but this they needed to hear.

"What—what is this?" Bella asked softly.

Her body stood, breathing rapidly and expelling smoke through an elongated snout. Black, beady eyes stared at Bella's spirit, then it threw its head back and laughed.

Fysica wasn't the only one at the table who winced at the grating sound. It was eerily similar to their uncle's and sent a shiver of fear up her spine.

A gravelly, deep voice boomed, making even the table vibrate with its projection. "*This* is magic. I'm finally free from that cursed mirror, and for that, I thank you."

The queen's body glanced at the pile of ash and waved its hand. It coalesced into a pile. From the ashes grew a tiny, green plant shoot.

Then the drakin twisted a wrist and whispered ancient words that made Honifery and Druexxa gasp. A golden strand lifted from Bella's spirit and dipped down to the rose, merging with it until the green bud glowed.

When it faded to normal, the drakin queen grinned, too many sharp predator teeth exposed. "Consider this a thank you present. You may remain here in this precious castle of yours until that rose dies. Then you'll go to the Deep with the others."

Bella's spirit lurched, her arms swinging wide as she somehow lost balance. It should've been impossible as a spirit, but it was a big transition. One that Bella never should've gone through, if Fysica had done her job right.

Regret twisted her stomach as she watched.

Bella gasped, finally gaining control of her new corporeal form. "What? Why? Where are you going?"

The queen's body stepped toward the door. At first, it was just a drunken stumble, but each step became smoother.

"Oh, I have plans. Promises to fulfill that are long overdue, my dear."

Bella floated to the door and held her arms wide. "No, wait! You can't leave me here and just take off. That's my—my body."

The drakin arched a brow and smirked. "Are you sure you want it back? I mean, just look at how hideous you are. No longer the beautiful queen. No, I think I'll hold on to it for now. It's been years since I've had a body, and I intend to fully use it before upgrading."

Then the drakin walked through the floating Bella, who screamed. The drakin's chuckle echoed off the shaking walls.

The smoke cleared from the table, and the image dissipated.

Fysica glanced at her eldest sister. "That was Crookilius. Three hundred years ago, he made a deal with our uncle for power."

"What kind of power?" Druexxa asked sharply.

"I don't know yet. I'm still researching. There are two remaining dragons. One has just become king of the forest."

"And the other?" Druexxa's sharp eyes looked so much like their mother's, it hurt.

Fysica reached for her teacup, but her hand shook so badly, she pulled it back to her lap. "The other dragon trapped Crookilius in the mirror. I've talked to him, and he explained Crookilius' plan."

"Why do I hear a but in there?" Druexxa asked.

Fysica wrinkled her nose and inclined her head. "But if Crookilius' plan is still the same, he is going to lay waste to the entire continent. It was part of his deal. If he controls the continent, then the Asshole can begin his campaign to take over all Celawynn."

Her sisters stared at her in horror, their faces almost mirror images as they paled.

Honifery rubbed her temples and shook her head. "This is what I was afraid of. My contact in the Deep has shown me that our uncle is trying to create a portal to release his daemon army upon Celawynn. We must stop him at all costs."

Fysica nodded. "To stop our uncle, we must stop Crookilius. I am keeping watch on my champions but might need to reveal myself. We will need them in the coming war."

Honifery shook her head. "I don't think that's wise. Maybe Dru's champions can go help?"

Druexxa shook her head. "There is another sin lord in the Zands that has recently come to power. My champions are going to find out if this one also made a deal with our uncle."

Honifery took a deep breath. "Always with the deals… Very well, help your champions however you can, but be smart about it. Try to keep from being seen by our uncle, because I don't want to lose either of you."

Honifery took her hand again, and Fysica squeezed it.

"We'll be fine." Druexxa sniffed and looked away as she blinked quickly.

Honifery released Fysica's hand. "However, that brings us to why I've called this meeting…"

Hours later, Fysica blinked past the pain in her body and the burning medallion on her chest. When her eyes adjusted to the dimness, she found herself back in front of the fireplace in her new cabin, flat on her back.

She looked at her hands and sighed. Her smooth, dark skin was now tan, wrinkled, and spotted with age. The golden veins of magic weren't visible in this form, but more than how she looked was how she felt.

Her back ached from where she'd slammed into the dirt packed floor on her re-entry to this plane. She got up slowly and laid on the bed. Someday, this old body wouldn't be necessary. But first, she had a war to stop and champions to save.

# Chapter One

Wulfric snarled and snapped at Brody, anger coursing through him. "How dare you," he growled. "I'm the alpha of the Ironpaws, damn it!"

Brody grinned maniacally and circled him in the small clearing on the edge of the river. "Correction. You were. I'm taking over."

Wulfric shook his head, blood splattering from where it dripped into his eye. He lunged, snapping his elongated jaws. He didn't have time for an alpha challenge, as illegal as this one may be.

It was his job to see the tribe through the winter. The Elders had said it was going to be the worst winter in centuries, and they'd been right so far. They still had weeks to go before spring.

Brody twisted and clamped down on his shoulder. The stupid pup wasn't trained enough to manage a throat attack, but Wulfric turned and took advantage. His bloody teeth latched awkwardly onto the back of Brody's neck and ripped the wolf off. Brody's jaws tore a chunk of Wulfric's fur and flesh as he went flying.

Wulfric didn't whimper. He'd fought many wars over the years, not that he could remember any from the time before. Pain was as familiar as food and almost as necessary. Both would keep him alive.

He limped back, watching Brody warily as he mentally assessed both their wounds. His head pounded from where the wolf and his two friends had ambushed him with a club. One of them was dead and the other lay near a tree, staring silently as he either bled out or healed.

Logically, he knew he'd only been defending himself. But his chest ached at the deaths of his people, the betrayal, the confusion.

Wulfric focused on Brody. "But why?"

Brody shook his head, his eyes glowing with rage as he stalked back to Wulfric. "You don't get it, do you? You walk around like a god, lording your power as alpha over the rest of us. We're tired of it."

A stab of anger made him growl. He played with the young ones, led the youths on hunts, trained the warriors, kept the peace with the other tribe leaders, and took care of the Elders. When had he lorded power over any of them?

He rolled his shoulders, testing his weight on his injured front leg. Pain stabbed him like a knife, but he refused to take his eyes off his opponent. "How was I abusing my power as alpha? Who thinks this?"

Brody howled, the sound echoing off the dark trees. "Butch, for starters, and now he's dead, thanks to you."

He winced and panted, staying as still as possible. He didn't want Brody to realize how injured his foot was or how much those words hurt. He had worked for years to protect and honor the people who had taken him in and loved him unconditionally, if harshly.

He would not be goaded into feeling guilty. "Butch's death is on your head. What did you expect when you ambushed the alpha?"

"I expected more than this!" Brody roared, blood dripping from his fangs as he prowled back and forth with hackles raised. "When I signed on to be a Growler, I expected more than this isolation and tyranny."

Wulfric arched a bushy brow, the movement barely visible in their wolf forms. New Growlers were welcomed with open arms because it was an instant family. "What isolation? Our family is enormous. We fill the entire lower half of the Feral Forest."

"And that's the fucking problem," Brody snarled, shifting onto his back legs as he prepared to pounce. "We've outgrown the forest. We're bursting at the seams. And on top of that, we're not family, are we? I miss my actual family, my flesh and blood. I'm tired of hiding, of giving up who I am."

Brody lunged half-heartedly, testing Wulfric's reaction times. "The time for hiding is over. Busparia's defenses are in ruins, the soldiers have all fled back home—except for us! We want to go home!"

Wulfric jumped back, wincing at the pain as he balanced on three legs. "The Growlers are our home now. You knew that when you accepted the blessing of the Elders."

Brody barked a laugh. "A blessing? Not if it keeps me from my family."

Wulfric froze, confusion and blood loss making his head pound. "What family are you talking about?"

Brody didn't give him time to ask more questions. He

launched into the air with a roar, and Wulfric twisted to the side. A massive paw landed a lucky blow to his temple, sending him out of the controlled roll. Wulfric hit a tree and grunted in pain, coming up on three weak legs.

Brody prowled closer, drool dripping from his muzzle. "Busparia's new queen has nearly destroyed the country, and we're worried about our families. They're no longer safe. Now is the time to strike, to save them, yet we can't just bring them back here. We're too cramped as it is, but in Busparia... they're still waiting for us. The land is ripe for the taking."

Something within him twisted at the mention of Busparia. Faint feelings of a past he no longer remembered threatened to drown him in sorrow. "No," he said to the memories.

"No? That's it?" Brody growled. "See, this is why you're a terrible alpha. How I've survived five years like this is beyond me."

"We're not going anywhere." Wulfric shifted to keep the tree on his bad side. It would help protect him. If Brody was smart, he'd attack the weak leg.

Wulfric tried to diffuse the situation. "We need to talk this through rationally."

"There's no more time to lose. Home is right there on the other side of the forest, and they may need us to save them from the queen or her monsters." Brody's mouth twisted in anger, his features harsh in the cold, crisp sunlight.

He snarled and leaped in the air, but Wulfric spun behind the tree, pain lancing through him. Brody hit the pine, the sharp whine of pain piercing his ears.

Wulfric winced, that sound an echo of his failure as a leader. He was supposed to protect them, not harm them.

"Stop before you hurt yourself. Remember the gift and be grateful for a second chance at life."

Brody snorted. "I know, I know. We were all dying soldiers who otherwise wouldn't have made it home."

Brody stopped, and his beady, black eyes peered into Wulfric's gaze, the emotion and yearning making Wulfric's breath catch in his throat.

Then the anger returned to Brody's face as he lowered his muzzle. "And what's the point of a second life if I can't see my family ever again?" Brody spat vehemently, anger burning hell-hot in his gaze as he clambered slowly to his feet.

The pressure on Wulfric's mind increased, memories fluttering just out of reach. He shook his head and relayed the message they'd heard over and over since being turned. "We can't go into Busparia. They'll hunt us down and destroy everything we know."

"Not everything." Brody's lip curled in disdain. "I know a lot more than just this damn forest. In fact, there are several of us who kept our memories, *alpha*."

He sneered the word and spat blood on the ground, turning to face Wulfric, stretching to test his injuries again.

Wulfric's body shivered in the cold, but his mind was frozen on the words. How had he kept his memories? That was the price of being turned into a Growler. The Elders had been performing that ritual for hundreds of years, but somehow Brody hadn't paid the price?

It didn't make sense. His head ached, and his body seemed to slow even as his heart raced at the danger.

He should end this farce of a battle. It wasn't worth calling it an alpha challenge, as it wasn't within the bounds of the law. Wulfric's shoulders stiffened, and he lifted his head, breathing deeply through the pain as he circled the tree. The pounding in his ankle kept his mind in the moment, even though it tried to draw him into the yawning chasm of darkness.

Damn it, he was supposed to uphold the law and keep them safe, love them as they loved him. Wulfric took a shuddering breath, the scent of blood flooding him, calling to him to turn feral.

*Focus, Wulfric, focus. Try to reason with him.*

"If we go into Busparia, we'll either kill or be killed. And we're not going to attack innocent civilians outside the forest who may see us as a threat. That will just keep the fear of Growlers going."

Brody took two steps closer, blood dripping steadily onto the pine needle covered ground. "The new queen and the general are taking control of more than just the capital. This winter is the perfect time for us to finally leave these cursed woods and go home."

"It's too cold."

"Exactly! It's keeping everyone inside, so we can slip into the country unnoticed. We're protectors, soldiers, and warriors, but we're stuck hiding in these woods like outlaws when our families are being killed in their own homes."

Wulfric shuffled on his feet, keeping his weight on his three legs as the dizziness increased. "That's not our home anymore. There's no home left for us in Busparia."

Brody's toothy grin widened, red with blood. "Perhaps not for you...but if you won't lead us home, I will. Step down as alpha. This is your last chance."

Wulfric shook his head, tightness pressing on his chest as his vision swam. Blood poured into his eyes, and he shook his head again so he could see. But he was too slow.

Brody attacked, and this time, his aim was true. His jaws clamped around Wulfric's neck as he viciously ripped at flesh and fur. Claws dug into muscle. Wulfric twisted, rolling them both on the ground.

He pinned Brody and dislodged him, smacking him into the dirt with a whimper. Then another wolf slammed into Wulfric's wounded side, sending him sprawling. Spots swirled with white lights behind his eyelids, the gurgling of the river the only sound to be heard over the pounding of his heart. No birds, no woodland chatter. All else was still.

He blinked, seeing double. No, two more wolves had joined the fight and paced beside Brody as he rose to his feet.

"Finish him," Brody said.

Wulfric's breathing grew ragged as his head spun. He'd seen these two wolves with Brody in the past. Why hadn't he opened his senses to inspect the area in a wider arc? They prowled to him, and he assessed his wounds, the situation, his surroundings.

He wouldn't be able to take on two more uninjured wolves. He needed to find medicine or magic. They wouldn't let him, and it wasn't guaranteed that the Elders would help him, either.

Even though the alpha challenge wasn't official and was completely illegal, he had no way of telling if the Elders would even side with him. They would likely say it was the will of their patron goddess and let him bleed out.

Where could he go? The gurgling river was the only sound in the night. The river. It would take him further from the Elders and their medicine, but he would at least be away from Brody and his minions. It was his only chance.

With a groan, he rolled to the edge of the bank and dropped off the ledge into the rushing current below.

The frigid, icy water enveloped him, numbing some of the pain. Gasping for air, he thrashed weakly with three legs, letting the raging water carry him away. He struggled to think, his mind became hazy from blood loss and pain, and his body grew weaker by the second.

Where could he go to lick his wounds?

Think, Wulfric, think. The river led through the center of the forest to the western border with Glathen, before turning more directly south and spilling into the sea. He had to get out of the river before the turn. The water flowed faster, and he grunted as he slammed into a rock. His vision blurred as he fought for air.

Get out of the river. And go where?

His vision began to darken on the edges. He only had a few minutes left.

Growlers avoided the old druid's cottage in the center of the Feral Forrest. It was forbidden, off-limits, part of a treaty from years ago.

Maybe the Elders had lied about that though? If Brody remembered his family and his past in Busparia, maybe the Elders had lied about the old druid too?

If the druid didn't kill him, she might offer shelter, warmth, medicine, and magic. The rushing water grew louder, and his heart raced, even as his body became dangerously cold.

He needed time to heal and grow stronger before he could reclaim his place as alpha and sort out the problem with Brody.

But first, he had to survive the waterfalls and escape the river before it turned south. Water swirled and tossed him from side to side. He fought against the darkness, desperately calling on all the spirits and gods he could remember as he clawed his way to the bank.

# Chapter Two

"Mistress Scarlet, welcome back," said the butler as he took her cloak. "How was your mission?"

"It wasn't as successful as I'd hoped." Scarlet stomped mud off her boots just inside the door of the castle. Every step made her head vibrate and bob side to side as she tried to keep her head upright.

"Oh?"

"It's hard to be inconspicuous with fucking antlers, bunny ears, and a wolf's tail," Scarlet scowled.

The butler sniffed and held her cloak, "Tell me about it."

He waved his two extra arms, which were really just two feather dusters that stuck out from each side of his ribs. Even as he shook out her cloak, the dusters were busy cleaning the dirt on the door and wall.

From his hips extended a broom on one side and a dust pan on the other, which also didn't stop moving.

Scarlet sighed and a stab of guilt made her stomach

twist. "I'm sorry, Hobbs. I know this curse is hard for you too."

He smiled and nodded his head to the wide hallway. "They're in the library, miss. I'll send in some refreshments."

"Thank you," she said, the weight of responsibility added to the heaviness of her antlers. She might have more curses than the others, but she was the one who'd been appointed to solve the problem. They were all relying on her, even though most of the others avoided her.

She walked down the wide, marble hallway. In the past six months, the haunted Hartsgrove castle had been cleaned and rebuilt from an attack by the skeletal dragon.

Now it shined good as new, thanks to Hobbs and the castle's ghost, Leopol. She looked around but didn't see the wispy man as she entered the library.

Her brother, Knox, stood behind his wife, massaging her shoulders. Eirwyn sat in one of the plush chairs in front of the fireplace, feet propped up with a forgotten book in her lap.

Her family turned at the sound of her boots on the floor and smiled. They were so damn happy and content together.

She didn't envy them, she really didn't. She'd never wanted to live the domesticated life, barefoot, pregnant, and reliant on a man. Her dad had raised her to be independent. Plus, there was her love for adventure and that sense of fulfillment from a job well done.

Even if that job was slicing the throat of some noble scum or making an abuser disappear. She was a hired Hunter, but she had standards.

The past few years, the hunt had been getting stale, though. She didn't want a home or babes, but she did want someone to have her back. She was so lonely, especially with these fucking curses.

They'd put a stop to almost all of it. Now she had responsibilities. People relied on her. She pushed down the rage that burned in her soul at the injustice of the curses and fear of failure at being unable to break them.

Knox smiled. "Scarlet, you're back! How was the trip? Did you have any trouble?" His smile turned into a worried frown as she stepped closer.

She sank into the opposite cushioned chair, turning sideways and dangling her legs over the armrest.

"Of course I had trouble. I can hardly ride through the forest without getting this fucking rack tangled in the trees, much less meet with the other Hunters."

She sighed, knowing they would think she had no propriety when in reality, this was just the most comfortable position for her giant-ass antlers.

The housekeeper, Helga, came into the room pushing a cart and swiping her tea leaf hair out of her face.

Eirwyn shifted on the seat to sit up. "Oh, tea is here. This will make you feel better. I'm sure you're hungry after getting all tangled up and traveling all this way."

Knox put his hand on her shoulder and shook his head. "No, you stay here. I'll serve."

Helga fussed, and Scarlet pulled out her dagger to pick at her nails. They weren't dirty, but making Helga glare at her put a smile back on Scarlet's face.

The housekeeper's hair kept falling into her face, and she kept blowing it away. But the tea leaves had a mind of their own.

Eirwyn had confided a few months ago that Helga had taken scissors to them repeatedly, but they always grew back like weeds overnight. So she'd put her curse to work and had packaged tea into bags to transport to the other two new villages in the forest.

Scarlet sighed and sat up, taking the offered tea from Knox. At least the tea leaf hair made a relaxing drink, she thought as she sipped.

"How is the little dragonling and the queen?" Scarlet asked.

Knox pulled up another chair as Helga parked the cart at Eirwyn's elbow.

Eirwyn rubbed her stomach protectively, shadows and light swirling around her as her nerves went higher. "Eh, as well as expected I suppose. Lailant says it's going well, but I would feel better with more information. We have read almost every book in this castle, and Leopol has been very helpful."

Although a ghost, Leopol was the only one who was an actual dragon, other than Knox. He knew what to expect from experience, if not the books in the library.

Scarlet sipped her tea as Knox stared at his wife with concern. She swallowed, the heat burning her tongue. "Yet you're still worried?"

Knox pushed a plate of olpertine closer to Eirwyn and moved a second plate between himself and Scarlet on a low side table.

He nodded. "Wouldn't you be? But everything will be fine. This has been done for thousands of years before, remember?"

Eirwyn nodded, distracted as she practically inhaled the olpertine's sugary fried dough.

Scarlet met Knox's worried gaze and understood. It was like watching her dad ride off to war, not knowing if he was going to come out unharmed or not. The reminder of her dad sent her own worry and frustration sky high.

She took a deep breath and tried to control herself. Her antlers weighed her down, causing a throbbing headache like always. Every damn day, she pushed her body, pushed past the pain and tried to live a semi-normal existence.

She could live with the tail and the nose. The antlers were the biggest problem. They spread as wide as her shoulders and had twelve points. Was it any wonder she was cranky all the time?

Not as cranky as Eirwyn. Thankfully Scarlet wasn't the one carrying a giant egg. That honor fell to her dear sister-in-law.

"Just ring if you need me, Your Majesties," Helga said, dipping a curtsy.

Knox and Eirwyn both nodded but didn't look up as she left. Scarlet smirked. She never would've thought her big brother would become king, but it suited him. He'd taken to it like a fish takes to water.

Unlike herself and the curses. She just couldn't accept that this was her life now.

Other villagers both here in Hartsgrove and over in Vidrland were cursed too, like Helga and Hobbs, but they all gave Scarlet a wide berth. She was used to setting people on edge when they found out she was a Hunter, but this was something completely different.

She'd had months to get used to these cursed changes in her body, but every time someone looked at her in horror, the hair on the back of her neck stood up. Anger seethed under her skin, making her scratch behind her long ears to find some sort of short-lived relief.

Eirwyn frowned, rubbing her stomach absently. "So what's the news in the capitol? Did you find out what's going on? Is Bella alright?"

Scarlet reached for an olpertine and popped it into her

mouth to keep from snapping about the queen. The confectioners sugar dissolved on her tongue as she chewed the fried treat, and her nose twitched as if phantom whiskers were tickling her cheek. She shivered at the memory and took a drink, re-centering the weight of the antlers.

Thankfully, the whiskers hadn't made a re-appearance since that day at the castle.

She cleared her throat. "Of course I found out what's going on. I may be a freak, but I'm still the best Hunter in the land."

"You're not a freak," Knox said. "You're just cursed like nearly everyone else here."

She almost crushed the next olpertine and glared at Knox. "No one else has multiple curses here. I'm the one who sticks out in a sea of weirdness. I'm the abomination in a crowd of tea ladies and candle and clock men. Of all the people who've been merged with inanimate objects, you can't seriously think that I'm just like everyone else."

Knox crossed his arms and leaned back in the straight chair. He certainly looks royal enough with that stern stare.

"It's not like you to have a pity party, Scarlet. You know we're going to break the curse."

Scarlet drowned her rage with another olpertine and drink of tea, but the roiling emotions finally broke free. "Yeah, yeah, that's what you've said for months."

"We're not giving up," he said.

Scarlet shot back, "Easy for you to say when you look so normal."

They both glanced in surprise at each other, then burst out laughing.

Knox scratched at his temples where green and brown scales spread around the back of his head. Brown hair grew on the top which he kept in a thick braid. But for years, he'd hidden his scales beneath a cloak and stuck to the shadows of the forest, rarely going in public.

"Well, that's a first. Never heard anyone call me normal before," Knox grinned.

Scarlet chewed another olpertine. They'd fought like this as kids a lot. Quick, heated words, then a laugh, and it was over. It was good to hear him laugh about his own appearance now.

The love of a good woman would do that to a man, though. At least, that's what she'd seen in her short thirty-five years.

Scarlet swallowed and drained her tea. "Well, as normal as you'll ever be," she teased.

Eirwyn had eaten almost her entire personal plate of olpertine and finally stopped long enough to chime in. "You're not normal, but normal is over-rated. You have to accept who you are, Scarlet. Embrace your curses and use them to your advantage, like Helga."

Scarlet arched a brow at her friend and sat her empty porcelain cup on the cart. "Queenie, some curses are easier to accept than others. I appreciate your optimism, but I need my old body back."

"And if you can't get it back?" Eirwyn asked softly. "What then?"

Scarlet stared into the fire, the food settling like a knot in her stomach as her lips pinched. Her heart pounded in her ears, too fast like the scared little rabbit she worked so hard to bury deep inside her.

She had beaten that fear within her for six months and made it her little bitch. But it was a constant, daily battle with her multiple instincts. Run like a deer, fight like a wolf, or hide like a fucking scared little rabbit.

That's what she'd been reduced to with these fucking

curses. It wasn't all about the physical differences. It was about eliminating that fear for good. The only thing that had helped keep it at bay was channeling it into anger, but that anger needed a focus, a release.

Her eyes burned with rage as she turned to stare at Eirwyn.

"I'm going to kill the queen, Eirwyn. Gods help me, if she doesn't fix this, I will kill her."

The silence was only broken by the crackling of the fire in the fireplace. A tear rolled down Eirwyn's cheek, and Knox sighed, handing her a napkin from the cart.

"You can't just kill her," Knox said, the disappointment in his voice making Scarlet's stomach twist.

But she just arched a brow and crossed her arms and ankles. Stretching her legs in front of her toward the fire, she took a deep breath. Her mind wandered as Eirwyn handed her empty plate to Knox, who tidied up the cart.

The silence was tense. She needed to make them see it was a last resort but maybe the best option.

"It's not just about the curses," she said quietly. "There are other things going on in Busparia. We thought the old king was a bad ruler because of the taxes and the war with Glathen? This is worse."

Eirwyn's shoulders sank at the mention of her brother.

Knox sat forward, his tea forgotten as he frowned. "In what way?"

"The king would throw suspects into the dungeon and torture them or hold them ransom until someone paid their taxes, right?" Scarlet's spine tingled at the memory of her own time in the dungeon, but she pushed the emotions away.

She continued. "The queen doesn't. Any infraction leads to sudden and instant death."

Eirwyn gasped, and Knox took her hand.

Scarlet shook her head. "That's not all. Every town in the country has a curfew. No one roams the streets after sunset. There are reports of monsters killing anyone caught in the darkness. Cattle and livestock are found every morning slaughtered and ripped to shreds."

"Monsters?" Knox asked.

Scarlet nodded. "I didn't believe the reports at first, but my team of Hunters and I barely made it into an inn our first night on the road. We could hear the flutter of wings and the growls."

"Growlers?" Eirwyn asked.

Scarlet shook her head slowly, staring once more into the fireplace as her spine tingled. "No, I don't think so. They didn't sound like Growlers. This was something entirely different."

She looked up and met their gazes one at a time, trying to make them see how bad it was outside of the relative safety of the Feral Forest.

"The queen is wielding that fear like a double-edged sword. She claims that those who die are those who oppose her rule and break the laws. It's no coincidence that the so-called monsters only descended on the villages and valleys after the queen passed through on her grand-tour of the country."

"How can the Council just let this happen?" Eirwyn asked.

Eirwyn was the former princess of Busparia. Her brother had ruled with the Council for decades before his death six months ago. That's when their entire world was turned upside down.

Scarlet replied, "I don't think the Council has a choice.

Between Bella, the General, and the Chancellor, it's practically martial law in Busparia."

She rubbed her temples, her head hurting yet again from the balancing act of antlers.

"The Chancellor is a yes-man. He'll do whatever he has to stay in power," Eirwyn said.

Scarlet nodded, "That power has finally settled in the capitol. There haven't been elaborate, fancy balls, but she has begun to wine and dine the nobles and the Council. Those who oppose her disappear, and it's not the Hunters still in Busparia responsible for it, either. Most of the Hunters who remain are no longer getting contracts. When we arrived at the Guild house, they asked us for guidance and help."

"What did you tell them?" Knox asked.

Scarlet shrugged. "Exactly what you said. There's shelter in the forest for any who swear fealty to the two of you."

"And what of the war? Any word on that?" Knox put his empty tea cup on the cart and stepped behind Eirwyn to massage down her arms. Scarlet sighed, ignoring the pain in her chest as she watched the two of them together.

It was almost nauseating to watch all the love between them. The little touches. The heated glances. The tender care.

It reminded her too much of her parents and of what she would never have.

"The General is preparing more troops to launch another invasion when winter fades in a few weeks, but I wasn't able to get as close as I wanted to confirm that rumor. I had to rely on other Hunters to get in and out, as these fucking antlers kept getting in the way," Scarlet muttered, scratching where one came out of her head.

Knox murmured and began to pace. "How are we supposed to get her to break the curse and stop the war once and for all?"

Eirwyn bit her lip and her eyes watered. "Maybe we can visit her? Surely she'll see us. It's been months, and we were friends for years before—before..."

Scarlet's lips twisted. "Before the king was eliminated and she cursed everyone within a league's distance?"

Eirwyn's face nearly crumpled as she wiped a tear from the corner of her eye. Scarlet's chest ached, but her friend needed to come to terms with what had happened last summer. She needed to accept her brother's death for what it was.

No one had let Scarlet wallow in grief when she'd lost either of her parents. Eirwyn had had months to process, and it was time to face the reality of life.

"You were friends before we declared the Feral Forest a separate country too," Knox said, scratching his temples again. "You know she's probably upset about that."

Eirwyn shook her head stubbornly and a tear rolled down her cheek, before she wiped it away angrily. "No, I don't think she'd care about losing this territory. She was a fair and honest woman."

"Before she got married," Scarlet said.

Eirwyn glared. "She can be again. Maybe once the devastation of my brother's death fades?"

Knox knelt in front of her, taking her hand gently. "Hey, maybe you're right. Maybe once she's back to her normal self, we can meet with her. After the egg is hatched, that is."

Scarlet shook her head. "And she'll suddenly be sane? Eirwyn, you of all people should know how grief can take a toll. You're both still in mourning. We can't rush into a meeting with her. If her emotions are too raw, who knows

33

what might happen. I mean, last time, she cursed us, remember? And now she's controlling monsters?"

Knox rubbed his hands up and down Eirwyn's arms, and she sighed as she leaned her head on his forehead, holding her hands under her enormous stomach. Scarlet's huge ass ears meant she heard every whispered word between her step-brother and his wife.

"I know," Eirwyn said. "But she's my friend."

Knox kissed her temple. "And you want to be there for her. It's understandable, my love. But we can't go see her until after the egg has hatched. You're due to deliver any day now."

Eirwyn's shoulders seemed to wilt, and Knox brushed her long black hair over her shoulder. "First, I have to give birth to an egg. Then we have to wait for it to hatch. I'm just so tired of waiting."

Knox held her gently, nuzzling his head to hers. "According to the dragon books, it'll just be a few more months. Think of it this way. It's almost the end of winter, and we need to focus on the villages while we wait. They're relying on us to see them through when food stores run low."

Eirwyn sighed, "I'm just so tired of not being able to get things done."

Scarlet's chest tightened. She wanted to get things done too, mostly reversing the curse. Eirwyn might have been friends with the queen back in the day, but Scarlet had sworn revenge on the woman who had cursed them all.

If the evil queen wouldn't reverse the curse, Scarlet would rain down vengeance and make her wish she'd died along with the king. Then after the pain and suffering, she would die for her crimes.

As much as Scarlet loved her brother and Eirwyn,

someone had to step up and take care of the situation with the queen of Busparia. Scarlet was perfectly willing to enact justice for all the lives that had been ruined. Not just those who'd been cursed, but those who'd died fleeing the curse too.

Delivering the first dragon egg in centuries was Eirwyn's primary concern. Knox could handle the villagers, and Scarlet could handle the evil queen.

Rumors flew through the villages in the forest, as no one really knew how long it would take to deliver the egg and then for it to hatch. This birth was stressing not just them but the entire tiny forest kingdom.

Scarlet sighed. "I'll keep an eye on the situation in Busparia. All you need to do is focus on the dragonling. Do you want me to get Grandma and bring her here for the birth?"

Eirwyn and Knox looked at her, Knox now sitting on the chair with Eirwyn sideways on his lap, his arms tightened around her protectively.

He nodded, "Yes, that would be helpful."

Eirwyn's lip wavered and her eyes glistened. "Yes, please. We're at an impasse with both the east and the west, I'm afraid. All we can do is prepare for spring and the baby."

Scarlet looked at Knox and tilted her head to the side in question. Before he could reply, Eirwyn struggled to stand. Knox helped, one hand on her elbow as his other pushed her up.

She finally sighed and brushed her hair back as she stood. "I'm going to the bathroom yet again. I'll be back."

Knox nodded, shifting on his feet as he watched her waddle away. He was so protective, it made Scarlet smirk.

When he looked back at Scarlet, he arched a brow. "What?"

She grinned and crossed her arms. "Nothing, it's just... you're already a great dragon king and husband, but you're going to make a great father soon too."

Knox sighed and sank into the chair again, even as his cheeks tinged pink. "You think so? You think your dad would be proud?"

Scarlet's chest tightened and a sudden knot formed in her throat. "Yeah," she said, her voice rough and low. She cleared her throat. "Yeah, he would. Now what aren't you telling me?"

She took a deep breath, despising the emotions, the vulnerability. The longing. She blinked, setting the thoughts aside.

He sighed, "While you've been scouting in Busparia in the east, our messengers from the west returned. They will agree to the trade agreement and formal recognition of the nation of the Feral Forest but only after we meet in person."

Scarlet nodded. "Which we can't do yet."

"Exactly," Knox said. "We've scheduled a meeting for the spring, after the hatchling is safely here. We hope. So in the meantime, we'll continue building the villages."

Scarlet read his aura and pursed her lips. It flared bright with jagged edges, radiating from his head. "You're more worried about the birth than you're letting on, aren't you?"

The dark circles under his eyes were deeper than normal, but she'd thought it was just because he was new to being a king. Not that he was new to leading people, as he'd led the band of merry outlaws for years without telling her. She was still mad at him about that secret.

He nodded. "I've read all the books I could find here and at the dwarves' place, but what if the birth of the egg goes wrong? What if it takes hundreds of years for the egg to hatch like it did me? What if—"

"You can't what-if this, Knox. You'll drive yourself sick with worry. Have you talked to the old medicine woman, Lailant?"

He nodded. "And the druids, and the dwarves, and Leopol. They all say it's going to be fine, that the mate bond will help her."

Helplessness made his shoulders droop, and she gave a wry smile.

"Well, you'll know soon enough."

"They think it'll be around the full moon."

"That's next week," Scarlet murmured. Knox didn't reply, both of them thinking through the possibilities, analyzing the situation and all the potential outcomes the way her father had taught them.

Scarlet sighed and looked around. A maid with leaves for hair stared at her with wide eyes from the closed glass doors to the garden. When she locked eyes with the girl jerked and turned away, sweeping the stone patio outside.

Scarlet's head pounded, and she just wanted to get away from the stares and into the peace of the forest. Not that anyone had ever called the Feral Forest peaceful before.

"I'll go get Grandma. She should be here," Scarlet said. "Between her, the other druids, and the medicine woman, Eirwyn will be fine."

Knox sighed, his shoulders lowering. "Thanks, Scarlet. I sure hope so. If anything were to happen to Eirwyn... well, let's just say that I understand how the queen could've cursed us with her grief."

Scarlet's jaw clenched. She didn't know what that worry was like. Since her dad had died years ago and she'd become a mercenary Hunter, she'd tried to shut down most emotions. Except anger and now the need for revenge, since it was what kept the fear at bay. Those drove her forward.

But for her brother, she'd put a pin in those plans. "I'll restock my supplies and head out at first light. I'll bring her back before the full moon."

The weight of responsibility was almost as bad as the weight of the antlers as he stared at her with hope. "Thanks, I owe you one."

She smirked, trying to lighten the mood as Eirwyn came back through the door. "So, what else is new?"

He chuckled, his eyes lighting up as he saw his wife come back into the room.

# Chapter Three

Scarlet frowned and pulled Rain to a stop outside her grandmother's cottage. Scarlet sat still, her long ears twitching as her eyes meticulously moved from side to side. No matter how long she searched, Grandma wasn't here.

The weather grew colder, the ground becoming slick with a mix of mud from the horse. The cottage and barn were blanketed in a thick layer of snow, ice clinging to the roofs and trees like a glittering cloak. Not even the animals had ventured outside to disturb its pristine appearance.

The feeling was back, that pit in her stomach that said get ready. It always hit before an ambush or a fight at the tavern. Her dad had always smiled with pride whenever she'd warn him about this feeling. He never doubted her, so she never did, either. It had saved her life more than once.

The stillness in the air was nearly suffocating, like all the Feral Forest waited with bated breath. Scarlet's heart raced, the emotions threatening to cloud her judgment, even as she stretched her senses as far as they could go.

Grandma wasn't in the house, the barn, or the garden...

but a brilliant blue and gray aura swirled within, barely visible through the walls. Someone else was in the kitchen, someone with *two* auras.

The swirling blue and gray was like two different auras in one. She saw it on Eirwyn to a degree, with the pregnancy. But this was vastly different. More entwined instead of two separate auras of two different people.

That couldn't be right. The thick wooden walls of the cottage must be throwing her off. Built into the side of a giant living tree, the roof intermingled with the pine branches above.

The hair on her nape stood up, and her tail swished against the horse's flank. She watched the house as she led Rain along the outer edge of the clearing to the back side of the barn. Nothing broke the stillness except the crunch of Rain's hooves on the frozen ground. Not a bird or a squirrel or a rabbit.

Her nose twitched as she sniffed the air. The aura hadn't moved in the house. It was alive, whatever it was, and it was unusual. Most people had a single aura. They came in a variety of colors and strengths, but this one... Being able to penetrate walls with her senses was a new gift.

She scowled and slowly slid off her horse, leading her to the warmth and safety of the barn. No, it wasn't a fucking gift. It was a curse, one that she intended to end. And if it couldn't be fixed, there was the matter of how to get revenge on the queen. She'd have to be careful in how she went about it, since she didn't want to alienate Eirwyn. Her sister-in-law still seemed attached to her childhood friend and brother's widow.

Eirwyn. Scarlet blinked and sped up her movements. She had to find Grandma and bring her back to help Eirwyn deliver the dragon egg. Maybe the person in the cottage would know where she'd gone. It was probably a Robin from the village.

The aura was all wrong, though. No other Robin looked like that. She'd just left the village that morning, and the villagers and the Robins were the only people who knew where the cottage was.

A Robin, most likely.

*Are you trying to convince yourself? What do your instincts tell you?*

Her jaw clenched at the echoing memory of her father's voice in her head. That feeling drove her heart rate up and her stomach twisted in anticipation for a fight.

The stranger was dangerous, perhaps had even hurt Grandma. If she was dead, that would explain her missing aura. The thought sent her into quiet action.

She slid off Rain's back and led her into a stall with food and water. There was no time to unsaddle; she had to find out if Grandma was safe.

She padded on silent feet across the clearing to the kitchen, the crunch of snow loud in the stillness.

The last time there'd been surprise visitors here... She took a deep breath, trying to calm her racing heart, but the fear remained. Her hands hovered over her dagger sheaths as she focused on trying to mute the sound of her steps.

She stopped at the window beside the back door and peeked inside, her heart in her throat.

A great, hulking dark shape lay on the floor. She could barely see the shadow of it through the window. Her mind warred with her rising panic as she cautiously withdrew her hidden daggers. One pointed down to stab and the other she held with the blade along her forearm to block or slash. Some of the fear abated with them in her hands.

She breathed deeply, evenly, waiting and watching, but

the threat didn't stir. There was no sign of struggle or Grandma either.

She crept to the rear door off the kitchen and cracked it open. It creaked, making her freeze in fear as her heart skipped a beat. But the figure on the floor didn't move. She bent her knees and turned sideways to fit her antlers inside, hugging the wall.

Her eyes fell on the body, and her breathing grew loud in her ears. Her body shook, but she couldn't move. Terror flooded her, reminding her of the dungeon, the helplessness.

The herbal scents of the cottage flowed over her, calming her with each panicked breath until she was breathing long and slow. She had to assess the situation and think logically like she'd been trained.

On the floor lay a real-life Growler, a massive gray and black wolf, larger than any normal animal.

This was the type of monster that had killed her mom. Tightness pressed on her chest, and her pounding heart morphed the fear into anger at having her mother ripped from her.

If the Feral Forest's magic didn't kill intruders in the forest, the Growlers would. They only knew how to hunt, kill, and fuck, and those who met Growlers face-to-face didn't live to tell the tale. She had to get rid of him before he jumped up and killed her or worse.

The thoughts raced through her mind as she took a deep breath. She would not give in to the fear or let this monster escape.

She launched herself at him, her mind a whirlwind of confusion and anger. She straddled his back, pressing the daggers against his skin with trembling hands. Her heart raced with adrenaline, urging her to hurt him, while her conscience—her grandmother's voice—tugged at her, reminding her that violence wasn't the answer. With each dig of the dagger, she felt torn between revenge and remorse.

The blades barely drew blood. It wasn't nearly enough to hurt him for what his people had done to her mother. She wanted to hurt him, to make him pay for what they had done, but as she pressed harder against his neck, her hand trembled and her heart raced.

As she stood in front of the giant, wolf-like creature on the floor, the flickers of humanity in its blue and gray aura swirled like a stormy sky. Despite his monstrous appearance, there was something undeniably human about him. She'd never second-guessed taking a life before. Thinking back to past missions, even her first kill hadn't given her this inner turmoil. Those jobs had all been thorough, cold, and calculated. She'd known exactly what kind of person she was hunting.

Although this Growler, this monster should be an automatic kill on sight… she couldn't bring herself to do it. Call it an unspoken bond, a familiarity like reuniting with a long-lost friend, a shared connection, an animal sense of understanding how hard it was to live with a dual nature—whatever the fuck it was, she couldn't kill him.

The scent of blood filled her nostrils, and she pushed aside her emotions to logically categorize the situation.

A thin layer of gray, black, and white matted fur oozed sticky blood in several places, not just from her knife. The fur was thick in some places like his chest but barely peach fuzz everywhere else.

Oh damn, how could a four-legged wolf have fucking biceps like a wrestler? A tail stuck out just below the waistline, exactly like hers. Her long, red tail swished from side to side, some part of her recognizing him.

43

She was not a Growler, deer, or rabbit, but some other abomination instead. Some deep part of her didn't want to hurt him. Her mind shied away from questioning why not. That way led to more emotions, and she didn't want to give into those.

He shifted on the floor underneath her, trying and failing to push-up onto four feet, and she stiffened on him.

"Don't move, you fucking monster."

Her gaze met the eerily golden eyes of the animal over his shoulder. Other than blinking slowly, he didn't move, but the sense of familiarity made her whole body run hot.

She licked her lips, her mind stuttering to comprehend. Try as she might, she couldn't kill him, not a wounded creature in her grandmother's kitchen. He was a monster, one she'd run from for years. She'd never been this close to one. They'd never been this *real*.

Braced between her thighs, he was hot as lava and clearly sick with fever. How many creatures had Grandma patched up in this kitchen? She'd be mortified if Scarlet killed one, even a dreaded Growler.

She cleared her throat and moved to take her weight onto her knees and off his body, shifting her head to re-balance her antlers. What good was a Hunter who wouldn't kill a monster? What the hell was wrong with her?

Disgust and anger warred within her.

She kept the daggers pointed at him, ready to pounce again if necessary. "What are you doing here?"

He blinked slowly and whimpered, the high-pitched whine of a dog. He struggled to lift his head, but he had no fight left.

Looking at his elongated face reminded her of who he was though...what he was.

The last time a Growler had pushed through the

magical boundaries around the cottage, Scarlet's mother had been killed.

She dug one pointed tip of the dagger against the jugular of his neck. "Did you attack my grandmother? Where is she, and why are you here?"

Dear gods, don't let her be dead. Emotions clawed at her throat, but the Growler's eyes rolled back in his head as he slumped to the floor. The pool of blood was spreading, and for the first time she noticed that the front door was open. A trail of blood and snow led straight to him.

She reached over to touch it and rubbed her fingers together. He'd been here a few hours already based on the blood, and he wasn't going to move on his own, not with those injuries.

With a quick glance around, she got up and strode through the kitchen to the living room, her eyes taking in every detail as she shut the front door. Tidy kitchen, clean countertops, and neatly stacked dishes in the open cabinets. The long, wooden table separated the living room, which had two plush chairs flanking the large fireplace.

Nothing was out of place, other than the Growler bleeding all over the floor. The scent of herbs filled the air, covering up the tangy metallic blood that always made her heart race. Both rooms were neat as a pin, and Grandma would throw a fit if she saw the mess he'd left through the great open room. Bloody footprints marred the shining wooden floor, mixing with melted snow and ice.

Scarlet took the stairs two at a time, jerking to a halt when her antlers tangled with some drying herbs.

"Son of a bitch," she muttered, going slower as she removed leaves and plants from around her head and searched the rooms upstairs. Grandma's hairbrush and toothbrush were gone, along with her favorite floral print carpet bag. Maybe she went to the old druid's circle again to talk to the spirits?

Six months ago, if she would've found a Growler here, she would've slit his throat with no hesitation and said good riddance.

But she wasn't just a Hunter anymore. She had responsibilities to help the other cursed villagers. Plus, the wolf part of her curse complicated things. It was the only reason she hadn't killed him, why her stomach was so knotted at the thought of ending him. That had to be it.

If grandma was at the druid's circle, she'd not be back for days. She needed to clean up his mess before Grandma returned. If she was going to be here in the cottage with him, she might as well patch him up too.

Scarlet went back downstairs and stood over him. He didn't move, so she nudged him with her boot. He didn't grunt or groan or open his eyes.

Her heart raced again, and she knelt to feel for a pulse. She breathed a sigh of relief to feel a thready and weak heartbeat. Then she scowled and jerked her hand away. What did she care if the fucker died? That would be so much easier.

She ran her hands over his head. The fur was more like a mane of knotted and matted gray and black hair. Her hands tingled at the tickle of his fur, and they came away from the back of his head covered in the sticky juice of life.

She searched the rest of him, down his neck, and over his back. Carefully, she rolled him over and winced. Her chest ached at the sight of so many injuries.

Several gaping wounds still bled steadily at the shoulder, ribs, neck, and foot. Red mixed with the black, gray, and white fur all over his muscular body. Smaller scratches had caked with dirt and congealed into crusty scabs, sticking to his thick layer of fur.

She watched his chest, barely rising and falling. Her chest tightened as she looked up at his battered and bruised face.

He was going to die. She should be relieved to be rid of one more monster in the world, but strangely the fear threatened to choke her again. She knew in her soul that she had to fight to save him.

Besides, Grandma would want her to fix this. It wouldn't have mattered to Grandma whether he was a Growler or not. He'd obviously come here for help, and with him passed out cold, he was harmless and close to the Beyond.

She pursed her lips and got to her feet, pulling out a pan to start boiling water. She'd work to save him, but she wasn't going to rush around in panic.

Instead, she set the pot on the stove and lit it with a match, before going to the medicine cabinet and setting out herbs and jars for a poultice.

# Chapter Four

Eirwyn shifted in her chair, her ass going numb again. Nothing felt right, nothing tasted good, and she was cranky as hell. She hadn't even felt like smiling and sending Scarlet on her way yesterday morning.

She finished her letter to the Confederation representative still in Glathen. She shook the paper to dry the ink, then slipped it into the envelope and sealed it with her wax stamp.

Helga knocked and poked her head around the door. "Have a minute?"

Eirwyn leaned against the pillow behind her and nodded as she arched her back. "Of course."

Helga turned and backed her way through the door, pushing it open with her hip. "I think what I eat influences the taste of the tea. I drank a lot of peppermint yesterday. Can you taste peppermint in this newest batch of leaves?"

She laid a tray on the desk, and Eirwyn nodded as a stab of pain shot through her back. Thankfully Helga was too distracted pouring to pay attention.

She added two lumps of sugar and a dab of milk to the cup just the way Eirwyn liked it. Helga had been her lady's maid since she was a young girl. Some days, Eirwyn had driven her mad with all her wild ways, but Helga had stayed and even tried to protect her from her brother, Gastone, when she could.

Eirwyn took the warm cup and sipped. The flavors swirled on her tongue, and she closed her eyes and sighed.

"Ah yes, I can taste the peppermint! It's wonderful, Helga."

Helga beamed, her round face shifting as the skin around her eyes crinkled. "Thank you, your highness. I'll go cut more and package it up directly, if you like it."

"Oh yes, please do. Can you find Leopol and send him in too?"

Helga nodded and bobbed a curtsy, leaving the tray on the desk for Eirwyn to pour more later.

She looked out the window of her sitting room. It was tall enough to see over the top of the helrose hedge. Two giant eagles flew to the north, swooping and playing with each other.

She rubbed her stomach and winced at another stab of pain. Since the false pains had started, Knox and everyone else had informed her she couldn't fly anymore until the egg was delivered. Flying had been one of the best benefits of mating with Knox. It was everything she'd imagined it would be.

"That's the first thing I'm going to do when you're out of here, little one," Eirwyn sighed as she rubbed her stomach.

"Pardon me, your highness? You wished to see me?"

Eirwyn turned to see Leopol strolling into the room, his incorporeal form shimmering in the bright light from the open windows. The breeze blew her black hair into her face, and she pushed it aside.

"Have you done any research on what Scarlet reported? With the monsters in Busparia?"

Leopol nodded and held up one of the two books in his hands. She had no idea how he could interact with objects.

"Yes, actually, but we need more details to narrow down what type of monsters might be terrorizing your people."

She frowned. Were the Buspartans her people? Or were her people now simply those in the Feral Forest? She wasn't sure anymore. The lines had been blurred these past six months.

She pulled out another piece of paper and said, "I can send a message to the dwarves to see if they've made progress on reverse engineering my brother's spy mirrors. Gods knows there were enough on every street corner. If they can tap into the frequency and see what's going on in Busparia, we might see what monsters are there."

He nodded and held up the other book. "Another thing, your highness. I had the last five years of almanacs delivered a few weeks ago, and I think the winter is dragging on too long."

Eirwyn winced as this stab of pain shot up her spine, not staying low in her back like it'd been all day. Leopol took her reaction as dismay at his words, and he continued.

"Yes, I know. It's very concerning. The question is, could it be tied to the monsters somehow? There are several winter type monsters that spread cold, ice, even blizzards."

Eirwyn hissed a breath as the stab of pain began to pass, but Leopol just continued.

"Blizzards are more the norm in the mountains, but perhaps we should warn the mountain town? If you're sending a message to the dwarves, could your messenger continue north to the town mayor?"

Eirwyn nodded and wiped her sweating brow. Why was she so hot? She needed to move. She pushed herself up with the help of the arms of the chair and gritted her teeth.

She leaned on the desk and breathed deeply. "I think that's a great idea. Can you fetch Lailant and Knox please, while I write these letters?"

Leopol snapped his heels together and bowed slightly. "Right away, your highness."

He turned on his heel and walked through the door to the hallway, but Eirwyn didn't watch. Instead, her whole body froze as a trickle of something slid down her legs.

Well, thank the gods she'd sent for Knox. She bit her lip and thought through all the things she still needed to get done before the dragonling arrived.

Then she was a flurry of activity. First, she scrawled the two messages. She'd just signed her name when Knox strode through the door.

She rushed to shove the letters into the envelopes, but another stab of pain snaked around her back to her stomach, like a hand squeezing her insides. The wax seal stamp fell to the floor as she gasped, her hands slamming down onto the table.

The light in the room shimmered as her magic flared.

"Eirwyn!" Knox shouted, running the few feet to her side. "Are you alright? Is it the babe?"

She nodded through gritted teeth. "He's coming."

---

Knox's stomach was a knot of anxiety as he helped Eirwyn

change out of her under clothes. She leaned on the side of the bed, her hips swaying from side to side as she moaned.

He rushed to the bell pull and then to the door anyway. He shouted down the hall to a maid halfway down the stairs, "Fetch Lailant now!"

He didn't stop to see if she obeyed. Instead, he was back beside Eirwyn, helping her into the bed. She sighed when she laid back on the towering pillows and closed her eyes.

"Are you—are you napping?" His whisper was barely heard over the thunder of footsteps outside the door.

"No," Eirwyn said, her nostrils flaring and her lips pursing. "I'm breathing through the pain, Knox."

Her body relaxed as she sighed and finally opened her eyes. She pointed a shaky hand toward her sitting room door.

"There's two letters on my desk that need to go out today, one for the Confederation in Vidrland and the other to the dwarves."

Knox shook his head, taking her hand in his as his green, noxious gas sunk to the floor. He was breathing too heavily, his heart racing at all the terror filled thoughts that flashed through him.

"It can wait. We'll send them with news of our babe's arrival," he said, squeezing her hand.

Eirwyn's eyes flashed, and she opened her mouth to argue. But Helga, Hobbs, and Leopol threw open the door and piled into the room.

"Is it time?"

"I've sent for Lailant."

"What do you need?"

Knox pushed the sweaty hair from his mate's forehead and barked orders.

Eirwyn squeezed his hand, and he took a breath. He looked down to see her smiling, her eyes twinkling.

"Relax, I'm fine and so is the babe."

"But you could—"

"But I won't," she said, her jaw firming and her eyes narrowing. "Just because I'm having the first dragonling in hundreds of years doesn't mean everything comes to a stop. You still have a job to do. Send my messages. See if the eagle rider has had any more success taming the things, because we'll need the way clear for visitors when spring comes."

She hissed and squeezed his hand again, her eyes closing as her body stiffened. This time, she moaned, and the sound sent terror through him.

Lailant pushed through the door, her gnarled hand gripping a walking cane tightly. Her pale purple dress was faded, but the white apron was clean aside from berry stains on the hem.

Gray braided hair, wrinkles giving evidence of her advanced age, and yet her eyes were clear and focused. She took in the scene in a blink, then pushed him aside.

"The queen is right. Go downstairs and take care of things while I take care of her. I'll call you if you're needed."

Knox protested, but then found himself on the other side of the door as it closed in his face. He blinked and paced in front of it, his jaw stiffening as he heard Eirwyn moan once more.

Green gas filled the hallway, and he waved a hand to disperse it. He turned on his heel, his tail whipping around and hitting the wall. He paid it no heed, as Leopol came up the stairs followed by Hobbs and a towering pile of fresh linens.

"I'll take it," Knox said, reaching for the stack, needing

an excuse to go inside the room. He pushed open the door, but the sight of Eirwyn's creamy thighs covered in blood made him swoon.

Hobbs took the stack and stepped inside. Lailant looked over and pointed her bony finger, her eyes flashing. "Get out, I said."

The door slammed in his face at the force of her words. Knox blinked. Had Lailant shut it with her magic? He didn't think healers had that ability.

Leopol's icy hand on his shoulder made him look over. "Come, Knox. Let's go downstairs. Time to hurry and wait, eh?"

Knox ran a hand over his neck and tilted it, cracking it several times as they walked to the stairs. "Tell me that's normal," he pleaded.

Leopol nodded as they went down. "Absolutely. Your father wasn't even allowed in the manor. He was absolutely feral when you were born."

"Really?" Knox asked as they went to the library, his father's former office and now his own.

"Oh yes. He snapped at the servants so much and threw magic wildly. It was the most out of control I'd ever seen him."

Leopol grew quiet as he thought of his previous life. Hundreds of years has passed, but Knox could only imagine how lonely and sad his friend was now.

He was more of an uncle, his father's cousin, but he'd become so much more. He was a fount of knowledge, knew every inch of the library and castle, and taught Knox new things every day. Leopol had helped him learn how to lead the new Feral Forest kingdom in a way that would've made his father proud.

Leopol was his one link to the dragons of the past, to his

heritage. Knox poured a hefty drink of liquor and downed it in one gulp. The smooth burn of fire down his throat brought him back to the conversation. He burped a green puff of smoke and wiped the back of his mouth with a hand.

"What happened then?" Knox asked.

Leopol turned, his eyes focusing once more as he smiled. "Oh, the druids threw him from the castle. Told him to come back when he saw the light in your mother's window."

Knox put down the decanter. His stomach twisted. "That's it. The druid. Grandma should be here."

Leopol stroked his chin. "You could fly and get her. You're fast, so you can return before the delivery progresses too much. She's hours to go yet."

Tingles raced along his arms, and he strode to the door. "I hate not being able to know instantly if there's an emergency. Someday, there will be a way to communicate right away if she needs me."

Leopol's hand slapped his back. "But not today, my friend. Today you must trust nature and us to keep her safe."

"Your highness," Hobbs called from the stairs. Knox turned, his brows rising as Hobbs moved faster than he had in the past six months living here. He reached the bottom of the stairs and held out a small hand-sized pouch. "Lailant says you need to deliver this to Scarlet."

Knox slid it into his pants pocket, not bothering to see what it was. "How is she? Eirwyn? The babe?"

Hobbs smiled, but it was strained and tight. "Just fine, your highness. Lailant said all is going as she expected."

Knox ran a hand over the back of his neck. "That could be good or bad. Alright, if she asks for me, tell her where

I've gone?" Knox asked, glancing up the stairs as a moan echoed through the halls.

Leopol and Hobbs both nodded as Knox threw open the front door. "Watch out for the eagles on your way out," Leopol said.

Knox scoffed as he strode into the bright but weak winter sunshine. "I rather hope they give me an excuse to tear them apart. I feel savage."

Leopol followed him down the stairs, his eyes sad as Knox changed into dragon form. "It's the helplessness. I know exactly how you feel, Knox, but fetch the druid and be safe."

Knox nodded his big green head and spread his wings. His legs tensed as he launched into the air. A few tense moments always sent adrenaline through him. It was a struggle to make it over the helrose hedge.

He circled the castle, spying the small cluster of cottages about a half-mile south. Well outside the eagle's breeding grounds to the north, it was their third settlement in six months. Their numbers were growing steadily as more and more Buspartans sought refuge in the Feral Forest.

He shook his head at the irony of it and turned southwest toward Grandma's cottage.

# Chapter Five

Wulfric floated in the water, struggling to keep his head up so he could breathe. No, it wasn't water. Clouds? He floated but with every tight breath, he sank lower and lower to earth. His mind fought to stay in the air, but he couldn't breathe.

He sucked in a shallow breath at the pain in his side. A weight pressed on his chest. A noise like an anchor dropping brought him back to the ground, and he pried his eyes open. Caked and dry, it took longer than normal for the world to come into focus.

A fire crackled in the hearth beside him. The hearth... it reminded him of a long-forgotten past. The grinding sound came again, and he turned his head to the side, groaning at the pain in his neck.

A goddess stood at the table, grinding lavender into a mortar. The stench of crushed ginger, turmeric, cloves, and oregano filled the air. On the table in front of her, oil jars and soaking salt were spread out. As he watched, she picked up the oil and added a few drops into the bowl.

Efficient, confident, capable, yes, but a goddess wouldn't be doing such work. His eyes flitted around the room, taking in the table, the kitchen, the comfortable chairs. He'd made it to the dreaded druid's cottage. She must be the one they'd all been warned away from.

Muscles rippled under her green shirt, sleeves rolled up as she worked. She was lithe, a small woman, but dressed unlike anything the female Growlers wore. The black leather vest was laced tight on the sides like some sort of armor, matching her black pants and mud-caked black boots. A green shirt under the vest had sleeves rolled up to her elbows.

But it was her face that captivated him. Pale with white freckles sprinkled across her nose like a newborn fawn.

He blinked, his mind too slow for his liking. Was her nose that of a rabbit? Or was it a deer? He frowned, not seeing any whiskers.

She wasn't human, but she wasn't quite like him, either. A wide rack of antlers stuck up from either side of her head, and long ears hung down to her shoulders like a rabbit.

A riot of red, curly hair was piled between her antlers like a crown. It was silky, wild, and unlike anything he'd seen before. Well, in the ten years he'd been a Growler. She picked up the mortar bowl and sniffed, her cute little pink nose twitching just like a little rabbit.

His body was on fire. Sweat or blood dripped down his temple, yet he couldn't move. He hated that he was lying flat on his back, vulnerable to her, a stranger, an enemy, a beautiful and terrifying druid.

But he didn't feel any threat from her as she walked over, her swaying hips making his heart race.

His breathing grew shallower, but when their eyes met,

his entire body froze. His breath, his heart, his entire world seemed to shift on its axis as their eyes connected.

Her green eyes called to the wild part of his soul. A growl rose in his throat, and his fingers itched to reach for her, hold her, claim her.

She slowed to a stop and frowned, tilting her head in confusion. Excitement coursed through his veins, and even with his injuries, his body felt the zing of desire and awareness. The hair stood up the back of his neck.

"You feel it, too?" His voice was ragged and rough from disuse, but it seemed to jerk her from the trance they were under.

She scowled and knelt at his side. "I don't know what you're talking about," she said, her eyes flitting down his body with awareness. "You're gravely wounded. If you were human, you'd be dead by now."

"Growlers self-heal," he said, never taking his eyes off her, his mind racing to comprehend these feelings. He watched for her reaction to his words, but she didn't run away screaming like most humans. She was an enigma that he wanted to peel back, layer by layer.

She nodded and dipped her fingers into the bowl. "So I've heard, but some of your deeper wounds are taking a while, and I'm worried about the fever. At least you're awake now, though. You've been passed out for hours. But it's a good sign that you're morphing back into a more human shape, right?"

He glanced down in surprise, seeing his hybrid form was back. Pain shot through his body in multiple directions at the movement of his neck. Teeth clenched together, he fell back onto the floor to wait out the wave of nausea.

It was several moments later that he realized her soft, chilly hand was rubbing the poultice on his shoulder and neck. Her voice was quiet, and even with his wolf hearing, he couldn't make out the words.

But he recognized it as a spell of some sort, the tone similar to that the Elders used in ceremonies.

Her hand moved down his chest to his lower ribs. The coldness of the cream seeped under his fur, soaking into his body. For the first time, he could breathe a little deeper, a little easier. It wasn't a miracle cure, but it was definitely better.

His body relaxed bit by bit, and he opened his eyes. The bowl was set aside, but her hand still rubbed up and down his chest slowly. She stared at her hand, his torso, as if confused on why she was still touching him.

His abs rolled at her touch, wanting more. His nose flared as he smelled her heady scent, heard her breath hitch as she stared at him. Her fingers made his body flutter but not from pain.

How long had it been since someone had touched him like this? It'd been months since his last mating, but Growlers were wild and ferocious, biting and snarling for dominance. There was no tenderness among Growlers.

He hadn't had a gentle touch since he'd become a Growler. She was so soothing, so caring and calm as she wound the gauze over the poultice. His eyes grew heavy as he relaxed under her magical hands.

---

Scarlet kept scrubbing the floor in the kitchen, trying to get the blood out of the wood before Grandma got home. She'd be pissed if she found a mess, and Scarlet had spent the past few hours cleaning. The Growler was still passed out, but his presence was like a beacon. She kept stealing glances at him as she worked.

Thank the gods he looked more mannish now. It had made her fear diminish enough to take care of him without shaking.

She sat back on her haunches and rubbed her shoulder, the pressure on her neck and head pulsing with a dull ache. Fucking antlers.

The door flew open with a bang and Scarlet jumped up, pulling her daggers and crouching in front of the Growler. Fear threatened to choke her as her heart raced.

A cloaked figure stood in the doorway, wind blowing the edges around a pair of muddy boots. Scarlet blinked and relaxed as the aura penetrated her brain. Grandma pushed her hood from her head and stepped through the door, shutting it behind her.

If her red hair wasn't streaked with gray, she could've passed for Scarlet's sister. They had the same green eyes and freckles, although Scarlet's had morphed with her curses. Both of them were average height and build, although Grandma had less muscle than Scarlet.

Scarlet slowly stood, putting her daggers away. "Grandma, where have you been?"

Olive arched her brows and removed her cloak to hang on the hook by the door, her muddy skirts swishing. "Is that any way to greet your grandmother, child?"

Scarlet rolled her eyes and strode over, taking the heavy basket from her with one hand and giving her a side hug with the other. "Welcome home, Grandma. I was worried about you."

Olive patted her back with a sigh. "I know, but I'm fine. I had a dream, so I went to find the glockenberry."

"What the hells is a glockenberry?" Scarlet asked, releasing her.

"A rare plant that only grows in one part of the forest. Is that him?" Olive slid the bag from her back and strode to the kitchen table, pointing to the fireplace.

"Who?"

"The Growler."

Scarlet shook her head, which just made the headache from the weight of her antlers worse. "Were you expecting him?"

Growlers had been banned from this part of the forest, and the magical protections around the cottage's clearing typically kept out any who tried to get in. As Growlers came closer to the cottage, the magic attacked them with gut-wrenching pain.

Normally. If Grandma had disabled the protections because she'd been expecting him, it would explain how he'd been able to get inside in such a weak state.

Olive stared at the Growler laying under the blankets near the hearth and shrugged. "He needs the glockenberry, according to the dream, but I was worried I wouldn't make it back in time."

Scarlet shook her head, pushing down her need to know all the details. The more she asked, the more confused she'd be. All she could do was wait for Olive to explain everything on her own. Her grandma talked in cryptic riddles when she was in full-on Druid mode.

Olive quickly washed her hands and strode to the shifter while Scarlet put the cleaning supplies back where they belonged.

As the sun had begun to set, his features had turned more human. His mouth had shortened to be less of a muzzle, although he still had the nose of a wolf and a soft layer of short gray and black fur all over.

His claws had receded into calloused hands. The erect ears of a wolf were visible above a full mane of gray and black hair that fell to his jawline. The even rise and fall of his chest revealed a white patch of fur and bandages though a blanket covered his lower half.

Olive knelt beside him, and Scarlet's gut twisted. She knew Olive would work to heal him, but the anxiety and worry over his continued sleep ate at her. It was why she hadn't been able to sit still all day.

Scarlet explained how she'd found him and what she did as Olive unwrapped his injuries.

"And he hasn't woken up since after you moved him this morning?"

Scarlet shifted on her feet and nodded, her hands behind her in a tight clasp, feet spread slightly in parade rest. "Correct. And his fever keeps climbing, I think. At least, he feels hotter tonight than he did earlier."

Olive hummed as she thought, then said, "The glockenberry... that's why I had to find it."

Scarlet frowned. "What are you talking about?"

Olive waved behind her. "Make some tea, child. We need to make a healing potion and mix the glockenberry in with it."

Scarlet strode to the kitchen and worked while Olive continued muttering.

"Don't make me regret this, Growler. You're her only hope."

Scarlet frowned and picked up the basket near the door, wondering what her grandmother was talking about. How could a Growler give hope to anyone? Their presence normally spelled painful death for their prey.

The hair on the back of her neck stood up, and she shivered at memories of running from the monsters. Being chased through the forest under the threat of death was among her least favorite activities. When she'd first gone with her dad on Ranger missions, they'd raced time after time through the woods to escape the Growlers.

Then just last summer, she'd escorted Eirwyn here, running from the pack of Growlers the entire way through the forest. Their howls had haunted her once more, bringing back nightmares she'd long suppressed.

As a kid, she'd grown tired of running and had learned to fight. She refused to be a weak damsel in distress. She could handle herself now.

But that underlying childhood fear had come back since she'd been twice cursed. It was the fucking scared little rabbit within her. Her jaw clenched as she reached for the now cleaned mortar and pestle.

Olive joined her and took over in the kitchen, so Scarlet stepped back, watching to see how she could help, waiting to see if Olive would explain more.

"Here, grind this please." Olive handed her the bundle of purple flowers, roots dangling, then worked quietly to make the tea.

"The glockenberry, I presume?" Scarlet asked, crushing the flowers into the mortar and picking up the pestle.

Olive hummed. "Yes, child. I know how you feel about Growlers, but I'm glad you didn't kill him outright. This is good, very good."

Unease shot through her spine as she ground the plant, and she glanced at where he lay on the floor. "How is this good? He's a monster, a Growler, and yet you don't sound surprised that he's here or that I spared him."

Olive shrugged, pouring three mugs of tea and sitting at

the table. "I'm not. It was actually heartwarming to see you jump up and protect him when I came in. I made the right choice, I think, but only time will tell."

Scarlet frowned, more confused at the cryptic words than before. She shifted on the balls of her feet and grunted with the flex of her muscles. If the plant was a fine powder, it'd be a more effective potion. Hope for him to be healed warred with her confusion, and she latched onto the one thing she did understand.

She asked, "What do you mean, protect him? I was protecting myself."

Olive snorted, "Don't fool yourself, child. Not over this. Not over him."

Scarlet paused, her mind working furiously. Why him? What did Grandma know that she didn't? She twisted her wrist and gripped the stone pestle tightly. "I don't know what you're talking about."

Olive hummed again, staring at the wolf by the fire as she drank her tea. Scarlet finished in silence, biting her tongue as the frustration swirled in her gut. Then she held the mortar to her grandmother. "How's this?"

Olive nodded and took the stone bowl, mixing the powder into the two remaining mugs. The steam curling up turned blue then green. Olive smiled grimly and looked at Scarlet, her eyes piercing her.

Scarlet froze and pressure increased on her chest, like when she'd been caught stealing cookies as a kid. Hair stood on the back of her neck under that intense gaze.

"You will drink one, and he will drink the other."

Scarlet's breath shuddered as her head shook automatically. "No." Her gut twisted again. This was a bad idea. That look in Olive's eyes said there was more to this than what she was saying.

Olive arched her brow. "No?"

Scarlet frowned. "I'm sorry, Grandma, but if the glockenberry is a super powerful version of a normal healing potion, shouldn't he take it all? He's the one that's gravely injured and getting worse."

Olive's lips twitched with pride, but Scarlet knew she was holding back information. Scarlet hadn't made it this long as a Hunter without having great instincts, and something was off about this.

"He will take enough of it, but this is something we haven't tried to break your curse. Don't you want to see if it will work?"

Scarlet's eyes widened. It might help her curses?

"Well, why didn't you just say that?"

With no further thought, she grabbed a mug and downed it, gulping the warm liquid. Her nose wrinkled as she drank, the smell assaulting her sensitive shifter senses.

She slammed the mug onto the counter as if she were back in the tavern. She smacked her lips, trying to get the bitter, gritty after-taste out of her mouth. Her throat spasmed, and she choked, her eyes watering. Olive passed over her own mug of regular tea, and Scarlet drank that too.

When her breathing returned to normal, Scarlet pulled on one of her long ears and scowled.

Olive chuckled and shook her head. "Give it time, child. Come, help me get him to drink."

Olive's eyes glittered with anticipation as she stood, taking the remaining magical mug to the Growler by the fire. Scarlet followed, kneeling at his head as Olive directed her to lift him enough to drink.

He moaned and his eyes fluttered at the movement, but he didn't wake.

"Come on." Scarlet grunted, pushing his wide shoulders up. She propped him up and watched as Olive held the mug to his lips, pulled down his jaw, and began to pour the potion slowly inside.

He grunted, eyes closed, but seemed to swallow fine. He didn't gag or choke or move.

When the mug was empty, Olive moved back. "Alright, you can lay him back down."

"Now what?" Scarlet asked. "How long does it take for it to work?"

The sharp tone of voice made her wince. She was terrified again, which made her angry.

Stupid fucking rabbit instincts that made her want to hide while she waited for the potion to take effect. Worry twisted her stomach in knots. She didn't want to get her hopes up. Not again.

"Not long," Olive said, her eyes flitting between Scarlet and the Growler and back again.

When she'd first been cursed months ago, she'd come straight to Olive's. They'd tried every spell, potion, and magic in the old druid's repertoire, but nothing had worked. Then Scarlet had gone to the other two druids at the Robin's camp, facing all the stares and horror-filled gazes, but with no success.

Scarlet laid the man's head on the floor and frowned, realizing that her hand was brushing his gray and black hair away from his face.

"Why don't you go up to bed, child? You look like you haven't slept in a few days."

Scarlet sighed and shook her head. "I haven't, but I'm not leaving you down here with him. If this magically cures him, he might wake and attack. No, I'm fine, but you can go up to bed. I'm sure you're tired, since you've been gone all day."

Olive stood with a grunt, stretching her back. The dirty hem of her dress brushed against the Growler's blanket, but he didn't stir. The fire beside her burned too hot as she thought about what lay under the blanket. With Grandma's return, she was suddenly glad that she'd thrown the patchwork over him when his wolf's body had begun to morph into a more human shape. A well-defined man's shape.

"That's a great idea. If you're sure you'll be alright..."

Scarlet blinked as she tried to remember what they'd been talking about. She cleared her throat. "I'm sure, Grandma. We're fine here."

Scarlet looked up and caught the calculating expression on Olive's face before she smiled innocently. Olive ran her hand down Scarlet's cheek.

"My precious child, the world is changing, and with it, what you thought you wanted. I hope I have prepared you enough."

Scarlet twisted to watch her, frowning at the cryptic words. Sadness and worry warred within those words, but Scarlet still didn't know why. Questions swirled in her mind, making her dizzy.

She dragged herself to the deep cushioned chair beside the fire. She leaned back, her vision swimming as her head pounded.

Before her eyes closed, she checked the Growler's aura. Her body relaxed as she watched it grow incrementally stronger.

# Chapter Six

Wulfric's nose twitched as the rich aroma of sizzling bacon, juicy sausage, and savory ham wafted through the air, filling the room with a tantalizing scent. Slowly, he blinked open his sleep-heavy eyes, feeling the crust of tiredness that coated them. With a deep sigh, he raised a hand to rub at his weary gaze before lifting his head to survey his surroundings.

The room spun as he blinked, taking precious seconds to get his bearings. Memories came back but only the recent ones yet again. The fight with Brody. The icy river. The druid's cottage.

Squinting, he took in his surroundings. A woman with curly gray and red hair stood at the stove, stirring a pot of soup and humming to herself. He rubbed at the stiffness in his neck as he tried to remember how she got there. As he stretched, he felt a dull ache in his muscles, but it was nothing compared to the agony he had felt before.

He heard the even breathing behind him and turned his head.

The younger red-haired druid who had taken care of him lay on a large, cushioned chair, one leg thrown over an armrest, her head hanging over the other. Black pants clung to her calves near his head, and awareness slammed into him.

This was the woman who'd nursed him back from death. He glanced at the woman in the kitchen, warily watching her. The way she moved reminded him of the younger woman behind him. A relative, perhaps?

His mind was fuzzy, and he couldn't remember talking to the younger one, but he must have. He felt like he'd known her for years. For once, he wasn't worried about being vulnerable to someone behind him.

He came up on his good elbow, his injured arm wrapped close to his side with gauze. Beads of sweat broke out on his upper lip as he rolled to his knees, and his breathing grew shallow. His vision tilted and his heart raced from the pain.

The old woman's skirts coming into view and a soft hand settled on his back, causing him to snarl and recoil in surprise. His body collided with the other cushioned chair, sending it skidding across the floor as waves of pain crashed through him. It felt like shards of glass piercing his skin, each one leaving a searing trail of agony in its wake. He could feel his muscles tense and shake under the intensity of the pain, his breath coming out in ragged gasps.

The sound woke the younger woman, and she jumped to her feet, daggers appeared in her hands as she jumped in front of the old woman, ready to defend her. Green eyes scanned the room, then she slammed him back onto the ground, her knee on his chest and daggers to his throat.

His entire body tensed under her weight, prepared to fight against her. The raw power and determination in her eyes only fueled his own determination to break free from her grasp. It was a battle between two fierce warriors, each unwilling to back down without a fight.

"No," the other woman shouted, making the younger one above him freeze. Gods, she was beautiful, like an avenging angel.

Bright green eyes as deep as the forest at sunset. A wild mane of curly hair piled on top of her head just begged him to bury his hands in it. High cheekbones, wide little rabbit nose that twitched as she breathed deeply, her breasts rising and falling in the confines of the black vest and green shirt.

Their eyes met, both of their hearts racing. He could see the pounding of hers at her neck, the wildness in her eyes. A deep part of himself recognized her, wanted to flip her over and wrestle for dominance...

Wanted to claim her as his.

He blinked in surprise, and his heart stuttered as his body went slack beneath her.

She was his mate.

The Elders had said when the bond hits, they'd know. By the gods, they were right. He'd seen the mate bond snap into place while on a pack run with a neighboring pack. There had been no tearing those two apart. They were lucky to both have lived through it.

He wrestled with control of his primal side, not wanting to hurt this woman or scare her away. She wasn't a Growler. She might not survive a rough claiming, even if she accepted him.

He'd seen a mate bond be denied, too. They'd both wound up dead within a few weeks. The need to protect her flowed through him, giving him new energy. Even if he had to protect her from a rough claiming from him or from herself, he'd see her safe and loved

He shuddered, renewed purpose and the weight of a new responsibility settling in his soul. His hand wrapped around her wrist at his throat, his thumb caressing back and forth on her skin.

The magic of the mate bond made his mouth water, and he desperately wanted to kiss her.

Her jaw slackened and eyes darkened, flaring in recognition. Her hands shook as she slid away from him, sitting on her ass beside him. She brushed the hair from her face and blinked with a stunned expression.

Did she feel it, too? Did she know what they were to each other?

His heart raced as he looked up at the older woman, concern clearly written on her face. But he could only drag his eyes away from his mate for a second before he looked back at her.

He blinked, trying to memorize the beauty's face, as the other woman sighed and wiped her hands on her apron.

"It's as the dream foretold," she said softly, solemnly. Then she cleared her throat. "Alright, breakfast is almost ready. I'm sure you're both famished. Growler, you can sit in the chair if you feel able, but don't push yourself. Just sit where you are if you'd like, and I'll bring you a plate."

He came up on one elbow and leaned against the chair behind him, never taking his eyes from the goddess of his dreams even as his vision swam. "Who are you?"

His voice was gravelly and weak, and the woman frowned. She came to her feet gracefully and walked to the kitchen table, putting one of her daggers away and grabbing a mug.

He smirked, glad she never turned her back on him. His Red was a smart woman. His eyes narrowed. She wasn't his yet, but she would be soon. He had to plan how to claim her without killing her or making her deny it. It wouldn't be easy. With her prickly nature, she'd be hard to get close to.

And those slightly curved antlers, two sticking up like a deer's but with no other points. They were only about the length of a hand and not very tall, but they could spear a man to death with how pointed they were. If he got too close and she didn't want him to be, he'd be gutted.

They were above the cute little rabbit ears that stuck up on the sides of her head, soft red curls falling around them as her bun was loosened. A long red bushy tail flicked behind her. What was she?

He'd never seen the like before. She was one of a kind, predator and prey, all wrapped in one neat little package. He wanted to know everything about her, why she was so quick to draw those daggers, why she was so tender when she applied the salve.

She handed him the mug, dagger ready in her other hand. He wiped the sweat from his lip and took the mug with his free hand. His bad arm, ribs, and entire left side throbbed where they were bound together with bandages.

"I'm Scarlet," the young woman said. "A Hunter and Olive's granddaughter."

She nodded to the woman in the kitchen, and he drank the water, gulping like it'd been days since his last drink.

Shit, she was a Hunter. They were the reason the Growlers kept to the forest now. Hunters had almost wiped their race out until the Elders had turned them with the gift.

Scarlet. Her name rang in his head like a bell. He couldn't wait to yell her name in the throes of passion.

He smacked his lips and lowered the cup. "How long have I been here?" His voice wasn't as rough, but he raised the cup to finish drinking anyway.

"I found you yesterday morning. Your fever was terrible,

but Grandma came home with a special herb. Seems like it worked."

He grinned slowly. "You don't have to sound so put out about the fact that I survived."

She shrugged and sat in the chair opposite of him, twirling her dagger between her fingers. "I have no opinion about your continued existence here."

"Shame," he murmured. "I'd be devastated if something happened to you, Red."

Her eyes narrowed, and the dagger stopped, trapped between her forefinger and thumb as if ready to throw at his head. Then she scowled, "Don't call me Red. My name is Scarlet."

His lips widened. She was feisty, and it sent a thrill through him. "And you can call me Wulfric, alpha of the Growlers." He frowned, looking down at the empty mug. Well, he may be the former alpha.

He'd need to reclaim his title so he'd have something worth offering her. Growler women had tried for years to chain him down, but they'd never felt right. Not even when he'd slept with a few of them. That had just been scratching an itch.

He looked up. Scarlet was a completely different matter. He needed to proceed with caution if he was going to convince her to claim him back.

The older woman returned and handed him a heaping plate of food, mostly meat and eggs. He set the mug on the floor and took the plate, but the older woman took the mug.

"I'm Olive, as Scarlet said. Why don't you tell us what brings you to seek help from this old druid? The Growlers haven't been here in thirty years, and with good reason. We're not exactly on friendly terms."

She turned and grabbed a pitcher from the table as she

talked, refilling his mug. Her words rang true, and he sensed no danger from her.

Then her words finally penetrated his still healing brain.

"Wait, you're the druid everyone says to stay away from? Not Scarlet?" He pointed with the fork, then looked at the utensil, a tingling feeling in the back of his brain as he stared at it. He knew it was a fork and how to use it, but he'd not used one in years. Not since turning into a Growler.

He took a deep breath, but pushed aside the thoughts as the old woman waved a hand. "Scarlet's learned basic healing and druidic practices, yes, but sadly, her talents weren't magical enough to become a full druid."

Wulfric watched as Scarlet's dagger paused in the back-and-forth pattern and her eyes lowered. She had feelings about that. Was she disappointed in herself or relieved?

Then her back stiffened, and she lifted her jaw. "A better question would be, how did you get through the protective barriers? They're designed to keep out Growlers, among other things."

Pride made him smile around a full bite of ham, but it was the druid that answered her granddaughter.

"Oh, I disabled them, child."

Scarlet sighed and briefly closed her eyes. "I was afraid of that. Grandma, that's—"

"Dangerous? I know," Olive sighed, walking back to him with the cup again. "But the dream showed me what had to happen, so I obeyed. And it's a good thing I did, isn't it? Otherwise, he would've bled out in the forest or been eaten by the forest itself."

Scarlet shivered and sank back against the chair, her jaw set in a sullen expression. Good, she had a healthy under-standing of how dangerous the Feral Forest could be.

He was a third of the way through the plate when the druid handed him the refilled cup, which he immediately chugged.

Olive snorted and turned back to the table, bringing the entire pitcher to refill it. "Wulfric, is it? Dreams are sometimes fuzzy on the details. What brings you here?"

He took a deep breath, feeling compelled to tell the woman everything. He recognized it as magic, but didn't fight it. The Elders used this type on them all the time.

"It was a normal night, and I was doing a perimeter check. A few other Growlers ambushed me in an illegal alpha challenge. I could only take out two and a half of the five who attacked. Felt like I might have more odds of surviving if I regrouped, healed, and then returned to take back my position."

He began to eat again, but didn't miss the look that the two women exchanged. Scarlet sat back in the chair and tossed the dagger, catching it easily by the handle.

"Why did they challenge you? Were you a terrible leader?"

He looked at her as he chewed more slowly, thinking over the past few years. After another drink, he said, "I don't think so but there have been grumblings over the past few months. Several of the newer Growlers think that the new queen isn't strong enough to hold the current boundaries of Busparia. They speak of an invasion, of taking control, but I think most of them just miss home."

Olive shifted on her feet, her face almost a mirror expression of Scarlet's. They both were so eager, wanting to know more.

"Is it true?" Olive said. "Growlers are both born and turned?"

He looked at her and nodded slowly. Even though he no

76

longer felt the compulsion, he owed them some answers, since they'd saved his life. "Yes, but I can't tell you how. That information is forbidden by the Elders and will never be discussed outside of the pack. Even as alpha, I don't know the spells or how it works."

Olive seemed to deflate as she tapped her chin. Then she looked at Scarlet with a contemplative expression as he continued to eat.

"What?" Scarlet asked, blinking. "What are you thinking?"

Olive pursed her lips and hummed. "Well, I'm thinking the same method that turns humans into Growlers might also be used in reverse to change your curse."

Scarlet's eyes widened, but Olive continued. "What remains of your curse, anyway. Your ears and horns have shrunk thanks to the glockenberry, but sadly it didn't cure it completely."

Scarlet's jaw dropped along with the dagger, her fingers flying to her head as the weapon clanged to the floor.

# Chapter Seven

Scarlet's throat threatened to close with emotion. Her ears no longer hung down to her shoulders, heavy and giving her way too many overwhelming sounds.

Now they stuck straight back from the sides of her head where her human ears had been. Even though they were a little longer than her old ears and still felt like small rabbit ears, she sighed in relief.

Above them, on the top of her head, stood two small antlers. She wrapped her hands around them, feeling the long, smooth points as they curved back slightly.

Gone was the wide rack of multi-pointed antlers that weighed her head down and made her neck hurt. Tears filled her eyes as she felt them, turning her head this way and that to get used to the new feeling.

How had she been sitting there, watching his every move, and hadn't noticed? He was too distracting, too mouth-watering for her liking. She was the best Hunter there was, damn it. She had great observation skills, but she'd completely missed the changes within herself.

She let the disappointment in herself go, the overwhelming joy of relief making her eyes mist. It wasn't a cure, but it was definitely more manageable.

Olive's gaze was filled with tears too, and Scarlet jumped up and wrapped her arms around her. "I—I, oh…"

Olive grunted and hugged her back. "Shh, it's alright, child. It's alright."

Scarlet's eyes closed as she tried to get a grip on the stupid emotions. The weight of her antlers was nothing compared to the weight of sticking out and not belonging. The smaller antlers would be hidden with her green and red cloak. She could go back to field work with the Hunters instead of managing teams. For the first time since she'd been cursed, it truly felt like life really was going to be alright.

"Thank you." She squeezed her eyes to stop the tears. She wasn't the crying type, even though her throat threatened to close and her eyes burned. All this emotion was unacceptable.

Olive patted her back. "I'm glad it worked," she said softly, holding her tight just like she'd done when Scarlet's mother had been killed.

By Growlers.

Her jaw clenched as she latched onto the anger and grief swirling inside. When they threatened to burst, she spun on her heel to flee to the washroom under the stairs.

She used the facilities, then splashed water on her face from the sink. She couldn't turn her back on the Growler. There was no telling what he might do.

But she had to get her emotions in check first. Weakness wouldn't do, not for a Hunter.

After a few more deep breaths, she was ready to go back out there and get some answers. Plus, she didn't want to leave her grandma alone with him for long, helpless though he may seem at the moment.

*Yeah, keep telling yourself that's the reason.*

Her body seemed to yearn to be in his presence, the ache in her chest at just being in a separate room made it difficult to breathe.

She opened the door and strode to the kitchen, carefully avoiding his heavy gaze. The way his golden eyes followed her every move made a shiver run up her spine.

She knew that look of interest, had seen it time and time again when she let herself be noticed by the nobles of Busparia or the tavern boys. Back when she'd been tasked with gathering information for various parties or taking out prominent society members, she'd not been above using her body to get what she wanted.

But there had always been safety in anonymity, the false identities and a sense of belonging when she was treated like any other woman.

This was different. The intensity of their connection was unlike anything she had ever experienced before. Every time he gazed at her, a wave of electricity seemed to course through her body, causing her skin to tingle with anticipation. And when she had him pinned beneath her thighs, she could feel herself melting into a puddle of desire.

This level of attraction to the Growler would be impossible to resist, but damn it, she was going to try. There was something about him that was too alluring, too dangerous for her to indulge in fully.

She loved skirting the edge of danger, but she wasn't stupid. She knew when to step back and regroup and when to attack and press her advantage. It's how they'd survived the last mission into Busparia.

She grabbed a drink and guzzled it, deliberating setting

her mind to all the Hunters had done last week. It was a needed distraction, and she still had to figure out what reconnaissance the Hunters needed to do next. They had to find out what those monsters were, for starters, and do it without getting killed. When she could breathe again, she grabbed a dish towel to clean up breakfast.

Even as she tried to shake off those thoughts, another danger loomed in front of her—him. She knew she needed to stay focused and keep her guard up, but her heart was pulling her in a different direction. By the gods, she had to find a way to balance these conflicting emotions

She shook her head, and the new lightness of her head reminded her of the changes and how that could affect the next mission. What did she need to know next, right in this moment?

She looked over at Olive. "Why didn't we try the glockenberry months ago when I first came to you for help?"

Olive sighed and joined her in the kitchen, loading another plate with food.

"The dream, child, the dream..." Her voice trailed off as she turned to put the plate on the table. "Sit, child. Eat, then we'll talk. Wulfric, would you like more?"

He grunted, licking the plate like the uncivilized Growler he was. Scarlet rolled her eyes and sat, picking up her fork and watching Olive as she sat at the table with her own plate.

Scarlet drummed her fingers on the table. "What aren't you telling me?"

Olive pointed at the plate with her fork and frowned, but didn't answer. Instead, she began to eat.

Scarlet sighed. There was no changing Olive's mind once she'd set it to something. It was a shared family trait.

Scarlet ate quietly, watching Wulfric out of the corner of her eye.

His aura was stronger today, and though he moved stiffly, he seemed fever free. Or rather, his swirling blue and gray auras were healthier.

But the way his golden eyes had looked up at her when she'd pinned him, like he was just toying with her and letting her have the upper hand...

Her core clenched at the memory, and her legs shifted restlessly. He'd been so solid between her legs, with muscles in all the right places.

A shiver raced through her body as she finished her food. There was no time for that kind of dalliance, especially with a Growler who'd just as soon kill her as fuck her.

The memory of racing through the woods last summer with Eirwyn, Growlers on their heels, made her squirm with unease. She hated feeling weak and vulnerable, but she had to remind herself who and what he was.

It was time to get him healed and send him home, but she couldn't do that without answers from Olive.

Scarlet set her fork down a little too hard and crossed her arms. "Well? I've eaten, so will you tell me what you're avoiding now?"

Olive wiped her mouth with a napkin and glanced at the Growler. "Very well, clear the table and bring a chair to the hearth while I visit the washroom."

Scarlet rolled her eyes at the delay tactic, but did as she was told. She took their empty plates to the sink, but when she spun around, the Growler blocked her way.

Her mouth dropped open in surprise. It wasn't often that someone could sneak up on her. She hadn't even heard him get up.

His human legs were covered in that soft layer of gray

and black fur, his thighs as thick as tree trunks. He was huge, a head taller than her own petite frame, wide as an oak, and just as solid. Her gaze drifted over his stomach muscles, her mouth watering as she looked up, avoiding looking at his crotch.

He glanced from her eyes down to her lips. Even with bandages wrapped around his shoulder and ribs, pinning one arm to his side, he exuded strength and vitality.

She sucked in a deep breath, and her tongue grew thick in her mouth. He smelled like grass and warmth, of a warm fire and safety. She wanted to melt into his embrace, even as the hair on the back of her neck stood.

He was a Growler. He was dangerous, unpredictable, a killer.

Her mind told her no, but her body swayed toward him as her eyes wandered. Her gaze dipped down to his lips, then her head jerked up, meeting his golden gaze.

Eyes crinkling in the corners, he smiled a wide, toothy grin as he leaned his one free hand on the counter behind her, caging her in and setting his empty plate down. "What's the matter, Red? Cat got your tongue?"

"You—you're naked," she said, fighting back a mewl of surrender and straightening her spine, chin tipped up as she gripped the edge of the counter behind her for support. Her hands wanted to reach out and touch him, but she held back, warring with herself.

*Snap out of it, Scarlet!*

"All the better to seduce you, my dear."

Her core responded like the hussy it was, but she frowned. "What?"

He wiggled his brows. "Do the smaller ears make you hard of hearing? If that's the case, just look down. The captain is eager to meet you."

She gasped and slid to the left, finding herself trapped in the corner of the kitchen, back against the medicine cabinet. "I'm not hard of hearing. And I'm not going to look down at—wait, did you say captain?"

His brows furrowed in confusion, then he shrugged. "So I did. Don't ask why, because I have no idea."

She blinked. He called his dick a captain but didn't know why? She had so many questions, but so did he apparently, as he turned to the sink and put his plate in the soapy water.

He took a shallow breath with a wince at the movement.

"What are you doing? Your knuckles are still raw and swollen."

He flexed his hand in the soapy water, his Growler nose twitching. "I know, but I thought I'd clean up after myself, so you wouldn't think I was uncivilized. I used to be human, you know, and not incompetent. But I can't seem to clean this one-handed."

She crossed her arms, trying to create a barrier between them. She wouldn't let him know she was rattled at the size of his... She swayed closer and panic made her stomach twist. "Tell someone who cares, Growler."

She scurried to the hearth and grabbed the blanket that had covered him before, ignoring how he made her body ache in places that had long since lost interest elsewhere. The hair on the back of her neck stood up, as if reminding her not to taunt him and turn away.

But she just tossed the blanket at him as he walked slowly back to the fire. The damned Growler walked on his wobbly feet past her, limping slighting, his ass rippling with muscles that she wanted to bite into. She kept track of him out of the corner of her eye as he wrapped the blanket around his waist.

Olive returned from the washroom as he practically fell into the other cushioned chair.

"Be careful," Scarlet snapped, glaring at him as she dragged a kitchen chair to the hearth and turned it backward. "You'll open your stitches."

She straddled the chair, resting her arms along the smooth wooden surface of the back. The stretch of fabric brought a delicious friction against her clit, and she squirmed against it.

His eyes twinkled even as his lips were pursed in pain. "Aw, I didn't realize you cared, love. If I did bust a stitch, would you kiss it and make it better?"

"When the hells freeze over," she shot back with a glare.

He grinned wider and chuckled. The sound sent a shiver down her spine, straight to her pussy. Damn him, why hadn't she just killed him when she had the chance?

Olive chuckled too but didn't take her eyes from her knitting basket. "I see I made the right choice. That settles that."

Olive pulled out her knitting and sat in the other cushioned chair as she hummed softly, the needles making a soothing click-clack that brought memories of her childhood.

Scarlet's body relaxed at the comforting sounds as she processed Olive's words. "What do you mean, right choice? In saving him?"

Olive waved a knitting needle. "Never mind that. Wulfric, you are going to reclaim the alpha title, yes?"

He nodded, wincing as he stretched his side. She watched him warily, surprised that he fit in the chair at all, and refused to acknowledge the worry about his stiffness and healing.

"Wonderful. You'll take Scarlet with you and convince the Elders to reverse her curse," Olive said.

Scarlet's jaw dropped. "Are you fucking serious? There's no way I'm going into the heart of Growler territory."

Olive frowned, giving her the look, the one that said there would be no arguing.

Not that Scarlet ever heeded the warning. "Come on, Grandma. You just want a human to walk into the Growlers camp and say, hey, help me break a curse, will you?"

Olive shrugged, "Except you're not exactly human anymore, are you?"

Dread settled in her belly like a brick.

Wulfric stroked his chin, the blanket thankfully covering his lower half with his enormous feet stretched toward the fire. They were hairy paws but long like human feet. The dichotomy was confusing and made her head hurt.

"I'm afraid I have to agree with Scarlet on this. It's not a good idea. I haven't seen a non-Growler in camp since I joined them ten years ago. I'm not sure what they'd do. Probably turn her into a Growler at the very least."

Panic crept up in her throat at the thought of losing control and causing chaos, yet a small part of her longed for the freedom and power that came with being a Growler. It would eliminate this rabbit's nature to fear everything and everyone. It was a never-ending internal battle for Scarlet, one that left her feeling conflicted and torn between four sides of herself. To be a normal human, to be a fearful rabbit, to run from trouble like a deer, or to face it all and fight like a Growler? Gods, she hated being pulled in all these directions.

Scarlet snorted and sat up, hands gripping the back of the chair until her knuckles turned white. "The hells I'll be turned into a Growler."

"You already are a quarter Growler, child," Olive said softly. "Your tail?"

Scarlet glared. "I'm nowhere near the mindless monster. Maybe a wolf, but not a Growler."

Olive arched a brow and slowly turned to stare at Wulfric. "You're not a mindless monster, are you, dear?"

He smirked. "Only when I have to be. Or when a girl begs for it."

While she didn't want to be seen as a mindless monster like the other Growlers, she also couldn't deny the animalistic tendencies that had been growing inside her the past six months. And now, with Wulfric's teasing smirk and Olive's pointed question, she couldn't ignore the undeniable attraction she felt towards him.

But as tempting as giving in to her primal instincts and desires may be, there would be severe consequences. She was already struggling with being accepted in this world, but adding on a Growler transformation would just alienate her even more.

Even if it would be fun to rut with him in mindless abandon, forget her curses, this human need to fit in, the desire for companionship and partnership.

Scarlet's chest tightened, and an image of him turning into an animal in the bedroom made her cheeks flush. "And that's not even addressing the fact that I'm female. They'll lose their heads! The full moon is next week. No, no, no, no."

Wulfric ran his hand through his hair, the thoughtful expression on his face sending her panic higher. "Actually, it might work."

Scarlet shook her head and pulled out a dagger to clean under her nails. Having the blade in her hand brought her comfort, settling her nerves slightly. She couldn't have them both agreeing.

"By the gods, you change your mind fast," she grumbled.

He shrugged, stretching his shoulder as his gaze was unfocused above Olive's head. "I take a while to process, Red. Let me think this through, but it might work."

Scarlet's breathing grew shallow. She couldn't go with him to the Growlers camp. Maybe she could entice him with something else? "No, it won't. You've been demoted and probably pronounced dead. This is your chance for a new life. Take it and run. Go somewhere new."

Grandma nodded. "Yes, he could come to Hartsgrove or Vidrland with us, couldn't he? I'm sure Knox and Eirwyn would love to have a Growler aid their cause. He could be useful. Who knows?"

"Vidrland?" Wulfric asked, his lips twisting. "You mean that upstart king that's taken over the northern half of the forest? You have to be mad, woman. That's enemy territory, and they have to be pushed back to the mountains."

Scarlet pointed her finger at him. "First, that's my brother you're talking about. He's no upstart. He's a dragon whose family has ruled this forest for hundreds of years. And second, what do you mean pushed back to the mountains? What are the Growlers planning?"

Wulfric's jaw stiffened with emotion. "The argument in our tribe was about which way we would expand. Either east into Busparia or north into dragon territory. We had settled on going north a few days ago, before I was ambushed."

Scarlet pointed the dagger at him. "And you were on the side of invading the dragon's lair? By the gods, you're dumber than I thought."

His eyes flared, and his hand gripped the armrest of the chair, claws growing as his emotions heightened. "I'm not. It's a calculated risk and the better option, considering Growlers are forbidden from leaving the forest."

"Other than to raid the Southern Road, pick off injured soldiers returning from war, turn them into more Growlers, and thus grow your numbers. You know, if you'd just leave them alone, your tribe wouldn't be running out of room."

Wulfric's eyes narrowed and his mouth and nose began to elongate. "You don't know what you're talking about."

"Yes, I do. I've seen the reports in Busparia."

"No, you don't. It's not like that."

"Yes, it is."

"No—"

"Enough," Olive laughed, shocking them both enough to turn to her with surprised expressions. "Oh, this is going to be fun to watch."

"What are you talking about now?" Scarlet asked, completely at a loss.

Olive smiled and set her needles down. "Wulfric can come with us to Hartsgrove to see Knox and Eirwyn, or you can go with him to the Growlers tribe. Those are your options right now."

Scarlet frowned. "Why can't he just run home, and I'll take you to Eirwyn? I think that's a much better plan."

Olive's lips twitched again as she looked down intently at her knitting. "Well, you see, the glockenberry only grows in one area of the forest. And the one plant was all I could find. It's very temperamental."

"How is a plant temperamental?" Scarlet asked. Exasperation made her voice higher than normal.

Grandma shrugged and shifted on the chair, still not

meeting Scarlet's gaze. A shiver of awareness went down her spine as dread spread.

"Well, this is the Feral Forest, after all. Plants and animals alike don't act like they should."

Scarlet glared at Wulfric, and opened her mouth to be a smart ass.

Olive said quickly, "The glockenberry doesn't release its healing properties and magic without consequences. It clings to itself until the very last moment. Since you both drank the tea made from it, you're tied together until the next full moon."

Scarlet blinked. "What?"

"Tied together? What does that mean?" Wulfric asked, his face now shifted back to the normal human mouth, the claws gone.

"The farther apart you two are, the weaker you'll be. If he goes to the Growlers and you go to see Eirwyn, the distance will literally kill you both."

Scarlet gripped the back of the chair and glared. "That's a load of shit."

"It's really not," Olive said, shaking her head but not looking up from her knitting. "With all magic, there are consequences. This is just the consequence of both of you ingesting the one plant. If I'd added it to my tea too, then we'd all be tied together."

Scarlet's eyes narrowed as she gasped. "You knew! You knew we'd be tied together! Grandma, why–"

"The dream," Wulfric said quietly. "She keeps muttering about a dream."

Scarlet looked from him to Olive who was nodding. "I can't tell you about the dream right now. Not yet, but you both needed to be tied together until the full moon. Which direction you go from here is up to you."

Scarlet's chest ached as she tried to catch her breath. Olive had been doing this cryptic shit all her life. Why couldn't she just bake cookies and heal hurts with magical kisses like other grandmas?

Olive put her knitting back in the basket beside her chair and stood, drawing Scarlet's gaze. "Talk it over while you clean his wounds and check his bandages. I'm going to feed the animals in the barn."

Olive grabbed her cloak by the door and slipped outside, boots crunching on the snow. Scarlet's head spun from information overload. She scratched her now-shorter ear, her mind spinning.

With a frown, she turned to Wulfric. "If she says the magic binds us, there's a fifty-fifty chance that she's bluffing. We could try to separate and see what happens."

His bushy wolf brows wiggled. "I'd rather you get closer. You heard her. Come check my bandages."

She pursed her lips and stood. He wanted her to check the bandages? Fine, she'd check them. But he wasn't going to like it.

# Chapter Eight

Wulfric grinned and sat forward on the chair. "Here you go. Now you can reach the edge of the wrapping."

Scarlet sank to her knees in front of him, her eyes spitting fire. Anticipation licked his spine. He held his breath as she reached her arms around him, her fingers carefully not touching anything but the bandages.

He breathed in her scent, his nostrils flaring. She smelled of late summer sun, of the earth and grass. Her closeness did things to him, things he couldn't resist. She was definitely his mate, and he felt like roaring in triumph.

Instead, he widened his legs and shifted to the edge of the chair, the blanket shifting on his lap and riding up.

Her lips pinched even as she sucked in a breath. The pounding of his pulse grew louder in his ears like a chant encouraging him to *kiss her, claim her, fuck her.*

She glanced up at him through those long, brown eyelashes, and he leaned forward. Then she jerked the bandages free, ripping flesh that had started to heal underneath. He gasped at the stab of pain along his left side.

The air rushed out of him under her ruthless hands as white spots appeared behind his eyes.

"Oh no, did that hurt? Oh, clumsy me." Sarcasm dripped from her words.

He grinned through the pain, enjoying being at her mercy like some sort of sadistic love-sick puppy.

She rose on her knees to unwrap the bandage that now dangled from his ribs. Vision swimming, he did the only thing he knew would distract him from the pain.

He leaned forward, his mouth meeting hers. Such soft lips, like the petals of a flower. She froze and gasped. He swooped in, taking advantage of her open mouth. The touch of her tongue was like a brand. It ruined him for all others, and in that moment, he knew she was it. All he needed was right here.

Joy mixed with the pain, sweeping through his veins like wildfire. He ravished her, pouring everything he had into the kiss. Without words, he told her how he felt. She was his mate. This was inevitable.

He wanted to cherish her, love her, take care of her, worship every inch of her body. He wanted to know her, claim her, feel her openly and gladly accept him. He wanted to ravage and ruin her tight little body until she thought of nothing but him.

His chest tightened, and he shifted on the seat, the throbbing in his body moving lower between his legs. She didn't move, like a deer frozen at the sight of a Growler. He angled his head, nibbling her lower lip softly and teasing his tongue inside. Yet, she still didn't move, and he wanted her full participation.

"Open for me, bunny. Kiss the pain away," he growled, desperate for her.

She shuddered at his words. He swirled his tongue

around hers, and his free hand lifted to glide across her confined breasts.

She jerked back, sliding along the floor to slam into the other chair by the hearth. Knees pulled up in front of her, she looked at him wild-eyed, surprise making her face slack.

"What—what are you doing?"

Her fear wafted over him like a heat wave. He shifted on the chair and frowned with worry, disappointed at himself for scaring her. When he'd teased her before, she'd verbally sparred with him and held her own. But now, her fear swarmed his senses, mixing with the scent of her desire and anger.

He was being too brazen, too much of an aggressive Growler. He rubbed his own chest where it ached to feel her fear. How could he salvage this and show her he was so much more than just a mindless Growler? Perhaps he could distract her and make her feel more comfortable?

He stretched, his arm no longer bound to his chest with the bandages. The pain had eased to a dull roar. Pain, he could live with. Pain, he was used to.

But he couldn't live with scaring her.

"I was kissing you," he said softly, watching her carefully as he thought through how to help her relax around him.

"Wh—why?" she whispered, her fingers flying to her lips. He took a deep breath as the fear faded from her. The only scent that lingered in the air was her arousal, confusion, and anger, the fire in the hearth, and the drying herbs hanging from the rafters.

He couldn't hold back from her. He wasn't compelled to tell her through magic, but he wanted no barriers between them. It might not convince her to accept him, but he wanted to give her the world. He would answer any question, complete any task she asked if it meant she'd give him a chance.

"Because you're my mate," he said.

She jumped up, her hands waving in front of her in denial, as if to hold him at bay as she watched him warily. "I'm not your fucking mate. You're crazy."

He shrugged, feeling the cold dribble of blood and glancing down at his ribs. "I know what I know, and in this, I'm right. But damn if you weren't right about these ribs. I pulled the stitches free."

She shifted on the balls of her feet, her hands wavering as her gaze caressed down his body. He felt the lingering gaze like lightning, and his dick jumped under the blanket in response.

She frowned and took a deep breath, her spine straightening. Then she stepped closer and batted his hand away to poke at his ribs with her fingers.

He raised his arm, testing the joint and flexing his stiff muscles to give her better access to his ribs. He enjoyed her fingers on his skin, even as he was hyper aware of her touch. It held its own kind of magic that healed the broken parts of his soul.

Her eyes fluttered as she straightened, following the movement of his bicep and chest. The thrill of the chase slid down his spine like warm rain. She might be surprised at his words, but she wanted him too. The scent of her desire flooded him, and he breathed deeply.

"I'm not your mate," she murmured, going to the medicine cabinet to take out supplies. Did he detect a hint of disappointment in her tone? Hope flared in his chest.

"You are," he said. "But we're not going to argue about it now. You need time to accept it and come around to the idea. I understand that. I'm a patient man."

Well, he might've been once. He really didn't know.

"Growler, not man," she said, stomping back over to him with a bowl of gauze, thread, needle, and a little jar of ointment.

How often did he lie awake at night worrying about having lost his humanity? He sucked in a breath at her words, but she didn't seem to notice.

She glared, "And there's nothing to accept. We're not mates."

He tilted his head to the side, but otherwise stayed still on the chair. He didn't want his little bunny to run away, and somehow, he knew she was prone to it.

But damn it, he couldn't let her think he was just going along with her denial. The words bubbled up inside him.

"Actually, you know what? I'm not a patient man at all. But I'll drop the topic for now if you can look me in the eye, and tell me you don't feel it," he growled.

She looked at him, her brow furrowed and her chin jutting out stubbornly. "I. Feel. Nothing."

Her nose twitched with every word. The smell of her lie filled the air. A slow smile spread across his face, making her scowl. "You don't really believe that," he said softly.

Her lips twisted as she gently lathered the ointment on the biggest tear on his ribs. "Of course, I do."

"No, you don't," he said, watching her face carefully. "You're just saying that because you've tried for so long to cut off the emotions. The pain, the heartache. It was the only way you could survive."

It was something he'd done too, why he'd jumped at the idea to become a Growler and forget all of it.

He didn't know how he could recognize that within her, but the realization settled in his soul. It was like he'd known her forever, although he didn't know what had caused her so much pain.

Her hands stilled, her fingers cold on his fur. She avoided his gaze, but he reached out with his good hand and cupped her cheek, tipping her face up until her beautiful green eyes looked into his soul.

"You don't have to pretend with me, bunny."

She glared and jerked out of his hand. "I don't know what you're talking about."

His heart ached for her, his tough little bunny. What had she been through that had toughened her so? He wanted to hear all her stories. He wanted to kiss her and make her feel better.

Instead, he just shook his head and took a guess. "You lost something and had to put on a tough persona to make it through, didn't you?"

Her eyes searched his. Did he go too far? Pressure on his chest increased as she stood up, the bowl and jar forgotten on the floor. Hands on hips, she glared at him.

"Yeah, I lost my mother. To a raiding pack of Growlers. Then my father to the war." Her pain-filled expression was like lightning to his gut.

His stomach twisted and dread spread through him. If Growlers killed her mother, would she ever see him as more than a monster?

His poor bunny, how did he not know everything about her? He should've known, should've asked more questions first, before kissing her and telling her of the mate bond.

"I'm sorry," he said simply.

She closed her eyes and took a deep breath, hands clenching. "See? You don't know me. You know nothing about me, and you definitely don't know what mates are because that's not us."

She spun on her heel and stormed out the front door. She went into the snow without a coat, and he didn't want her to get too cold.

He half rose from the chair, but his vision started spinning, and he sank back down. He breathed through it, his mind racing through different things he could say to her, ways he could get to know her so she'd accept the mate bond. Then they could claim each other.

A tingle in the back of his head spread, and for the first time since becoming a Growler, he worried about the family he might've left behind. When he'd been turned and lost all his memories, he'd taken it as a fresh new start on life.

But now he wondered what he'd lost. He had no way of knowing what town he'd come from, what his job was, or what kind of man he'd been. Had he had a mate before? The humans called them wives, didn't they?

He sighed and grabbed the ointment from the floor. Slowly, he began to lather it on his open wounds. They were closing up nicely on their own and would probably be completely regenerated by tomorrow morning, other than a few scars.

He'd gathered several in the past few years, and he wondered if they bothered Scarlet. She'd been so gentle with him, taking care of him like the softie she was. She didn't want anyone to know, but he knew. He could see under the hidden layers.

No, his bunny wasn't bothered by his scars. She had a tough shell, was a powerful warrior in her own right, but inside she was soft, sensitive, and caring.

Now he just needed to convince her of the truth of their matehood, complete the mate bond with her, and reclaim his position as alpha. Then he could spend the rest of his life peeling back her other layers and getting to know her.

The key was going to be fixing her curse. She'd cried when she'd realized her antlers and ears had changed from the tea. If he could convince the Elders to fix her, she might open up to him and see him as something more than just a savage Growler. She might see him as a fucking hero.

# Chapter Nine

Scarlet stomped through the snow, the crunch the only sound in the stillness of mid-morning. Stupid fucking Growler thought he knew everything, but he didn't. He didn't know her.

And he never would. She had to keep him at arm's length. Because the way her lips had tingled at his kiss... She'd seen stars, just like she'd always heard girls talk about at the taverns.

She shook her head and pushed open the door to the barn. Grandma was brushing Rain but didn't look up when she came in.

"So what do you think?" Olive asked, the wind outside picking up with a howl.

Scarlet scowled and began to pace in front of the stalls. "He thinks he's my mate. What the fuck? There's no way the fates would be so cruel."

"The fates don't make mistakes, child," Olive said softly. "It's as the dream foretold."

Scarlet glared at her, then spun on her heel. So that's

what Olive hadn't wanted to talk about in the house? The fucking mate bond. "I refuse to accept it."

Olive's sad eyes glowed in the lamplight. "Then you're both doomed, child."

Doomed? Surely she was being overly dramatic.

The whipping wind outside increased, and Scarlet used her hand to make a cutting motion. "No, I won't let it be. Not that it matters right now. What matters is getting you safely to Eirwyn. They're anxious about delivering the egg. You're the only living person who's even seen a dragon egg hatch before. You need to be there."

Olive nodded and waved to a bag by the door. "I know, that's why I packed my bag a week ago. I'm ready when Knox gets here."

Scarlet paused and rubbed her temples. She was getting whiplash from the conversation. "What are you talking about? Knox isn't coming. He sent me to get you."

The ground shook, causing them both to stumble on their feet. Scarlet looked through the open barn door. Faint light shone off green iridescent scales, blocking the view of the cottage. Scarlet's heart raced. He wasn't supposed to be there. Something must be wrong with Eirwyn.

Olive tossed the horse's brush into an empty bucket and strode to the barn door, completely unfazed. "Ah, there you are. How's Eirwyn?"

Scarlet followed Olive out of the barn as the dragon transformed, a curl of green smoke sweeping over him. When it dissipated, Knox stood in only a pair of pants. He raked his hands over his scaled temples, sliding along the topknot mohawk braided down his back. His green eyes flashed as he turned to the barn.

"She's in labor. Please, can you help?" His eyes were wild with fright.

She hadn't seen him this scared since they'd heard the screams of the first carriage accident on the Lone Road.

They'd been children when they'd saved Eirwyn as a baby. They'd been too late to save the king and queen, but she could see the same fear on his face now. He was afraid he wouldn't be able to save his wife.

"She's going to be alright, Knox," she said softly.

He stared at her, his brow furrowed as he shifted on his feet. "You're probably right, but we have to go. Are you ready, Grandma?"

Olive handed her bag over to Knox and said, "Aye, of course, child."

Knox put his hands on his hips and stepped back into the open clearing. Frowning, he pulled a small pouch from his pocket and held it out to them.

"Oh Lailant sent this for Scarlet. I don't know why when you'll be back at Hartsgrove tomorrow, right?"

Olive handed her bag over to Knox and took the pouch, "I'm trying to convince her to run an errand for me, so she might take a week or so to get back."

Olive looked inside the small purse, then looked up at Scarlet with a mischievous grin. Scarlet's spine straightened. That look never boded well. Olive stepped closer, gripped Scarlet's wrist, and pressed the bag into her palm.

"There are no coincidences, child. Lailant knew you'd need this. I'll see you soon. Do what you need to do, but don't rush to get back to Eirwyn. She and the dragonling are going to be alright."

"Did the dream tell you that too?" Scarlet asked, twisting the drawstring on the bag.

Olive nodded and smiled. "Yes, so stop worrying, and go figure out this situation."

She jerked her head toward the cottage, then released Scarlet and turned to Knox. "Knox? I'm ready."

Knox nodded once and disappeared in a flash of cold, green smoke, turning back into the giant, green dragon.

Olive waved her hand and coughed. Her green eyes looked into Scarlet's soul, the soft daylight making them bright.

"Listen to me, Scarlet. All your life, you've been fiercely independent, but in this—with him—you must learn to work together. Talk to him. Get to know him before you reject the mate bond, child, or you'll regret it for the rest of your life. Trust me on this. Trust him."

"But Grandma, a Growler? I can't forget what they did to Mother."

"Nor should you. But saying all Growlers are bad is like saying all humans are good. We both know neither of those are true. Give him a chance to prove himself. That's all I'm asking. And use this if needed."

She squeezed the bag in Scarlet's hand, and Knox snorted his impatience. Green gas sank to the ground as he crouched on his four feet, belly to the ground and Grandma's bag looped around one of his horns. His head jerked like an overly large impatient horse, and Olive stepped onto his wing and threw a leg over his back. She moved the bag and settled her skirts.

Scarlet didn't want them to leave. Then she'd be alone with the Growler. Of course, she could handle him if he attacked. She didn't doubt that. But what if the mate thing was true? Was it something she could resist? Or was it inevitable, fate, ordained by the gods?

"Be safe and listen to your gut," Olive said as Knox lumbered onto his feet and tested the weight on his back.

Scarlet saw a movement by the cottage, and her heart

jumped into her throat. No, he couldn't be seen. Knox was too on edge with the impending birth and wouldn't think clearly. He'd just snap Wulfric in half with his massive dragon jaw. Knox started to turn his head toward the cottage, and Scarlet jumped back into his line of sight.

She waved her arms to get Knox's attention and yelled loudly, "Bye! I'll be behind you soon! Go on, go to Eirwyn."

Her heart hammered in her chest, driving her to make a commotion of saying goodbye as Knox launched them into the air. With a few heavy beats of his wings, Scarlet nearly buckled under the whipping frigid air. Then they disappeared into the pale sky, clouds heavy with snow shielding the sun.

Heart still racing, she glared across the glen at the Growler and slipped the pouch into her pants pocket. He stood by the back door to the kitchen, a blanket wrapped around his waist. She couldn't quite make out his expression.

"I didn't quite believe the rumors of the dragon king. I guess I was wrong," he said thoughtfully, his deep voice echoing across the clearing.

She stomped closer, drawn to him like a magnet. "One of the many things you're wrong about."

He smiled, and her feet slowed. A thrill raced up her spine at his smile. Did the clouds part and let the sun shine on his face? No, that was just a trick of the light.

"Oh, I don't doubt that I'm wrong occasionally. But not about us, bunny." He grinned wider, and she scowled.

She crossed her arms and glared, her heart still racing. "You've got a big mouth for a monster."

His grin only widened. "All the better to eat you with, my dear."

A thrill went up her spine at his words, but her throat went dry.

"In your dreams, wolfie," she said, crossing her arms and cocking a hip.

The blanket dropped as he tipped his head up, stepped toward her, and sniffed the air. "The druid is gone."

It wasn't a question, but Scarlet barely processed his words. Her eyes swept down his body. Holy mother of the gods, she had avoided looking at his dick when she was patching him up.

But now, it was just right there.

Her senses seemed to go into overdrive. The auras around him flared before she suppressed them enough to see him. The short layer of gray and black fur over his body made her want to slide her hands all over.

Would it be soft or wiry? The mane of hair on his head blew in the wind, and she shivered. She glanced down at his dick, thick and long as it hung heavy against his thigh.

Damn, he didn't seem to be bothered by the cold at all. And she, well, she was so hot from being near him, the cold felt good.

Was this the mate bond? This undeniable tug in her gut that felt like she was tied to him with a string, and someone was pulling on the string to bring her closer.

No, she couldn't give in to it. No matter how much her mouth watered and her hands tingled to taste and touch him. It would be disrespectful to her mother's memory.

She pursed her lips and looked back up, meeting his gaze with a challenge of her own.

"So she is, but it means little. Get back inside before your busted stitches start bleeding and attract predators."

"Bunny, I *am* the predator."

His jaw elongated as he stepped outside and spoke, the

kitchen door shutting behind him. His grin widened play-fully. As much as a predator could, anyway. But the slam of the door reverberated through her as if sealing her fate.

She licked her lips and shifted on the balls of her feet, her nose twitching. She expected the surge of fear, but that familiar emotion didn't greet her. Her head said to run and hide but her body felt the lick of desire ripple through her.

He stepped barefoot onto the frozen grass, the faint light flickering over his muscles and gray fur. "The dizziness is the most concerning, but my skin is almost completely scabbed over, thanks to your help."

With each step he took, Scarlet's heart thumped harder.

She stepped back, her hands going to her daggers. "You busted the stitches—"

"And I put on the ointment when you left. Even as I did, the last one sealed over. Should be completely healed by morning."

She froze, her hands shaking slightly as she grabbed her daggers and held them, combat ready. She'd never had a problem with nerves before, so what the fuck was wrong with her? She took a deep breath and narrowed her eyes, bending her knees to prepare to jump. Whether at him or away from him, she didn't know.

She shook her head on the exhale. "No, you're weak, an invalid." She didn't know who she was trying to convince, him or her.

He grinned as his jaw completely shifted into a wolf's even though he remained upright on two human legs covered in that gray fur. "That tea must've kicked in all the way. Even now, the dizziness is fading. Hells, I feel like I could run for miles."

Panic clawed at her throat, and her nose twitched furi-ously. The stiff brush of fear slid down her spine like ice.

Damn it, she didn't want the fear or the desire. Why couldn't she just be? She refused to give in to this fear, this rabbit side of her that whispered to run and hide.

What side of her wanted to bend over and just let him rail her with that big dick?

Her cheeks heated at the thought, and he stalked toward her. She backed up, daggers gleaming in the faint light.

He stopped in his tracks, lifting his nose to take a deep sniff of the crisp winter air. "You're hesitant, but not completely terrified like you were in the cottage. We're making progress."

She shot him a glare and took a step back. "I'm cautious, not scared. And I'm not stupid enough to freeze to death out here. Get back inside."

"But it would be so much fun to play," he exclaimed, grinning mischievously. "We could test the druid's theory and see how far we can push our boundaries."

She snorted in response. "It's too cold and it looks like it might snow soon. Only an idiot would think playing in the Feral Forest is a good idea right now."

"Ah, but there's so much room out here compared to inside. So much better to chase you down and eat your pretty pussy, my dear." He prowled closer and sniffed again. "Interesting, you like that dirty talk, bunny? Do you want the big bad wolf to chase you through the woods and pin you down until you moan?"

She gritted her teeth and shook her head vehemently. "Hell no, you don't get to know what I like and don't like, Growler. Let's get that straight right now. You and I will never happen."

He leaned down, his arms turning into paws as his body morphed into his giant wolf form.

She sucked in a breath. "What—what are you doing?"

Damn her breathy whisper. She was not scared. She just didn't like surprises.

"If we're not going to happen or take a fun run through the woods, I suppose I can get comfortable then."

Her eyes widened as his tail wagged and he stretched, never taking his golden eyes off her. Fuck, he could talk while shifted?

Knox could only speak to Eirwyn while shifted because she was his mate. But that was all in her mind.

Scarlet could literally hear him. "Can all Growlers speak while shifted?"

He sat on his haunches and scratched behind his ear as he nodded. "Of course." The movement made him seem like an overgrown dog instead of a dangerous monster.

But she wouldn't let down her guard. He yawned, then shook his entire body.

"There, that's so much better. A little sore, but the shift will help speed up the healing. When I turn back, the stitches will be gone along with the open wounds. Then I'll be well enough to play with my mate."

Her hands fisted at her sides. "When are you going to get it through your thick skull that we're not mates? It's not gonna happen, Growler."

He prowled closer, so she bent her knees, bouncing slightly and ready to spring into action.

"Perhaps you don't understand what being mates means for Growlers," he said softly, his eyes sharpening and some of the playfulness falling away. Her nipples perked at his tone, making her grind her teeth in frustration.

"I don't care," she said.

He lowered his head and breathed deeply, then sat on his haunches and looked to the sky. "Growlers rarely find their one true mate. They can mate with anyone, but that's just sex and reproduction. True mates, that's rare."

"So says you," she snorted. She wasn't going to fall for that trick. She wasn't special, other than being twice cursed.

He looked back at her, freezing her in place with those piercing golden eyes that seemed to read her soul. "So says the Elders and everyone in the tribe. In the ten years I've been a Growler, I've only seen three mate bonds snap into place. One couple was already mated when I joined. Another couple met on a hunt with another tribe and immediately sealed the bond."

"And the third?" Damn her curiosity. She pursed her lips, daggers never lowering even as he just sat there.

He stood and faced her, prowling like she had no choice in this. "The third couple denied the mate bond and refused to complete the ritual. They were dead within weeks."

Her breath caught in her throat as fear spiked through her. Then anger turned the paralyzing coldness in her veins to lava.

"If you think I'm going to fall for that, think again. You're not getting in my pants, so you can fuck off or fight me. Bring it on, wolfie."

# Chapter Ten

Wulfric licked his lips as a shiver ran down his spine. Their eyes locked, something primal stirring in the depths of his soul. He couldn't shake the feeling that this moment was bigger than both of them, that their fates were entwined in a way neither of them fully understood. Stubborn warrior Hunter that she was, she refused to surrender to it, not yet. He loved the challenge that hung in the air.

"Don't tempt me to take what's mine, bunny," he said softly.

Now completely a wolf, he circled her with a predatory grace, his eyes never leaving hers. Each step was a silent promise, a tantalizing mix of danger and desire. The air between them crackled with electricity, and for a heartbeat, he wondered if he would truly lose control—and if she wanted him to. The heavy lidded desire on her face said yes, and he licked his lips in anticipation.

She turned with every step he took, her face wary as she refused to turn her back on him. "I'm not yours, dickhead."

He chuckled. She was just so adorable with her little

bunny ears and antlers. She looked so innocent, like the most delicious prey ready for him to take a bite of.

But her fierce expression and words were a delightful contradiction. She was a trained warrior. What would she do if he poked her? How would she react? Which of her natures would hold the lead? Rabbit, deer, or wolf?

He snapped his jaws near her heels, and she jumped as high as any deer. His heart raced with adrenaline and excitement, but her strong gaze faltered, a flash of vulnerability breaking through. It was enough to send a jolt through him, a reminder that beneath her tough exterior, she was still fragile, still afraid. His wolf growled in frustration, torn between the urge to protect and the desire to conquer and make her his.

She pointed a dagger at him. "Hey, watch it. Don't you dare bite me, Growler, or it'll be the last thing you do."

His mind flashed a warning, and he knew she spoke the truth. His heart pounded with the thrill of the hunt, the primal desire to claim what was his. But then a shadow of doubt flickered through his mind. The Elders typically performed a magical ceremony to turn someone into a Growler, but one bite *could* turn her into a Growler. Unlikely, but possible.

There were rumors of Growlers chasing someone in the woods, biting them, and then that person becoming a Growler. If he bit her and she was turned into a Growler, she might never forgive him, might never trust him again. The thought of losing her completely sobered him, quelling the fire that burned within.

He didn't want to chance it. Becoming a Growler wasn't a decision he wanted to make for her. It was always a choice, and some did turn the offer down, choosing death instead.

He backed up, some of his playfulness fading at the memories of his own turning. He sat on his haunches again and whined.

She frowned and stood straighter. "Don't you whine at me, wolfie. You're the one who nipped like some pup."

He chuckled. "I'm no pup. Want me to show you just how much of a man I am?"

Scarlet just rolled her eyes and snorted. "Hard to be a man in your shifted form."

"I'll show you hard."

Her lips twitched, and victory smelled so sweet. She wanted to smile!

Her lips pursed as she looked away, refusing to. "I can't have this conversation with a dog. You know what? You can stay like this. Dogs sleep outside with the other animals. I'll go inside like the civilized person I am. You can go to the barn, but stay away from my horse."

He growled. "I'm no dog."

She shrugged. "Whatever, wolfie. Do whatever, be whatever. Just leave me alone. Hells, you can run back to your tribe for all I care."

She sniffed and walked with head held high to the back door of the cottage. He grinned when she still didn't turn her back to him.

When she let the door softly close behind her, he paused to catch his breath. She had filled his nose with her scent as his eyes had feasted on her like a starving man.

It was overwhelming, but he wouldn't want to go back to before he knew she existed. His responsibilities to the pack had to be balanced with wooing his mate, though. Today, he was far from his tribe and could focus on her. So how could he convince her to take a chance on them?

He glanced up at the sunlight just barely peeking over

the trees. Like always, being outside settled to his soul. Had it always been like this? When he'd been human, had he craved being outside? He frowned and sniffed around the clearing. He pushed away the pain of the empty hole in his mind that should've been his memories and instead focused on Scarlet.

He had pushed her, flirted with her, kissed her, played with her, and tested her responses to determine which method might be the best way to convince her. Nothing had worked.

He howled in frustration. He didn't know how to convince her to accept the mate bond, but he had to stay near her. The magic of fated mates would help increase their attraction to each other, and perhaps that would help. It had to.

But all the pent up energy that demanded he bend her over and fuck her senseless sent him into the woods instead. Perhaps distance would make the heart grow fonder. He tested his muscles and took it easy.

Just a slow loop in widening circles around the clearing. There were no other predators out and the forest didn't mess with him in this form. He was one with the forest, moving silently over the frozen ground with barely a crunch from each step of his paws.

After a few minutes slinking away from the cottage, lethargy overwhelmed him. He powered on for a few more minutes but eventually had to stop because of the growing dizziness. His vision spun, and his entire body screamed to go back to her.

Damn it, the druid was right. He breathed slowly as he turned around and walked straight back through the forest to the cottage. Each breath became easier and his mind cleared the closer he came to his mate.

This could work to his advantage, though. It would ensure she would stay close to him and wouldn't just ride to the dragon's camp tomorrow, leaving him to fend for himself.

She would have to go with him and help him reclaim his title, right? He snorted as the cottage came in sight.

He didn't know her very well yet, but one thing was certain. If he told her she had to, she would dig in her heels and refuse.

He paused on the edge of the clearing and licked his aching paw. He could feel the sun setting, even though the trees blocked the sight. The wound was getting better, but he'd probably pushed himself too hard too fast today.

It couldn't be helped though, if he wanted to reclaim his position before the full moon. He had to get into his best fighting form, which meant a quicker recovery.

Mating would help. He stared up at the soft light in the upstairs window and sighed. If nothing he'd done had convinced her, then he had to let it be her idea.

Hm, yes, that was exactly what she needed. She needed to be in control. For the moment, at least, until she began to trust him.

The wind whispered to him as he thought of their future. She would eventually surrender to him, and it would be worth the wait.

He could flirt with her. She seemed to enjoy the verbal sparring, if her change of breathing and smell of desire were any sign.

With that decided, he let the coldness of the shift wash over him. The crunch of bones echoed in the clearing. He sent a silent prayer up to the gods that she would accept the mate bond before they both wound up dead.

Then he turned to the back door on two feet. He picked up the blanket where it'd dropped earlier and walked inside.

She wasn't downstairs by the fire, but he stopped to warm himself. His human form was more susceptible to the elements.

Sounds from upstairs eventually drew him through the cottage. He wanted to be near her, smell her, talk with her. Fuck, he wanted to taste her so bad.

He took a deep breath and reminded himself to let her decide. He stepped quietly on creaky steps, following her scent and sounds to push the door open to a bedroom.

She stood between two windows at a wash stand and splashed water on her face. Her dark black pants stretched tightly over her curves, emphasizing her feminine figure as she bent over. Her long, red tail moved gracefully and fluidly behind her, enticing and mesmerizing. The air was also filled with a musky aroma, hinting at her primal nature and drawing him into the room like a moth to the flame.

The animal urge to claim her seized his gut, and he gripped the door, his claws digging grooves as he breathed through the urge. Fuck, she better decide soon because his patience was already fraying. He growled and licked his now human lips.

She spun at the sound, droplets of water glistened on her skin, highlighting her smooth features. "What are you doing? Get out of my room."

He grinned and shook his head. "I think not, mate. I'll sleep here with you."

He flopped onto the bed with the blanket in hand, feeling it bounce like a cloud. Growler beds were stretched hide tied to a frame with layers of quilts. He didn't remember sleeping in such a fluffy bed, but somehow this felt familiar, like a far-off dream. He saw a vision of bouncing a little girl on a bed, making her laugh as he tossed her into the air to land on it safely.

Scarlet made a gurgling sound in her throat as she glared, pulling him from the unexpected memory. "When the hells freeze over. We are not sharing a bed. If you must sleep here, I'll take Grandma's bed across the hall."

He sat up on an elbow, the blanket draped over his waist. "Come now, bunny. This isn't the mate bond talking. Be practical."

Perhaps an appeal to logic would help convince her. She was a smart woman, and she wanted him to heal. It might convince her to get near. If he could just cuddle her for a few hours, it would keep the pressing need to claim her at bay.

Her eyes narrowed. "How is sharing a bed practical?"

He pulled back the covers and felt the soft, cool sheets. "If you're to come back with me, you need to carry my scent. Otherwise, the pack will tear you apart. The closer we are, the more my scent gets on you, and therefore, the safer you'll be."

A flash of fear crossed her features in the soft glow of the lamp, then it was gone as her jaw set stubbornly. "I don't believe you."

He shrugged and laid on his back, putting his hands behind his head and crossing his ankles where they stuck out from under the blanket. "The mate bond also makes us both stronger. So the more we're together, the stronger I'll be when we arrive. If we complete the mate bond, it should give me the edge I need to defeat a proper alpha challenge. Of course, I could've defeated him the first time, if he would've followed the rules."

He appeared nonchalant, but that stab of fear slammed

into him again. If he kept pushing, she would start fighting him again. Somehow, he had to let her lead.

Damn it, letting someone else have control was harder to do than he cared to admit. But for her, he would try.

She snorted. "That's a lot riding on a stupid mate bond. Sounds like a bunch of excuses to get in my pants."

Disappointment speared him, but he fought his instinct to throw her on the bed and fuck her. Instead, he stared at the ceiling, not looking at her. "Suit yourself, but don't come crying to me when they attack."

The seconds ticked by, and he could've sworn he heard her racing heartbeat. But he didn't move. He could be patient, he had to be patient. It would be worth it.

Finally, she turned back to the wash stand and wiped her face and hands. "I've not even decided to go with you," she mumbled.

Her belligerent tone was like a child who knew she had to do something but didn't want to. He grinned in triumph behind her back, but otherwise remained still as he responded.

"Yes, you have. You want the Elders to change you back into a human. Or are you satisfied with the changes from the berry tea?"

He didn't tell her that they'd never done that in all the years he'd been with them. He didn't even know if they had that ability. But they had to stay together so he could convince her to accept the mate bond.

"No, I'm not satisfied."

"I can satisfy you, if only you'll take the chance."

She didn't reply for several minutes. Then she picked up the lamp and strode to the door where she paused.

She looked at him with her big green eyes, and he carefully kept his expression neutral. Every fiber of his body screamed at him to jump up and keep her close, but he denied himself. If his time as a human in the army had taught him anything, it was self-discipline. He thought, anyway, since he couldn't remember those years at all.

Finally, she sighed. "I'm not keen on walking into a death trap. I'll think about it more. Good night, Growler."

She slammed the door behind her, and his entire body tensed at the separation. He was mostly healed, but shifting had drained him. Without the attraction between them to keep him awake, his eyes grew impossibly heavy.

The pressure on his chest tightened at being separated from her, but he wrestled with his mind. He would not be a savage, a barbarian, a mindless monster. That would not win her favor at all, not with what Growlers had done to her mother.

He had to bide his time with her, wait her out, even though it went against his nature. He doubted she'd be able to resist the mate call for long, if the stories from the tribe were true. How those two fools had run away from each other and then died would not happen to them.

He couldn't lose her. Not when he'd just found her and could finally feel the icy fingers of loneliness easing from around his heart.

Damn, it was going to be a long night while he waited for her, though.

# Chapter Eleven

Scarlet floated through the clouds, different auras flying by on the snowy breeze. Snippets of conversation floated with them.

*"She may be a Hunter, but she won't take the risk."*

Scarlet tried to frown, but she wasn't in her body. Were they talking about her?

*"But this is her chance to break the curse. All she has to do is mate with the Growler and let the Elders perform the ceremony."*

What the fuck were they talking about? All she needed was the ceremony. She didn't need to mate with Wulfric.

*"Exactly, so she'll never break it. Ten gold says she'll dig in her heels and refuse to even go to the Growlers' camp."*

The wind shifted and the auras floated away. The clouds parted to reveal the night sky, and the constellations came alive. The wolf chased the woman across the sky, catching her dress with a paw until it slid from her body. She stumbled, and the wolf pounced on her.

Only the woman opened her arms and accepted the wolf with a smile.

Scarlet sat up, drenched in sweat and the fresh rush of desire. The room was dark, as the moon didn't shine on this side of the cottage. The chilly wind whipped outside, but inside she was too hot.

Did she have a fever? Had she contracted some sort of wolf sickness from being close to him? Fleas, ticks, who knew what kind of infection she could pick up from the fucking Growler.

She rubbed her burning eyes but the image of him standing outside, proud and naked, tormented her. The look in his eyes said he knew how to use that dick to please a woman. Her breathing grew ragged and her breasts felt heavy.

She threw back the covers and paced across Olive's room from the bed to the door to the window while her grandma's voice echoed in her head. *Trust him. Open to him. Take a chance on love.*

She wiped her eyes and shook her head. Grandma hadn't actually said those words, so why were they on repeat in her mind?

Suffocated by her tight clothes, they were a constant reminder of her need to be on high alert. She had slept in them, unsure if she would have to defend herself from the Growler. The heat and sweat trapped against her skin only added to her discomfort as each step caused friction between her pants and her sensitive clit. Her body was aching with desire and she struggled to keep control, taking shuddering breaths to calm herself down. The conflicting sensations between her body's arousal and the need for self-preservation left her in a state of inner turmoil.

And she *was* in control. She could do this.

Desperate, she pulled her shirt over her head and pushed down her underwear and pants.

Pacing naked, her tail swished, tickling the back of her thigh and lower back. She shivered at the light touch, and she grew hotter. It was like her brain was still floating through the clouds, her body the only thing she could focus on. Her nipples pebbled in the open air, heavy and aching.

Wulfric's big, rough hands would feel good on her breasts. She gasped, shaking her head and turning away from the door. No, absolutely not.

She'd thought taking her pants and underwear off would ease the pressure on her clit, but it just made things worse. Her core ached with every step, torturing her to find relief.

Relief that she would find across the hall with Wulfric.

His name echoed in her head now with every step. The way he'd prowled toward her with singular focus, as if she held the answers to life and was the most important thing in his world.

Not like she was a freak. Not like he wanted to avoid her which was what all the people she'd met in the past six months did. Not like she was a disease and could pass her curses to someone else just by being in the same fucking room.

No, he'd looked at her like he wanted to devour her. He'd talked so openly about what he wanted to do to her.

Fucking hells, was she getting hotter? She wiped sweat from her forehead with a wet cloth, then dipped it into the cold pitcher of water under the window. The coolness of it should have made her calm the fuck down.

But the scrape of the cloth along her skin made her core clench and her nipples pebble.

Damn it. She threw the cloth to the pitcher, making it wobble. She jumped, stabilizing it before it fell. Her hands were shaking, and now she was both sweating and had goosebumps.

She held her head and scratched the hollow behind her ears. Maybe she could bring herself relief? She slid her hands down her breasts and pinched the hard nubs.

Her head fell back with a gasp, and her eyes fluttered. She slid a hand down to her folds. Fuck, she was so wet. Wulfric would howl to see it, smell it, taste it. She shuddered in anticipation as she circled her clit and pressed firmly, making her hips buck.

Then she eased off. One hand on her breast, one on her clit, she set up a steady rhythm. The heat grew higher between her legs, threatening to combust.

But then the wave faded. She'd done this more times than she'd slept with actual men, so why wasn't it working?

The mate bond.

She spun on her heels and went back to pacing. The damn Growler had ruined it. All she wanted was to throw open the door and mount him.

Would he let her? Could she sleep with him without accepting the mate bond? Scratch the itch that was crawling under her skin?

She paced. No, that was ridiculous. There was no telling what the mate bond even entailed. But this burning heat in her body that screamed at her to go to him was proof that the mate bond did exist. It explained how she was feeling.

That, or an infection.

Of course, she could ask him if this was normal for mates. Her steps faltered near the door. She could ask him if there was a way to ease the burning need without completing the mate bond too. Sex could just be sex, right?

Her mind latched onto the idea like a drowning woman grabbing a life rope.

Before she could talk herself out of it, she opened the door and stepped into the hall. With a creak, the door to her old room opened, and she slid inside.

Light from the moon spilled through the windows and across the floor. It fell on his face, relaxed in sleep. But the moment she took a step into the room, his golden eyes flew open.

He didn't move, just watched her shut the door behind her and stand stiffly along the wall. Fuck, what was she doing? She was still naked. Her breasts ached for his touch; her pussy was on fire. This was a bad idea.

She tilted her head up and tried to slow her breathing, but it was damn hard to do when his scent filled the room. The smell of grass and pine filled her, calming her even as it drove her desire up.

She wasn't going to back down. She couldn't. Her body would revolt, and she'd get no sleep.

He sat up but didn't say a word. The blanket pooled at his waist, and she could almost see the imperceptible lengthening of his mouth and chin.

It sent a thrill of awareness through her, and her sex began to weep with need down her legs. She could almost feel the phantom movement of his cock inside her, and it made her gasp.

He jerked at the sound, and her eyes widened at the tenting of the blanket. He sniffed, and his golden eyes began to glow.

"Fuck, you smell delicious, bunny. Have you changed your mind?"

Oh gods, he could smell her? She flattened herself against the wall, excitement racing up her spine.

She shook her head, nearly panting. "No, yes, maybe. Ground rules, I need ground rules. Information. Answers."

Fuck, what was wrong with her that sentences were too much?

He grinned, the predatory nature of it making her whimper. "Cat got your tongue again?"

She sucked in a deep breath and asked on the exhale, "What exactly does a mate bond mean?"

Her voice was barely a whisper, but his wolf ears quirked at the sound as he went eerily still.

"It means we are mated for life. Our souls entwine, and we give each other strength."

She breathed deeply, her mind racing like she was running through mud. "And the consequences?"

She fought her body's response to him. The clawing hunger in the pit of her stomach that urged her to straddle him and ride like nothing else mattered.

"All magic comes with consequences," she whispered.

He nodded, "Mates rarely outlive each other. Most cannot live without the other, so if one dies..."

She swallowed hard and frowned. She had to get revenge on the queen and fix the curses on the rest of the people too. She wasn't the only one who needed to be turned back.

If the Growlers could turn her back to normal, they could help the rest of the villagers too. Then she could take care of the queen. But if they mated and Wulfric failed in the alpha challenge, he'd be dead... and so would she.

She couldn't afford that now, not when so many people were relying on her to find a solution. Well, they were looking to Knox and Eirwyn, but they were tied to the Feral Forest for now. It was up to her to solve this, and she couldn't do that if she were dead.

Focus, she needed to focus.

She took another calming breath of his intoxicating scent.

"Is there a way to have sex without completing the mate bond?" she asked, praying to the gods that the answer was yes. Lust burned in her brain, making her barely comprehend their conversation.

He nodded slowly. "If I can control myself during it, yes. If I go feral, then no."

"How...how does the mate bond become complete?" She only knew vague details of how Eirwyn had mated with Knox. There were rumors of other shifters, but no one talked about how mates claimed each other.

"We bite each other at climax," he growled. "We claim each other, accept each other, love and protect each other. The bite symbolizes that trust."

Her stomach flipped at his words, and it had nothing to do with physical desire. Her soul yearned for that kind of acceptance. Wasn't that why she wanted to reverse her curse and get her old body back, get back to normal? Become the hero of the people instead of the freak?

So she could slink in the shadows and do her job as Hunter. So she would be accepted in Knox's kingdom as an ally and friend, instead of a monster to be avoided. So she could hold her nephew when he finally hatched, without scaring the poor thing.

"No biting. Got it. Think you can handle just sex, wolfie?"

His ears twitched at her words, and he pulled the blanket aside. She stepped forward and paused beside the bed, her tail tucked down beside her leg.

Was she really going to sleep with a Growler? What would her mother say if she knew? What would her father say?

As soon as the thoughts came, they floated out the window because he moved. His muscles rippled under the faint light until he sat at the edge of the bed. He looked up at her, then his gaze dropped like a caress along her skin.

She was surprised he hadn't pounced as soon as she'd come into the room. He was letting her set the pace and waited for her to make the next move.

More than anything thus far, it challenged everything she thought she knew of Growlers, but she didn't have time to be confused or think about it as he reached for her.

## Chapter Twelve

His hand hovered in the air, his golden eyes watching her, waiting for her.

She stared at him, wondering if there was more underneath that Growler surface. In this moment, they stood on the edge of a cliff. If they went over it, she knew her life would never be the same.

She was so fucking tired of everyone avoiding her. But the way he looked up at her, as if she hung the stars in the sky...

She arched her back, offering her breasts to him.

He licked his lips, his jaw shifting back to mostly human, then leaned forward. His long, canine tongue swirled around her nipple, sending goosebumps spreading along her skin like lightning.

She gasped and jerked, her hands sliding into his mane of wolf fur. It was so soft and silky. She scratched behind his ears, and he froze before his jaw and body shivered and his tail thumped on the bed behind him. She squirmed, her hands diving deeper into his hair.

He growled and tugged her nipple into his mouth, his hands settling on her hips to hold her still. His breath was hot as fire, making her shiver with delight. His hands wrapped around her ass, cupping the mounds and pulling her between his legs.

His mouth switched to the other breast, working the tip to life and swirling his tongue around it before sucking hard. Her fingers tightened on his hair, pulling his head closer.

Fuck, this felt good. Beyond good. It was incredible. Like the stars in the sky burned brighter, and even with just his mouth on her and his hands on her ass, she was closer to that burst than she'd been on her own.

Holy hell, she was in trouble.

It was the last conscious thought she had because in the next moment, he dipped his fingers between her thighs from behind, the tip of one finding her dripping wet core. She moaned and clenched around him. It was torture, not enough friction, too slow. She needed *more*.

He growled and clamped onto her nipple, making her jump. His fingers dug into her ass as another finger joined the first and dove in and out.

Gods, it still wasn't enough. She needed all of him. She breathed deeply of his mane, gripping hard as she tried to control herself, slow down, not go insane from his touch and the need for him.

Fuck, she didn't *need* him. She was an independent Hunter, a survivor in any situation. She didn't do team work, and she wouldn't let herself become dependent on him.

But damn it, she knew his dick would be the only thing to ease this burning fire inside her.

Desperately, she lifted a shaky knee and set it on the bed in a half-straddle. She grabbed his cock and traced her slit with it. Gods, it was so big and heavy, thick with that glistening tip.

"My, my, what a big dick you have."

He growled, his hips tensing as she squeezed. "The better to fuck you with, love."

She moaned and licked her lips, but her pussy ached too much for her to taste and explore. She was too desperate. Her hand barely wrapped around it, but she squeezed and pulled him closer to her dripping center. She was bold, insistent as she teased them both.

He growled as his hands bit into her hips. "Put me out of my misery. *Please*," he said as he switched to her other breast.

His mouth grew frenzied the closer she brought him to her core. And still he waited for her, let her decide when it was time to put them both out of their misery.

The fingers that teased her gripped her ass and urged her closer, a soft nudge and nowhere near the barbaric Growler she thought he'd be. Her foot came off the ground, her weight only supported by her knee on the bed.

He released her breast and leaned back to meet her gaze as his hands on her hips morphed into claws. His patience combined with the burning desire etched on his face melted her. Something inside her chest seemed to dislodge, making it tight and breathing difficult. Panic clawed at her at the flood of emotions. She blinked, and lined him up with her entrance.

Together they moved as one, and she sank down inch by delicious inch. Time stood still. Neither of them breathed as they both tried to process their feelings.

With only the tip inside, she whimpered at the stretch. It was too much, too big. She couldn't do this. It was simple biology.

"Fuck, you're so tight," he murmured against her breast. "Breathe, bunny. Let me in. You can do it, and it'll be so worth it."

She tried to obey, but fuck, he stretched her too much as she eased down another few centimeters. They both moaned, and his claws bit into her ass.

She put a hand on his shoulder and shook her head. "Fuck, I can't do this."

He immediately paused, looking up into her eyes. "Stay with me," he growled.

She took a breath and said, "I'm trying to, you fucker, but the fates are wrong. This isn't going to work."

He grinned, his golden eyes going soft. "It's going to work, bunny. Trust me."

She met his golden gaze, her heart stuttering at the words. Trust him, a Growler, a monster.

Except he'd done nothing to violate that trust. He'd been nothing but patient with her tonight. Could she trust him?

She tried to relax and sank down a little more, hissing on a breath and shaking her head as her nails dug into his shoulders.

He kneaded her ass and grazed her puckered hole with a finger. It made her core flutter and clench, which triggered a growl from him and made his eyes flutter. The wildness flared to the surface, and she hesitated.

*This* was the look of a Growler, the one she'd always dreamed of in her nightmares. Wild and almost beyond logical thinking, that look made her clench again as panic shot through her core once more. He leaned back on his elbows as his jaw shifted to wolf. He howled, and the windows shook.

The sound sent a shiver up her spine, and she clenched

again, sinking deeper onto him. He blinked and panted, and she saw him return to his right mind.

She took a deep breath, calming a bit to know that she could drive him to the edge of his control. It wasn't just her. He felt it too.

"Fuck, tell me you're alright, bunny. Tell me what you need, if you're ready," he sat up and licked her hard nipple, rocking his hips slightly.

She gasped, needing more. But even in the heat of the moment, even as she settled her other knee on the bed to fully straddle him, she marveled that this beast, this monster was waiting for her.

He was letting her lead. He could easily flip her over and take control. The thought made her core clench, and he groaned, biting down on her nipple.

She gasped and jerked, the movement pushing her down all the way. Finally, she was fully seated on him. She gripped his hair, arched her back, and rocked onto him.

The fire swept through her, burning her soul with the rightness of it. He was like coming home, exciting and calming, safe yet dangerous.

She melted into his arms and rested her elbows on his shoulders. He easily lifted her by the hips, then he thrust and eased her hips down on his dick. It was so slow, and she felt every inch stretch her impossibly wide.

She moaned as he speared her, still adjusting. It was beyond anything she'd ever known before. She'd been with men, but this was no man. He was a beast, and she knew there was no turning back now.

He was impossibly huge, and it hurt so good. His cock seemed to pulse within her as he filled her completely. The tendons on his neck stood in sharp relief as she jerked back, holding back the scream as he moved again, lifted her and brought her back down for the second time. She felt his knot push against her opening, and he paused.

His eyes glowed in the darkness, but she wasn't scared. Not when he watched her with such reverence and awe.

"Are you ready, bunny?" His voice was deep, and his eyes flashed wild once more. "Third time's the charm because I don't think I can keep up this slow pace. I'm—I'm going to break."

She gripped his hair and drew his wolf's face to her breasts. "Gods, yes, fuck me, wolfie. Fuck me hard."

Before she could blink, he set up a bruising rhythm like a runaway horse. She held onto his neck as his fingers dug into her ass with each hard stroke. Stretched to near breaking, she lost all ability to think.

The blunt promise of a soul-bending orgasm was within reach. Dear gods, don't let it float away like earlier.

His relentless thrusts rammed into her, and she held on for all she was worth. The animal fierceness welled within her, clawing at her body from the inside out.

Her fingers dug into his back. The tension pooled between them, growing higher and higher.

Every pump inside sent pleasure through her body, and he pistoned harder, his shaft sliding in and out. Her pussy swallowed, and she was stuck between torment at the stretching and ecstasy at the fullness.

Her body ached like a run up the highest cliff, demanding more, begging to be filled completely. The furious flood of need drove her higher and higher. Tortured moans slipped past her lips as she matched his rhythm and rode him.

The need to explode built, and then his teeth grazed her nipple again. He sucked hard, biting and sending stars behind her eyes. The pain of the bite and the stretch of the knot on her opening made her mind burst with colors.

She exploded with a screaming orgasm. Clenching, thrashing, fire flowing from her core through her veins like lightning, her body shook with soul-wrenching satisfaction.

"Fuck." He bucked and moaned, his face buried in her chest as he thrust upward once more. It was like he wanted to drive his knot deep into her, but she was too tight and spasming too much. He was too erratic and desperate for release as her orgasm went on.

He swelled within her, and his teeth scraped her breast again. She gripped his head, and he jerked back with a howl. Canines sharp, nose and jaw elongated, eyes wild as the hot, pulsing seed unleashed inside her, virile and volcanic love.

Even as she spasmed around him, her back arched. Staring at this gorgeous creature who accepted her as she was, she basked in the triumph of seeing him undone. She'd done that. She'd sent him over the edge.

His body tensed in pulsing waves that mirrored her own. They came hard, each fueling the other's climax. The pulsing storm settled slowly into gentle waves, and his hands flexed on her hips, the claws gone.

Then he slid them over her back in a caress so gentle, she felt tears in the corner of her eye. She hesitated to name why, focusing instead on what his caress meant. Acceptance, joy, and peace flooded her. Somehow, she knew he felt them all. The fact that her presence could bring him those emotions differed completely from what she'd known for so long.

He stroked her back up and down, and she sank her head onto his shoulder. His hand came up to cradle her head into the crook of his neck, holding her like a well-loved child and angling her small antlers away from him.

His arms could crush a man to death, but he held her so gently, her chest grew tighter. He didn't treat her like a ferocious monster, like the other villagers who avoided her.

Could she trust him, trust these feelings?

She sighed, pushing the question away. She'd worry about it tomorrow. Holding him just as tightly, their breathing began to slow. Damn, even their hearts beat in sync.

The power of their shared release left her breathless. She'd never climaxed that hard before. But more than that was how he made her feel.

Her tight rein on her emotions was paper thin. The wall around her heart crumbling steadily with every stolen glance, every caress of his hands. The fear of that would return. She knew it would be short-lived, but she was too tired to be afraid and pull away.

Her body felt deliciously sore, and for the first time in hours, in the months since being cursed, her mind was at peace. She would bask in it for as long as it remained. Then she'd pull away, go back to her life, and forget about him. She couldn't let her emotions get tied up in this Growler.

## Chapter Thirteen

Wulfric woke to find Scarlet sprawled limply on his chest, one leg thrown between his. Her petite, little calloused hand lay on his chest, and a faint memory stirred of some other woman long ago. A brunette with bountiful curves had sprawled just like this. She was...

His wife.

His body went stiff as he tried to picture her face. It was fuzzy, but he remembered a beautiful smile and thick hair that smelled of bread.

Sweat beaded his lip, and his breathing grew ragged. Scarlet stirred, and he held still as she nuzzled against his chest and murmured.

His wife must've done the same. It must be what had triggered the memory.

Yes, this contented feeling was definitely familiar. Holy goddess, he'd been married. Was he still married? No, there was no way he would willingly become a Growler if he was leaving behind a wife.

The familiar empty ache in his chest tried to pull him down into the darkness as he tried to remember.

The pain of loss pressed on his chest again, and for the first time in ten years, he understood why. A sudden image of a funeral pyre blazing in a temple seared through his mind, causing his arms to tighten on Scarlet. Pain pulsed through his body, but he fought to suppress any outward signs of distress.

The image of fire triggered a torrent of memories that overwhelmed him, sending bursts of light dancing behind his closed eyelids. The past flooded back in a rush, each one feeling like a slap to the face. He closed his eyes, trying to push them away, but they persisted with a vengeance. His heart raced as he tried to steady his breathing, caught between the agony of the past and the comfort of Scarlet's presence.

The villagers offering their condolences as they all got roaring drunk at the tavern.

Training to be a soldier outside the capital.

The march to war with his friends.

The blood, the death. Battle after battle.

His body shook, and he slowly eased out from underneath Scarlet. She turned on her side and sighed, still asleep.

He lifted a shaky hand and raked it down his face. He paced to the door and back on silent feet. No more images came, and his breathing got easier the more he moved.

Were these the type of memories that the ambushers had had? If so, how had they gotten more memories faster?

Sleeping with his mate couldn't have unlocked the vault on his past, because Brody and his friends weren't mated. His mind ached as he tried to remember every interaction over the past few years. They had all been turned within the last two to five years, compared to his own ten. He'd been alpha for five years now, beta for the two before that. Before becoming a Growler...

Images flew through his mind. Battles. Bars. Women, but with one woman—*his wife*—featured more than any others.

Damn this Growler side-effect of being turned. When he'd been turned and lost a lifetime of memories, he'd not been prepared for the painful gaping chasm where they'd been stored in his mind. The more he realized he'd lost, the more painful it became.

Perhaps that was why he didn't want to turn Scarlet. He liked her just the way she was, and he definitely didn't want her turning into the same old she-wolves that made up the Growler tribe.

Vicious. Back biting. Sneaky.

He couldn't let that happen to Scarlet. She was his mate, and he had to protect her from them. Protect her like he couldn't protect his wife.

His heart skipped a beat. Damn, he'd had a wife, one that he'd loved... and failed to protect. Rationally, he knew he couldn't stop the fever that had spread through their village. But in his soul, he knew there was more he could've done.

He couldn't let anything like that happen to Scarlet. She mewled in her sleep and turned onto her back. The last streaks of moonlight fell on the bed. A red bite mark around her nipple made him grimace. Guilt hit him like a blow to the head. He'd lost control and bitten her in the heat of the moment. He'd tried so hard to be careful, to keep the wolf caged.

His end of the mate bond was done, wasn't it?

Maybe. He really didn't know enough about the process.

Damn it, he needed to talk to the Elders. It was supposed to be such a natural thing, instinctual for animals like them. But he was so worried about hurting her and taking away her choices. She was so independent; losing that would hurt her.

His heart started racing, and the walls closed around him. Carefully, he eased off the bed and walked on silent feet out the door. Slipping down the stairs, his heart pounding in his ears, he pushed open the front door and shifted onto four feet.

The bracing, frigid air was still in the early morning light. Birds chirped in the trees, no longer caring about the Growler in their midst.

The cold seeped under his fur, sharpening his mind. Shit, why hadn't the Elders warned them that fated mates would be this instant, this futile to fight?

He didn't want to fight against it. But admitting he'd had a wife whom he'd loved had forced him to compare the faceless woman to Scarlet.

There was no escaping this. He wanted Scarlet more than his own breath, which currently puffed white into the freezing air. He'd known her for less than a day, yet the Elders had spoken the truth about mates at least. When he knew, he knew. She was his mate, his world.

Frustration welled inside, and he wanted to howl. He refused, instead sucking in an icy breath and jogging around the house in ever widening circles.

Why was he so upset? Was it just because he'd realized some of his past?

His mind tried to search for more of his past but to no avail. It was like the flood had been damned, but there were leaks here and there.

He knew he'd been a soldier, and he'd lost a wife and

child. The gnawing loneliness that had left him feeling so empty wasn't just because he was a Growler and had lost sight of who he was as a man.

He remembered feeling like this after his wife died.

The ripping pain in his chest was now a dull and familiar ache. He'd mourned his wife for the past ten years of being a Growler, even if he couldn't remember her. This heartache was as familiar as his own face.

No, this frustration now was because of Scarlet, his beautiful bunny who didn't realize her own power and might. He would do anything for her. If she realized that, would she use it against him?

If she'd been a Growler woman, she would've. But with her unique characteristics, he couldn't be sure.

Either way, he had to get to know her. He had to win her trust and her heart. That mission hadn't changed even though they'd slaked their lust in the dark of night.

He also had nothing to offer her yet. Nothing but a Growler life that she feared and despised.

Thank the gods he'd not lost his mind and turned her by accident during their mating. She would've seen it as yet another curse thrust on her. He needed to speak to the Elders to see what would happen if she never claimed him back. Would he be the only one to die of a broken heart or would it be Scarlet because she rejected him?

When the other two Growlers had refused to mate, they'd both ran in opposite directions. They'd been from different tribes, but the strength of the mate bond had scared them both. Their families had recognized it, tried to convince them both to go to the other.

But they had remained stubborn and separated, and eventually they both wasted away to nothing. The Elders had said the gods had punished them for going against the goddess. When word had come from the other tribe, the Elders said they'd both died within the same hour.

He didn't want Scarlet to die for not claiming him. And if he died, he couldn't protect her. Silently, he sent a prayer to any gods who'd listen, asking for answers...and for Scarlet to claim him back before it was too late.

The gods smiled on those who helped them out, though. He had to convince Scarlet to take a chance on him, and he only had a few more days to do it.

When the full moon rose and broke the bond of the berry, she'd bolt like a deer running for her life.

He lengthened his stride, dodging silently around tree after tree. He needed to eat. If he was going to prove himself as a worthy mate, he needed to feed her too. A plan formed in his mind, and the first stop on the campaign to win her heart was breakfast.

Thankfully, he was fully healed with only a few scratches and scars left of his fight. The light outside grew brighter as he hunted, sniffing out a worthy offering to his mate.

Rabbits wouldn't do. Somehow, he couldn't imagine her eating one of her own kind. Same with deer. What would she want to eat?

It had to be something he could find nearby. He couldn't go too far away or they'd both end up sick. A fresh scent caught in his nose, and he turned to track it.

Two hours later, he trotted back into the clearing with a lynx slung over his back. It was the biggest he could find, and it had almost taken him out. The further he'd gotten from Scarlet, the more his stomach had rebelled and his vision blurred. Weakness had made him stumble, letting the lynx get in a good swipe of the claws.

But he'd triumphed in the end. He shifted with the cracking of bones by the back door, dropping the corpse to the ground. Then he stepped inside to find a knife to finish the job.

Scarlet glanced up, one boot laced up and fire in her eyes as she glared at him from a kitchen chair. "Where have you been?"

His heart pounded at her tone, the ferocity of her expression, and he paused just to soak up her presence. She was such a beautiful vengeful goddess, and she was all his. He wondered if she could see the adoration in his eyes, if she'd take advantage of him in this state. He'd never fallen so easily or so completely.

He froze, remembering his past dead wife. At least, he didn't think he had. Guilt licked his spine, making his frustration come back full-force.

Her eyes scanned up and down his body, and awareness made him grow hot as the memories of the past faded.

She stomped to him, grabbing his arm and turning him this way and that. "Are you hurt? Is this your blood?"

"No, I'm fine. Just a few scratches from our breakfast. Do you like lynx?"

"Of course, I like lynx, but that doesn't excuse you for disappearing."

"Aw, were you worried about me, bunny?"

His lips twitched with a smile, but he knew better than to let her see. So he stepped close and pulled her into his arms.

She scowled, stiff and unyielding. "Not on your life, wolfie. But you heard what Grandma said. We're not supposed to be apart."

She muttered and cursed as she pushed away from him. His chest hurt from the rejection as she stalked to the sink with one shoe on. His precious, fierce fighter was hurting them both by fighting this bond.

Why couldn't she see it and accept him? If she hated Growlers for what they did to her mother, perhaps he'd never be good enough for her. His emotions threatened to choke him at the thought.

Unease slithered along his spine like cold water.

She dunked a rag into the water bowl and rang it out as she spun on her heel. "Imagine my surprise when I woke up alone, feeling like I was being torn in two."

He frowned and stepped toward her. "Are you alright? What happened?"

She punched him in the non-injured shoulder and glared. "It's the fucking tea we drank. You went too far away just like Grandma told us not to do. Didn't you feel it?"

She started to run the wet rag over the bloody streaks on his chest. Her dainty hands made his spine tingle with desire, and his dick lengthened while his tail twitched.

He growled, his hands sliding up her biceps in a caress. "I felt it. It's why I got scratched in the damn hunt. The lynx almost got me when the dizziness hit, but I'm fine. See? The scratches are already closing."

If she was worried about him, perhaps there was hope for them yet.

She harrumphed and scowled up at him, her eyes big and showing her hurt and pain. "Why did you leave? Stupid Growler. If you'd waited, I would've made breakfast. There's more than enough provisions here."

He had to fix this sad look on her face. "I will never leave you again," he murmured, turning and trapping her against the counter once more. He gently tugged her closer, hugging her tight and stroking the back of her head.

"Don't be ridiculous," she whispered, not returning the hug. But at least she wasn't fighting him. At least she melted into his arms and let him hold her. It was like a salve to his soul, being pressed up against her. Some of the heartache and chaos of the morning eased.

His head dipped to nuzzle her neck. "I need to provide for my mate, Scarlet."

"You don't have to take care of me. I can't take care of myself."

"I know I don't have to, but I want to." He ran his nose down the side of her head, avoiding her antlers and nuzzling her jaw.

"Oh really?" Her words were a breathless whisper, her tone softening from anger to desire. As he kissed along her neck, she tilted her head back and let out a sigh of surrender. Her hands gripped his back, pulling him closer.

"Really." He continued kissing, moving up to her earlobe where he gently tugged on it with his teeth. She shivered in response, and the intensity of their connection deepened.

"I want to take care of you, but it's more than just a normal want. It's something deeper, something I can't ignore or deny. I might want wild blackberries, but if I don't have them, I'll be fine. What I feel with you is so much more."

She shuddered, and he tugged on her ear with his teeth. "More?"

"This bond between us is like a fire burning deep within me," he confessed hoarsely. "I need to provide for you, protect you, worship every inch of your body." As he spoke, his lips traced down the column of her neck and over her collarbone, igniting new sparks of desire within them both.

"Oh," she said, breathless. "What are you going to do about it?" The hint of challenge in her tone was unmistakable, and it sent a thrill through him.

"Going to woo my mate, for starters" he said, nipping

down the side of her neck. "Do you think talking about a deep, aching need will make your pussy weep for me?"

She gasped, her hands spasming in his hair. "Nope, not going to happen."

He chuckled and ground his hips into hers, making her mouth drop open. He licked her bottom lip. "Are you sure, love? It's so cold outside, and I've been gone for hours. Help me warm up, bunny."

Her lips sought his, but he just peppered soft, short kisses to her bottom lip, her jaw. Her hands fisted on his back.

"Damn it... fine, but no biting. This doesn't mean I accept the mate bond."

His chest grew tight at her words, but he swooped to take her mouth in a bruising kiss. Too late for biting on his part. As soon as the thought came, it flew away. He swept inside, stealing her soul and trying to fan the flames.

Her hands settled on his chest as her knees buckled. He pressed her against the counter, his mouth sucking gently on her jugular. He could almost taste the blood flowing through her veins, and he felt his incisors grow.

The need to bite her neck while exploding inside her was quickly becoming something he couldn't ignore.

He had to show her all he could offer, convince her that there was no living without him.

He let his hands shift and shredded her pants, spinning her around. "Hands on the counter," he growled as he sank to his knees.

She did one better, pulling her knee up and laying her lower leg on the counter too. He growled in approval, "Fuck, yes."

Then he pulled her cheeks apart and licked up her dripping slit. He growled as the nectar flowed like honey on his tongue. "You little liar. You're definitely dripping."

"Shut up and suck my clit," she panted.

He chuckled. "Happy to oblige."

Slowly, he lapped at her pussy, twirled his tongue around her clit, then shifted his tongue to lengthen it and slide it as deep as it could go. He took a finger and circled her clit, adding pressure until she groaned.

His mouth worked its magic on her until she was moaning and thrusting her ass back against him. When she began to chant, "Oh gods," he knew it was time.

He stood and thrust his cock into her, pushing slowly but steadily into the tightest vise-like grip. She was so narrow, it was almost painful to work his way inside. His lip beaded with sweat as he held her hips, claws digging into her soft flesh and mouth shifting into a wolf's jaw.

He flexed, focusing on receding his claws and controlling his wolf until his dick was fully sheathed inside her pussy.

He pulled out, then plunged into her wet heat, a scalding hotness that gripped him, milked him, welcomed him completely. He withdrew again, then rammed himself home. His body, hard and primal against hers, released the beast within him.

He fucked her hard and fast like the animal he was. Hard, rough strokes matched the pounding of his heartbeat. He took her with a pounding need and driving hunger he'd never felt before. The tension built quickly as the pulsing root of his cock surged within her. It called to the most animal part of him, driving him to claim her. His body began to shift and his knot rubbed against her opening with each thrust.

Blind to all else, he no longer had control over his baser

instincts. She grew tighter, her gasps shallower, and his vision blurred with the need to bite her.

Fangs at her shoulder, blood flooded his mouth like ambrosia. Like before, the bite triggered her release. She screamed and thrashed under him. Her body jerked and shivered. Quivering waves rippled up and down his shaft, and he tried to hold back.

His vision swam as her body clenched and writhed around him. He couldn't fight the orgasm any longer. His balls tightened in response to her quivering muscles. He came in a rush of hot, salty seed, exploding as he coated her core. No woman had ever felt so good, so perfect. He knew that down into his soul, even if he didn't have the memories to confirm it.

She was his everything, his entire world. He stayed inside, letting her body milk him, but he pulled his teeth from her flesh. He licked the bite clean, pulling back to watch as the punctures closed over.

He felt her knees buckle, so he pulled her back against him and swept her into his arms. He took her back up the stairs, her shredded pants falling to the floor and dragging, caught on her one boot. When he tucked her into bed, her head lolled, making him smile. She was back to sleep, and all was as it should be.

He pulled the blanket over her to keep her warm, then went to make breakfast like he'd originally intended. He would take care of his mate, and soon she would accept the mate bond. He just knew it. She was already falling for him, otherwise she wouldn't have been so worried about his disappearance earlier.

He grinned while he skinned the lynx and prepped the meat. It was going to be a great day.

## Chapter Fourteen

The aroma of sizzling meat and eggs filled the air as Scarlet walked downstairs, one leather boot in her hand. The sound of clinking plates echoed with her steps on the stairs. She'd fallen back to sleep until nearly noon, which she hadn't done since she was a child.

She was definitely not a child now, not with how deliciously sore she was. She shivered as images of their indecency in the kitchen floated through her mind. Grandma would throw a fit if she knew what they'd done.

Then again, that was probably why she'd left in such a hurry yesterday. She probably would've said it was inevitable. Scarlet scowled as she stomped down the stairs.

She'd woken up disoriented, washed her face, and changed into a spare set of clothes. When she'd found one boot still on, her annoyance had turned to anger. The familiar emotion wrapped around her like a hug, and she grasped it with both hands.

It was much better to face the unknown downstairs with

the comforting emotion that had sustained her for years. Ever since losing her mother then her father.

She hit the landing and stopped at the water closet under the stairs, leaving her lone boot outside the door.

The other had been left downstairs by the table. When he had come through the door in all his fucking naked glory, blood soaking his fur, making him look rugged, fierce, and dangerous, all her senses had gone haywire.

It was an irresistible combination. She threw the washroom door open and kicked her boot into the living room. When she turned the corner, she paused, her chest growing tight.

Her stomach growled and lurched, but not entirely from hunger. Her mate was cooking breakfast, Olive's apron around his waist. His naked ass didn't seem to bother him, but it sure bothered her enough to freeze in place.

Fucking hells this was ridiculous. She couldn't have a Growler for a mate. She wasn't a shifter and shouldn't have a mate at all. Humans like her with weak ass magic just got married or didn't. They weren't supposed to have mates.

Wulfric turned and smiled, his face mostly human now except for his wolf ears and mane of gray and black hair. Fur or hair? She didn't even know how to describe him.

"Hungry?" he asked, his voice sending a shiver up her spine.

She frowned and sank onto a kitchen chair as he scooped something onto a plate. He set it in front of her, then turned back.

"Do you want some coffee or tea?" he asked.

She poked the food with her fork, her nose twitching in appreciation, her mouth salivating. "No more fucking tea for me, thanks."

He chuckled, and she squirmed on her seat. She wouldn't give in to his trap. He was lulling her in with a sense of familiarity, making her think he was domesticated.

She knew better. He was a wild Growler, a monster, and she had to keep her walls up.

If she didn't, she'd end up hurt. Or dead like her mother.

She scarfed down her food and ignored him. It was simple but delicious. Chopped potatoes, scrambled eggs, and diced meat. Even when he sat beside her, knees touching, she moved to avoid touching him.

"Do you like it?" he asked between bites, his voice subdued.

She looked up and around. "Like what?"

He pointed with his fork. "The food. I have to keep my mate well fed and happy."

"I'm not your mate. But yes, it's delicious. Thank you," she said, wiping her mouth and taking her empty plate to the sink.

"You're delicious too," he said, his eyes glowing. She didn't want to talk or think about it, but he'd just set her cheeks afire with the memory of his head between her legs. It made her want another round with him, and she couldn't have that.

She washed the plate and snorted. "We need to make plans."

She looked at the clock, frowning as she thought.

"To go to the Growlers?"

She took a deep breath and slowly exhaled. With a purse of her lips, she finished washing the plate. "Yes, how long will it take to get there? What will we do when we get to the camp?"

His hand slid his empty plate in the water, and she froze, her breath stuttering in her chest. He was right behind her again, but this time, she knew what his body felt like pressed against hers.

She was cocooned by his arms again, and the safety they provided made her yearn for so much more. It'd be so easy to lean into his strength, to be taken care of for once instead of the one taking care of everything and everyone else.

Her nose twitched, a reminder that she couldn't trust him. She had curses to break, people relying on her to find a solution. She slid to the left, away from the heat of his body and the feelings he stirred within her.

She couldn't give in. She had to focus and plan the mission.

He cleaned his plate and answered her questions. By the time she'd put on both her boots, their plan was made. She frowned as she finally looked at him, leaning casually against the counter with ankles and arms crossed.

"Does everyone walk around at the Growlers camp naked?"

He snorted and shook his head. "No, we have bags of clothes stored throughout the woods if needed."

Scarlet pursed her lips. "You can probably fit in my brother's clothes upstairs. We can take them with us."

"But not to wear now?" he grinned, his big teeth sending a shiver up her spine. Had he bit her with those teeth? Wasn't that part of the mating process?

Her mind shied away from the answer. She didn't want to think about it. No, they needed to focus on the mission. Curing her curses was her number one priority.

What had he asked? Oh, the clothes.

"You can shift and lead the way to camp in wolf form, but I can't follow you as quickly on foot. Is my horse going to be safe at camp or should I leave her here and walk?" Scarlet stood and brushed her hands down her thighs as nerves threatened to swarm her.

She'd not gotten nervous on missions since joining the Hunters. Traveling with her dad had prepared her well. Years of work as a mercenary, and the thought of going into the Growlers den sent her into a tizzy. It was ridiculous, and it made her mad.

Wulfric shrugged. "Not sure. We've stolen horses before, but they don't stay in camp very often. We don't have a village with wooden buildings and a stable."

He frowned, rubbing his hand along his jaw. "I remember buildings."

Her skin tingled and itched, so she began to gather supplies for her pack that was still in the barn. "Fine, I'll leave her here with enough food and water for a few days."

"Then I'll walk with you for a while. Stretch my human legs."

She nodded jerkily. "Go upstairs and find some clothes, then."

His steps echoed up the stairs, but she refused to turn and watch his fine ass walk away. She felt panic clawing at her, but she focused on breathing evenly and planning every step of their journey.

Her movements were still jerky as she gathered healing potions and ointment. The bag that Knox had brought from the old medicine woman was on the corner of the counter next to her shredded pants. She opened it and pursed her lips.

Shit, she hadn't thought of that, but somehow Lailant had known.

She popped the cork on the vial and downed the

disgusting ginger and fennel gel. A swish of water washed it down before her stomach knotted in pain.

She sank into a chair and put her head between her knees, holding her stomach as the magic swirled through her body. This never got easier. All she could do was breathe and try to unclench one muscle at a time. Slowly the roar of magic through her body subsided until she could sit up.

With a shaky hand, she took another drink of water. The spasms through her stomach grew fainter, more manageable. The spots on the edge of her vision disappeared. She blinked in the dim light of the kitchen as steps echoed through the room.

When Wulfric came around the corner into the open, her jaw dropped. He looked almost human, wearing brown pants and a dark green shirt. The sleeves were a tad too short, and the pants only came to his ankles. His bare feet weren't quite human but neither were they wolf. Some sort of in between that made her feel akin to him.

But it was his expression that caught her attention the most. Frowning, he asked, "Are you alright? I got a stomach ache, but we're nowhere near being separated."

Her eyes widened, and she swallowed her suddenly dry mouth. "You felt that?" Her voice was soft, barely a whisper as he nodded.

She closed her eyes and leaned back in the chair. "Fuck," she whispered.

It must be true. They were mates, and even though they hadn't bonded yet, they were feeling each other's emotions and pain. It wasn't tied to the glockenberry.

Fucking hell.

She rubbed her forehead and sighed. "Yes, it was me, but I'm fine. It was just a potion."

She spun the empty vial in her palm. Anti-pregnancy

potions tasted like shit, but she would be safe for another month. Hopefully she'd be long separated from him by then.

She pointed to his feet to distract him. "What about shoes? Do you wear shoes? It's freezing outside. Do Growlers get frostbite in this form?"

He shrugged and ran his hands down his stomach, drawing the shirt tight over his abs. Moving from foot to foot, he frowned at himself and wiggled his toes.

"When it's cold, we stick close to the warmth of camp. Unless we're hunting, which we do as a Growler. The cold does hurt us more like this, so shoes are probably a good idea."

She waved to the front door where a basket of shoes sat under the coat rack. "You're free to try Knox's boots, but they might not fit."

He walked away. Just a few more days, and they'd break the spell of the tea. By then, she'd know if the Growlers could turn her back to normal.

She reached up to feel her shorter horns, thankful for the changes already. But it was a reminder of what she had to fix for everyone else. They were counting on her.

Thank the gods she wouldn't have to solve the problem with a babe too.

What would a baby between them even look like? Would it have antlers? Or be fully one animal shifter over another? She'd heard of other animal shifters living in their own communities in Glathen, but hadn't ever seen a bunny or deer community.

She was the only one. Still a freak of nature, an abomination to be avoided.

Unless she had a baby. She stared at the vial, thankful but somehow sad at the same time.

Wulfric put his hands on her shoulders, and she jumped up, spinning to face him with her hand held out. "Don't touch me."

He frowned, and she felt a stab of pain to see the wounded look in his eyes. It was partly guilt over hurting him, but somehow she knew it was what he was feeling.

He held his hands out. "I can see how worried you are, but I will protect you from the pack. Growlers are vicious, but they're not all bad."

She breathed deeply, refusing to tell him she hadn't actually been worrying about the Growlers.

Instead, she grabbed the heavy bag of supplies and glared. "You can't even protect yourself. How are you going to protect me?"

"You're my mate. They'll respect the mate bond," he said, crossing his arms.

He was so tall and intimidating. With his rugged good looks and rippling muscles under that thin layer of fur, she couldn't think of anything he couldn't handle. He was full of life, strong and virile. He could probably take on the entire army of Busparia by himself and still live.

She shook her head and reached for the dried fruit on a shelf. Her dad had been like that too, larger than life, wise and strong. But he'd still been killed.

She had to prepare for every possibility. She met his golden eyes.

"I'm putting a lot of trust in you, Growler. If I die on this foolish mission, you better believe I'm going to haunt you and make your life miserable."

He laughed and nodded, the sound making her core melt and some of the tension in her shoulders ease. She scowled and turned away, adding the fruit to the bag of supplies.

He sat on the chair she'd vacated and laced up the boots as he talked. "I'll keep that in mind, but we're both going to be alright. I've just found you, and I'm not going to let anything happen to you now."

Her heart stuttered and her breath caught in her throat. The look in his eyes, the set of his jaw—he was completely sincere.

She didn't trust it. These kinds of feelings just ended up hurting people. She'd watched it over and over through the years as a Hunter. Death came easily and ripped families apart. She wasn't always proud of her role in that, but there was no changing it.

She tossed her bag on the table and strode to the stairs. "Let me get a set of spare clothes, then we can head out."

Her steps were heavy on the stairs, but she didn't care. She was pushing him away, keeping him out, but it was better to do that first, before he realized this wouldn't work. Her life wasn't with him or the Growlers.

She had things to do for Knox, a village to heal, and a queen to kill. She didn't have time for a mate or love.

She came back downstairs and tossed him the leather pouch of clothes. He caught it easily and peeked inside. "If you wolf out and rip the clothes you're wearing, at least you'll have extra. No sense in freezing on the journey."

He nodded, rubbing his chin. "Thanks, I'll carry the heavier bag."

She schooled her features to hide her flash of anger. Of course, he'd want to show off his manly muscles and take the bigger bag.

But it wasn't worth picking a fight over. Instead of telling him to fuck off, she just shrugged and gathered the other bag on the table. "I'm going to make sure my horse has what she needs. I'll meet you outside."

She escaped into the bitter wind, the door slamming behind her. Fuck, what was she doing? Was she seriously about to travel through the Feral Forest on foot with a Growler?

It was madness, pure madness. Almost as mad as having a Growler for a mate.

# Chapter Fifteen

Wulfric laced up the other leather boot over his new brown pants and felt the pressure on his chest increase. The dizziness swept over him like a tidal wave and memories faded in and out.

A wife laughing at the hearth, a baby crawling on the floor. An old woman pulling a death shroud over his wife's face.

He shook his head as the images flooded through his mind. Why now? Why were the memories coming now after ten years of being a Growler?

Sweat beaded on his lip, and he wiped it away, his head pounding. His stomach lurched, breakfast settling like a weight in his gut. He was too hot, the clothes too restrictive. He stumbled to his feet and pushed through the door.

The frigid air hit him, and he breathed deeply, eyes closed as he focused on staying upright.

"Wulfric?" Scarlet's voice was soft, grounding him in the present. "What's wrong?"

How quickly she went from cold and distant to concern for him.

He blinked in the blinding sunlight falling through the trees. The images and rushing in his ears faded as her small hand settled on his bare forearm. He looked down into green eyes so deep, he could drown in them.

His hands settled on her elbows, afraid to pull her close but needing to touch her, needing to be reminded of life. She was real, warm, and vivacious. She was more than just a beautiful woman in the right place at the right time; she was a lifeline, grounding him in his humanity and easing the ache in his chest caused by painful memories.

The past was easier to face in her presence.

He blinked as a bird flew overhead, a robin trilling softly and breaking the hold of the past. Even with the sun shining, snow began to fall softly, already forming a crown on the red hair piled high between her antlers.

"Talk to me, wolfie. What's going on in that big brain of yours?" Her voice was softer than it'd been earlier. When they'd been packing, she'd been tense and jumpy.

But now, with those green eyes staring at him with worry and tenderness… maybe there was hope for them yet.

He raked a hand through his hair. "I don't know how to talk about it."

She arched a brow but didn't say anything. So he took a deep breath. He had to trust her, talk with her, let her in. It was the only way to win her affections and convince her to complete the mate bond.

"Growlers don't remember our lives before we were turned, but I do now." His voice was harsh and deep.

"What do you mean?" she asked, shivering in her thick, fur-lined red and green hood as she reached for one of the two bags on the ground.

He licked his lips and swallowed, trying to choke out the words to explain. He wanted her to understand him, to bare his heart and soul to her, but damn if it wasn't hard to do.

Wulfric grabbed both bags and slung them over his shoulders. "Let me carry them. We need to get moving before we freeze where we stand."

She pursed her lips and nodded. "Very well. We can take the path to the Lone Road. Can you find your way from there?"

With a nod, he wiggled his toes in the boots. They were uncomfortable, but he was trying to adjust to living like a human for her sake. "The Lone Road is the boundary of our territory, so yes. I can find the way. If we push ourselves, we should reach camp by tomorrow night."

Her brows rose as she stepped back, pulling gloves cut of her pocket. "So close? I thought they were several days away."

He shrugged. "Depends on the time of year. This month, we're in the most northern camp."

Adjusting the green shirt again, he led the way out of the clearing and into the woods. The grass crunched under their feet, breaking the silence around them. Each step pinched his toes in the too tight boots, and he had to consciously make sure his feet stayed shifted into human ones. They left the birds behind and even the rustling of small game grew fainter the deeper they traveled along a faint path.

"I'm here when you're ready to talk about the memory thing," she said as she led him along the path.

He scanned the woods, watching for predators and for the magic of the forest to attack. But it might be easier to talk about his feelings this way. If he wasn't facing her, he wouldn't need to analyze her expression and see how she was interpreting it.

This way, he could just talk. Freely. It had been years since he'd done this. He took a deep breath, some of the tightness on his chest easing.

"When Growlers are turned, we give up everything we were before. The magic of it erases all memories of our human lives."

Their steps crunched as the trees grew thicker and closer together.

"So you don't remember anything from before? Your life as a human?"

He shook his head and offered her a hand over a fallen log. She stared at him in fascination, uneasily taking his hand.

She stepped onto the log, but her foot went straight through the decaying wood. Beetles swarmed out of the hole, spreading over the log and up her leg.

She cried out, and Wulfric grabbed her hips and swung her away from the log. Some of them flew off her in the motion, but too many kept clinging to her, their tiny legs scurrying over her skin.

With a quick flick of her wrists, she drew out her gleaming daggers, their sharp edges glinting in the dim light. Wulfric deftly maneuvered around her as she frantically flapped her hands, narrowly avoiding her horns. He lunged forward, swiping at the crawling pests that threatened to latch onto his own legs.

"Fuck, fuck, fuck," she muttered, each word a slash of her palms.

Several of them crawled on his own legs where he knelt on the ground, but he paid them no heed.

"There's more," she yelled, panicking and pointing to the log behind him.

He turned his head, and his stomach clenched. Hundreds were still pouring out of the hole in the log. He spun back around to see that she was now spider-free. Without hesitation, he leapt to his feet and scooped her up, throwing her over his shoulder and running to safety.

"Ah!" she screamed again, her tiny hands landing on his back, daggers bouncing as he jogged toward the road. "What are you doing? Put me down."

"Not until we're free from the swarm. Hold tight, bunny." He ran faster, trying to keep his gait smooth so as not to hurt her. He felt the stinging bite of beetles lessen on his legs, but he didn't stop until he got to the road.

Then he put her down on her feet, turning her to inspect every inch of her legs. "All gone?" he panted.

She scowled and nodded, patting her thighs and stepping away from him. "I could've managed on my own."

He sighed in relief and took her hand again. "I know, but you don't have to do it alone now, Scarlet."

He didn't release her hand. She scowled, but tipped her head up as he tugged her to follow the road. "This doesn't mean we're done with the conversation. Keep talking, wolfie."

He looked up over his shoulder, ever vigilant. "The river is this way. We'll meet it and follow it South. The Growler camp is just off the river."

"If you want to talk about your human life, I'd be alright with that."

His lips twitched at her attempt to appear nonchalant. He wanted her to trust him, which meant opening up to her about his former life. The knot in his stomach made him nervous, but he had to push past it.

He squeezed her hand and sighed. "When I was ambushed, the leader, Brody, said that he remembered his past. I didn't believe him. But the past few days of being with you–"

Vines stirred above, reaching for them. He spun her with their joined hands as it stabbed down, narrowly avoiding them. He tucked her behind him, but her hand reached up toward the vine, palm out.

It receded back into the canopy as the rest of the vines slowed their movements to a crawl. His brows rose, and he looked back at her. "Did you do that? Is that druid magic?"

She grinned and shook her head, revealing a brand on the inside of her left wrist. "It's dragon magic. My adopted brother, Knox, the dragon you saw yesterday? Grandma raised him from a hatchling. I was five when my mother died, and Knox hatched. When we were kids, he had a dream and burned this onto my wrist. We figured out it bypassed the magic of the forest."

"The magic that tries to kill trespassers?" Wulfric asked as they walked West on the only road that went through the forest.

She nodded. "Yeah, when I became a Hunter, he apparently formed the Robins and escorted people safely through the forest on this very road. For a fee, of course."

"Of course," he grinned. He rather admired the dragon for creating a business while also protecting the forest. Although the Robins had been a pain in the Growlers' side the entire time, he wished he'd thought to offer escort services through the forest.

She nodded at the bags still slung over his shoulder. "Want me to take a bag now?"

He shook his head. "No, I'm good."

They walked in silence until they came close to the river, then he led her South, far enough away from the river that they could still have a conversation while keeping it within sight.

He took her hand again, and this time she didn't tug it away. "Tell me more about the dragon. We've heard the rumors of what happened this summer, and why there's so many humans in the Robins' camp."

She grew quiet and nodded, then said, "It all started when the king of Busparia hired me to kill Eirwyn."

Wulfric's brows rose. "The princess? His own sister?"

Even the Growlers knew of the major players at the courts of both neighboring countries. But they hadn't heard this side of the story.

Scarlet nodded and continued. How they'd fled through the woods with Growlers on their heels. How they'd sought shelter at the cottage, and Eirwyn and Knox had gone to find a hidden magic manor in the forest.

How Scarlet had gone back to the king with a stag's heart and told him the deed was done.

"But he knew," Scarlet said softly, her steps slowing to a stop as she stared through the trees with unseeing eyes.

He squeezed her hand, and she looked up at him. The growing shadows made the angles on her face grow sharper. A sense of dread filled him at the darkness in her eyes.

"What happened?" His voice was soft in the stillness as snow fell through the thick trees.

She looked up at the sky and blinked rapidly. His strong warrior woman would hate the tears pooling in her eyes.

"He threw me in the dungeon for a few days. Normal torture, darkness, the stink of decay, and death everywhere."

She said it so flippantly, but Wulfric's heart ached for

her. He wanted to wrap her into his arms, but she stepped away, tugging his hand to keep walking.

He waited a few steps to reply but didn't push her. "Well, it's a good thing the fucker is dead already. Otherwise, I'd have to kill him for hurting you."

Her lips twitched, but didn't quite form a smile. He bumped his shoulder with hers. "How did you get away?"

"Knox rescued me," she said softly. "He and the Robins. They rescued all of us. The king had arrested dozens of people to flush the Robins out of hiding."

"Let me guess. The dragon saved everyone?" Wulfric asked softly. He wasn't sure he could ever measure up to her brother. The way she spoke about him with a little irony and awe? He wanted her to talk about him like that too.

She nodded. "Yeah. Knox distracted the king while we escaped. Then the Robins and I went back to the palace and started the rebellion."

Wulfric nodded, impressed with the strength she'd revealed in just that explanation. She'd gone from a broken prisoner to fighting. His warrior goddess was unlike anyone he'd ever known.

The Growlers had heard of the rebellion, how the people had stormed the castle and set it on fire. He wondered how much of that had been her responsibility.

"The king was killed by a Robin, but the queen blamed us all. It was... life-changing for everyone, I guess. So many people were cursed, and they fled to the forest for safety."

She laughed suddenly. "I never thought the Feral Forest would be a haven for anyone but the druids, Knox, and I. But crazier things have happened, I guess."

"Like being mated to a Growler?" he asked.

Her back stiffened, and she nodded, but didn't say anything for several steps. Wulfric was afraid she was going to close herself off again, get angry and distant. He desperately did not want her to withdraw from him.

But she didn't let go of his hand, and that gave him hope. They walked side by side, and he kept the river to his right.

# Chapter Sixteen

As they moved through the forest, Scarlet slashed at the thick vines that reached out to grab them while Wulfric used his meaty fists. Assassin vines disintegrated in his hands as he ripped them apart. Sweat glistened on his brow as he worked, his muscles rippling with each powerful stroke. Scarlet couldn't help but steal glances at him as she hacked away at the vines with her dagger.

Scarlet moved like a crimson blur, her twin daggers flashing in the dappled sunlight filtering through the canopy. Her breath came in short gasps as she ducked and weaved, always one step ahead of the writhing vines. The vines fell away and they continued their trek through the forest. Sweat cooled as the temperatures dropped.

There wasn't an awkward silence, but an unexpected easy camaraderie. The more they talked, the more relaxed she became. It was all light-hearted, such as why she hated bees and why how his toes hurt in the boots. The weak winter sun shone down on them, chasing away the cold as they laughed and shared stories. It was as if they had known each other for years, despite having just met. It was like catching up with an old friend rather than getting to know a stranger. She knew that this was the start of something special, and it terrified the shit out of her.

Before she could catch her breath at the realization, a horse-sized snake slithered toward them, but they stood back to back and fought it off. They made a great team, their movements in sync as they battled against the ever-increasing number of creatures emerging from the shadows. The snake's defeat seemed to trigger a frenzy, as if the forest itself had awakened with a hunger for their flesh.

Scarlet's heart pounded in her chest, adrenaline coursing through her veins as she gripped her daggers tighter. Wulfric's solid presence at her back gave much need reassurance that she wasn't alone, his warmth a stark contrast to the chill of the air.

"We can't keep this up forever," she panted, slashing at two giant eagles as they joined the fray, the snake twitching in pieces around them.

Wulfric grunted in agreement, his claws sending blood over the white snow as he slashed a monstrous bird with razor-sharp talons. "Any bright ideas, bunny?"

Despite the dire situation, Scarlet felt a flutter in her stomach at the way he said bunny. It was more like a term of endearment than a derogatory nickname like the villagers had made up behind her back. The bird squawked and attacked them while the other grabbed two pieces of the snake and flew away.

Another swipe of her daggers, and then it too flew away, joining its mate. With each enemy defeated, they formed an unspoken bond and learned each other's strengths and weaknesses. It reminded her of when she was a kid with Knox. They'd often explored the forest, growing bolder with each year, especially after they'd realized the forest protected Knox.

Panting, back-to-back with Wulfric, she replied, "How far away are we from your tribe? When should we stop for the night?"

He stopped to sniff the crisp air and nodded. "Let's keep going a little further so we don't waste daylight. Maybe we'll get a break before the next thing in the forest tries to kill us."

"Doubtful," she said, following him South.

When the lengthening shadows of the trees grew longer and the sun was gone, they made camp near the bank of the river.

Wulfric glanced around at the small clearing as Scarlet blew into her hands. "I'll make a fire so we can get warm, then I'll hunt for dinner," he said.

She shook her head. "I'll take care of dinner. You make the fire."

He took a step toward her, frowning, but she held a hand out and shook her head. "Don't even argue, wolfie. You hunted breakfast this morning. I'll take care of dinner. Just have a fire going when I get back."

He frowned, the shadows making him look regal and intimidating. "Don't go too far. This isn't in the normal Growler perimeter check, but there could still be some loners around. Yell if you need me."

She rolled her eyes. "I practically grew up in this forest. I'll be fine."

He reached for her elbow and drew her closer, nuzzling her neck. She gasped as her hood fell back from her face, the inside red lining showing bright.

"Yeah," he growled near her ear. "But not on this side of the road. You're in my territory now, bunny, so pay attention and be on alert."

Her heart fluttered like an untried maiden. She pressed on his chest and forced a wooden laugh. "Like there's any other way."

With a tug up on her hood, she slipped away from him, taking an uneasy breath to clear her confused emotions. Being so near him was like walking in the fancy heels the ladies at court wore.

She felt wobbly on her own legs. One minute, she was her normal, strong self, striding purposefully through the woods.

The next, she was letting him help her over a fucking log like a dainty princess.

Ugh, what was wrong with her? Not that Eirwyn was any less of a badass for being a princess, but still. That wasn't her.

She didn't get far before her stomach roiled and her vision swam. The stupid glockenberry was literally keeping her tied to him.

She stopped, taking a deep breath to calm her emotions. Just a few more days, and she'd be free to leap over her own damn logs and go wherever she wanted when she wanted.

An hour later, she walked into the clearing with three eggs and two squirrels.

He looked up from the fire, a stick in his hand as he poked at the logs. She paused just to admire the way the firelight flickered over the rugged beauty of his face. The high cheekbones, the pale pink lips, and black eyebrows framed those piercing golden eyes that saw too much.

Then he smiled, his wolf's tail wagging. His incisors were too large, reminding her of the predator he was.

He had probably been a gorgeously rough human once. If it weren't for the long black and silver hair and the pointed wolf's ears, he did look mostly human.

"Ah, dinner is here."

The way he said it sent a shiver up her spine. She didn't know if he meant her or the food in her hands, but she refused to ask.

She just nodded and set the eggs beside their bags. Then she turned toward the river. "I'll just go skin these."

She slipped through the trees to the bank. She found a path down to the water, just five steps down, and crouched with one of her daggers. A noise above drew her attention, and she spun on her heel. Wulfric jumped and landed a few feet away with a grunt.

He grinned, his mouth too wide and a wild look in his eyes. "Hand me a dagger and that other squirrel."

She hesitated. He was still a Growler.

Before she could follow that train of thought, she was handing over one of her precious daggers. He beamed at her, making her preen under his proud gaze, and took the other squirrel from where it lay on the ground beside her.

Preening at making him happy? Ugh, what was wrong with her? She frowned and ignored him as he crouched down and got to work. As best she could ignore him anyway, with the way her body was hyper aware of him.

Then there was the emotional aspect. Her emotions were piling one on top of each other, adding to her confusion. Desire, sexual tension, and anticipation warred with anxiety, fear, and anger about the future. None of them were more powerful than the others.

They reminded her of how his aura shifted and twisted with the two colors. She glanced at him after every swipe of her blade.

He made quick, efficient, clean cuts. When she was done washing her hands in the water, he began unlacing his boots.

"What are you doing?" Gods, was that *her* voice? So low and seductive.

He nodded to the river. "This part is shallow. I think I can catch a few fish to go with the squirrels."

She sighed in relief. He hadn't picked up on her tone of voice. He set the boots aside and wiggled his toes in the small pebbles.

Her lips twitched in an unbidden smile. "You just want to get out of the clothes, don't you?"

He laughed and pulled the shirt over his head. Muscles rippled, taking her breath away. "Maybe I do. Can you take them up to camp for me?"

She nodded, her gaze roaming over his body. "Mm-hmm."

He gave her a sly look as he shoved his pants to the ground and tossed them on top of the boots and shirt. Damn, his dick was just right there. No embarrassment, no shame. She blinked, unable to look away as he strode into the water, sank to his haunches, and shifted into wolf form.

She shivered as she watched the magic. Just washing her hands had chilled her to the bone, but his wolf magic must keep him warmer. She craved his heat, but she didn't want to give in.

She frowned, cleaned her daggers, and gathered the now gutted squirrels.

With one hand, she grabbed his boots and clothes before slowly climbing back up to the top of the bank. With one last look at him in the river, she turned to the warmth of their camp.

It had been fun at the cottage. They'd had some great conversations on their hike so far. Then there was the team work to get their camp set up.

It wouldn't last though, and she wouldn't—couldn't—let

herself fall for him. If she let herself hope for something better, it would only be ripped to shreds. It wasn't worth the pain, she knew from experience.

She was slowly turning the squirrels over the fire when he came back into camp, dripping wet and still in wolf form. In his jaws were three good sized fish, which he promptly dropped next to her.

His tongue lolled as he panted, sitting on his haunches with so much pride in his eyes.

She chuckled and reached out a hand to scratch him behind the ears. "Good boy," she crooned with a grin.

He froze, his pupils dilating as she scratched, that wild, predatory gaze sharpening as his tail wagged furiously. The intensity of his gaze sent a shiver up her spine, and she pulled away.

He turned his head and licked the inside of her wrist. She shivered at the hot, wet slide. That rough texture had felt so good on her clit.

She took a shuddering breath as he pulled away and gave a whole body shiver.

Freezing water went everywhere, and she shrieked a laugh as it hit her face. When she wiped her face with a smile, ready to chide him, the words stuck in her throat. He'd shifted back into his more human form, that big grin on his face so wide it had to hurt.

"Sorry to get you wet, bunny."

She snorted. "No, you're not. You wanted to get me wet."

He wagged his thick eyebrows and ran a hand through his hair. "That I did. You should always be wet for me, bunny."

She swallowed hard, her stomach twisting at the race of heat through her body. It was too intense, whatever this was between them. She had to focus on the mission at hand.

She blinked away from him and pointed. "Take the squirrels while I gut and string the fish up to cook."

He sat in the dirt and took the two sticks skewered with meat, holding them over the fire. Was he treating her as an equal warrior because he believed she was? Was that why he'd listened to her suggestions and opinions today, or did he see her solely as a sexual conquest like most of the human men she'd been with? He definitely saw her as a piece of ass, but he kept saying it was so much more than just sex. And she was starting to believe that too. The connection they'd had today had surprised her.

As she sliced the fish, her stomach twisted at being both respected and objectified. As he sat there semi-naked, she struggled with her own conflicting feelings towards nudity—a concept so different from her upbringing. She forced herself to look away from his semi-hard dick.

They came from two different worlds. It would never work... not that she wanted it to. Despite her attraction to him, she wondered if their differences would ultimately cause more harm than good in their relationship.

Gods, what was she thinking? They didn't have a *relationship*, despite what he said about being mates. It had to be a ploy of some sort, and she was determined to figure out why even if it meant interviewing every Growler in his tribe.

She deftly wove the coil of twine through the mouth and out the gills, laying the twine down the slit of the body. She handed him one end, then stepped around the fire to stretch the fish across it.

Then they sat staring at each other, the silence settling between them full of tension.

Could she be his mate? For just a moment, she let

herself imagine it. If it was just the two of them like this, it would be rather fun. Hunting, camping, working together to survive.

"What are you thinking?" His voice was soft, but she refused to look up into his golden eyes.

She kept her gaze trained on his shoulders. So wide, like he could carry the weight of the world without even trying. It'd been a long time since anyone had shared her burdens.

She sighed and checked the fish. "I'm thinking about my dad, actually. He would've loved this."

"Eating fish and squirrel?" His brows raised as he glanced down at the pitiful meal. It didn't look tasty, but the smell of smoke and roasting meat made her mouth water.

She chuckled and nodded. "Yeah, he was a Ranger, the best in the land. When I was about ten, I started going with him. We'd camp like this, working together, talking about nothing and everything."

Her voice trailed off, and she looked up, trying to count the stars in the sky and keep her emotions locked up tight.

"Tell me about him. What was your earliest memory?" His wistful look made a crack in her armor, a crack that caused her mouth to open and stories to spill out.

---

While the meat roasted over the fire, Wulfric watched the light dance across Scarlet's face. She was gorgeous, and he grew very aware that he was naked. He pulled his shirt over his lap as he checked the skewers.

She stared into the flickering flames and told stories of her childhood. Many of them made him laugh, but there was an air of sadness to them too. Like she wasn't used to sharing the memories and ached to talk about them.

He definitely understood how she felt. He wanted to tell her stories of his own, but the memories wouldn't come. No matter how hard he tried, he didn't seem to have the keys to remembering.

So he sat back and listened, asked her questions when needed. The memories would come or they wouldn't, and all he could do was wait. He handed her the bigger skewer of meat.

"And that's how Knox came to have that scar on his eyebrow." She bit into the squirrel and wiggled her nose as she chewed. His bunny might have grown up in the woods with a Ranger and a druid, but she didn't like the tough food.

He must remember that. If it came down to it, he would ply her belly full of more than just his cock. The delicious food from the tribe could be a powerful weapon in his favor. Anything to keep her with him.

Proximity would probably help. He shifted to sit next to her, settling the fish on his thighs between them. The shirt remained draped over his hips, as it seemed to make her more relaxed than when he was naked.

He liked her relaxed, liked hearing her stories and learning of her family. The dragon could be a powerful ally... that is, if he didn't outright attack when they met.

Wulfric pushed the thoughts aside. No sense worrying about it now.

He tore into his own food, the smell wafting over him and making his mouth water. Meat was meat, as far as his wolf was concerned. They passed the canteen of water between them as they ate, the silence stretching easily.

Finally he asked, "Why did the dragon come to get the druid yesterday?"

Scarlet swallowed a bite and said, "Knox's wife is due to

deliver her first egg any day now. They needed Grandma's help, which is why I was sent to fetch her. Apparently, I wasn't fast enough, so Knox came to get her."

Deliver an egg? A baby?

He blinked at the flash in his mind. A long-lost brown-haired little baby, squalling and wiggling shortly after being born. Pressure increased on his chest with the flood of emotions. Pride, awe... love.

Pain. So much pain and loss. He reached for Scarlet's hand, linking their fingers and swallowing hard to force the suddenly dry meat down his throat.

She handed him the canteen, and he drank. When he could finally talk, he handed it back to her.

"When your brother landed yesterday, I thought it was an earthquake. Then when I saw the dragon, my first instinct was to protect you and kill him. I didn't realize he was your brother."

He was glad he had hesitated. He didn't want to take a father away from his kid, much less hurt Scarlet. She clearly saw Knox as her brother, biological or not.

It reminded him of his Growler family. They weren't related by blood, but he would protect his pack with every-thing in him.

It was how he felt about Scarlet too.

The play of emotions at his words fascinated him, and he paused mid-bite to stare at her. The softening at the corners of her eyes encouraged him, but then she scoffed and scowled, hand hovering over the dagger on the ground beside her. "Don't even try attacking Knox. I'll kill you right now and won't bat an eye, if that's your plan."

He tossed the scavenged bones of the squirrel into the fire. "Don't be absurd. He's your brother. I'm not going to attack him."

She pointed her finger under his nose and glared. "And you're a Growler. You can't change your nature."

He grabbed her finger and jerked her sideways, making her stumble onto his lap. He wrapped his other arm behind her, holding her like a bride across his lap, legs dangling to the side. When she gasped and looked up with those big green eyes, surprise warred with self-righteousness.

She was irresistible. He swept his mouth down to hers.

Wulfric kept his lips tender, coaxing her to open with patience that was wearing thin. He wanted to roar into the night and claim her in the primal way he'd dreamed of for years, but she needed to know he wasn't only a Growler. He could be tender, gentle, and loving. With her, he would be for she was precious.

She trembled in his arms, reminding him that patience was worth it. It gave him hope to hold on and wait her out.

And oh, was it worth the wait.

Slowly her mouth opened beneath his. His tongue swept inside in triumph, the intensity building until his chest tightened.

# Chapter Seventeen

Scarlet's heart raced as Wulfric's free hand explored her body slowly. It wasn't a frenzied race to the finish like before, nor was it a light-hearted flirting.

This was a hot, dreamlike kiss of promise. It spoke of a future together, a life spent on the same side, back-to-back fighting against the world as one unit.

With his mouth and hand, he told her how precious she was to him. And with this single, never-ending kiss, he hesitantly sought comfort and acceptance.

The same acceptance she craved.

Her heart ached to open to him, but a sliver of fear held her back.

This impossible kiss defied all reason and logic. The Growler and the Hunter, two that were never meant to be but had somehow been fated by the gods. It shouldn't work.

But who was she to deny the fates? Maybe they knew what they were doing. They had taken her parents, but maybe this was their way of making up for that. By giving her a mate, a lover, a soulmate.

She wrapped her arm around his neck and pressed her breast into his palm. She moaned into his mouth as his thumb flicked back and forth across her fabric covered nipple.

The promises of connection and love lingered even when he pulled away and broke the kiss. He carefully avoided her horns as he touched her forehead with his own and sighed. Her emotions swung back and forth from wanting him to wanting to run away from him.

She felt him smile against her cheek. With eyes closed, she savored the sounds of the forest, the breathing of her mate, the scent of their desire. She'd never been one to just sit and enjoy the touch of another. She wasn't a cuddler.

But in his arms, maybe she could learn to be because this felt pretty damn good. Like she was exactly where she was supposed to be.

She bristled, as their previous conversation invaded her desire-fogged mind. "If you kissed me to shut me up, think again. You're not getting out of the conversation that easily, wolfie."

He tightened his arms around her in a sideways hug that made her feel small and dainty. She should've felt mad about it, but she didn't feel fragile. She felt protected and loved. Cherished even.

He chuckled, his breath tickling her neck. "I didn't kiss you to shut you up. I'd never do that, bunny, just like I'd never harm your brother. What hurts you will hurt me. It's part of being mates."

If an ancient dragon and a magical princess could be together, surely there was hope for the wolf who had invaded her dreams and the weird freak of a woman that she'd become.

She pulled back and scowled, cupping his cheek. "We're not mates. How many times do I have to tell you?"

He held his hand over hers on his face as he kissed her palm. "We are mates, whether you believe it or not. You're part of my pack now, and so is your brother, his wife, and even your grandmother. I'll keep you all safe, don't worry, bunny."

She stared up at him, afraid to hope, afraid to believe. The familiar flick of anger up her spine brought comfort, and it mingled with the grief and heartache that never left her alone.

They may be mates, but that wouldn't stop the heartache. She was the only one who could protect herself, the only one she could rely on.

She eased off his lap and sank into the dirt, grabbing a dagger and picking at the leftover meat. "My dad said something similar before he went to war and ended up dead. You can't control everything, Wulfric."

She glanced over at him, but he jerked and stared into the fire with a distant gaze. Her chest grew tight at the look on his face, so reminiscent of her own pain.

---

Her words triggered another memory. His wife had scolded him like this too.

"You can't control everything, Wulfric."

Frustration climbed his spine as he raked a hand over his face. He closed his eyes, praying the memory of his wife's face would come.

Surprisingly, it did. He'd given a free round of drinks to the soldiers who had just returned from war, and his wife had been mad because he was getting drunk with them.

"What is it, Wulfric?" Scarlet asked softly, her hand settling on his forearm and grounding him in reality.

He felt the tension melt at her touch. "I remembered," he finally choked out.

She frowned and poked at the fire. "Remembered what?"

"My wife used to scold me like you just did," he growled.

Scarlet's jaw dropped. "You're married?" she gasped, her hand falling away from him.

He turned to the fire and shrugged, leaning back on their pack and tucking his hands behind his head.

"I don't know if it was the tea Olive gave us, the head injuries and being so close to death once more, or something from the mate bond. But for the past few days, I've been remembering my past life for the first time in ten years of being a Growler."

"What do you remember?"

He told her of the few snippets he'd had so far. It wasn't much, but it was more than he'd ever had before.

"And you've never had memories pop up like this before?" She handed him the canteen, but he just shook his head as he took it and sipped.

"No, never. The more I remember, the more hopeful I feel about the future. It's like puzzle pieces are finally snapping into place. I don't know if I can describe it very well."

She handed him a cooked fish, an egg cooked in the stomach cavity. He sat up, and they ate in silence for a few more minutes. With his Growler metabolism, he could've easily eaten four times that much.

But it was a simple, delicious meal made all the better by being shared with his mate. By having a piece of his past back.

She finally leaned back against a log and nursed her canteen. "And that's all you remember?"

He nodded and sighed, tossing the bones into the fire as he settled back next to her. "I know I was married, and we had a daughter. I hope I worked in the tavern; otherwise, I was there a lot. I don't want to think I was the type of person who would leave a wife and babe at home while going off to the tavern, but…"

His voice trailed off as he worried.

"But you don't know," she said softly.

He frowned, staring into the fire and nodding. "Exactly. I just don't know who I was. What if I was the kind of guy who screamed at his wife? Or ignored her? Or worse, hit her?"

Her hand settled gently on his knee, and some of the tightness in his chest eased. He linked their fingers and breathed deeply of the crisp, pine-filled air.

"I don't think you'd do that," she said begrudgingly. "Don't take this the wrong way. I mean, you're still a Growler, and we're not mates. But the man I've gotten to know the past few days wouldn't do any of those things."

He shrugged, uncomfortable at her praise even as the hair on the back of his neck stood up. "Maybe," he murmured.

He could hear the half-hearted agreement in his own voice. "But there's no way to know for sure. Not until all my memories come back. Maybe then I'll be a better alpha, and they won't try to kick me out again."

She tugged on his hand. He looked up to see her frowning fiercely.

"Well, I don't need to know your past to know what kind of man or alpha you are. I don't need to meet any of the other Growlers to know that you'd be patient and fair.

You observe and take action based on what you think is right."

He scoffed, "You don't know that."

Her eyes narrowed, "I know you listen and do what I tell you to. Earlier, we compromised on chores, hunting, and gutting. You aren't afraid to follow when someone else suggests something. You don't pretend that all ideas except yours are dumb. Do you know how rare that is in a leader?"

Wulfric frowned and shook his head slowly. "I remember some of my military commanders acted like that."

She nodded and crossed her arms. "Exactly. That's probably what led to your injury and being left on the side of the road for the Growlers to find."

He stared into the fire. Was he that type of leader? Was that why he hadn't seen the attack coming? Her soft hand on his arm made him look into her deep green eyes.

"You're a good leader, not like those commanders. Not like the former king of Busparia or even the leaders of the Hunters. Memories or not, you're a good leader, Wulfric. Don't even think for a second otherwise."

She tossed her head, and he grinned. Her fight was a balm to his soul. He leaned over and kissed her swiftly on the cheek.

Her outraged expression softened in surprise.

"Thank you," he said softly.

Scarlet's lips twitched in almost a smile, then she cleared her throat and took a drink, breaking their linked fingers.

"Well, I'm sure your wife loves you a lot. I bet they're still waiting for you to come home from the war."

A sharp stab of pain made him rub his chest with the heel of his hand. "No, I'm pretty sure they died. I remember the funeral pyres. A fever swept through the village, I think. So many funeral pyres."

When her fingers linked back with his and squeezed, some of the pain eased in his chest. He wasn't alone, at least not tonight. He had someone to share the recent memories with, someone whom he trusted.

Ironic, considering how quick she was to wave her daggers at him.

He cleared his throat and tried to take control of his emotions again.

"After that, I was drafted and went to war for Busparia. Left my—hm, maybe a shop? I might have been a shop keep, and my wife might have owned the tavern. I don't know exactly."

Her thumb traced his skin back and forth, easing some of the pain of the past. "And that's how you became a Growler?"

He nodded. "I don't know how long I fought before I was gravely wounded and shipped home on the Southern Road. Only, I didn't quite survive."

"The Growlers captured you? I've heard the rumors. I know that's how they grow their numbers."

He shook his head. "No, I wasn't captured exactly. They found me on a litter on the side of the road, waiting to die. The caravan had ditched a few of us. I had nothing more to live for. My family was dead. When they offered a chance at a new life, I took it. I never questioned them or regretted it until now."

They talked about their lives long into the night. He told of the memories that had come back and of life as a Growler. She told more stories of her Ranger father, then how she became a Hunter after his death in the war.

"Do you think my father became a Growler?" Her voice was soft as she lay on her side facing the fire. She yawned, and her head bumped his. Somehow they were both facing the fire, their heads close together so they could hear each other, their bodies curving around the fire.

His chest grew tighter. "I don't know, bunny. No one in our pack looks like you with that red hair, but there are other packs."

She snorted, "No one looks like me. I'm twice cursed, remember?"

He growled an acknowledgement but fell silent.

Part of him wished she would walk into the Growlers' camp and find her father. But as strongly as she felt about Growlers, he wasn't sure that she'd like her father to be one.

He didn't want to ask her if she hoped or dreaded it.

Their stories grew further apart, and the silences lengthened. He looked over to see her head in her palm, her eyes closed. He got up and added more logs to the fire.

The temperature would drop through the night, so he put on the itchy clothes and boots.

Then he grabbed her cloak and laid down behind her. He spooned her, draping the thick, warm fabric over them both. He hoped more memories would come in his dreams, but he slept like a rock.

As dawn approached, he nuzzled into Scarlet's back, her hair tickling his nose. She was so warm, and for the first time since being turned, he didn't want to get out of bed. The cold on the back of his neck finally drove him to rise in the pre-dawn darkness and stoke the fire. Then he left to wash his face in the river, refill the canteen, and relieve himself.

When he came back, Scarlet was sitting up, stabbing the fire like she wanted to kill it.

"Good morning, bunny," he said softly, handing her the container. He wanted to laugh that she was so clearly not a morning person, but the look on her face kept him silent.

She glared at him, swiped the canteen, and rubbed at her eyes with her free hand. After a few minutes, she stomped around and grumbled, refusing his help for even the simplest task. She stomped down to the river, and he let her go. There had to be a way for her to wake up happy. Would it help if he served her breakfast in bed? Did she need coffee before she was human? She obviously wasn't a morning person, but maybe some food would help her relax.

When she stomped back into the clearing, he pulled out the dried fruit from the pack and offered it to her. She sat next to him with a grunt and began to eat.

The easy banter they'd had yesterday had given him hope. He honestly hadn't expected to feel this kind of connection until she claimed him back. He felt like they were getting to know each other the way mates should. There was still so much he needed to know about her, her heart, her fears, her dreams.

Time was running out, though, and this morning, it was like she'd put the wall back between them. She was pushing him away again, and it frustrated and worried him more than he cared to admit.

He clung to the hope that she'd finish the mate bond, that she'd accept and love him before it was too late. The gods didn't make mistakes. She just needed time. Maybe by the full moon, she'd realize they were meant to be together. He just had to hold out a few more days and get to know her.

He gave her space as they broke camp and hiked through the forest. He didn't push her, instead occasionally carrying the conversation about life with the Growlers. It was easier to talk of the past ten years than the fuzzy memories of his human life.

As they marched south, the trees became larger and wider. This was the oldest part of the forest and the most sacred. The sounds of nature became more muted, the animals here used to the roaming Growlers.

By the time the sun started to go down again, hunger and anxiety were gnawing at his gut. The closer they'd gotten, the higher his anxiety had grown. How could he protect her and still gain back his alpha status? Their conversation grew more sparse as they walked.

The trees cast dark shadows as the almost full moon rose.

"We'll be within pack perimeters soon," he said quietly.

"We should make a plan for tonight," she said, the first time she'd spoken in over an hour. She'd gotten more tense the further they'd gone too, which was how he'd known it was more than just waking up on the wrong side of the fire.

Perhaps they both sensed that what lay ahead could kill them both and put a stop to all their newly budding hopes and dreams.

He stopped and opened the bag. He handed her the last of the dried fruit. She ripped it in half and handed him a piece. They ate in silence as he listened to the sounds around them.

No one was nearby, which was good. She handed him the canteen, and asked, "How do you plan to take your place as alpha?"

He drank before he answered. "Fight Brody, at a minimum. In a normal alpha challenge, the Elders create a magical circle that prevents others from interfering. Everyone watches the fight to the death. Whoever lives wins."

She frowned and pulled a dagger from her hidden

sheath. She twirled it as she thought. He could almost see the gears turning in her mind.

She finally spoke up, her voice strained with worry. "I don't like that you could die."

He brushed a piece of hair from her eye, tucking it behind her ear. "Brody's a pup. He knew he wouldn't win an official alpha challenge, which is why he ambushed me with so many of his friends."

"But still," she paused, her eyes dropping to the dirt where she drew with the tip of her dagger. "If it'll give you an advantage, I guess—I mean, we can finish the mate bond."

His heart beat faster, and he froze in surprise. The lump in his throat wouldn't swallow away, so he took another drink. He didn't want her to mate him for just this purpose though.

He took her empty hand and kissed her knuckles, drawing her beautiful green gaze to his. "Thank you, Scarlet, but I want you to mate with me when you're ready, of your own free will. I'll be fine if I have to fight him before we complete the mate bond. It's already half-done already."

She frowned, and he stroked the back of her hand with his thumb. "What do you mean, it's half-done?"

It was his turn to look away. He took another drink and dropped her hand to his thigh before he answered. "I bit you when I climaxed, both times actually. The wolf took over, and I couldn't stop it, so my half of the mate bond is done."

She tugged her hand from his, and it left an emptiness in his chest. She frowned and avoided his gaze, going back to drawing in the dirt as her face settled into a stoic mask that hid all emotions and vulnerabilities. He could practically feel the emotional walls going back up between them.

He sighed, "Can I have your dagger? I'll draw a map of the camp and tell you what I'm planning."

She nodded and handed it over with barely a pause, which made him breathe easier. The only way they'd get through what lay ahead is if they trusted each other. He'd known he shouldn't have bit her, but it'd been nearly impossible to resist.

He crouched in the frozen dirt and drew with the tip of the dagger, his voice soft and low as he talked through a plan.

# Chapter Eighteen

*Five months ago...*

"Blast it straight to the hells," Bella said, throwing one of the two potions at the stone wall. It smashed, splattering and dripping down the dining room wall.

She startled at the wide-eyed wild haired man as the door to the kitchen swung behind him.

As she turned to face him, her hands instinctively went to her hips, immediate remorse flooding her. How could she have been so foolish and reckless? He was one of the few who had stayed behind when everyone else fled the castle, and she couldn't shake off the guilt of trapping him there. Yet, in that moment, she also felt a surge of anger towards him for witnessing her moment of weakness and putting himself in harm's way. She didn't know how to make it right by changing his curse and giving him freedom. She sighed and rubbed her forehead.

"I'm so sorry. I didn't mean to make such a mess for you to clean up," she said, waving a hand to activate a silent spell. The spell opened the drawer to the buffet table and out flew several napkins. She used the animated napkins to wipe up the wall as Ignot rubbed his heavily wrinkled forehead.

"I take it the newest potion isn't ready?" His wry question made her snort and shake her head. He'd never treated her like the queen, since he'd often snuck to the tavern to drink when the royal family wasn't in residence. She'd known him since she was a child.

"No, Ignot, it's not ready yet. It's too dangerous," she admitted. There was one bottle left, but the one she'd thrown had bubbled on its own, growing bigger and bigger. Part of throwing it had been to dispel the magic as quickly as possible, as it'd shown signs of impending explosion.

Still, it didn't make the regret of her decision fade. The weight of the world was on her shoulders, and nothing had gone right since she'd met the king. She was already so weary after only a few weeks stuck in this form.

"Are you sure, your highness? I'm not sure how much longer I can hold on."

He stiffly walked across the room, holding tightly to the broom as he slowly swept the broken glass.

Her hand fluttered in her skirt. "What do you mean?"

"I feel less and less human every day. Soon I'll just be an empty husk of a knight."

"No, don't say that. We'll figure this out."

When the castle curse had settled, he'd been merged with a metal knight in the hallway. His skin was metal, his white hair sticking out oddly from his head, and his movements stiff and awkward.

His eyes remained human, and it was unnerving. He'd been the under-butler before, his old age preventing him from taking the prized position of head butler. Having armor for skin pained him greatly, though he was too proud to complain about it.

"Are you sure we can't just try this other bottle?" He didn't meet her eyes as he knelt to the floor.

"I'm sure. I tested it on the stuffed eagle in the hall. It didn't work," Bella said bitterly as she put the dirty napkins on the edge of the table for Sharlo to find and clean later.

Ignot waved the broom handle to the potion still sitting on the table. "Perhaps you should test it on the cat or any of the dozen kittens, then."

Bella shook her head and gripped her skirts in both hands now, staring at the dining table. What had once held grand dinners with dignitaries and nobles now was strewn with ingredients and supplies for potions.

It had been too difficult for Ignot to go up and down the stairs. After he and Sharlo had cleaned up her room from all the rotting flesh and blood, she'd wanted to make things easier on them. So she'd moved her workshop down here so they could still assist with collecting ingredients.

The guilt gnawed at her as they sat trapped in this cursed place. It was her decision that led them here, that turned Ignot into a rigid metal knight and Sharlo into a dangerous hat stand. The pregnant cat's transformation into a footstool only added to the weight of her regret. How could she have known the consequences of her actions? It was all her fault.

One footstool kitten pushed through the swinging door as Ignot knelt to sweep the glass into the dustpan. The kitten snuggled against his clunky metal leg, and Ignot scratched its head.

"I can't risk them," Bella said. She was so afraid to test the reversal potion on anything living. She'd already tested it on the plants that had morphed and merged with inanimate objects.

The chives and lavender had merged with the stone bench in the kitchen gardens. She'd watered it with the last potion, only for it to die and turn to dust.

The hydrangeas in the flower garden had merged with a bucket that had been abandoned by a servant. She'd tested the next potion on it, only to fail yet again.

"I've tweaked the formula over two dozen times with the same result. If I had even one success with the plants, then maybe I'd test it on a kitten," Bella murmured, twisting her skirt and staring forlornly at the supplies on the table.

"But what is left to change?" She wondered aloud. She'd adjusted the amount of magic she'd used, one word at a time of the old spell she'd found in the spell book in the library.

Lost in her own thoughts, she didn't pay any attention to the clank of metal behind her until it was too late.

The kitten's cry rang through the room, and she spun in horror, the walls shaking as her breath caught in her chest. Ignot had poured the potion onto the floor and the kitten had licked it up. It took two steps, weaving as if drunk. It hacked and choked, and Bella's eyes watered.

"What have you done?" She choked out past the knot in her throat.

Ignot's cold blue eyes didn't meet hers, which she was grateful for. He crossed his arms and stared at the cat. "You wouldn't have done it. Someone had to try."

She held her breath as it shuddered and hacked. The fur ball finally fell out of its mouth and rolled on the tile, then it jerked violently as it separated into two halves.

The kitten fell to the ground, unmoving beside a small footstool. *Two separate beings.*

She sucked in a breath. "It worked," she whispered.

Ignot knelt and stroked the cat's side as he sighed. "Sort of. They separated but the cat's dead, poor thing."

Anger made her shake, and the chairs in the dining room followed suit. "Poor thing?" Her voice was deceptively soft but rose quickly.

"Poor thing! You had no right to test that potion on it! I told you it's not ready."

"I know that, your highness, but—"

"But what? There should be no but. I'm the queen, or have you forgotten? If I say do not touch something, do not blasted touch it. Do you understand?"

The cold eyes finally met her own as she fisted her skirts, trying to hold on to her emotions. He nodded slowly, but his gaze was stubborn.

"I know you are, but I had to try, your highness. Every minute is torture. I can't take it anymore."

The old man's wiry white hair pointed in every direction, and his eyes were wild and chaotic. Desperate.

Bella held her hands out shakily, palms up. "You think I'm enjoying this state of being? I'm working day in and day out to find a solution, but it has to be safe. Fysica protect us—"

Her rage reached a crescendo, and she flew out the open dining room door. She had to get outside before she blew.

Her emotions were building, and her control was fractured at best. She reached the terrace and fled down the steps to the garden. It stretched all the way to the castle wall, but before she reached it, she screamed.

Loud, angry bellows that made a handful of bricks on the wall crash in front of her as she stumbled to a halt. She yelled again, her hands wide as she released the anger, heartache, and despair over her failures.

This was bullshit. She'd simply wanted someone to see her worth and teach her magic. She'd trained with the priests and had been allowed to read all their books if she kept the church in town clean. Then she'd trained as a healer with Lailant, the crazy old woman whom some whispered was a witch.

Bella hadn't cared. She'd just wanted to know more, needed to know more. If she'd known more at five, maybe she could've helped save her mom and everyone else from the fever. If she'd known more, maybe she could've followed her dad to war and saved him too.

Now she was cursed. And she'd been the one to curse who knew how many people and animals and plants. The entire town had been destroyed.

Despair washed over her as the tears fell. She rested her head on the wall, but she tumbled through it. Damn, she hadn't animated the wall; thus, she couldn't interact with it.

She laid on the dirt outside the castle walls and blinked as a dark cloud slowly crawled toward her from overhead. She winced and scrambled to her feet. She shuddered, took a deep breath, and ran through the wall again.

Cold washed through her, and she shivered, blinking as she appeared back in the garden. She did not feel up to battling the shadow creature today. She was too raw from losing the kitten.

But it had died as a kitten, not a monstrosity footstool kitten.

There had to be a way to separate a living and non-living thing that had been magically joined. Perhaps she'd been going about this all wrong. The spell book had been vague, after all. Perhaps it was a combination of spell and potion?

She walked slowly back to the castle, her mind not stopping for even a second to take in the beautiful overgrown garden or the grass growing between the cobblestone walkway.

---

*Four months ago...*

Bella bit her lip and carried the magical bowls up the stairs to her sitting room. She'd untangled another kitten, and it'd lived the past three days.

Hope blossomed in her stomach, but she couldn't let Sharlo or Ignot know yet. It would devastate them if it didn't work out, and the kitten had been weak ever since.

She went through the open door—the servants had long since left all doors open so she wouldn't have to walk through them—and set the bowl on the floor by the empty hearth.

The kitten's eyes didn't open at the smell of milk and fish. She pulled a spoon she'd affectionately nicknamed Gus out of her pocket and used it to prod the kitten, stroking awkwardly down its back.

Its eyes opened slowly. They looked feverish, but she couldn't feel it to see. Perhaps a healing potion in the milk would help? It was worth a shot.

She went to her bedroom and the vanity that had changed her life forever. She pursed her lips and animated the bottle the healing potion was in. It slipped into her pocket, and she turned back to the kitten.

She paused at the door and blinked. No, it couldn't be. She looked back at her vanity. The potion bottle she'd used on the cat sat empty where she'd left it. Its match... was gone. It wasn't where she'd left it.

Sharlo didn't come upstairs anymore to clean, the layer of dust evidence of that. In fact, the servant tried to stay as far away from Bella as possible. But Ignot...

Ignot.

Her chest ached and the windows rattled. There was no telling when he took it. She hadn't been in her bedroom in at least a day, maybe two.

A soft mewl drew her attention, and she went to the tiny ball of fluff in the next room. Her steps slowed as she neared.

It lay still, no breath rising from its chest. She was too late.

Ignot.

Maybe she could still save him. She raced out the door and down the hall, yelling his name. Had she seen him that day at all? She'd been holed up with the cat, documenting the kitten's changes by dictating to the magical pen.

A scream rent the air, and Bella turned toward the kitchen, dread filling her stomach like a lead weight.

---

*Two months ago...*

Bella stood silently, tears running down her cheeks as Sharlo buried the last of the kittens in a pot in the kitchen garden. It'd loved to chase the mice in this spot.

She rocked on her feet, hands twisting in her skirts. She'd been so close to finding just the right spell combination and ratios of ingredients for the potion.

This kitten had lived for three weeks, and it'd been strong the entire time. No fever that she'd seen. It'd been so happy with boundless energy. Ignot would've been so excited.

She'd followed the little thing around every day, had watched over it as it slept. And this morning, she'd looked up from her book, and it had just been gone. Dead between one chapter and the next. No complaining, no mewling, no convulsions like the others. Just gone.

She'd animated an ash bucket to pick him up and take him outside. Sharlo had found her using an animated shovel to dig a hole, but her magic wasn't enough to get the angle right. Her hands had been shaking too much, her tears too thick to see enough.

Sharlo had started silently weeping, and here they both stood as the last dirt settled on top of the hole. Sharlo leaned on the shovel, her shoulders shaking.

Bella wanted to reach out and offer comfort, a hand, a shoulder. She wanted so desperately to not be alone anymore. But even if her current form had allowed such a gesture, Sharlo never would've. Her family had all worked at the castle for generations. She'd been horrified by the low-born Bella becoming queen.

"I'm so sorry," Bella whispered to the kitten as she wiped her cheeks.

Sharlo's hands tightened on the shovel's handle, and her voice was harsh as she said, "Nothing for it now, your highness. No time to dilly dally. Let's gather all the ingredients you'll need for the next several batches of potions, shall we?"

Bella blinked at the servant as she walked to the smoke-house, leaned the shovel against it, and picked up a bucket to gather whatever herbs Bella pointed out. "I—I have enough for this week, Sharlo. I've been neglecting my duties in making any more, since I was monitoring the—cat."

Sharlo's shoulders hunched, and she bowed her head. Then she turned to Bella, her square jaw firm, her lips pursed, and a line between her forehead as she frowned.

"I took the potion and said the spell two days ago," Sharlo said harshly.

Bella's stomach knotted and the gardening tools around them began to shake. Her vision tilted as dizziness swam through her.

"No," she whispered, shaking her head.

Sharlo's face twisted into a bitter grimace. "Yes. The cat was fine for three weeks, so I took it. I've been fine, have felt fine, still feel fine. I've made the same amount of daily progress on the caved-in escape passage in the cellar as I have every day for the past four months."

Bella's mouth opened and closed, but no sound came out. Sharlo was the last living, moving thing in the castle. There were no more cats, no one else to talk to. She'd be utterly alone after she died.

She was a fool, a selfish fool, to think such a thing. Her head ached and her stomach twisted to imagine what Sharlo must be feeling right now. More tears fell down her cheeks. She'd cried so much in the past four months, more than she had in the previous four years combined.

Sharlo waved a gnarled and straightened into the ramrod posture only a servant can maintain. "None of that now, your highness. When I go, I go and not even the gods can change it. Let's get you set up with anything you might need before I kick the bucket. Perhaps you can even use more potions on me and see if these hooks will at least disappear."

Bella frowned and nodded, following Sharlo into the herb garden. Her mind latched onto that last detail. Sharlo took the same potion and said the same spell that Bella had used on the last cat, which had separated into a normal cat for three weeks.

But the cat had separated within just a few hours.

"You did it two days ago, you said? And the hooks are still there?" Bella asked, a million questions running through her mind. Sharlo should've separated from the coat rack by now. Maybe she wasn't dying and would be fine. Maybe Bella could save her with another spell or potion. There was still hope.

---

*One week ago...*

Bella coaxed the fork and spoon to pour one more ingredient into the bottle.

"That's it. Thank you so much. You're invaluable. Price-less. I appreciate you so much," she murmured.

A few kind words went a long way with semi-conscious inanimate objects. She only wished she'd praised Sharlo more while she'd been here. Losing her had been the hardest to take, possibly because she'd been so accepting of it. When she hadn't checked in before going to bed for the night, Bella had gone to find her.

She'd fallen in the cellar, chisel and hammer nearby.

Bella had animated a carpet and wrapped her in it, then magically flown it outside to the hole Sharlo had dug. Bella's stomach clenched at the memory, how she'd argued with Sharlo but the woman had demanded Bella stay practical.

Indeed, the lessons in practicality had helped her tame her wilder emotions. In those last weeks, the woman had opened up about her life too. It had given Bella even more perspective on the past year's events.

The fork and spoon clicked together in a series of

sounds as they talked to each other. These two were now permanently animated as she didn't have the heart to make them go back the way they'd been before. Then she'd be truly alone.

She'd had enough of death in the past few months. Her husband, Gastone, had been killed in her bedroom right in front of her. Then she'd wrapped his killer in her sheets and squeezed the life from him until he burst all over the room.

There'd been dozens of dead in the courtyard and throughout the bottom floor from the rebellion. Sharlo and Ignot had helped dispose of them, but then she'd lost Ignot, the cats, and finally Sharlo.

She shivered, throwing off the memories as the lights in the room flickered. She clapped as the fork and spoon finished pouring the precious liquid into it. It was the last of the cat's whiskers. After this, there would be no more potions available to test the separation spell. She'd gone back to testing the dead animal heads on the walls in the hallway, but had had no success.

She sighed and said the spell to heat the stone underneath the bottle to a low boil. The fork tapped his tongues together in a clacking that somehow translated into her brain.

There was no explanation for it. Magic hadn't worked normally since that fateful day when she'd lost her body to a mad magical mirror.

She rubbed her forehead and waited for it to boil. Once all the supplies were gone, she'd have to start pulling down the books that had been out of reach. She'd focus on reading every blasted book in the library. Perhaps there was an obscure spell book or something to assist in her search to reverse the curses. Ideally, she'd find something to help her get her body back.

# Chapter Nineteen

Wulfric's voice was deep and melodic as he outlined a plan to go into the Growler camp. Scarlet was so tired and cold, she wanted to just curl up and listen to him as she drifted off to sleep. Her fuzzy brain was probably why she let him take the lead.

They had some reconnaissance to do. He pointed with the tip of the dagger.

"These are the Elder's tents, and this is the only wooden permanent structure in camp. The longhouse is where we take most of our meals, so there's always a crowd there."

"And you want to walk right past it?" She shook her head. This is not how she'd accomplished missions for the Hunters.

He drew in the dirt on the edge of the camp's circular shape. "Ideally, no, but I need to see who's on watch first. If it's some of Brody's friends, then I'll need to go around them and talk to one of the Elders."

He marked seven spots around the camp drawing. "These are where the guards normally roam. They're evenly spaced and make clockwise circles. Then there's the outer perimeter watch in a wider circle here, going in the opposite direction. I'll have to sneak past both of them."

She bit her lip, her stomach flipping from nerves. That was a decent technique that she needed to share with Knox when she got back to Vidrland.

If she got back. She might not survive the night. Her skin crawled being this close to the Growlers' camp. All her instincts were screaming at her to run away. Well, the deer and rabbit sides of her anyway.

Part of her wanted to march straight into camp and demand they help break her curses. But that wasn't the only reason she was here. She had to help Wulfric first and trust he knew what he was doing.

She hated that feeling of helplessness, of needing to rely on him. She ground her teeth together and nodded.

"Alright, so you need to find a guard and talk to them. Find out what's been going on the past few days. Don't go through the guard circles into camp. That's too dangerous. Just do a reconnaissance mission tonight, alright?"

He beamed at her and nodded. "Yes, that's exactly it."

The way he looked at her made her swell with pride, but she tamped it down.

She nodded, and her other dagger flashed in the shadows. "Great, let's go then."

He frowned and shook his head. "No, I need to find the guard alone. They'll smell you from a mile off."

"But what about the glockenberry bond? If you go too far, we'll both be weak and sick." She did not want to feel that nausea anymore.

He shifted to his knees and cupped her face with one hand, the dagger hanging loosely from his other at his side.

"We should be able to skirt the edge of the bond and

keep you downwind so they don't smell you. Don't worry, bunny. We'll both be alright."

She opened her mouth to argue, but he leaned forward and kissed her softly. It didn't feel like goodbye, but she was more nervous than she'd been since her first mission as a Hunter. She'd woken up with this feeling of dread that had lingered in her mind all day. Something was going to happen. She could feel it in her soul. That same warning that had put her on alert the night Knox had broken her and the rest out of the dungeon. The same feeling that she got on missions, that had warned her of her parents' deaths...

He pulled back and smiled reassuringly. "Come on, let's circle around to get downwind. Then I'll head to the first set of guards and do some talking."

He stood and offered his hand. She took it, frowning in surprise. He was such a gentleman, and it still surprised her. He handed her dagger back, and she felt more at ease with it in her hand. "Right, talk. You sure you don't want me to come and watch your back?"

He grinned and hefted the bags. "Nah, it'll be better this way. We don't want to hurt them, after all."

He took a step then turned back to her with a frown. "You won't hurt them either, right?"

She sniffed and twirled a dagger. "Only if they give me a reason to hurt them," she said, her lips pressed into a thin line.

He sighed and shook his head, but the grin on his lips betrayed his true feelings. "Gods know I love how fierce you are and how you can handle yourself, but don't forget that they're my family, the only one I've had for ten long years. Come on," he said, taking her hand in his once more.

He was proud of her, Hunter skills and all. She blinked,

feeling a knot loosen in her stomach. It had been a while since someone had been proud of her like that. Not since her dad had taken her on Ranger missions. They walked away from the river and deeper into the forest, their feet silent.

Eventually, he took the bags off his back and slipped his shirt off, shoving it inside. The pants and boots followed, and she couldn't take her eyes off him.

She hadn't asked him about shifting, but then he knelt on the ground and lifted a small bush. He pulled out a canvas bag, and her eyebrows rose.

Silently, he pulled on loose brown pants. The way the sound carried in the stillness, they were probably canvas or leather. It was too dark to tell.

When he secured the pants with the drawstring and stood barefoot and shirtless, he grinned and leaned in.

His intoxicating scent enveloped her like a comforting hug before his lips met hers. The kiss felt giddy, and she knew he was looking forward to the hunt. Even if it was only hunting information, she had to trust him to come back to her.

He wouldn't leave her alone in the middle of the Feral Forest with her enemies all around. Not with how adamant he was about protecting his mate. He leaned back, his bright teeth flashing with a grin before he saluted.

Knees bent, Wulfric held his finger to his lips in the universal gesture to be quiet. His eyes glowed in the darkness.

"Wait here," he mouthed before slipping around a tree on silent feet, walking silently toward the southeast.

Scarlet left their bags at the base of the tree and pulled her daggers out. She trusted him to come back, but she wasn't going to be caught defenseless just in case something happened.

She barely heard Wulfric as she moved on the balls of her feet to watch his shadow move from tree to tree.

Then she lost him.

The hair on the back of her neck stood in awareness. It was eerily quiet, not even his steps echoing in the darkness. She blinked and stretched her senses, straining to find his peculiar double aura.

But it was gone. She pushed her other senses, desperate to smell him or sense his heartbeat.

For almost half an hour, there was nothing. Not even forest animals roamed nearby. They'd probably left this part of the forest to the larger predators long ago.

She had never wanted to be the little wife who was left waiting by the fire while her husband went off adventuring. That was what had killed her mom, and she wasn't going to fall prey to the same mistake. At the moment, she wished she was inside by the fire though. It was so cold, and the longer she waited, the colder and darker it became.

She blew into her hands, her gloves not even close to being thick enough. She took a deep breath to blow again, but picked up the scent of someone else. Her nose flared, and her daggers came up slowly. The scent grew stronger, and panic threatened to claw at her throat. She hesitated to even swallow or breathe, afraid the nearing enemy would pick up the movement or sound.

This was it. This was how she would die.

She frowned and shook her head. Fuck that, she wouldn't go down without a fight. She sensed the creature coming closer, and Scarlet leaned around the tree to see the target, reaching for her dagger.

A shadow launched itself, throwing her off balance and

making them both roll as they landed on the frozen ground. Claws bit into her shoulder, and her hood twisted to half cover her face.

She couldn't see her attacker, but there was no doubt it was a Growler. She swung her daggers, the familiar feel of flesh ripping beneath her hands. The coppery scent of blood hit her nose, and her nostrils widened as she panted, rolling them both until she straddled the creature.

It was definitely a Growler, but this one was smaller than Wulfric's shifted form, closer to Scarlet's own petite frame. She sliced shallowly and then back-handed the thing with the butt of her dagger.

A loud yip ripped through the air, piercing her ear drums. Scarlet winced and settled back on her haunches, one forearm pressed into the throat of the small thing.

"Stop fighting me, damn it. I'm not here to fight," Scarlet whispered, shoving a knee over the lower legs and another over the left arm. She slammed her elbow into its throat, and it made a garbled noise even as Scarlet reached over and pinned the free arm.

"Stop, you little fucker. I only want information," Scarlet hissed, expanding her senses to see if others were around. This one might be a decoy to distract her.

But no other scents, sounds, or auras flared. The wolf beneath her whined, and she eased up on the elbow to the throat. Scarlet frowned, seeing the same two-toned aura that Wulfric had but in red and gold instead of blue and silver.

"Who are you?" hissed the wolf, licking its lips.

Scarlet gave the only answer that might get her some answers. "Granddaughter of the druid."

The wolf's eyes went wide and another whine slipped

free. The creature seemed to shake with fear as it gasped, "Please, don't hurt me. I'll do whatever you want."

"Why are you so scared of the druid?" Scarlet asked, not for the first time wondering why this reaction. She'd sensed some of it with Wulfric at first, but he'd been so injured, she'd thought it was because he was afraid of dying.

"She... there are tales of when she came here years ago. She almost wiped out the tribe before a truce was called."

Scarlet blinked and frowned. What the hell? Why hadn't she known this? Had her dad known about it? What had her grandmother done?

She shook her head. There was no time for that. She applied slightly more pressure on the throat then let up, her dagger gleaming next to the Growler's cheek.

It swallowed hard as Scarlet continued. "So you know what I'm capable of and you'll cooperate?"

The wolf nodded, flailing as it choked. Scarlet let off her throat but kept the dagger close.

"What's the political climate in the tribe? Who's in charge?"

The Growler whimpered, "The—the druid knows?"

Scarlet's eyes narrowed. "Knows what?"

The Growler wiggled, but Scarlet didn't let it up. "The alpha is missing. Brody says he was killed on patrol and took over with his three friends."

Wulfric had mentioned that name. Dread settled through her spine like ice.

"Then yes, the druid knows. How does the tribe feel about alpha's absence and Brody's leadership?"

The Growler licked its lips, but didn't answer, golden eyes wide. Scarlet applied more pressure, and magic swirled under her.

She couldn't watch the morphing features but she held

onto the arms and legs with a firm grip. When she felt the wiggling and warmth of magic stop, she opened her eyes.

A youthful girl stared up at her with tears in her eyes. Black hair was spread on the ground with pine needles, and one of her wolf's ears was flopped over, slightly twitching. She was like a hairy human girl, but with a fur-covered nose and pointed animal ears.

The girl sobbed, "Brody says alpha Wulfric is dead. The Elders aren't happy. Please, don't hurt me." The words broke on another sob, and Scarlet frowned.

"I'm only going to hurt you if you move without my permission. Don't move unless I say to move, understand? If you do, it'll be the last action you take."

The girl's jaw dropped as she blanched but she nodded, tears pouring down her temples into black hair. Scarlet eased back, crouching in front of her with daggers ready. The girl's face began to crumple as her mouth opened to suck in more air, preparing to cry, but Scarlet had to stop her. The sound might attract others.

"Hush and sit up slowly. Cover yourself." Scarlet said softly, expanding her senses and feeling no one else nearby. The girl did so, covering her breasts and bringing her knees up protectively as she hid her face in her hands.

"Now, I'm not going to hurt you, but there's more that I need to know. You're going to answer all my questions. Yes?"

The girl nodded, wiping her tears and nose. Quickly, Scarlet grilled her with question after question. Wulfric had been right about the situation. Brody had taken over, but the girl didn't know much.

Young adults were apparently focused on their first shifts, the opposite sex, and the upcoming full moon run tomorrow night.

"What are you doing out here? This is outside of the camp's perimeters." Scarlet spoke with the weight of authority. She didn't doubt what Wulfric had said.

The girl nodded again. "Yes, my dad is on outside watch, but I was going to meet some friends. There's a popular spot to the east, a small set of ruins."

"Ruins? The ones by the cliffs and the Southern Road?" Scarlet asked, remembering when she'd gone there with her grandma as a child. It had been a year after her mom had been killed, and Grandma had simply walked through the forest like she'd owned the place.

Scarlet had been terrified, despite Grandma's reassurances.

Her jaw clenched as the girl nodded, ducking her head to stare at the ground.

"Like those, but smaller. In the forest. It's where we go to escape the adults and meet the other tribes' youths."

Scarlet tossed her dagger, catching it easily as she thought. The girl watched her warily, scooting back inch by inch slowly.

Scarlet didn't stop her as she spread her senses once more to check their surroundings. No one, not even Wulfric. He should've come back by now. He was only supposed to find information, but she had a sinking suspicion that he had continued on into the heart of camp.

Stupid Growler. He was the one who'd said they'd be stronger together.

"What's your name, girl?" Scarlet asked as she stood.

The girl froze, then whispered, "Sasha."

Scarlet offered her a hand, but she just stared at it. "Here's the deal, Sasha. You're going to take me to your father and convince him not to attack me. I have more questions."

Sasha scrambled to her feet without taking Scarlet's hand. "But I'm not supposed to be out here. My friends—"

"Will respect you for helping the druid's kin. You can tell your parents you heard me calling to you if you'd like."

"Can—can you do that?" Sasha asked, fear tinging her voice as she bounced from foot to foot.

Scarlet smiled and spun her dagger but didn't answer the question. Sasha whimpered once more, eyes watching the blade, and nodded before stepping away.

"Don't attract the attention of the other guards. Only your father," Scarlet warned.

The girl didn't turn her back fully to Scarlet but still led her through the trees. Scarlet left their bags where they were.

If she had to fight her way out, they'd only slow her down.

# Chapter Twenty

Scarlet saw the aura growing closer, but it wasn't Wulfric. She'd been following the Growler girl for gods knew how long, and had seen no sign of him. The girl had shifted back into wolf form. After Scarlet had seen her shivering and her lips turning blue, she'd insisted.

Of course, the girl knew that Scarlet would kill her with one throw of the dagger if she tried to dart away. When they'd skirted around two other Growlers, Scarlet had whispered, "Is that your father?"

Sasha had paused, staring at her in amazement.

"You—you know they're there? But we're too far away to smell them. How do you know?"

Scarlet arched a brow, spinning her dagger once more while the other stayed at the ready. "The more important question is, can they smell us?"

Sasha shook her head and kept going. Now they were definitely within smelling range of the Growler as they approached. Sasha seemed to grow more sullen, but when the large, black wolf growled and sniffed the air, she stopped.

They were twenty feet away from him when Scarlet pushed her hood back and stepped out from behind the tree. His gaze immediately went to her, his muzzle sinking toward the ground as he shifted into a battle stance.

Ready to pounce, Sasha shifted into her human form and stepped between them, hands up.

"No, Papa, she is the druid's granddaughter. To hurt her will be a death sentence."

The wolf paused, and Scarlet nodded, gathering all her skills of deception to convince him to help. "It's true. I called to Sasha to lead me to you. The druid needs your help to bring peace to the Growlers before it's too late."

The wolf shifted into a human form. The fine layer of fur that covered the Growlers' bodies hid their breasts and genitals, especially in the dim light of the moon.

He stood tall and proud, but he wasn't as imposing as Wulfric. Probably a few inches shorter, thicker around the middle, older.

"The druid forced the treaty on us years ago. We've had an uneasy peace ever since, so I'm unsure what you're talking about."

Scarlet held both daggers within the folds of her cloak, careful not to brandish the weapons. Sasha knew they would be at the ready, and she watched Scarlet warily.

Scarlet shook her head. "Not that peace. The Growlers are divided."

The wolf snorted and stepped closer to his daughter, "What does the druid care of the divide within the Growlers?"

Scarlet watched as Sasha eased closer to her father, but

she didn't stop them. Her thoughts tumbled over themselves with indecision. She wasn't a fucking diplomat. Hunters typically got their assignments, planned the mission, stealthily attacked, then went back to the Guild Master for payment.

This talking through a problem was more Eirwyn's style. Scarlet had no idea what to do, so she just tried to think of what Eirwyn might say.

"There is a bigger threat in Busparia than the Growlers can comprehend. The tribe needs to unite with the Robins in the north and—"

The male grabbed his daughter's wrist and jerked her behind him as he turned to snarl at Scarlet. "Never. The new alpha says Busparia is ripe for the plucking."

"Your new alpha is dumber than a rock, then. And he's not the rightful alpha. Wulfric is."

The wolf paused, his expression turning sad as he shook his head, "Wulfric is dead. Brody's two friends saw the alpha challenge."

Scarlet put a hand on her hip, still holding the dagger. She knew it must've shone under the moonlight, because the wolf's eyes dipped down then back to her face with a new hardness around his mouth.

"The alpha challenge was illegal, and you know it. Without the supervision of the Elders, Wulfric remains alpha. He's the only one who has the wisdom and strength to do what's necessary."

"And what's necessary?" the Growler asked softly, easing slowly closer to his daughter.

Scarlet sighed, the weight of the world pressing her closer to the ground.

"Unite both types of Growlers, the turned and the natural born, and join the rest of the Feral Forest to finally stop Busparia."

The wolf barked a short laugh. "That's impossible. Brody is going to move camp with the new moon. Warriors are going into Busparia to find more supplies, better territory…"

"Their previous families?" Scarlet asked softly.

Sasha frowned and peered at Scarlet around her father's shoulders. "What previous families?"

Scarlet's brows rose. "So Brody hasn't let everyone in camp in on that agenda, has he?"

The male shook his head slowly, one hand behind him as he held Sasha protectively.

Scarlet pressed her advantage. "Brody isn't thinking of the Growlers. He's only thinking of himself and what he left behind in Busparia. The magic of the turning isn't working right. Why do you think the druid sent me?"

She let the question hang in the air.

Eventually he said softly, "The Elders aren't doing anything. The magic is breaking down, but they're not going to stand in the way of the will of the goddess."

He said the last with a bitterness that caused Sasha to frown. Scarlet drew on all she's heard from Wulfric and tried to think like Eirwyn. She raised her brows, standing proudly as she replied.

"The Elders would let the magic fade. Then what will happen?"

The man growled, "Then the tribe will be wiped out by disease or famine or this damn winter. If the Buspartan defenders find out the magic is fading, they'll invade the forest. We can't have that."

Scarlet tilted her head. "That sounds too practiced. You've heard that argument a lot over the past few days, haven't you?"

The man's jaw snapped shut as his lips pursed, but he didn't answer.

Scarlet lifted both daggers and bent her knees. The Growler stiffened, but before he could move, Scarlet threw both daggers. One embedded in the tree to his left and the other in the tree to his right.

Sasha gasped and gripped her father's arm, but the wolf didn't look away from Scarlet.

Scarlet lifted her head and thought of Eirwyn and Knox. The events of the past year. The fears Wulfric had shared. Her stomach churned at the chaos, the needless bloodshed, and a sliver of worry for the Growlers made her stiffen.

"A war is brewing right here in your camp," she said harshly. "Are you really going to just let it come or will you do what's right to stop it? It's why the druid sent me. I'm to lend my assistance, but I can't do it alone. Are you willing to help or do I have to go through you to protect the forest?"

The silence stretched but Sasha stepped beside her father. "It will be a great honor to help the druid," she said.

The wolf stiffened and tried to push her behind him. Sasha shook her head and her jaw firmed.

"No, Papa. You know it's the right thing to do. I've heard you and Mama at night. You're worried about Brody's plan. This is the choice you've been looking for."

"It'll be dangerous," Scarlet warned.

For the first time, the girl smiled and nodded eagerly. "Growlers don't mind danger. We're taught to fight early."

Scarlet waited. This girl was barely an adult, yet she'd snuck up and attacked well. Her father should be proud. But if he didn't work with her, she wasn't sure that she'd reach Wulfric in time to help. He might have gone to the camp with the intention of speaking with the Elders, but if there were as many in camp as he said, he wouldn't make it out without fighting Brody.

Finally, the man sighed and nodded. "Fine, let's walk while you explain what you need from us. I'm still on watch."

Scarlet pulled her daggers free of the trees and fell into step beside the Growler as Sasha shifted to her wolf form. She outlined her plan and explained that Wulfric was alive and he'd gone to the Elders for answers.

"Sasha can go back to where I left our bags. If Wulfric shows up, she can tell him what's going on. Sir—what's your name?"

"Todd," he said.

Scarlet nearly stumbled in the dark at the entirely mundane name. "Alright, Todd, you can go into camp and see if Wulfric is there without raising suspicion."

Todd shook his head. "No, you should go back to your pack, and Sasha can go into camp. I have to continue the watch."

Scarlet stretched her senses once more. "There's a Growler half a mile that way, and another that way. If any living creature gets within that radius of me, I'll know what kind it is."

Sasha frowned but didn't point out that she'd gotten the jump on Scarlet.

"I'll stay between the two outer perimeter Growlers, keep pace with them. They'll never know it's me or that you've left the post. But if Wulfric dies from another illegal alpha challenge, the entire fate of your tribe dies with him."

Todd sighed once more and shifted to his wolf form without another word. He nuzzled the wolf girl, then they loped off in opposite directions.

Scarlet breathed a sigh of relief. As time passed and the

night grew colder, she worried about Wulfric. Where had all this diplomatic talk come from? These thoughts had been in the back of her mind as they'd talked over the past few days but it had surprised her when they'd all spilled out.

Did she really believe Wulfric should work with the Robins and Knox? It was definitely better than the alternative of Growlers running all over Busparia and being captured by the crown. Or worse, by some other Hunter, the few that were still operating in Busparia.

What happened to letting the glocken tea wear off, having the Growlers reverse her curse if they could, then leaving this place? She wasn't seriously considering working with Wulfric to help the Growlers, was she?

If she did, she could probably take a small, select team of Growlers with her into Busparia to destroy the queen.

If they'd listen to her and obey.

If Wulfric became alpha again.

If they accepted her for who and what she was.

Her head ached, and she reached up and touched an antler. Neither Sasha nor Todd had said a word about them, although they'd both stared in horror.

Half an hour passed, and Scarlet was growing weary. Her bones ached from the cold and her stomach was in knots. She was also growing too far from wherever Wulfric was.

Stretching her senses for this long was draining her energy. She glanced up and pushed, realizing that she'd tightened the boundary around her as she'd grown more tired.

Her spine stiffened. Coming toward her along the outer perimeter was an aura. It wasn't the Growler she'd been following in the circle around the camp, but it wasn't Wulfric, Todd, or Sasha either.

Shit, what was she supposed to do now? The wind was at her back. The Growler would've smelled her by now. She pulled her hood back up and held her daggers ready in the folds of her cloak.

Then she waited, continuing her slow walk forward as if nothing out of the ordinary was going on.

Too soon, the brown Growler came through the dark trees, his mouth bared.

"Easy now," she whispered softly, coming to a stop on the balls of her feet. "I'm no threat."

The wolf paused and glanced to the side. Scarlet looked to the left as a flash of brown fur slammed into her. She slammed into the frozen ground, gripping her daggers tightly. Damn it, she'd been so focused on the one, she'd missed the other. A flanking attack was classic, and she'd fallen for it. Anger and adrenaline shot through her as she hit the ground, her teeth chattering and pain radiating from her shoulder.

The familiar magic surrounded them, then the Growler's now human arms wrapped around her tightly, trapping her arms to her sides.

She kicked but grabbed the cloak with her finger tips, careful to hide her daggers. She had to bide her time.

"Well, well, well, what kind of freak do we have here?"

"Look at the prey that wandered into the big bad wolf's territory, Greg."

Greg? What kind of Growler name was Greg?

"Put me down, you stupid oaf. I'm the granddaughter of the druid."

The two males laughed, then one said, "If that were really true, you would've killed us before we even got close.'

Shit, what exactly had her grandma done thirty years ago?

The arms tightened around her as they tossed her over a shoulder and started marching toward camp. Damn it, her arms were trapped in one long, bulky arm, pinned to her side with the butt of the daggers digging into her thighs. She squirmed to lay the blades flat against her thighs, careful not to alert the stupid Growler too soon.

"Let's see what Brody has to say about her. Maybe we can have a bit of fun before killing her."

Scarlet's feet swung wildly, kicking at her captor's stomach until he wrapped his other arm around her knees. She was held too tight to escape.

With only her mouth free and unable to angle her head to bite him, she attacked with words.

"You're so going to regret this," she seethed, her jaw clenching. Oddly enough, she wasn't afraid, the familiar rush of anger heating her from the inside.

How dare they capture her? How had they been so fast with it? How had they snuck up on her?

She was the best Hunter in the land, damn it. She had never failed an assassination, never caused a scene or gotten caught.

Except last summer with the king.

This was unacceptable. No matter that she had grown weak and her aura readings had started to fade the farther she was from Wulfric. No matter that she was cold, weary, and weak. She had to reclaim her title as the best of the Hunters and use this to her advantage.

She pursed her lips as they drew closer to a hollow. The tents were densely packed, but there was a sort of order to it. The tents seemed to be arranged in clusters of four with a small campfire built in the center, each of the groups of four neatly organized in rows.

The closer they came, the stronger she felt. That made

her angrier too, because that meant Wulfric was in camp. He'd sworn he was just going to gather information from a guard or two. He'd lied.

The well-worn walking path they followed led straight through the camp. The closer they came to the center, the larger the tents became. Still she struggled, her heart racing as she cursed them under her breath.

"You fuckers are going to regret this."

A lone wooden building was nestled under the trees. Beside it were three of the largest tents. On the other side of those three was the largest tent in the camp.

In front of the large tents and the building was the largest bonfire. There were no tents nearby, just a large open area for congregating.

They'd passed a few people around the smaller camp-fires, but as they went closer to the center of the camp, more people followed them. Most of the men wore loose canvas pants while the women wore simple hide or canvas dresses that hung to their knees. Slits up the side revealed a lot of leg, but the simple soft leather shoes on their feet were the most surprising. The way Wulfric had complained about the boots, she would've thought they'd all be barefoot.

Women, children, and even shifted Growlers in wolf form came to see the prisoner as she was carried to the bonfire. When they reached it, one of her captors let out a sharp bark. She jumped, her stomach quivering as an answering set of growls swept through the camp. Fear threatened to choke her, and her rabbit nose twitched.

Shit, were they going to rip her to pieces? Roast her alive?

The crowd's noise died down as someone came out of the biggest tent. A wiry man with shaggy brown hair walked

221

forward, his golden eyes cold and calculating as the crowd whispered and pointed. Two others followed him.

"What do we have here?"

"Intruder, boss," said the one holding her. He slapped her ass hard, making her jerk.

"Get your fucking hands off me, Growler, and let me go," she ground out. If she could just angle her head around, she'd be able to bite him.

"She's a freaky little thing. Can we rough her up a bit before…"

The man's voice trailed off as he sought guidance from the leader.

"Don't even think about it, you upstart. Are you the little bitch Brody I've heard so much about?" Scarlet asked.

The crowd gasped and looked at the leader. Two other Growlers stood behind him, arms crossed, but Brody just threw his head back and laughed. It sent an icy shiver down her spine.

He waved his hand toward the bonfire. "I see my reputation precedes me. At your service, my lady."

He did a mock bow, but Scarlet snorted. "Let me go."

Brody's eyes glittered in the glow of the fire. "For your impertinence, I believe we'll have a bit of sport first. We're not monsters, after all, no matter what the outside world says. We'll give her a fighting chance."

Suddenly the men holding her dropped her to the dirt too close to the fire. She rolled away from the flames and to her feet. Her hood had fallen back, revealing her antlers and ears. She lifted her daggers as her eyes darted from target to target.

The crowd gasped and began to murmur, several falling back a few steps. A mother tugged a child back into the crowd. She searched the gazes for any open faces, anyone who might be able to help. But all that stared back was horror and a freakish fascination. The familiar wave of not belonging washed over her.

Dread settled in her stomach as she realized there would be no help coming. The Growlers wouldn't let her leave. The civilians were too scared or too stupid to help or let her go, and the warriors would follow Brody.

But she wasn't going anywhere until she found Wulfric. He was here somewhere. She just had to live long enough to find him. Hands spread and daggers gleaming in the firelight, she shifted her feet to prepare for an attack.

# Chapter Twenty-One

Wulfric slipped through the woods and crouched next to a tree to watch the guard slink slowly through the forest. Wulfric stayed down wind and sniffed. He didn't recognize this guard.

He settled down to wait, watching the guard disappear as he continued his patrol. Cold seeped into his bones, but at least the wind stayed consistent.

Scarlet was to the north. He could feel her presence like a beacon, calling to him. He hated leaving her side, but it was necessary.

He had to figure out what he'd missed, what Brody had done in the past few days.

The next guard lumbered past, making Wulfric wince. Jamison. The old, grizzled natural-born Growler always watched the turned and pointed out their mistakes. He'd grumbled about the newcomers for as long as Wulfric had been part of the tribe.

Ten long years. Wulfric watched him continue on the patrol, his lips pursing. He wouldn't find support there.

A conversation from last year echoed through his mind.

*"I don't care if you are the alpha, it's wrong, and you know it,"* Jamison said.

*Wulfric crossed his arms and leaned back in the oversized chair in the longhouse. "That's where you're mistaken. What's wrong is denying the new Growlers equal rights. What's wrong is insisting on the old ways that see the natural-born as full citizens but the newly turned as beneath you."*

*Eyes watched them around the room, the rest of the Growlers growing quiet as the conversation grew louder.*

*Jamison waved his arms wide, claws shifting as his emotions heightened. "There's nothing wrong with the old ways. They've worked for hundreds of years."*

*Wulfric growled, "And they were changed when the turned saved the Growlers from extinction."*

*Wulfric glanced around the room, acutely aware that the past few months had seen an increase in the division between the two types of Growlers. The turned now sat almost entirely on the right of the longhouse and the natural born on the left.*

*"The turned are ready to branch out and form their own tribe,"* Jamison said. *Several of those on the right nodded, but Wulfric slammed a fist to the wooden table. It shook as the dull thud rang out, the only sound in the room.*

*"I hear your concern, Jamison, but the turned have nowhere to go."*

*"Not yet, but the Feral Forest can only support so many of us, alpha. Someday you'll realize that. I just hope purifying the tribe doesn't destroy us all."*

*Jamison shifted into his wolf and ran out the door. There had been three others who were supposed to bring grievances to him tonight, but no one else stepped forward.*

*Small groups of Growlers whispered to each other around the tables, no doubt discussing what had just happened.*

But Wulfric had had no choice that day. Jamison had

proposed going back to the old ways, back to when the newly turned had been just barely better than slaves.

If the grumbling over the past few months were any sign, Jamison was more likely to side with Brody. Brody would've had him convinced that sending the turned into Busparia would allow the natural-born to go back to the old ways when they ruled the forest.

Fuck, he was tired of hearing the older generation grumble about purifying the turned Growlers out of the forest...

Time was passing, the night growing colder as the snow began to fall. He needed to get back to Scarlet, but not before he got the information he needed.

When Jamison was well out of ear-shot, Wulfric slipped between the trees and passed the path the guards had taken.

He had to sneak into camp and speak with the Elders. Or at least Elva. She was the one Elder who'd always had his back.

The other two had often sided with the natural-born when disputes escalated to the Elders, but Elva had been more impartial and fair.

He stalked on silent feet, the edge of the camp coming into view. He wove around the grid pattern of tents, sticking to the shadows along the tree lined edge. The only solid building was the cedar longhouse where they had almost all meals, dances, and community discussions.

He paused on the edge of the forest, listening to the soft sounds of people gathered around the various campfires. The camp would be bedding down for the night, but sounds in the alpha tent had him gritting his teeth.

He watched as a female Growler stumbled out of the alpha tent and shook her head, her mane of hair wilder than most wore it, her long, leather dress ripped at the shoulder.

Another female Growler said something as she walked past, and the first female growled and launched at the second. They tumbled into battle, teeth bared and both shifting to wolf form, clothes shredding.

Three males hooted and cheered them on, but the alpha tent flap opened. Brody strode out with a bowl and tossed the contents on the two females as two other males walked up, flanked by four others.

The women shrieked and jumped apart, both now wet with what appeared to be vegetable soup. Brody's voice didn't carry but his tone was harsh. After being chastised, the two females slunk away and Brody turned to the alpha tent.

The two males with the four escorts called to him, and Brody's spine stiffened. Wulfric's eyes narrowed as he took in the clothing from his safe hiding spot near the edge of the forest. What were the emissaries of the Nightstalkers and Duskkeepers doing in camp?

Wulfric pursed his lips and scanned his surroundings once more as Brody led them into the longhouse. He stepped out of the underbrush to the back side of the longhouse, following the shadows of it toward the three large tents. It was now more important than ever to talk to Elva the Elder.

He stopped at the back of the last tent, closest to the forest and sniffed, waiting to see if anyone saw or smelled him. The night seemed louder somehow. Faint sounds of laughter around various fire pits echoed through the camp, most of it on the opposite side of camp.

It was always quieter near the Elders, and Wulfric

wondered how Brody's presence had changed that. A change of leadership always made people push the boundaries, which would explain the two other tribe's sending someone to check out the state of the Ironpaws. Rumors of Wulfric's absence must have already made it to the other tribes.

After a few seconds, Wulfric lifted the back flap of Elva's tent and stepped silently inside, stooping in a crouch. He blinked, his eyes adjusting quickly to the fire in the middle of the tent, smoke curling up and out through the smoke hole.

The bed of hides and stretched canvas on the opposite side was made, clothing folded neatly at the foot of it. To the right was a small work station with Elva's beads, needles, and fabric. To the left was her cooking area, only a handful of bowls and cups stacked on a shelf.

Her dress, made of a thick hide material, was the deep brown color of tree bark and adorned with intricate patterns that reflected the culture of the Growlers. As she sat cross-legged, the slits in her dress revealed the pants underneath, providing warmth and protection from the frigid temperatures of their surroundings. The crackling fire in the nearby pit cast dancing shadows on her peaceful face, giving her an ethereal glow. Despite the harsh conditions outside, Elva seemed at ease and connected with nature as she communed with the elements around her.

Her wrinkled skin hung at the jaw, and her gray hair was kept in several braids down her back. The Elder's rope on the crown of her head and the heavier beadwork bodice was the only thing distinguishing her from any other woman in camp.

She'd lost weight in the past few months. Before he'd

been injured, several in camp worried that she would pass soon. But he knew she was stronger than she appeared. She took a deep breath and opened her golden eyes, peering at him with brows arched.

"Alpha, welcome home." She nodded, the skin of her chin swinging slightly.

"Elder," Wulfric nodded, then bent knees, palms, and head to the ground in respect before sitting back up on his haunches.

She waved a hand to the fire, and it flared green with magic.

"Join me, won't you?" It wasn't a question, but an order.

He sank to mirror her seated pose across from the fire pit. Her eyes had closed again, but he watched her carefully above the flames.

"You don't seem surprised to see me," he said quietly.

Her lips curled up on the ends, but she didn't open her eyes. "I'm not. We knew you weren't dead."

"We?"

"The other Elders and I. We've discussed it at length and sought the advice of our ancestors and the gods."

Wulfric waited but when she didn't continue, he asked, "And did they answer?"

She simply nodded. "They did. I'm glad you've returned now, as the other tribal leaders will be arriving sometime tomorrow to discuss what happened. Care to tell me your version?"

More questions flew through his mind, but he had to focus on the information he needed. He'd been gone too long from Scarlet already. He should've brought her with him. He took a deep breath. There was no more time to lose.

"Elder, Brody attacked me in an illegal alpha challenge along with several of his friends. It was an ambush, and I'm blessed by the gods to have survived. I take it Brody thinks I'm dead?"

Elva nodded, eyes still closed with palms resting on her knees. "Yes, I suspected when they came back from patrol without you what had happened."

"And you didn't use a spell to insist they tell the truth?" No one ever knew what the Elders would do in a situation. The truth spell was possible, but it had been equally likely that they'd just wait and see what shakes out.

"No, I didn't. I wanted to wait for your return before the Elders revealed their hand to Brody. I am glad you survived, Wulfric. He claimed it was a fair fight, of course, but the deliberate decision to disobey the rules of an alpha challenge didn't sit well with several in the tribe."

Some of the tension in his spine eased. "Good, that's good. Yet he still claimed the alpha tent?"

"Yes," she said with a weary sigh. "When you didn't return the following day, there was nothing we could do. He's had nightly meetings in the longhouse and has whipped most of the tribe into a frenzy."

The tension was back, making him sit straighter, his hands fisting on his knees. "What's his plan? Is he going to invade Busparia with the turned?"

Elva's eyes opened, and Wulfric's brows rose at the twinkle in them. Her smile widened as she replied.

"So many questions. It's like the first day you were turned. Do you remember?"

He pursed his lips and nodded, tamping down his impatience. "Of course."

The memory came unbidden, and it took his breath away.

*The pain in his chest as death had come closer. The feverish body, the pulsing in the wound in his side that had spelled his doom. The blistering sun beating down on him by the side of the road, the roar of the sea and the coughing of the others the only sounds.*

*He closed his eyes and awaited death. Then a shadow fell over him and the sea breeze sent a chill down his spine. Elva stood over him, her magical staff glowing with energy.*

*She leaned over him, a frown on her severe face as she said, "You're dying."*

*He chuckled, ending in a cough. He didn't bother wiping the blood from his chin. ".No shit, woman."*

*She'd arched a brow and leaned on her staff. "Don't sass me, young man. Unless you want to die?"*

*His vision swam and he closed his eyes. "What other choice do I have but to pray to the gods and wait?"*

*It was her turn to chuckle. "Well, the gods sent me. I offer a second chance at life, if you're man enough to take it."*

*He blinked, bringing the woman back into focus. "You must be crazy."*

*She shrugged. "Wisdom comes in many forms, soldier. It's up to you to decide to take the chance or not. I will go check on your comrades while you think on the decision. You still have an hour before death claims you."*

*He'd thought, fighting through the pain to lift his head and watch her move from litter to litter. They'd all been injured in battle, but the medicine tents were constantly overrun. They had been sent back home to recover.*

*Or die along the road. Those who had already died had been pushed off the cliffs into the sea below. But the four of them had been left here next to the old ruins while the rest of the convoy had pushed on to Busparia.*

*Home. Images of his wife and daughter flashed through his mind along with the aching pain in his chest. Was he ready to join his wife?*

*His eyes fluttered, then the old woman was back.*

*"Well? What will it be, soldier? Do you want to live or die?"*

*The tip of her staff glowed green with pulsing magic, and he licked his lips. Sweat beaded his brow. He couldn't leave yet. There was... something... left to do. What was it?*

*"What's the catch?" His voice was rough with pain.*

*She'd stared at him, her lips pursed. He'd not seen most of her features with the sun behind her. But he'd felt the strength of her presence.*

*She wasn't just some crazy old beggar lady. Perhaps she was a goddess in disguise, here to tempt him?*

*"You'll gain incredible strength and ancient magic that will knit your body back together. Self-healing will be yours for as long as you live. And you will live for hundreds of years, as only magical weapons will kill you. Man cannot hurt you ever again."*

*He closed his eyes. "The catch, woman. I asked what is the catch?"*

*She chuckled again. "You're wise to ask. Not many do. But to answer the question, you'll lose all memories of this life."*

*He took a shaky breath, his entire body shivering in pain from his injuries. But it was the pain in his heart that made him nod. No more nightmares of the battlefield or his dead wife's unblinking eyes.*

He blinked and the green smoke settled back into a normal fire. Elva's golden brown eyes watched him carefully from the other side of the fire.

He licked his lips, the memory of the thirst and pain a dull ache inside him. "I remember," he said softly.

She tilted her head, but her expression was the same calculating one he'd come to love.

"What do you remember, alpha?"

He took a deep breath and peered into the fire. "I remember being human. The memories from my life before are slowly coming back. From the way Brody talked when he ambushed me, his memories might be back too."

She arched a gray brow, her tiny braids falling over her shoulder. "I suspected as much. One of the other turned has admitted as such. The magic that binds us all is failing, alpha."

Her words made his stomach twist and his heart race.

# Chapter Twenty-Two

"Why is the magic failing?" Wulfric asked, fear tinging his words and turning them harsher than he intended.

Elva's eyes grew unfocused, swirling with green. "The time of the prophecy is here."

"Prophecy? What prophecy?" His mind raced with conflicting emotions—fear for the future, anger at being kept in the dark, and a touch of excitement at the possibility of something new, something that would help the tribe accept Scarlet and vice versa.

She blinked, her eyes coming back into focus as she stared at him. "Nomani and Barley aren't going to like this, but I told them it was coming. I have felt it building for months. They'll finally see I'm always right."

She slowly got onto all fours and pushed herself up. Wulfric quickly went to aid her, taking her elbow and helping her stand as she stretched her back.

"Thank you, son. Will you hand me my staff?"

He grabbed it from the bed, the green emerald at the

top glowing from the light of the fire. An intricate pattern of wood wrapped around the tip to hold it in place.

He wondered what Scarlet would think of the staff and Elva. He'd left her for too long. He had to find her, make sure she was safe.

"Elva, I have to challenge Brody, but I need to leave for a few more hours. May I stay in your tent tonight? A good night's rest is just what I need before the alpha challenge at day break."

She sighed and tilted her head as she listened, her eyes piercing him as they saw into his soul.

Elva took the staff and her golden eyes flashed green then back to gold. She shook her head. "I'm sorry, but no."

Wulfric frowned and opened his mouth to ask why not when a sharp bark came from the main fire. Loud growls followed, causing the hair on the back of Wulfric's neck to stand. He'd left Scarlet too long. He had to make sure she was safe.

"Ah, that will be our cue, I believe." Elva shook out her dress and took a drink of a nearby cup.

"What are you talking about? I need to slip out for a bit, but I'll be back later." He frowned and looked down at Elva.

She set the cup down and gathered her ceremonial robe, a pattern of various hides and beadwork like a cloak settling onto her frail shoulders.

"It is the night before the full moon. When we inquired of our Growler patron goddess, we all three received signs that the next three nights would decide the fate of our entire people."

Wulfric's ears echoed at her words. He frowned and shook his head in denial, not understanding how a single alpha challenge could make or break a tribe that had existed for thousands of years.

She tilted her head and stared at him, seeing too much of his raw and aching soul.

"There's no time like the present, alpha. You need to follow me while I gather the rest of the Elders. Your past has been preparing you for this for years. You will succeed... or else, we will all perish."

He crossed his arms and snorted. "Thanks for the vote of confidence."

She arched a brow and smiled at his tone as she stepped toward the tent flap. The murmur of a crowd grew outside, but she looked back at him expectantly.

He sighed, the weight of responsibility heavy on his shoulders. "Fine, yes, I *will* succeed as I am the rightful alpha. The goddess chose me for a reason. That's what you said five years ago when you appointed me alpha."

He said it accusingly, but her smile didn't waver.

She just nodded. "And it's still true, more so now than ever. Come, let's not drag this out. You will follow me and challenge Brody now."

She didn't wait for a response before she ducked through the flap. It ruffled behind her, settling back in place.

He ran a hand down his face and his stomach tightened, but he didn't have a choice. She was the Elder for a reason. She'd helped lead this tribe for over a hundred years. Surely she knew what was best.

Besides, he wasn't the type to shirk his responsibility. Perhaps he could win this alpha challenge and then go find Scarlet. It'd be safer for her to stay outside of camp until it was over anyway.

He ducked through the tent flap to see Elva already walking with Nomani to the third tent. By the time he caught up to her, she was inside Barley's tent, the eldest of the three.

Wulfric stuck to the shadows along the wall of the building, but his gaze went to the big fire pit in the center of camp in front of the longhouse. A crowd had gathered, even though snow was falling steadily and the almost full moon was high. Growlers didn't mind the elements as much as humans, although both wolves and their human forms walked through the camp.

All three Elders walked toward the bonfire, and the crowd parted for a few precious seconds. A flash of red drew his attention. Scarlet stood too close to the fire, daggers drawn and glare in place. His heart stopped and his breath turned into a low wheeze.

Hells, what was she doing here? The crowd closed ranks, and he lost sight of her. Panic clawed at him from the inside out.

The blood rushed to his head, cutting off the sound of the crowd chanting. His world seemed to tilt on its axis as his senses went haywire. Only when he sneezed was he able to snap out of it.

The Elders slammed their staffs onto the ground in unison, sending a shock wave through the camp. He couldn't see the Elders anymore, but the familiar shockwave sent him into action. Silently, he stepped into the crowd as it quieted and the group took a few steps back from the center.

Wulfric slid between people in the confusion, desperately searching for Scarlet. When he finally drew close enough to see her, his fists clenched.

The crowd had formed a wide circle around the fire. Too close to it on the right stood Scarlet. She stared down two wolves that prowled in front of her, never turning her back to any of them.

Across the fire and inside the empty circle, Brody stood

in human form, wearing only a simple pair of pants with bare arms crossed. His grin was wide and unhinged, reminding Wulfric of some of the barbarian warriors he'd seen go berserk on the battlefields all those years ago. The visiting tribesmen stood with arms crossed.

Elva and the other Elders stood to the left side of the fire. Elva raised her staff and asked, "What's the meaning of this?"

Normally it was Barley who led, but the power dynamics seemed to have shifted in his absence. He sent a silent thanks to the goddess for that small mercy.

Brody sneered, "Intruder. We're just having some fun before eliminating the threat, Elder. Nothing to worry about."

Wulfric's hackles rose but with the noise of the crowd, no one heard his growl. Brody wanted to show off his new power as alpha in front of the visiting tribesmen, but Wulfric had to protect Scarlet. He stepped forward, trying to push his way through the crowd.

Scarlet scoffed, "I'd like to see you try. If you don't like Brody the bitch, maybe Brody the dickwad could be your new title?"

Brody snarled and lunged at her half-heartedly. Wulfric pushed through the crowd. By the time he reached the front, Scarlet had easily parried, slicing Brody's wrist neatly. She barely drew blood before spinning around the fire.

The crowd around him whispered. "Did you see that?"

"She drew first blood. Who is she?"

Elva stepped in front of the other two Elders and slammed her staff into the dirt.

"Enough," she said. "You will not hurt the druid."

The crowd gasped, their whispers growing louder.

Brody spat in the dirt. "She's no druid."

"I'm a Hunter too," Scarlet said. The crowd took several steps back, and a few shrieks rippled through the air.

But Elva shook her head. "Doesn't matter, child. You're under the druid's protection, and we will honor the pact made thirty years ago."

The crowd grew louder.

"The hell we will," Brody yelled above the noise. "This is an intruder who has the nerve to walk right into our territory and jeopardize our safety. And you're going to allow it?"

Wulfric felt the anxiety roll off the crowd as Elva nodded. "Yes, she is a guest in our camp, and we will honor her as such."

Brody snarled, "She's no guest."

He lunged at Scarlet. Wulfric didn't think. He leaped over the two in front of him and into the circle, shifting just enough to gain speed and intercept. He slammed his good shoulder into Brody, who staggered into the other two wolves that threatened her.

He stood shoulder to shoulder next to Scarlet, their backs to the fire. The crowd had gone silent.

Wulfric's breath was shallow but steady as Brody untangled himself from the wolves.

"You won't touch her," Wulfric said into the silence of the night.

"A-alpha," one wolf shifted into the human form, surprise and fear on his face. No one cared that he was naked, as all eyes were on Brody.

Brody jerked at his words, swinging his head to Wulfric in shock. "You—you're alive," his voice was soft as his jaw dropped.

"Surprised to see me?" Wulfric asked softly, his eyes burning hot from anger. Scarlet's steady presence beside him comforted him. He wanted to reach for her, but they both were focused on Brody right now.

Brody glared. "You're not the alpha anymore. I am, and as alpha, I say we do not have to honor the fucking treaty with some druid who's probably dead now."

Scarlet laughed and her hood fell back, revealing her ears and two pointed antlers.

"Antlers!"

"Those ears!"

The crowd took another step back from the fire, making the circle bigger. "Oh, she's very much alive. You see, we found alpha Wulfric and patched him up. The druid *saved* him. You really want to threaten him right now?"

Brody's hands shook, whether in fear or rage, Wulfric didn't know. But his voice was firm and clear as he said loudly, "Oh, I definitely do. The druid can't save him now. I formally challenge you, Wulfric, for the position of Iron-paws tribe alpha."

The crowd gasped, and the silence broke like a dam. The gossip flew on the wind, growing with a roar.

All three Elders slammed the butts of their staffs on the ground again, and a flash of magic shimmered in a circle around the bonfire. Wulfric's heart raced. The official alpha challenge was about to begin.

# Chapter Twenty-Three

The crowd backed up as the yellow glowing ring of magic edged toward them, zapping a few of the slower ones. Tails smoldered and one wolf yipped in pain before prancing away.

Inside the circle, Elva looked at Wulfric and raised her voice to echo over the camp.

"A challenge has been issued. Standard rules apply. It will be a fight to the death or to unconsciousness. You have two minutes to prepare."

Her words were so final, and Wulfric's spine snapped to attention. Some of his memories of previous battles while human flitted in and out of his mind along with the two other alpha challenges he'd participated in before.

The same sense of cold calm settled over him now as it did then. Elva and the other two Elders each went to the edge of the circle, forming a triangle between them with the fire in the center.

Wulfric turned to face Scarlet. He had to make sure she was alright. But she just looked up at him with those fierce green eyes, one brow raised. "You didn't tell me Grandma was a fucking legend here."

He grinned and shrugged. "Wasn't sure you'd actually come all this way if you knew."

She rolled her eyes, then looked over at Brody who stood talking with his two friends, now both in human form. She looked back up at Wulfric, the concern on her face making his chest ache.

"How is this going to go? Will you be alright? Are you recovered enough? Can I help?"

He grinned, his feelings for her filling him with hope, purpose, and determination to succeed.

"I'm going to win," he said with confidence. "It'll just be the two of us in a fair fight, and that, I can handle."

"But your injuries—"

"Are healed. Don't worry, bunny. When this is over, I want to show you the camp and introduce you to some friends."

She looked over at the crowd nervously, the flash of vulnerability nearly making his knees weak. He wanted to pull her into a hug and protect her from the world, but she was more likely to punch him for it than seek comfort.

Elva's voice rose over the crowd. "It is time."

The Elders lifted their staffs and said an incantation together. A magical barrier erected itself from the circle, straight into the sky. Then Brody's two friends each were pulled by magic. One was forced to Nomani's side and the other went to Barley.

Scarlet struggled as magic settled on her, but Wulfric just shook his head. "This is normal," he said. "Elva will watch out for you."

Scarlet's feet slid along the compacted dirt. Elva smiled at her and nodded when Scarlet stopped beside her.

Wulfric turned to face Brody, and faintly heard Elva say, "Welcome to the Growlers tribe known as the Ironpaws, my dear. I'm Elva the Elder. I'm sure you have many questions, but all in due time. Prepare yourself. It's—"

Brody roared and attacked without warning, shifting in mid-air. Wulfric reacted and shifted, meeting him head on as a wolf. Brody swiped, but Wulfric was done messing around.

They'd already fought once. It was time to end it for good. He wrapped his claws around Brody's shoulder and took him to the ground. Brody rolled, and his claws slashed at Wulfric's ribs.

Wulfric grabbed his paw with his jaws and bit so hard he felt the crunch of bone. Brody yelped and clawed Wulfric's face with the other paw.

He jerked back with a howl and pushed off Brody. Pain shocked his body once more as Brody's claws ripped flesh, and Wulfric stumbled away.

Brody leaped off his back legs, one of his front paws held loosely, and slammed into Wulfric. They both tumbled into the fire. It licked at his feet and heels, singing his tail in seconds, and climbed swiftly up his body.

Howling in pain, they rolled out, twisting in the dirt as each tried to put out their own fire.

Brody shuddered and gasped as he swiped his still smoking tail in the dirt, but Wulfric came to his feet first. He patted his body furtively, then took a char-filled breath and pounced, knocking Brody onto his back.

The crack of bone made Wulfric howl in triumph as he rained blow after blow onto Brody's still smoldering side.

From the corner of his eye, Wulfric saw movement. He ignored it, lifting his paw to swipe once more.

Then someone slammed into his side, and a burst of

pain exploded through his body. He slid over the dirt, breathing shallowly as the pain pulsed in his ribs. A wolf lunged for him, but Wulfric blinked and rolled, stirring up dirt and ash.

The snarls and growls of fighting wolves were familiar, but the flash of red in the dusty air made him rub his eyes.

His heart raced as he pushed past the pain and blinked to clear his vision. The magic circle had changed colors to purple, something he'd never seen in an alpha challenge before, and Brody's two friends now circled Scarlet. They were no longer held by magic but participants. He opened his mouth to yell at the Elders, to ask questions, but her daggers swiped as she spun and slashed at the other two. They toyed with her, testing her defenses and skills.

Wulfric's mouth snapped closed as he focused on his mate. He had to save her. He circled the scattered fire, looking for an opening to leap in and help when movement to the side drew his eye.

He turned to look but another pain slammed into him. Fuck, love had made him blind. Brody had pounced at Wulfric's distraction.

Wulfric couldn't let him win. Not when Scarlet was on the line. He went feral, reaching into his primal nature to find the spark of wildness he needed to win.

Wulfric's bloody jaws clamped onto Brody's throat. Flesh ripped and shredded, blood seeped into his fur and filled his mouth as he tore into warm meat. Then there was nothing else but this joy in the snapping of teeth and tearing of flesh. Brody whimpered, but Wulfric flung him side to side, holding tight with his jaws locked, slamming him into the ground hard enough to make his own head pulse.

And still he didn't release his opponent. A flash of red penetrated the blood-lust haze, and he blinked swiftly, his gaze landing on Scarlet, still fending off the other two Growlers with her twin daggers of death.

The feral mindless bloodlust lifted, and Wulfric leaped into the air, slamming Brody down to the ground with his mouth still locked around where his shoulder met his neck. He felt a snap, then Brody went limp in his jaws.

Something tugged on the edge of his consciousness, and he tossed Brody away. The winds pulled his attention to Scarlet. When a glance confirmed that Brody lay still, he turned to find his mate.

She slashed at one wolf and went low, drawing blood and making him yip as Wulfric jumped over her, landing on all fours behind her. Back-to-back, they each swiped and slashed at the two remaining wolves.

A thump, and the ground shook with magic again. They rode out the wave, and all four of them stopped to glance at the Elders.

Elva stepped forward and lifted her staff. "Brody has failed the challenge. Wulfric remains alpha. When someone is raised to an Elder, we make a pilgrimage to the ruins of the goddess. We each received separate visions from the goddess with instructions once this alpha triumphed in his third alpha challenge. Now is the time for the prophecy."

The three Elders chanted in the ancient tongue. Wulfric's hackles rose as the magic swept through the camp like a pulsing wave, knocking those closest to the Elders to the ground.

He shifted back to his semi-human form as he flew through the air, grabbing Scarlet's cloak to pull her close to his side as they rolled on the ground. She shivered as magic pulsed, and he prayed that she wouldn't pull away.

Then she turned her head to his chest as the magic washed over them. One arm around her back, one on the back of her head, he breathed in the comforting scent of her. It grounded him, even as the world seemed to tilt and spin. The magic flowed through him and threatened to turn his stomach.

A searing pain in the back of his skull slammed into him, as if someone had taken a pick and hammer to his head. He howled and stiffened.

Scarlet's hands on his back pressed him closer, and he whimpered, bowing his body around hers. He wasn't proud of it, but it wasn't because she still held her daggers in her hands, pressing them into his back.

No, it was the flood of forty-five years of memories. Almost all of them came back like a hurricane. His parents' shop, his friends from the village carousing at the tavern, wooing his wife, the birth of his babe... He choked down the bile and tears, each memory choking him as his mind spun out of control.

Then the overwhelming feelings receded like a gentle, outgoing tide. He opened his eyes as the glowing magic faded. The circle keeping the rest of the crowd out had dissipated. Scarlet pulled back and glanced over at him. "Are you alright?"

He swallowed hard, but couldn't speak, his throat too choked with memories. He ran his hands over her head to check for injuries, but she was fine. He sighed in relief and groaned as he moved to his knees, then his feet, not releasing Scarlet's hand. His head pulsed with pain.

Wulfric glanced over the crowd as everyone stood, but it took a few seconds to comprehend what he was seeing. All the turned Growlers were holding their heads. Some were retching, some fell to their knees with tears in their eyes as they sobbed. A few howled in anguish.

Wulfric blinked and pulled Scarlet into the safety of his

arms. His mind went blank with what to do next, what to say, what questions to ask. He was paralyzed by the changes, but holding Scarlet kept him from panicking over his failure to lead.

She mumbled into his chest, "Too tight."

He immediately pulled back, loosening his arms and sucking in a deep, shuddering breath.

"Are you alright? What happened?" She searched his face, then scanned down his body for injuries.

Pain still flowed through him with every beat of his heart, but it was dull and achy. An old pain that would never really go away. A familiar ache of lost family and friends.

"Wulfric?" she asked.

He looked down at her in bewilderment. "I—all my memories. They're back."

Her brows rose. "All of them?"

He nodded, dumbfounded as emotions swirled in him. He remembered his parents, his childhood growing up in the shop. He remembered being good with money and making deals for supplies.

He remembered meeting his wife behind the tavern, sneaking away from her parents, the fight with her parents over her hand. He remembered their baby girl and happy days singing in the tavern with his friends.

Then he blinked as tears ran down his cheeks. He remembered the fever that swept through the village. The death, the heartache, the loss. He choked back a sob and pulled Scarlet tight into his arms once more.

---

The old woman, an Elder, stepped closer with a soft, sad smile on her face, but Scarlet barely paid attention. She could almost feel the pain radiating off Wulfric. He swayed, and she held him up in her arms.

"It's too much," Scarlet said, seeking the eyes of the Elder woman. "He needs rest and healing."

The old woman nodded and stepped toward the crowd.

Wulfric mumbled, resting his forehead to her shoulder with a sigh. "I'm fine, bunny, we're both fine."

Scarlet's chest ached at the endearment as the Elder's voice rose over the wailing.

"Tomorrow at noon, we will meet in the longhouse, and the Elders will explain the prophecy. For tonight, go back to your tents and rest. Remember and get warm. All answers will be given tomorrow, and the alpha will decide what's to be done. All hail the rightful alpha Wulfric."

"All hail alpha Wulfric," the crowd murmured, shifting uncomfortably. Most still held their heads, snow now piling on top of them all.

Winter was supposed to be almost ending after this last cold snap. But now that the fight was over, she shivered.

Wulfric bowed his head to the crowd. "Thank you. I tell you now the same thing I said five years ago. I am here to serve and protect."

The Elder woman raised a brow at them. "Alpha, do you have something to say about our guest?"

Wulfric growled and nodded, wrapping his arm across Scarlet's shoulders and gripping her to his side. He took a deep breath, lifted his head, and stared at the crowd.

He stood proud and naked in front of the fire, full of vitality, virility, and confidence as he commanded the crowd's attention. Blood covered his chest and face, but Scarlet found him all the more enticing because of it.

"This is Scarlet, granddaughter of the druid, and one of the most feared Hunters. She is an honored guest… and my fated mate."

The crowd gasped and then whispered furiously. Several children pointed at her, and a few looked at her in fear. Wulfric's voice rose over them all.

"You will treat her with the same respect you treat me. I know how you are feeling. I feel it too. When we were turned, we gave up our humanity, our memories, but they are back."

Half of the Growlers didn't appear affected but they looked warily at those who either held their heads or stomachs. Some stood with heads held high, openly weeping even as they looked to their alpha for guidance.

Pride made her see him in a new light. He had the same burden of leadership that Knox had. She recognized that same look in his eye as he addressed the crowd.

Damn, he really was so much more than a mindless monster.

Wulfric's voice commanded respect and honor. "I don't know what the prophecy is or why we have been given our memories back. The Elder is right. Those are questions for tomorrow. For tonight, I want to lay in my warm bed, honor my past, and remember who I was. What I gave up."

The crowd grew quiet, and Scarlet knew his words resonated with many of them.

He nodded curtly and blood dripped off his chin. "May you all do the same. Rest easy, knowing we will get through this together on the morrow. Now go to bed."

Wulfric's knees buckled, and Scarlet held him up as everyone shuffled away. Wulfric looked at Brody's prone body, his two friends kneeling at his side and quietly checking his injuries.

"Does he live?" Wulfric asked softly.

One of the now shifted men, a gangly, black-haired boy who couldn't have been more than twenty, nodded.

Wulfric sighed. "Nomani, will you heal him?"

She nodded and moved to his side, waving two from the crowd to come and lift him. While she gave direction, the two who had fought beside him stood to their feet.

They glanced at each other nervously, and Wulfric frowned, meeting each of their gazes. "Come here. Stand and accept your fate."

Their heads hung low but they shuffled to stand in front of Wulfric and Scarlet. Wulfric dropped his arm from Scarlet and laced her fingers with his own.

He said, "You broke the law when you assisted Brody with the illegal alpha challenge. Do you deny it?"

"No, alpha," they said in unison, their gazes on the ground.

Wulfric sighed, his shoulders deflating. "The law states that you are to be killed."

Scarlet froze. This was the type of Growler she'd heard about. Heartless and ruthless killing. Justified, but the idea of their deaths twisted her stomach.

She didn't want to analyze why. Probably her stupid curses making her weak.

"Yes, alpha," they both said, voices tinged with fear and dread. They didn't look up as they sank to their knees in front of Wulfric and waited to die.

Wulfric shook his head. "Brody went about this entirely wrong, but some of his ideas are good. Tomorrow, after the Elders explain things, I'd like to discuss those ideas and how we might find a compromise. I am not a tyrant or a king or a monster. We are a family, a tribe, a pack. One people united into the Five Uncivilized Tribes. You will swear allegiance to me tomorrow, or you will be exiled. Do you understand?"

His gaze bored down at them, his face fierce with blood and dirt drying to his fur, his eyes burning from the ash and smoke. Their heads jerked up in surprise, jaws open as they nodded, hope clear in their eyes.

Then Wulfric nodded. "Very well then. Go back to your tents and think of what you will say tomorrow and what choice you will make."

Scarlet looked up. Most of the crowd had dispersed. The other Elder woman had disappeared with Brody. The male Elder stood watching the crowd, tall and expressionless as he held his staff.

The last Elder woman—had she introduced herself as Elva?—stepped up to them and smiled. "Well done, alpha. Now let's get you to your tent and patched up."

Scarlet's breath caught in her throat as Wulfric's arm came around her shoulders once more. He leaned heavily on her as they followed the woman to the largest tent in camp.

# Chapter Twenty-Four

The closer they drew to Wulfric's tent on the other side of the building, the heavier he leaned on her. When the Elder held the flap, Wulfric practically fell inside. Scarlet followed, the flap closing behind her.

The tent was round and made of some sort of canvas material. The sides of the tent were probably seven feet tall, then the roof arched in a type of dome. A hole in the top was open to the sky, and smoke from a fire in the center of the room curled toward it.

Wulfric swayed on his feet, muttering. "Stupid, fucking Brody. He's made a mess of everything."

The Elder clicked her tongue, then gently pushed him to the enormous bed on the opposite side of the fire. Furs covered it, strewn about in disarray. The Elder quickly tossed the dirty, sticky blankets to the floor, stripping it down to the stretched canvas on the frame. Wulfric swayed, and Scarlet stepped forward to hold him upright.

"Easy there, wolfie, you're alright now," she murmured

while Elva grabbed folded, clean blankets and furs from the chest at the foot of the bed.

The floor was packed dirt, but several woven rugs overlapped here and there. Wulfric leaned on her, and she stumbled on one. "Fuck, you're heavy. Hold on, wolfie."

"Here, it's ready," Elva said breathlessly, flipping the last of the blankets onto the bed. Scarlet leaned forward, and Wulfric fell onto the now clean bed with a groan.

"Oh, stop your moaning. You're going to be fine," Elva said, poking his leg until he settled on his back. He held one hand over his side as the Elder pulled a blanket over his lap.

Scarlet looked around, biting her lip and trying not to breathe. The smell of musty, sweaty wet dog filled the room, competing with the smell of the wood burning in the fire and something else.

"What is that smell?" Scarlet asked, her sensitive rabbit nose wrinkling in disgust.

Wulfric grunted. "Fucking Brody."

The Elder walked to the side of the tent where dirty bowls and cups were stacked. "The bucket in the corner probably. Can you take it to the attendant outside and ask for a clean one?"

Scarlet jumped at the chance to do something. She wasn't the type to sit by the bed and hold his hand. She needed a purpose, and she didn't know how to help Wulfric recover, but this she could do.

She found the source of the smell and nearly gagged. She picked up the bucket half-full of piss and shit and kicked her way through the door flap, careful not to slosh it.

Three Growlers stood nearby around a communal fire in the center of the four largest tents in camp. As she drew closer, two of the Growlers saw her. Their amiable expressions shifted to wariness as they straightened. The third one with his back to her turned.

Relief surged through her, but the look in his eyes was unreadable. Todd nodded but otherwise didn't acknowledge that they knew each other. She nodded back and set the bucket on the ground.

"The Elder said you'd know where to find a clean bucket. We also need fresh water to clean his wounds."

One snarled. "We don't take orders from the likes of you."

The other elbowed him. "Shut it. The alpha said to respect her."

Todd dipped his head in a pseudo-bow. "Yes, we'll bring fresh water. Probably need fresh blankets and linens too. We'll take care of it, Luna druid."

Scarlet shook her head as unease slid up her spine. What was a Luna? "I'm not a full druid, so none of that. Call me Scarlet."

Todd made a fist and touched his chest with it. "Scarlet, let us know if you need anything else."

Scarlet squared her shoulders and took a deep breath of the fresh air. "Thank you."

She spun on her heel, but as she walked away, her ears picked up the whispers.

"She can't be his mate. Look at her."

"You heard the alpha," Todd replied. "Frigurd, go fetch clean water. Clancy, you take the bucket. Clean it and bring it back."

"What? Why do I have shit duty? Frigurd can take it, and I can get the water."

"No," Todd said firmly. "You insulted her, even though the alpha gave explicit instructions regarding her treatment. You get the shit."

Scarlet grinned as she opened the flap and stepped back inside. Somehow the male Elder had slipped in while she'd been dealing with shit. The man was imperious with his head in the air as he looked around the room disdainfully.

"Disgusting," he muttered, gripping his staff tightly.

"Then clean it," Elva said, slipping around him to sit next to Wulfric. She lifted his head and made him drink from a bowl.

"And get my hands dirty? I think not," the man sighed. "But I will get someone in here to air it out. Give me a few minutes, and I'll be back with reinforcements."

He turned and spied Scarlet. The firelight flickered over his face. Disgust was clear. He was repulsed by her and slightly afraid.

All of the feelings of unease amplified at his expression, reminding her of everywhere she'd ever tried to fit in. First as a kid in the villages, then with the Rangers, the Hunters, and the Robins. She tilted her chin up as her cheeks flushed. She knew her faults, knew she never measured up and wouldn't be welcomed.

But for Wulfric, she would try. Eventually he stepped closer, nodding curtly. "Maiden."

Then he slipped back through the flap and into the night.

"Does he always have a stick up his ass or is this special treatment?" Scarlet asked, striding over to the bed.

Elva didn't look up as she inspected the oozing deep gouges on Wulfric's torso. His breathing was shallow but even. She looked closer and frowned as she realized he'd passed out. She couldn't stand there not helping, so she walked to the kitchen and stacked dishes, holding her breath against the smell.

"Barley? Oh don't mind him. He's always like that."

Frustration licked her stomach, or perhaps it was worry for Wulfric. There was a large, stone bowl with dirty water. She found a pitcher and tipped the dirty water into it before sitting it outside the tent flap.

Scarlet took a deep breath of fresh air and let the flap close, turning back to check on Wulfric. "Good to know. I wasn't sure if he didn't like the fact that I'm a cursed freak or that I'm supposedly Wulfric's mate. But if he's always like that—"

"Always," Elva chuckled. "Why is the mate bond not complete?

Before Scarlet could answer, two females and the two guards she'd given the bucket to came into the tent. Scarlet stepped to the wall of the tent as it became much too crowded too quickly.

Elva met her gaze over the activity and shook her head. She turned to the newcomers and gave orders for cleaning, taking a clean bucket of water from one of the guards.

Scarlet stood, legs wide and ready to bolt out of there as they cleaned the room. Elva woke Wulfric up, and the two guards helped him stand so they could inspect the injuries on his back.

Wulfric wavered on his feet, but his gaze found Scarlet along the wall. He smiled his wolfish, wide grin, and some of the anxiety in her stomach eased.

"There's my bunny. Come cuddle me and make it all better."

One man chuckled, but the two women gave her knowing smiles and grins. The Elder man came through the flap carrying three jars and two vials.

Scarlet shook her head, not taking her eyes off Wulfric. "Your tent is filthy. Let's get it and you cleaned up first."

Wulfric frowned but the one holding him eased him down to the clean bed. He groaned, holding his stomach.

Elva sighed, grabbing the two vials from the other Elder. Their voices were lost over the sounds of the men settling Wulfric onto the bed, someone clanging the bowls as they cleaned and another hauling the dirty blankets out the door.

Scarlet felt helpless just watching and observing. She'd done this countless times in taverns and villages across Busparia. She'd sat and watched, gathering information and making a plan.

But this was so different. She didn't have a plan, didn't know what would happen after tomorrow. And underneath it all was worry over Wulfric.

Worry? Hells, she was terrified he'd die and leave her in the middle of the Growlers' tribe alone. It wasn't just the thought of being alone that scared her. She genuinely didn't want him to die. Ever.

Logically, she knew his wounds weren't that bad. She knew the biggest threat would be internal injuries, the way they'd pummeled each other.

She'd been helpless to stop it, and it made her angry that she'd had to watch and do nothing.

She frowned and crossed her arms. Fucking Growler, making her care for him. The urge to protect him, hell, even the urge to gather him into her arms and just hold him, was unnerving. It made her feel raw, vulnerable, and weak, and she hated feeling like that.

Finally, the others gave that little nod bow and left, leaving only her, Wulfric, and the two Elders.

The man assisted Elva but turned in the silence and met Scarlet's gaze. "If he survives the night, then he'll be fine. There's no internal bleeding that we can see, but there's a rattle in his chest that I don't like."

Elva settled her hand on his chest and muttered under her breath. Green magic spread from her hand over his skin, making the soft, short fur ripple with the wave.

When it faded, she looked up and smiled at Scarlet. "He should sleep fine. I'll stand watch, Barley. You get some sleep and come relieve me in a few hours?"

The man frowned, still looking at Scarlet, but nodded. "Very well. I'll check on Nomani and Brody first. Maiden."

He gave the nod bow and slipped through the door.

"Come, child. Let's sit by the fire. We have much to discuss," Elva said as she leaned her staff against the bed frame and sank onto a cushion close to the fire. She crossed her legs, the slit up the sides parting for her knees.

Scarlet sat next to her on another cushion as the woman smiled into the fire. "Now, tell me your story."

Scarlet took a deep breath and forced her shoulders to relax as she crossed her legs too. She put her chin in her palm, resting her elbow on her knee.

"I'm not sure where to begin. Maybe it started thirty years ago when Growlers killed my mother at my grandmother's cottage?"

Elva nodded, "Hm, I see. And what do you know of those events?"

Scarlet shook her head as an icy chill ran down her spine. "What do you mean? It was a simple attack of opportunity. Mother was at the cottage alone, unprotected, and slaughtered."

Elva sighed and lumbered to her feet. "Actually, there's more to it than that. Let me put on a pot of tea, as this may take a while."

Scarlet's heart raced for new reasons now. She took a shaky breath, trying to regulate her emotions. She was so tired and shaking from hunger, but at least she wasn't cold anymore. At least they were safe… but some sixth sense told her she'd not like what the Elder had to say. Dread spread through her stomach, twisting it like a vise.

# Chapter Twenty-Five

Elva hummed as she poured the tea, then sat back on her cushion with a sigh. "Drink up, dear. You look bone tired and dead on your feet."

Scarlet sniffed, the spices making her nose twitch. The first sip burned as it went down, smoother than any ale she'd ever drank.

When she opened her eyes, there was a green haze in the tent.

Green flared up and the smoke formed images. It was similar to Eirwyn's magic with light, but softer. The image sharpened but was still like looking through water.

Scarlet blinked. "Grandma's cottage," she whispered.

Elva nodded, but Scarlet wasn't paying her any attention. There was her dad on a horse. He was tense and reined in hard, his mouth opening on a shout.

She ached to hear his voice, but she couldn't catch her own breath to ask the Elder if that were possible.

Her mother came rushing out the door, wiping her

hands on an apron. Dad pointed behind him, and Ma shook her head then raced inside.

Dad swung down from the horse just as Ma came out with a tiny little redheaded girl sleeping in her arms. Dad took the girl and nodded for Ma to get on the horse. Ma shook her head and pushed him toward the horse.

She waved to the barn, where the door burst open. Another horse pranced nervously outside toward the cottage. She waved to the horse, frantic as she clearly told Dad to leave.

Both of them froze and turned to stare to the right. A shiver went up Scarlet's spine, dread settling like a knot in her stomach.

Elva whispered, "They heard the howls of the Growlers."

Ma turned and shot a white ball of energy at Dad and the horse. They flew through the woods as if blown by a gust of wind, somehow missing every single densely packed tree.

Scarlet's hands shook as Ma turned to the howls just as Grandma stumbled into the clearing and collapsed.

Blood dripped down her face, and Ma raced to her, mouth open in anguish as she gathered Grandma into her arms. Frantic yet gentle movements, she practically carried Grandma to the cottage, each step shaking and weak.

The horse nuzzled Ma's shoulder, and she glanced up. With a flurry of magic, she had Grandma draped over the back of the horse, then slapped its flank. In an instant, they were off, galloping into the woods with a trail of glowing magic left behind in their wake.

Ma turned in the clearing just as a dozen Growlers came through the trees. But they weren't just any Growlers. they were larger, more muscular and formidable than any

Scarlet had ever seen before—all except for Wulfric. Fear gripped Scarlet's heart as she gazed on her mother's killers.

They wore the colors of the Buspartan army. There were no weapons, but they were Growlers. No weapons were necessary.

The image hovered in the air as they closed in on Ma, and she turned and ran into the cottage. The door slammed, but they burst inside. Scarlet felt her throat close up with each step.

Elva whispered again. "Those are not our Growlers nor do we know where they came from. We can guess. When your grandmother came to our camp, she killed dozens of our warriors before I could calm her enough to listen. This is what I showed her, the truth of that day."

The image dissipated, and Scarlet could finally take a breath.

"The truth?" The question was raw, and Scarlet sipped the tea with a shaking hand to dislodge the knot. But it wouldn't leave.

"Aye, those were Buspartan men. Not ours. Your grandmother and I interrogated the other four Growler camps, but none of them could identify those men. We even sought the help of the goddess at the ruins."

"And what did you find?" Scarlet asked harshly. Anger welled within her to mingle with the grief. Why had her grandma kept this from her all this time?

"More about the prophecy. More about the dragon hatching, which sent your grandmother racing home to the cottage."

Scarlet stared unseeing into the now normal fire. "That was when Knox's shell had begun to crack, the first crack in hundreds of years of the druids protecting it." Emotions swirled through her, and it took several minutes for her to breathe through them.

The Elder finally broke the silence. "The slaughter of our warriors birthed a legend among the Growlers. The druids were always revered, but now even more so. You will be safe here, especially now that Wulfric has claimed you as his mate."

Scarlet looked at the woman. "Except we haven't really completed the bond, have we." It wasn't a question, but she did have one for the woman.

"What will happen if we don't?"

Elva's brows rose. "If you don't finish the mate bond?"

Scarlet nodded, hoping that Wulfric had lied about that too.

Elva frowned. "Then you will both die. No other Growler has ever lived through a mate rejection."

Scarlet swallowed hard and turned to stare into the fire again. A knot of dread settled in her gut as the truth hit her. She would *have* to complete the mate bond process. It wasn't such a big deal, was it? After all, she enjoyed fucking him.

She frowned. "And we just bite each other in the heat of the moment?"

Elva's lips quirked and her eyes were mischievous. "That's about it. You'll need to say vows to each other to seal the magical bond, but that's all it is."

"I will leave you to contemplate your choices and these truths." Elva shifted onto her feet and went to the corner, settling into a wide, wooden rocking chair.

She settled her hands on her lap and nodded to Wulfric. "Wake me if he needs me, dear. Or you too, for that matter."

Scarlet stared into the fire and took a deep breath, the

images of her mother playing through her mind. As a Hunter, she was trained to pick up on details, and she needed to go through each image of those Growlers one by one.

She leaned back against the side of the bed, Wulfric lying near her head on the canvas mattress. His breathing was deep and seemed to be stronger than before her chat with Elva.

In her mind, she analyzed each of the Growlers who had attacked her mother. The detailed combing of her memories made her eyes grow heavy until she finally fell asleep.

A soft hand stroked her hair, just behind her rabbit ear. Her foot bounced as she drifted slowly awake. A soft mewling sound made her eyes flicker awake.

Elva snored in the rocking chair in the corner. The fire had died down. She swallowed hard and straightened, grabbing a few logs and adding them to the fire.

When it blazed brighter, she finally turned to see Wulfric staring up at her from the bed.

He smiled softly and patted the bed with a palm. "Come lay down, bunny. We need rest for tomorrow."

"How are you feeling?" She didn't deny him. Her sleepy state made her more pliable to his demands. She frowned even as she climbed over him to lay down next to the canvas wall of the tent.

"Much better now that you're here," he said, drawing her head down to rest on his shoulder. He sighed a deep breath, his body relaxing once more.

"How are *you* feeling?" He stroked her hair, adjusting her head so that her horn didn't stab him in the neck or eye.

She yawned and snuggled closer to him, pulling a blanket over them both. "Tired. Elva... she showed me how my mother died."

He tensed beneath her. "Oh?"

Scarlet nodded, closing her eyes once more. "It was the Buspartan Growlers. They wore the dragon circlet on their shoulders."

"What's that mean?"

She yawned again. "It means they were Hunters, sent to kill my mother or my grandmother."

"Hunters? Like you?"

She nodded, pain pressing on her chest. "Yes, I've heard whispers of an elite band of Hunters known only as Dragon Claws. They don't answer summons from the Hunter's Guild Masters, not in any of the cities I've worked in. They're elusive, to say the least. I thought they were a myth until I saw the circlet."

The more she spoke, the more tense she became. "Shh," he said, kissing her head and stroking her hair once more. "We'll find them and figure out why together. Don't worry, bunny. You're not alone in this."

Not alone. She relaxed into his arms. It was nice to not be alone.

---

"Are you sure I have to be there?" Scarlet asked, tugging at her new Growler's clothing. She'd chosen to keep her black pants and green shirt under it.

He just smiled as she cinched the leather vest over the top of it. It was her armor, and she wouldn't feel comfortable without it, he knew.

"Yes, as my mate, you need to stand by my side."

"But we haven't completed the mate bond," she pointed out.

He splashed water on his face and arched a brow at

where she sat on the bed, lacing up her boots. "Not from lack of trying on my part," he murmured.

She sat up and glared at him. He wiped his face with a towel and then strode to the end of the bed to fetch his fancier clothes. He wanted to impress her, and this was a big pack meeting. He had to remind his people what the alpha looked like.

He pulled on his soft leather pants, tying on a beaded belt.

"Look, I know we're not mated yet, but if anyone asks, we'll tell them that we were waiting for the full moon to complete it."

"That would be a lie," she said, glaring at him. "I don't like that you lie so easily, Wulfric."

His brows rose. "I do?"

She nodded. "You lied about only going to recon the guards. You said you wouldn't come into camp, but you did."

He frowned and pulled on his beaded doe-skin shirt. She gulped and paled, then glanced away with arms crossed.

He shifted his gaze from her to the shirt, noting how its color almost perfectly matched her skin—a delicate and natural shade of doe-like brown, with a hint of rosy under-tones. With a frustrated huff, he swiftly discarded the shirt back into the chest and pulled out another one. This time, it was a crisp white shirt with shimmering silver beads and thread delicately stitched into intricate patterns.

"I'm sorry about coming into camp without you. It was not intentional. I had to roll with what was happening in the moment. I did not intend to lie to you, bunny."

She looked up at him, her frown deep as she demanded, "Do you intend to lie to me again?"

He shook his head, as solemn as her. "Never."

She pursed her lips and then dropped her hands into her lap. She dug at her nails, then pulled her dagger from her pants' sheath to clean under them.

"Bunny? What's really wrong here?" He asked, sitting on the side of the bed.

She took a deep breath and sighed. "I don't like crowds. I freeze up, can't talk. If you need me to say something in that meeting, I—I probably won't be able to."

He reached over and stroked her cheek until she looked up at him. Her gaze was fierce as she pointed the knife at him, but he didn't pay it any mind.

"If you need someone to have your back, I'll be there every time. I'll protect you," she said, biting her lip and looking down at the knife. "But I can't speak up."

He gently took her chin between his finger and thumb. "You can speak or not, it doesn't matter to me," he said softly, peppering gentle kisses to the edges of her mouth.

She swayed closer, but the flap of the tent flew back. A guard stepped in and narrowed his gaze between the two as Scarlet pulled back and put her dagger away.

"Alpha, the Elders said they are ready for you," Todd said.

"Thank you. We're on our way." Wulfric took her hand and stood, striding toward the door.

She sighed and barely dug in her heels as they strode the few feet to the longhouse.

Many were already sitting on either side of the room. Wulfric tucked her hand in his elbow and circled the room, talking quietly with each table.

He chuckled where needed, asked after children and how certain people had been treated in the past few days under Brody's reign of terror.

When they finally turned to walk to the raised dais at the end of the room, Scarlet leaned closer.

"Brody didn't treat them too badly, did he?"

Wulfric shook his head and led her to the empty seats beside the Elders. "No, a few of my loyal supporters were knocked around. Two of the females were fighting over him, but no one was killed, which I'm relieved about."

They sat and several people brought food. Soup, ale, venison, potatoes, and gravy. Wulfric nearly inhaled everything that was set in front of him. After days going without, he was famished.

Scarlet ate all the soup, but pushed the venison to the side to eat the rest of her food.

Wulfric leaned back and waved to the head server. When the man came closer, he said softly, "No venison or rabbit for my mate. Is there any other meat for her?"

The server paled, glancing at her horns and ears, then nodded and spun on his heel.

Elva looked at him from around Scarlet and nodded her approval. Then she pointed her head toward the crowd.

He wiped his mouth and leaned back in his chair while Elva stood. The chattering crowd quieted as she spoke.

"Last night, the alpha challenge question was settled. Wulfric is the uncontested alpha of the tribe. Are there any other challengers?"

The crowd remained silent, and the server brought Scarlet an entire roasted chicken with savory mushrooms, carrots, potatoes, and herbs.

He crossed his arms and said, "Alright, does anyone want to represent Brody's faction and actually discuss the problems and solutions?"

The chatter in the room died almost instantly. No one

moved for a few precious seconds. Elva elbowed him, and he sighed, raking his hand through his hair.

"Look, I know this tribe has always been ruled by the Alpha and the Elders. But I meant what I said. We're a family, and families talk about these things. So please, if we're going to move forward as one, we need to work through this. Why did Brody say I was a bad alpha? If I've done something that led any of you to think that, please come forward now so I can be better."

He let his words ring through the room before he continued. "There are a lot of changes and more to come. I know it can be scary, especially since I'm going to propose a treaty with the dragon king to the north, but—"

The gasps from the crowd rose, and Elva stood, staff in hand. "Alright, before we get into what to do for our future, I feel that we must settle what happened with our past, both the turned and the natural born."

Several people shifted uneasily in their seats, the air thick with tension and barely concealed doubt. Murmurs stirred along the edges of the circle until Elva rose and tapped her staff once on the stone floor. It pulsed green, casting a shimmering light upward, and in the center of the room, an image unfolded like mist drawn from memory— an older version of their camp, wild and untamed, but brimming with life.

"Long ago," Elva said, her voice calm but heavy with meaning, "Growlers lived in harmony with the forest. We were not just protectors, but partners—working beside druids, dragons, and the spirits of root and river. Our blood ran warm with the blessing of the gods, and our kind were born, not made."

Nomani stood, her staff glowing violet as she added her

magic to the vision. The image shifted—dragons overhead, fire in the distance, the trees shrieking in silent agony.

"When the dragon war scorched the land, we fought to protect the forest, but the damage was done. The ley lines twisted. The gods retreated. And our numbers... they fell. Too few births, too many lost. We were dying out."

Barley stood, his staff burning blue as he fed his power into the flickering vision. "The gods heard us. Or perhaps just one. A way was given—rituals, herbs, and firelight. The druids helped us decipher it. With their guidance, we learned to turn others. Desperate humans, broken souls. We offered them strength, and in return, they became Growlers."

"But the first turned..." Elva's voice softened. "They lost everything. Their past, their names, their faces. The transformation replaced their essence. They had only two shapes: beast and hybrid. The human part—gone."

"The tea sustains them," Nomani added. "A sacred brew that mimics the Morphyx gland. Without it, they died. They're not like us, not truly. They weren't born shifters. They were made."

The image twisted again, turning to a vision of frost creeping through the forest, blanketing trees in white as a storm darkened the skies.

Barley grunted. "Look outside. That storm doesn't feel like normal weather. We've all noticed that the winter isn't lifting but growing stronger. It's the prophecy."

Nomani nodded solemnly. "The Elders have sought answers. The goddess gave us this: 'When dragons ride once more, Growlers will regain what they've lost. Only when the dragons, Growlers, and druids unite will they stop the evil one and turn back the ice.'"

Gasps rippled through the crowd. The image faded slowly, but the chill remained. Nomani's voice dropped.

"Some of the turned started regaining their memories last year. The old blood stirred, the time of the prophecy drawing closer, ever since the dragon king of the north reclaimed his rightful throne."

"Rightful?" someone cried out.

"This is our forest, not his!" someone else shouted.

Elva slammed her staff to the ground. "His parents were the dragon kings of this forest before we were ever created by the gods. It is time we worked with the dragons and druids once more."

Barley sniffed. "Brody swayed many of you with talk of regaining your place in society, of leaving the woods."

Elva turned to him expectantly, her bright eyes shining in the half-light. Wulfric stood, and every eye fixed on him.

"Brody wanted to go back home to Busparia once he realized what he'd lost. After we regained all our memories last night, I understand how he felt. However, if we want to be accepted, we must be cautious. We can't just go running into Busparia trying to claim what was once ours. Growlers who leave the forest are never heard from again. We need allies."

"Aye, and what makes you think the dragons are going to help us?" someone shouted.

"You have homes there, families even. So just go already. Why wait around for some dragon who may not even listen?" Jamison said, crossing his arms. There would always be a few dissenters from the old guard who were more vocal about all the turned Growlers just leaving.

Elva grabbed Scarlet's hand and lifted it in the air, drawing her to her feet. Scarlet didn't speak, and her face blushed, but she didn't back away. She stood tall, her scent revealing her terror, as Elva spoke.

"The dragon will listen because the alpha's mate will help bridge the gap between our worlds. It's as the goddess decreed ages ago."

Wulfric nodded and took Scarlet's other hand, linking their fingers together and letting her know that he was right there by her side.

"I don't know what the goddess said," he said loudly, not taking his eyes from Scarlet. "But she will learn our ways and help us form a treaty with the dragons to the north, as the dragon king is her brother."

More gasps from the crowd before the chatter grew louder. Scarlet's eyes flashed, and her lips pursed, making him frown. What had he said that displeased her? It was all the truth, wasn't it?

# Chapter Twenty-Six

Scarlet fumed, caught between a rock and a hard place. What the fuck? They hadn't talked about this at all.

He knew she needed to break her curse and gain revenge on the queen. Didn't he? Had he not been paying attention? She'd thought he was a decent listener for a man, but she had no plan of staying in the Growlers camp, no matter the mate situation.

Although… his talk earlier of living their lives together had melted something in her chest. *Did* she want that? Would she ever be accepted here?

Her lips pursed in annoyance, but she didn't interrupt. Being the center of attention made her clam up, paralyzing her. Frustration mounted in the crowd, then questions flew at them.

"What in the hells is she?"

"Is the dragon as dangerous as they say? He's real?"

"Where is the druid? What of her? Is she going to attack us again?"

"What about going into Busparia?"

Wulfric held up the hand that wasn't holding hers. "We have to work with the dragons first, gather information on Busparia and the political climate. I'm assuming everyone got their memories back last night, if you hadn't had them before?"

The crowd nodded, and one Elder said, "The time has come, and the memories were finally released by the gods as the prophecy says. When dragons ride once more, Growlers will regain what they've lost. The born Growlers and the turned are truly one people now."

"I lost my people when I was turned," someone yelled as the crowd's voices rose to a crescendo. Elva slammed her staff to the ground, and magic burst out from the center images, scattering and quieting the group.

Wulfric finally turned to address the people. "I know you must be eager to rush back to your families, but it's been years. We can send inquiries and check on them, but we can't go ourselves. Not yet."

Scarlet tugged on his hand, and he leaned over to her. She whispered, "Tell them about the Growlers that killed my mother."

Wulfric nodded, and she sat down, forcing Wulfric and Elva to release her hands. She wiped them on her pants as he shared the still-raw information. Her stomach twisted at being the center of attention.

"The king of Busparia has an elite band of Hunters known as the Dragon Claws. Has anyone heard of them?"

No one spoke up, but several shook their heads, so Wulfric continued. "They are a threat to us because they are Growlers too."

Gasps around the room echoed in the mighty chamber, making her flinch. Wulfric put his hand on her shoulder and brushed his thumb back and forth. It soothed her even as he continued to speak to the crowd.

"They are the Growlers that attacked the druids thirty years ago and killed Scarlet's mother."

Elva said, "We don't know why, but every Growler that has gone into Busparia from various tribes has never returned. We only assume the Dragon Claws either took them or killed them. It would be a fool's errand to go check on your families without ensuring a way to survive."

"How are we supposed to go home, then?" The crowd's murmurs grew louder, but Wulfric didn't give them a moment to gain momentum. He was a good leader, like Knox but more confident. Of course, he'd had several years of leading them whereas Knox had only been officially king for a few months.

She stood and whispered into Wulfric's ear. Then he turned to address the crowd, telling them what she'd said.

"The dragons in the northern half of the forest have a better network because they have the Hunters on their side. Scarlet brought them with her when they left Busparia. They can blend in better with the locals, find information on our families, and see if it's safe for us to come out into the open."

"How can they blend in with the locals? Just look at her." She flinched at the words and sank back into her seat, her shoulders hunching.

Wulfric's eyes flashed golden bright as his hand settled on her shoulder again. She wouldn't have seen it had she not been looking at him. His jaw elongated and his hands shifted into claws as he barked out, "Don't you dare speak of her like that."

Scarlet laid her hand on his where it rested on her shoulder. He looked down, and his claws receded.

He cleared his throat and frowned, taking a deep breath before he said, "The former king of Busparia cursed her twice, which is part of the reason she's here. She seeks to break the curses, which I'm hopeful our Elders can assist with."

"And if they can't be broken?" The jerks in the crowd were really starting to annoy her. Her fingers hovered over her daggers, itching to spin them.

Wulfric looked down into her eyes and smiled softly. "It doesn't matter to me whether they can be broken or not. She's perfect the way she is, and she is my mate regardless. The gods don't make mistakes."

The reminder of the gods' role in fated mates caused the crowd's murmurs to die down. Wulfric squeezed her shoulder gently, pride filling his gaze and making her chest ache. This wouldn't last, but she soaked up his support.

"My mate is one of the best Hunters in the land," he said proudly. His posture dared any of them to argue, but the crowd was silent for once.

"You saw her fight last night, but that's not even the half of it. She will be a great asset to our tribe, trust me." His words were a balm to her soul, making her yearn for acceptance and a home. She wasn't sure she wanted that to be here in the Growlers camp though.

The crowd grumbled once more. "Only if you finish the mate bond."

"Aye, if you don't, you're both dead."

"Then we'll go into Busparia and surely die from these other Growlers."

"Or the Hunters."

"Or the army."

"Or the winter."

Scarlet stiffened, and Wulfric arched a brow, reminding

her of their plan from earlier. He'd somehow known it would come to this. She pursed her lips, sniffed, and nodded slightly. His grin widened as his eyes darkened with desire, locking with hers in a promise that made her toes curl.

His chest puffed out as he turned to the crowd. "We had planned to complete the mate bond tonight with the full moon. What could be more romantic?"

The crowd chuckled and seemed to relax at the news.

Elva cleared her throat. "Now that that question's settled, there are two betas from other tribes here today, and the other two will arrive tomorrow, after the full moon tonight. Our alpha will discuss what's to be done with them."

Wulfric nodded, turning to the crowd. "I'll meet with the other tribal emissaries and discuss a possible treaty with the dragons. Once negotiations are over and we're all in agreement, I will go to the dragons with Scarlet and propose the treaty. Scarlet will help organize the Hunters to check on the turned families and see how we can safely find them."

Someone in the crowd interrupted. "What if they kill you? What if they won't work with us?"

Wulfric grinned, and Scarlet's heart pounded at the wolfish, predatory gleam on his face. "Oh, they will work with us, if they know what's good for them. We're Growlers, after all."

Uneasy chuckles rang through the crowd, but she saw several smiles as the tension dissipated. They were a proud people, she was coming to realize. The murmurs around the tables about a treaty made them nervous. They were afraid they'd lose their identity and culture. They were already struggling to reconcile their memories and previous identities.

Barley and Nomani sat down while Elva explained how

the Elders would start collecting a list of people to check on in Busparia. They would be in the longhouse tomorrow morning for brunch after the full moon run tonight.

The crowd's temper seemed to lighten at the mention of the full moon, and soon dancing broke out in the center of the sunken floor. A stringed instrument and hide drums added to the noise, and soon there were smiles and ale flowing wherever she looked. Wulfric sat beside her as a berry dessert was laid on the table. She ate and a line formed to the side of the table.

One by one, Growlers approached them. Some simply came to chat and opened up more than when they first entered about what Brody had promised them.

Some shared their experiences as humans, how they were turned, and told Wulfric how much they approved of this plan to restore them to their families.

Then the two Growlers who'd helped Brody—the ones she'd fought—both came forward, flanked by a guard. Each of them swore allegiance to Wulfric, one of them explaining that he'd left a pregnant wife when he'd gone to war and been injured less than a year after leaving.

He accepted their fealty, but assigned them to shit duty for the entire camp for the next month.

Sasha came up to the table and smiled shyly at Scarlet. She waved to the rather round woman behind her in the soft doe-skin dress.

"This is my mam. I wanted to introduce you, and let you know that I dropped your pack inside the alpha's tent." She bobbed a crude curtsy with one fist to her chest, then backed away.

The woman eyed Scarlet, making her spine straighten. Then her pinched lips softened and wobbled slightly. She leaned over the table, and Scarlet leaned forward. Wulfric frowned and tensed beside her, but Scarlet simply took his hand and squeezed.

"I'm grateful to you. My girl should've been at home where she belonged, and it was within your right to—to..." She trailed off, pursing her lips once more.

Now that everyone wasn't staring at her, now that she was one on one, she found her voice.

Scarlet sighed, her own lips softening and she whispered, "It's alright. I'm glad she was the one I met. The goddess must've sent her there for a reason."

"I'm glad too, Luna. Me too." She likewise bobbed a shallow curtsy with fist on chest and stepped aside for the next person in line to speak with them.

Scarlet leaned over to Wulfric to ask, "Luna?"

He grinned and nipped at her neck, just below her ear. "Alpha's mate and queen." She blushed and leaned back as the next person stepped up to talk to him.

Hours later, dusk was falling and the moon rose as Wulfric led her past the central fire pit where they'd fought Brody the night before. He tucked her hand into the crook of his elbow like a gentleman. She'd seen lords escort ladies at balls like this, when she'd snuck in for a kill. It sent a thrill through her that he treated her with such reverence. They explored the rest of the camp, and she kept pinching herself in a reminder that this was real. Not just him and how he treated her, but this village.

Instead of the bloodthirsty savages she'd expected, the werewolf camp bustled with... domesticity. On the other side of the tents, fluffy white sheep grazed peacefully in fenced pastures, werewolves in human form using pitchforks to toss hay off a cart.

"What the hell is this?" The surprise in her voice made it higher than normal.

Wulfric chuckled at her shock and patted her hand. "Surprised, bunny? I told you we're not the monsters your grandmother warned you about."

"But... but you eat people," Scarlet muttered.

He rolled his eyes. "More so in the old tales than in modern times. These days, we prefer mutton. Less screaming, more wool sweaters. Besides, we only attack people who step into our territory. Those deaths or turnings are entirely justified."

Now she was the one to roll her eyes, but she didn't argue with him. She'd often used such logic with her own mercenary assassinations.

Scarlet's mind reeled as she tried to reconcile this bizarre reality of Growlers with everything she thought she knew. The fearsome werewolves... were sheep farmers? It was too absurd.

"And you pack all this up to move every few months?"

He nodded, "Everything except the longhouse. We have three primary locations and two secondary ones per each of the five tribes. We move based on seasons, hunting availability, and livestock rotations so we never deplete the land's resources. It's been getting leaner with each year though."

"Because the population is growing so much?" She'd deduced as much from the conversations in the longhouse.

He led her around the perimeter of the sheep pens. "Yes, when the Busparian king withdrew from the war with Glathen, we watched the Southern Road and saved as many of those they left to die as possible. But we were already maxed on our resources by then. The past year, we've spent so much time trying to stretch every last resource."

"But sheep?" Her voice was still high with incredulity.

He chuckled. "We're tied to each camp long enough to cultivate feed, but the livestock is the only way we're able to survive the harsh winters. All the wild animals hole up or hibernate, and it's tough to hunt when we're all freezing our balls off too."

She chuckled as they left the pens, passed the chicken coops, and went back around the tents. The joyous chaos around her increased as the full moon crested the trees, the Growlers nearly vibrating with energy. Wolves and humans alike raced by them, laughing and chasing each other. Even the kids who weren't able to shift yet were awake and giddy, just waiting for the full moon to rise fully.

He rubbed his jaw and said, "Every year, there's a debate about cutting down our seasonal moves and staying in one spot longer. Perhaps now it's time to encourage that. Put down roots. Would you like a house or a home base for your Hunter work?"

She frowned and looked to the ground as the sun set through the trees. Her stomach twisted at his words. She hadn't realized how much his announcement in the long-house had bothered her.

She blew out a breath slowly. "I don't like how you just said that in front of everyone."

"Is that why you were upset with me in the meeting," he asked softly, tensing under her hand.

She nodded, watching more kids kick a leather ball. "You said I was going to stay here when you know very well I have no intention of it."

He paused, turning to face her and gently lifting her chin so he could meet her gaze. "I did, yes, but I spoke out of hope, not from certainty."

She frowned. "Hope?"

"Yes," he said nodding, taking her hands in his and blowing hot air to warm them. "I want you here with me, Scarlet. I won't lie about that."

"And do what? Sit by the fire, darn your socks, and pop out your babies?"

She frowned and tried to pull her hands away, but he held firm. His grin drew her actions to a halt. Her stomach twisted with that smile. She didn't want to stay here with him. She didn't.

*Yeah, keep telling yourself that.*

"I'll darn your socks if you darn mine." His grin was wide and his eyes twinkled, making her stomach flip.

She rolled her eyes and scowled. "You don't even wear socks half the time."

He chuckled, and the sound slithered down her spine and straight to the aching need between her legs.

"I want you to have my pups, yes. I want to see you round with my babe. But I also want to fight by your side, and I'd never ask you to give up the Hunters. Although I'd like you to be my eyes and ears with the people so I never have a surprise like Brody again. I want to be a better leader, Scarlet, and I think you can help with that. Can't we do all of it?"

She frowned and shrugged. She'd been the power behind the throne for the head of the Hunter's Guild for years, and now she juggled that and helping Knox. Was it really any different?

Reluctantly, she said, "I don't know, Wulfric. I don't know if I—I can live here."

She liked feeling useful, but it wasn't the same as being accepted. Whether the Growlers accepted her or not was another matter entirely. She'd gotten some shy smiles from the kids while they'd waited by the fire for the moon to rise, but most stayed away or stared warily.

He grinned and tugged her closer, wrapping his arms around her waist and back. "Give me time to convince you. You were made for me, bunny, and we belong together."

She stared into the fire and swallowed hard, avoiding his gaze. "Were you serious about finishing the mate bond tonight?"

His smile faded, but he didn't release her. "I was, Scarlet. We need to complete the process. If we complete it tonight, we can sort out the treaty details over the next few days, then travel together to see your brother. If after all this is settled and your curses are cured, you still want nothing to do with me or the Growlers... well, we can discuss it when the time comes. But until then, let's work together to survive, and that includes completing the mate bond. Can you do that?"

She felt a knot build in her throat and her eyes burned. It wasn't a declaration of love. It was practical, and something she could definitely understand. It made sense, and she didn't want an emotional entanglement anyway.

Yet her chest was heavy as she nodded and pursed her lips. "Very well. We'll complete the mate bond. I'd hate for you to have lied to your people, after all."

He grinned and dipped his head, his lips meeting hers and sending a zing of awareness. She licked her lips, her tongue flicking against his. He groaned and dove inside, plundering her mouth like a starving man, right there in front of the entire tribe.

Her stomach flipped, and her heart raced. It was more than just the sexual need building within her. He tasted like acceptance and love, even though he'd not said the words. Several Growlers hooted nearby, breaking into the overwhelming feelings this one kiss evoked.

"Alpha, alpha, alpha," the chant built in intensity. Wulfric groaned, and she felt it reverberate through them both. It made her giggle, and he broke the kiss to lean his forehead against hers.

"Gods, I'm sorry," he whispered.

She laughed softly. "For what?"

He leaned back and grinned, that mischievous look sending a shot of pure desire straight to her core. "For this."

Then he leaned over and tucked her stomach against him, throwing her over his shoulder and standing. She squealed, her hands settling on his lower back as he strode toward his tent. A roar went through the crowd, clapping and taunting him.

"There ya go! Get your Luna!"

"We have a Luna! Finally!"

Their words carried on the wind, and Scarlet laughed as Wulfric slapped her ass, saying over his shoulder, "I'll join the run later. First, the mate bond."

A cheer rang through the crowd, and Scarlet's cheeks flushed. She felt lighter than air, and not just because Wulfric carried her so effortlessly. The other Growlers had seemed happy to have her here, even if they were wary and hesitant. Perhaps this was where she'd finally be accepted and welcomed. She wouldn't trust it, but their words gave her hope.

She sighed as he set her on her feet and held the tent flap. It was time to finish this.

# Chapter Twenty-Seven

When they entered the tent, the fire was roaring. Someone had stoked it while they'd mingled with the pack outside. It was almost fully dark, and he could feel the moon rising. Soon the full moon would beam down at them through the hole in the ceiling. He wanted to time it so that they completed the bond at that exact moment. He wanted it to be perfect for her.

The glockenberry would be wearing off any day now, and the need for her to claim him back had risen with every hour they'd been in camp. A sense of urgency stole over him, and he led her to the bed, his stomach in knots.

She tilted her head. "Are you nervous?" The incredulity in her voice made him wince and shrug.

"Gods, yes. I don't even remember being this nervous when I got married."

She sat on the edge of the bed and leaned forward to unlace her boots. "Tell me about her?"

Wulfric reached behind his head and tugged his shirt off. It was probably against some rule to talk about a previous

285

wife to his new mate, but he wouldn't deny her. She could ask for the moon itself, and he'd hunt the heavens and Celawynn itself to bring it to her.

He tossed his shirt into his chest of clothes. "She was the daughter of the tavern owners. I first noticed her at our village school before I could even read, but never talked to her until we were older. She always had her group of friends, and I had mine."

Scarlet set her boots by the chest at the foot of the bed. "Was she beautiful?"

He paused, picturing her easy smile with the dimple on one side. "I always thought so. Deep brown hair like newly varnished oak and eyes to match. Gods, those eyes. She could've had anyone in the village. Hells, in all of Busparia. Yet she chose me, much to her parents' dismay."

He shoved his pants down, throwing it into his chest.

"They didn't like you? Why ever not?" Her surprised anger made him chuckle as he laid on the bed, hands behind his head and ankles crossed. He watched as she unlaced her vest and set it on top of her boots, her face indignant on his behalf.

"I wasn't good enough. My parents had raised me to run the general store, but her parents had lofty goals for their precious daughter. They wanted a noble who would provide for her. She loved to read, and they wanted someone who would let her read to her heart's content instead of working her hands raw."

"So they spoiled her." Scarlet's voice was flat now as she pushed her pants down and folded them, adding them to her pile of clothes.

He shifted on the bed, growing impossibly hard as he watched her undress. "Not really. They just loved her so much and wanted the best for her."

Scarlet paused and frowned in confusion. "But that would've been you. You're the best."

Her sincerity made his chest swell with emotion, and he leaned up on one elbow. "Ah, bunny, your words are a balm to my soul. Look at what you've done to the captain now."

He waved a hand at his crotch, and her eyes dropped as she grabbed the bottom of her borrowed shirt. She licked her lips as his shaft lengthened out of its sheath, growing thick and heavy. She shook her head and chuckled, eyes glancing away and head going high as she pulled her arms out of the shirt.

"Seriously, that nickname is ridiculous."

He grinned and palmed his dick, sliding his hand up slowly. "At least I remember now why I call it that."

"Your wife?" Scarlet paused, but he shook his head.

"No, actually. Shortly after I arrived in the army's camp in Glathen, I was promoted to captain. Then the camp followers started hounding me. They gave it that nickname, and it sort of stuck."

Her shoulders relaxed at the explanation, and she swept her shirt up and over her head. It only caught a moment in her little antlers, then she was tossing it to the floor with the rest.

"Did you fuck the camp followers?" When she met his gaze, her cheeks were flushed and her gaze accusatory.

He sat up, his hands settling on either side of his hips on the bed. "I did, yes. I'm not proud of it, but I'm not going to pretend that I've been celibate since my wife died or in the past ten years since I've been a Growler."

Her breathing changed, growing shallow, and her pupils dilated, pushing the deep green aside. "Very well, but if any of the Growler women in camp make a reference to intimately knowing *the captain*, I'll gut them before they even see the blades."

He laughed, reaching for her hips just to be able to touch her and swinging his knees to brace her between them. He looked up into her fierce face, his chest full of emotion. "Ah I love when you get all protective and growly."

She scowled and tried to pull away. "Well, don't get used to it. Just because we're completing the mate bond and are working together to keep the forest safe doesn't mean we're going to live happily ever after."

He heard her words, saw her stiffen and hold herself away from him. The scent of fear emanating from her was palpable. Not the frantic, fight-or-flight fear of imminent danger, but a more subtle and complex fear. The fear of vulnerability and potential heartache, the fear of taking a chance on someone new. It wafted off of her in waves, mingling with the natural fragrance of her skin and creating an aura of trepidation around her.

His fingers flexed on her hips, his claws growing as his own flare of possessiveness made his chest burn. He wanted her to give in and trust him to not leave, to take care of her, to be a true partner in life. He didn't want to take away her independence, but there was no way he could let her go now that he'd found her.

He tugged her nipple into his mouth, making her back arch as she gasped. Her hands fisted at her sides as she stood proud, not bending to his will.

Gods, she was amazing.

The smell of her wetness rose to slap him in the face, and he sucked in a breath. He nuzzled her breast as he went to the other, saying, "If you think I'm letting you go, you're crazier than I thought."

She arched a brow, her soft smile slipping into a flash of vulnerability. "Are those the vows we're supposed to say to finish this mate bond?"

He licked his lips and shook his head, his hands spreading around to knead her ass. "Our vows are our own. There's no set order or requirement for them. I'll go first. I promise to always protect you and put your needs before my own. The goddess might have thrown us together, but I *want* to spend the rest of my life with you. This I vow."

Her eyes went dark as the canopy of the forest outside as she softened, yet still she held herself stiffly in front of him. They didn't touch, except where his hands stroked her ass.

"Very well. Here's mine. I promise to always protect you and fight by your side for as long as we're together. This I vow."

He felt the magic weave between them, hovering like a caress. Her eyes turned from side to side, widening, and his brows rose. "Can you see it?"

She licked her lips and nodded. "I can't always see magic like I can auras, but I see this one."

His chest swelled and he pushed her hair behind her rabbit's ear. "That's amazing, bunny, and now you're all mine." What else didn't he know about her? It'd take a lifetime to peel back all her layers and learn everything, a lifetime he was looking forward to.

She swallowed hard, the scent of her fear to believe in them flooding his nose. She planted her hands on her hips. "We'll see if it lasts. Are we going to finish this or what? I need to bite you or something?"

He slid back on the bed, releasing her hips and trying to draw her to him. Like their first night together, he had to let her come to him. She had to realize on her own that they belonged together.

"Yes, at climax we'll both bite each other. It'll be an urge neither of us can refuse, from what I understand."

"Fine, but I'm in charge." She crawled on hands and knees to him on the bed, the scent of her nerves mixed with her desire. Gods, her emotions were all over the place tonight. It made his mouth water, needing more of *her* in every way possible.

She kept herself from touching him but slid over the top of him, straddling his waist. His cock jumped and his knot and balls pulsed. By the gods, she was glorious. Wild, red hair tangled in her little horns, the haze of desire in her eyes, naked above him, breasts heavy and just begging for him...

"You're a goddess sent to torment me, aren't you?"

His need for her grew by the second, and on the last word, she ground her breasts flat on his chest. They both groaned at the contact, and he gripped her hips. One hand went around to her ass and the other rose up to tweak a nipple. He rolled it between his finger and thumb, and finally, *finally*, she rubbed the rest of her body against him.

The length of him as their hips aligned, and he growled as her slickness coated him. He lifted her breast to his mouth, so perky and ready to be worshiped. His tongue swirled around her nipple, making her groan and squirm closer.

His other hand slid around her hip, encouraging her to rock against him and tease them both.

"My, my, what a big dick you have," she panted.

He grinned and released her nipple as he bucked, making her squeal. "All the better to fuck you with, my dear."

Without another word, she rose to her knees and whimpered. He reached between them and guided himself inside. Only the tip, but she eased down inch by inch, not stopping until his knot pressed against her opening. He stilled, his hands gripping her waist as he sucked in a breath. His nose flared, and he fought hard to control his shift. He wanted to howl *mine, mine, mine.*

She rocked forward, her delectable mouth forming a breathy *O*. Fire raced between their bodies, demanding more and more as she leaned back. He cupped the underside of her sweet mounds, feeling the weight of them in his palms as he rolled her nipples.

Her head thrown back, her hands on his chest, he groaned in ecstasy. Her breasts bounced with each savage thrust. His hips slammed up into hers, seeking more, wanting to find that secret spot inside her soul that made her cry out his name.

She stretched and melted around him, but when his fingers shifted to claws and drew blood on her chest, he went crazy with lust. The scent of her blood pushed him toward feral. He struggled for control. He needed to bite her before he lost himself.

He rolled her onto her back and thrust inside with a savagery that made her scream, his knot stretching at her opening. Her pussy tightened around his shaft as he pumped with hard, rough strokes.

"Yes, yes, more." She clawed his back and began to shake violently.

Each thrust pressed his knot against her opening, and her inner muscles squeezed him wildly, preventing him from pushing the last of him inside. His mouth grew, shifting into a muzzle as he bowed to her neck. He bucked and clamped his teeth into the tender flesh as he exploded inside her.

She screamed at the bite, shaking uncontrollably beneath him as her orgasm went higher. Then she bit his shoulder, piercing the skin and making him jerk inside. He held himself still, growling and grunting as he was paralyzed by the pleasure rippling through him.

Stars burst behind his eyelids as the mate bond snapped into place. Magic wove around them, binding them together until it was finally finished.

He felt her contentment and satisfaction, and he sighed, happy for the first time in a long time. The stress of the past melted away, and he fell onto his side, tucking her against him and staying inside as best he could. Still panting, he drifted into a dreamless sleep.

# Chapter Twenty-Eight

Scarlet woke with a big stretch, smiling as she felt the weight of Wulfric's arm and leg over her. She shivered and realized the fire had died. She eased out from under him and added more logs to the coals. Her legs were shaky and her center of balance felt off. She smiled at the soreness as she cleaned the evidence of their mating with a rag she'd found beside the bed.

Her body felt off, but she wasn't sure what it was. Dizziness swarmed her, and her stomach growled with hunger. Her nose twitched, and the need to hunt, to run filled her.

She felt different, but not like she'd been before with the giant antlers. Remembering how she'd felt this disoriented when she'd first been cursed by the king, she bit her lip as apprehension crept up her spine. Tentatively she reached up to touch her antlers, but her hand froze halfway up. The light caught her arm, her hand. A soft layer of fur covered her, a pale red with spots. It was thicker than what it'd been before.

She found a pitcher of water and poured a drink with a

shaky hand. When she tried to drink, it spilled down her jaw, making her jump. She swiped at her jaw and froze. Then her world tilted, jarring her into action.

"What the fuck?" The cup dropped, spilling on the rug as she touched her mouth with both hands. Her heart raced, and she almost jumped toward the door just to have a reason for it to go that fast.

Wulfric leaped off the bed and landed in a crouch, his head swiveling. "What? What is it?"

She stroked her elongated jaw and stepped closer to him on wobbly legs. "What the fuck? Fuck, fuck, fuck."

Wulfric turned to her and his eyes widened. Panic raced up her spine, and her breathing shallow. "Wulfric?" The note of fear in her voice must have shaken him from his reverie because he straightened and stepped toward her.

Hand outstretched, he said softly, "Breathe, bunny, it's alright. You're shifting."

Her hands went wide as she balanced precariously. "How? Why?"

No sooner had she asked the question than her stomach felt like it was being ripped open from the inside out. She fell to her knees and threw her head back, screaming as pain streaked through every cell of her body. The pain and magic twisted her body and bones cracked. Her scream softened to panting and moaning.

When the flashing magic and pain faded, she blinked. Her vision was sharper but there were more grays and blues. The reds and yellows of the rugs and blankets were now monochrome.

Wulfric stood tall, still in his human form with his jaw dropped in surprise. "Scarlet? By the gods, you're beautiful."

The reverence in his voice softened some of her panic,

and she looked down. She had red fur, big paws. A flick of her hips, and she looked behind her. The Growler tail she'd had for six months finally matched the rest of her.

She frowned and sat on her haunches. Reaching up with a front paw, she scratched at her ear. Her heart raced as she jumped. "Antlers?"

Her voice was breathless and a little garbled, a little deeper, but she didn't care as long as he understood her.

Wulfric grinned and shook his head. "Nope. They're gone. You look like every other Growler, except for the color of your fur. I've not seen that particular red in any of the five tribes."

"I—I need to run. Hunt. Eat."

He nodded. "Let me shift, and we can join the pack. There's probably some of them still out there."

He glanced at the hole in the ceiling and then shifted. A sliver of moon was barely visible. She looked back at him, and his Growler form prowled toward her. She was still smaller than him like in their human forms, but there was something irresistible about this. To be dwarfed by his wolf size, larger than the other Growlers she'd met about camp. Her new body recognized him as the alpha. She wanted to roll onto her back and submit to him. Instead, she nuzzled under his neck, and he put his head on her back.

"By the gods," he murmured the prayer reverently, a prayer of thanksgiving to the , the goddess, to whoever had made this happen.

It was a logical observation, as she was disconnected from her emotions in this form. She wasn't anxious about being a Growler. Right now, in this moment, all she wanted was to run, hunt, and eat. Maybe fuck a little too.

Gods, was this why the Growlers were known as mindless creatures who just wanted to fight or fuck?

He turned and slinked to the tent flap. "Come on then. Let's see how you hunt in this new body of yours. Don't be surprised if it takes a while to get the hang of it. It took me months before I caught my first deer."

Her mouth watered, and for the first time in months, she actually wanted the taste of venison. They went through the doorway and into the cold night, snow falling softly. The sounds of camp were muted, as most of the pack had already returned from their run.

The guards nearby straightened as they went toward the edge of the woods. "Alpha," one of them gasped, staring at Scarlet.

Her lip pulled back in a small snarl as Wulfric nudged her shoulder with his. "And the new Luna," he said proudly.

Both guards held a fist to their chest and nodded. "Luna," they said in unison, surprise and delight evident on their faces.

They reached the woods, and their paws were nearly silent on the soft crunch of snow. She let him lead as he knew these woods better than she, but her nose picked up intoxicating scents left and right. She could smell birds in the trees above, the paths other Growlers had taken over the past few hours, and more that she couldn't identify yet.

They ran past the inner and outer perimeters before they caught the scent of a boar. No words were needed. As one, they followed the scent to a small depression with a dense cluster of trees. Mushrooms grew in abundance, and there at the base of one, a large boar nuzzled noisily.

It obviously didn't hear them approach, and the wind was blowing toward them. Wulfric looked at her and jerked his head to the left. She nodded and followed his silent instruction, slinking on silent paws. She paused before she drew closer and looked back at Wulfric. He crouched low to the ground, but kept glancing between her and the boar. When he met her gaze, he nodded his head, but didn't move forward.

The first emotion in this form filled her. He was letting her take point on this kill. He was proud of her, believed in her, and supported her. The nuzzling sound paused, and she looked back at the boar. It was turning its head to the right. Heart racing with anticipation, she attacked, taking off in a sprint and leaping on its back.

It screeched and bucked, but her claws were already deep in its tough hide. She felt the warmth of its hairy body, as it squirmed. Her jaw tensed, her teeth too big for her mouth and saliva making her tongue thick.

*Finish him.*

She didn't think. Her incisors pierced the skin of its neck, and hot sticky liquid filled her mouth. It should've disgusted her, but her eyes rolled as it cried out and jerked. It slammed its back into a tree, and she saw stars behind her eyelids. She didn't let go, but instead bit down harder. A snap in her mouth as its neck broke, and it crumpled to the forest floor. The pulse under her claws and in her mouth slowed.

"Well done, love. That was quite impressive for your first shift. Can't say I've seen that in the past ten years of being a Growler. You can let go now," Wulfric said, stepping into her field of vision.

Slowly, she unhinged her jaw and sat back, panting. Wulfric stared at her, assessing but with pride obvious even on his wolf's face.

"How do you feel?"

She blinked, catching her breath. Her stomach was jumping around in giddiness. She wanted to laugh and jump and play. Instead, she just grinned and said, "I feel really fucking good."

Wulfric chuckled and nodded at the boar, muddy snow turning red beneath it. "How do you feel about eating fresh? Do you want to drag it back to camp to roast?"

She licked her lips, the tangy taste of blood still making her tongue thick. She didn't answer, but just bent down and tore into the shoulder. It took a few angle adjustments before she could pull the chunk away.

She sat back on her haunches while Wulfric nodded in approval and tore into the back flank. They ate in silence, slowly but surely working their way down one side. A scent floated past her, and she turned her head back to the trees to the west.

Three auras angled toward them, Growlers by the size and sight of their distinct double auras. They'd soon merge with the three. She licked her lips, her stomach twisting as she waited for the Growlers to connect. For the first time in months, she didn't have even a hint of fear in her chest or stomach.

When the brown and two black Growlers met them, their wolf heads bobbed low. "Alpha," they said.

Scarlet recognized them and grinned. "Sasha, Todd, ma'am."

The smaller black one gasped, "Luna Scarlet?"

Wulfric nuzzled her neck and grinned. Scarlet didn't even care that he'd just gotten blood all over her. It was kind of hot actually, and she shuffled her back feet to apply friction to her core as she looked at Wulfric.

Even in this form, his smile made her stomach flip. "Aye, my Luna is gorgeous, isn't she? The mate bond worked incredible magic tonight."

The other Growlers yipped and several bounced around her in a circle, laughing.

"Call me Muddia. Welcome to the family. I'm so happy for you both. Congratulations," said Todd's mate.

She felt their giddiness in the air, and Scarlet yipped in reply.

Wulfric grinned. "Thank you both for the warm welcome. It does not go unnoticed."

Scarlet felt his joy and the weight of responsibility roll off of her shoulders, and she threw her head back and howled. The others joined in, then Todd pounced on Sasha. Muddia laughed and pounced on Todd. Then the three of them rolled and played, laughter randomly breaking out.

This was a side of Growlers she never would've known existed if she hadn't experienced it herself. If the rest of the forest or Busparia knew how... normal it all was. They weren't mindless monsters, but families trying to teach their kids the only way they knew how.

She nuzzled Wulfric, gratitude filling her yet not having the words to explain it. He licked her face, and she reared back. "Ugh, that's disgusting. Is that how Growlers kiss?"

He laughed and then tackled her into the snow. She shrieked at the suddenness of it, but surprisingly, it didn't feel cold at all. She was warm and for the first time in more than her six months of being cursed... she had fun.

Wulfric nudged her, then jumped away, turning to put his ass in the air, head on the ground between his paws. The look in his eye was so playful, even with his jaws covered in blood. It was so similar to that morning outside the cottage when Grandma had left with Knox. Had it really been less than a week ago?

She nipped at Wulfric's back leg, and he jumped, his tail between his legs. She laughed but ran around the thick copse of trees when he turned to chase her. She panted, her heart racing but from exertion instead of the constant fear she'd lived with for the past six months.

Wulfric tackled, knocking her near to Sasha, who nudged her back up. Scarlet laughed at the irony. This little Growler was helping her up when back in Vidrland, no one even wanted to get within touching distance of her.

Muddia panted beside her and asked, "Are you going to finish the boar?"

Wulfric waited for Scarlet to answer so she shook her head. "No, it's all yours, if you want the other half. Enjoy."

Muddia pranced happily to the corpse. "Oh thank you, Luna, thank you. I'm starving."

Todd snorted and followed with Sasha. "You're always hungry."

Muddia glared, but was too busy picking at the carcass to sass her mate.

Wulfric nudged Scarlet, nuzzling under her jaw. She tipped her chin up, submitting her jugular to him. She trusted him, this mate of hers that she didn't see coming. He'd blown into her life like a blizzard, and now everything was different but in a good way. Not like six months ago.

The reminder of her curse brought a chill and she shivered. She still had a responsibility to seeing the curse reversed for the rest of Knox's people. The thought made some of her lighthearted joy dissipate. She turned into Wulfric's chest and tried to burrow closer, suddenly so cold.

"You alright, love?" His voice vibrated his chest, and she hummed an answer. She was content and not quite ready to go back to camp. What if this shift into a Growler wasn't permanent? Was it the mate bond that had changed her?

There were so many questions, and each one made her feel heavier and colder. She took a deep breath and leaned back to answer him, but some strange scent came through her nostrils. The noise of the others eating stopped, and all was still.

She stepped back and looked around. Wulfric's silver and black fur stood on end as his hackles rose.

"What is it?" Her voice was a whisper, but she wasn't afraid. Not in this form.

Todd growled, "That's no animal I know."

"Shh, let the alpha lead us, as is his right." Muddia scolded, and all three of them turned to Wulfric, looking at him for guidance. Scarlet waited, nerves making her jittery for the first time as a Growler.

Wulfric snorted softly, scenting the creature. "It's moving toward camp. We can't let it get even as close as the outer perimeter guards. Flanking maneuver: Midnight 3. Sasha, you stay three leaps back. Watch how we handle this, as you're not done with training. Scarlet is with me."

The three others spread to the left, Sasha flanking behind her parents.

Wulfric turned to her. "Stick to my side. We're going to find out what that is."

"I hope I can eat it," she said. He chuckled and led the two of them to the right. She lost sight of the others but could still see the soft glow of their auras through the trees.

# Chapter Twenty-Nine

The temperature dropped with every step they took back toward camp. Scarlet stayed close to Wulfric, practically touching him with every silent step through the frozen tundra. Wulfric sniffed and turned slightly. The creature was moving toward camp and didn't seem to have noticed them flanking it from the west.

She could see its aura, or rather, its lack of an aura. While the Growlers, humans, druids, any sentient being had a distinct aura that she could see from a mile away in open land, the closer they drew to this one, the colder and darker it became. Its aura was like a shadow standing clear as day against the stark white of the snowy forest.

Gentle snow turned to icy sleet when they were a half mile away. It pelted their fur, and even with the thicker skin and her new ability to better regulate her body temperature, she shivered and pressed closer to Wulfric. He nudged her with his nose, and she gasped at the coldness of it. It was like ice.

He sniffed but turned back to track the creature. She

shivered and let him stay a few inches ahead. The thing was definitely heading toward camp, but in an ambling sort of way like it hadn't quite committed to it or it was simply taking its time getting there. Wulfric kept them on a path to intercept, and now that they were a quarter mile away, she could see the other three's auras a bit further out.

The sleet pelted them, stinging ice that tiny knives not quite strong enough to cut but still painful. The wind picked up, pushing her into Wulfric and then trying to push her away from him. She battled the wind, trying to stay right at his flank, trying to keep touching him since the ability to see was diminishing with every step.

When they were close enough to hear it clomping loudly on the frozen grass, she pressed closer to Wulfric's side and squinted through the biting ice. It was smaller, barely the size of the boar, but the swirling ice around the empty black void of its body was hard to look at. It made her want to run away.

But she wasn't a scared little rabbit anymore. Wulfric crouched and drew closer until they were just a few feet away. The creature paused, and the wind swirled harder around them, growing to blizzard proportions. It was only because they were so low to the ground that they weren't thrown about with the wind.

Wulfric ran low straight at it, and a paw came up to swipe at it. Scarlet didn't wait but crawled low. Wulfric connected with its torso and it bent over, shadows coming up to where its head must be. She still couldn't see it through the shadows, ice, and snow.

She was working by touch only, but it wasn't the first time she'd make a kill without eyesight. She narrowed her eyes to slits to protect them from the sleet, then sank her jaws into its ankles. Her teeth grew impossibly cold, like biting a block of ice. She increased the pressure of the bite until she felt the crack of bone and with a forceful pull ripped the ankle, tossing a foot into the storm. Slick blood gushed from the wound, and the smell of rancid meat rushed over her as a shrill howl of wind set her jaw shaking. Before she could draw a breath to relieve her senses of the nauseating odor, the bleeding stump kicked her in the throat.

Scarlet flew through the air and slammed into a tree with a grunt. The impact reverberated through her bones, causing an intense crunching sensation in her ribs. Gasping for breath, she fought against the pain and shook her head to clear the dizziness that overwhelmed her. Through blurred vision, she frantically searched for Wulfric among the trees and underbrush.

He was still locked onto the monster with his claws, one paw clenched deeply into a black shoulder while the other ripped and tore at shadows. The monster thrashed wildly, its long icy talons raking across the wolf's flank. But Wulfric held on with dogged determination, shaking his massive head from side to side.

The ice monster let out an ear-splitting shriek as the werewolves' razor-sharp claws tore into its crystalline flesh. Shards of ice went flying, tinkling as they hit the frozen ground. Black, viscous blood oozed from the deep gashes, steaming as it met the frigid air.

She took a few shallow breaths to prepare for her next attack and saw that Todd, Muddia, and Sasha were closing in. She had to end this now, before Sasha became involved.

She crawled low, wind battering her with ice and sleet slashing at her thick red fur. The creature twisted and shadows wrapped around Wulfric's throat. Still, he didn't let go of the creature, but just kept slashing and clawing.

If there was a time, it was now. Scarlet jumped, taking advantage of its distraction to dig her claws into its chest and lunge for the jugular. She clenched her jaws tightly together and thrashed her head side to side. Unlike the boar, it wasn't a quick snap of the neck.

The ice monster fought back, slashing with icicles at them both. Thick blood filled her mouth, coating her tongue as she fought to keep her hold. It didn't taste anything like the boar either. It tasted like coals, death, and decay. She gagged, fighting not to throw up as she shredded more shadows with desperate swipes of her razor sharp claws.

Shadows swirled freely into the icy blizzard, and her senses were overwhelmed. Jaw locked, she choked on bile as icy slashes cut her head, back, and legs. Wulfric moved at its back, then the neck under her jaw ripped. There was a sickening crack as the ice monster's neck snapped. It let out one final gurgling howl before collapsing in her mouth.

She stumbled back, the unlocking of her jaw allowing the vomit to spew in an arc. Claws still slashing, she went down to the ground, turning her head so she wouldn't throw up on herself. The wind and ice dropped like a washer woman tossing a dirty bucket. She gasped and covered her head even as she heaved again.

When all was still and she regained control of her gag reflex, she wiped the back of her mouth with a paw and looked up.

Wulfric stood on two back legs, half-shifted in a pile of snow and ice above her and the half-buried creature, holding its detached head high in one hairy hand, claws extended. When it died, the black aura had faded. All that remained was a solid white and icy blue creature, icicles sticking out from the hands, elbows, shoulders, ears, knees, and one remaining foot.

Todd approached with the other foot, holding it in a paw and spitting. "Bah, this thing tastes worse than shit."

Scarlet scooped up a pile of snow with a paw and scraped her tongue with it, trying to remove the bitter after taste. "No kidding," she said, voice low and shaky.

Wulfric's eyes glowed as his gaze swung to her. "Mate," he panted.

She scraped her tongue more but kept her eyes on Wulfric. She wasn't afraid, but she didn't know why he looked so animalistic, much more so than his normal Growler.

Todd stilled, holding his arm out to stop Muddia and Sasha. He said softly, "Luna, talk to him. He went feral, and you need to bring him back."

She lowered her paw slowly, but Wulfric looked at Todd when he spoke. He growled at the other Growlers, ready to leap to her defense again. Before he could pounce, Scarlet kicked a spray of ice and snow, hitting him in the shoulder. Wulfric looked back at her and blinked slowly.

"That's right. Eyes on me, wolfie."

His breathing was too fast, and he stood ready to leap to her defense again. But he also seemed to be waiting for her, like he would burn the world down if she asked him to. She smiled, her stomach twisting and turning.

"Hey there wolfie. Did you have fun killing that stupid ice monster? He fucking deserved what he got, didn't he?"

Wulfric grunted and his chest puffed out. He held up the head and shook it, black blood slinging around. "Good?"

"Yes, you did good, wolfie. Can you stop wolfing out and come back to me?"

Her chest grew warm even as she shivered. She really

did want him to go back to normal. Was it possible for Growlers to stay feral? How long did it normally take? She had so many questions, and Wulfric was the only one she wanted to ask about it.

"We have so much to talk about, Wulfric. Come on now. We have to figure out how to take this thing back to camp so we can figure out what it is and why it was here. We need you, alpha."

Nervously, she pushed more snow together in her paws. It was harder to make a snowball without opposable thumbs, but she needed something to do with her hands while she talked to him.

"Need you?" Ah, he'd said two words! That was progress, right?

He blinked and slowly lowered the severed head, gripping it by one icy horn. His hand was turning blue the longer he touched it, and she had to get him to let it go.

"Yes, wolfie. I need you. Drop the head now."

He frowned and looked down at the head in his hand. He dropped it, but didn't step away from the creature's body. Todd yelped and threw the foot, shaking his own paw that was now blue from cold. Wulfric's hair raised at the sound, and he crouched low, shifting into full wolf and turning to Todd with teeth bared.

She threw the snowball. Her aim was better, hitting Wulfric in the face. He blinked and howled, the trees above shaking with the vibration.

She laughed, "For fuck's sake, you're the alpha. Snap out of it already. That's Todd. He's a friend as are his family."

Wulfric frowned. "Friend?"

"Yes, friend. Leave him alone." Scarlet took a wobbly step toward camp.

She swayed and shook her head, still dizzy. Perhaps it

was the fight or vomiting or this being her first shift, but she was suddenly exhausted. She fell onto a foreleg, too weak to move.

Wulfric was beside her in a flash, holding her up on one side with his massive wolf's body. She sighed, drawing warmth from him and shivering at the touch. He shuddered and slid his ears under her neck, whimpering and shaking.

"Mate," he growled.

Scarlet panted, her head fuzzy. "I'm fine, I'm fine. Just tired."

"Oh you poor thing. You're probably exhausted. The first shift always takes so much out of you, and to have had not one but two fights?" Muddia shook her head and stepped toward her, but Wulfric bared his teeth.

Scarlet nudged him to get him to back down. "Enough of that, wolfie. We need to focus, get back and get some rest."

Sasha peeked behind her mother. "We can run to camp and get a litter for you. I had to be carried home on pa's back after my first shift."

Scarlet winced and shook her head. "I doubt the alpha will let me go long enough to ride a litter. Besides, I don't want the tribe to see me being brought in on a litter."

Wulfric wasn't able to take control of the situation now, but she could. She knew what Knox would do in this situation. She stood, legs still shaking, and raised her head high.

"Todd, take your family and get help. I may not need a litter, but we obviously can't touch this thing if it's still freezing us with every contact. Do you think the Elders can identify it?"

Muddia nodded. "I'm sure. They know a lot of unexplainable things."

Wulfric shuddered next to her, and Scarlet looked into

his face, assessing. He wasn't attacking, but just stood next to her, smelling her and running his nose over her neck and back.

She tilted her head for better access and tried to keep her voice even. "Go fetch a litter then. The alpha and I will stay here and guard it. Todd, we need to know if there are any other threats on the tribe, increase the guards, send messengers to the other tribes to see if they had similar possible attacks tonight..."

"Right. Was this a mindless creature with an attack of opportunity or a coordinated effort." Todd nodded and moved back and forth on his feet, ready to run.

"Exactly that," Scarlet said, glad the Growler thought like a soldier. She yawned.

Muddia pawed the ground. "Will you two be alright here with it? Stay upwind from the smell, don't touch it."

Scarlet wrinkled her nose, filling her nostrils with the woodsy scent that was Wulfric. It helped cleanse her senses from the ice creature. "Definitely. I might take a nap while we wait for you."

"Right, a nap. That's what we're calling it now?" Todd snorted. "If it's alright with you, Luna, we'll send Sasha back with the reinforcements and litter. We could use the alone time."

Muddia giggled, and nudged Todd. "Growlers always get a bit randy after a good fight."

Sasha groaned. "Gods, how embarrassing. You didn't even do the fighting!"

Todd shrugged and smirked, making Scarlet laugh.

Wulfric jerked and stumbled a step away, blinked, and shook his head. When he straightened, his eyes were back to their normal golden glow. She sighed in relief as he smiled, face still covered in boar's blood and black ooze.

"Bunny," he said reverently, bowing his body around hers as much as he could in their four-legged state. "You're alright? Are you injured?"

She sagged against him, her body shaking. "Just so tired and cold, wolfie. Gods, let's get a little farther from this thing."

She stepped a few trees away with Wulfric beside her every step of the way, still able to keep the corpse in sight.

"Right, now that he's back to normal, we'll leave you two to guard it. Sasha will be back soon with help." Todd said before the three of them bounded through the trees.

Scarlet sighed and sank to the cold forest floor. "Oh thank the gods. I was afraid I was going to collapse in front of your people."

He sank to the ground behind her, spooning his big wolf's body around hers. "Shh, I've got you, love. I'll keep watch."

She shivered, leaning into him as his warmth slowly spread through her.

# Chapter Thirty

A log split in the fire, and Scarlet rolled over on the bed. She was finally warm, and didn't want to wake up. She moved her cheek back and forth on the pillow, but her antler caught. She sighed, reaching up to dislodge it and rolling onto her back, a large loose shirt twisting around her.

Her eyes flew open. Antlers. She felt the small tips, her small rabbit ears, and her eyes watered as she traced her nose and jaw. She was back to the way she'd been after drinking the glockenberry tea, back to what she'd been before mating.

"Ah, I see you are awake," a soft voice said from the corner of the tent. Scarlet blinked away her tears and lifted her head. Elva sat in the rocking chair, slowly pushing herself. Her eyes glowed softly in the firelight, but the wisdom and understanding made Scarlet tear up more. She laid her head back on the pillow.

"Are you alright, Luna?" It was the hesitancy and pity that made her jolt into action.

She sat up, her fist hitting the bed as she glared across the room. "Am I alright? No, I'm not alright. Look at me! I'm back to whatever freak this is. I thought the mate bond had fixed it, had made me a Growler. Or did I imagine all of last night?"

She wiped furiously at her cheek to remove the offending tear as the Elder tilted her head.

"The entire tribe is singing your praises right now."

She frowned. "Why?"

"You took down a full-grown boar and an ice monster on your first shift. No one else in the history of our people has done anything like that before."

With a heavy heart, Scarlet sucked in a sharp breath. The pain in her chest was a constant reminder of her cursed nature. She yearned to be like the other humans—or hells, she'd be alright being like all the other Growlers. It was a never-ending internal struggle for acceptance and belonging within any species that she'd finally achieved... only to have it all melt away like snow.

Her throat was tight as she asked, "Will I be able to shift again? Why don't I look mostly human like all the other Growlers? Why do I still have these fucking antlers and ears and nose?"

Elva stood and walked slowly around the fire to the small kitchenette area. She riffled through another chest and turned with a plank of smooth wood in her hands, a scattering of dried meats and a mug of something on top.

She brought the tray to Scarlet and placed it on her lap before sitting beside her on the bed. "Who knows why the goddess blesses as she does?"

The Elder patted Scarlet on the knee, but Scarlet swallowed hard at the pitying action. That look was almost as bad as the mean comments from villagers back in Vidrland.

Scarlet took another bite of the meat and chewed while she thought.

She took a drink, then said, "It's not a blessing. It's a curse."

"A curse is in the eye of the beholder. One man's curse is another's blessing. It's been said of the Growlers for hundreds of years. Don't the people in Busparia talk about us like we're cursed? And yet, to the man dying on the side of the road, we're a blessing."

Scarlet looked away, her chest tight as she shook her head and continued to eat. "This is different. It wasn't a choice of salvation when I was twice cursed."

"And you cannot live like this? Take what you see as a curse and turn it to your advantage?" Elva asked.

Scarlet frowned, swallowing more of the tea. "Before the glockenberry tea, my antlers were a fourteen-point spread and my ears hung to my shoulders. Everything was so loud and my head and shoulders hurt every day. I couldn't sleep."

Elva waited while she took another bite. She couldn't deny that these two small antlers and tiny ears made life much easier. "To knowingly live like this? I can't do it. I'd constantly be wondering if I tried every option, exhausted every avenue to fix it. When I shifted into a Growler last night, I was finally *free*. I was a normal Growler just like everyone else. I was accepted and welcomed on the run. I— I can't go back to *this*."

Elva's eyes glowed brighter and the fire flashed higher. "You're a Growler now, and the tribes will accept you as the amazing Luna you are. You'll learn how to control the shift. Just be patient."

Scarlet tried to run her hands through her hair, but grabbed her horns instead, scratching the skin around each.

"Ugh, I've been patient for six fucking months. I've tried everything to get rid of these cursed antlers, and I finally felt what it was like to be normal and accepted for once in my fucking life. Can't you—yes, you can do the Growler spell!"

Elva's brows rose. "What?"

Scarlet took her hand. "Yes, you can turn me into a Growler."

Elva frowned and shook her head. "No, I don't think it works like that. The mate bond already made you a Growler. You just need to develop the skill."

"But not enough of one, or I wouldn't have these fucking antlers back. The goddess can do it, you know she can."

Elva jerked back and crossed her arms with a scowl. "The goddess frowns on turning those who don't need it. The spell is only supposed to save someone from death. Anyone who turns into a Growler outside of the spell is the work of the goddess. To perform the spell when she's already blessed you? It's sacrilege."

Scarlet's heart beat fast. "It's not if the goddess just started the process, and you're supposed to finish it."

Elva frowned, and Scarlet knew she was wavering. She pressed her advantage. "Please, Elva. I came here to get help. Wulfric promised you could help, and Grandma sent me here knowing the spell would work."

Elva hesitated, so Scarlet continued. "We both know the Growlers won't fully accept me like this, no matter how many things I killed on my first shift. Doesn't Wulfric deserve a mate who can make him proud?"

Scarlet held still, letting her words hang in the air. Wulfric wanted her to stay here as a Growler, learn their ways and be his mate forever. If she wasn't a true Growler

314

but an outsider, then she'd never be accepted as his mate or his equal.

She knew her words were true, and it was callous of her to use them as a weapon against the sweet woman. But she'd come here for the spell, and she wasn't going to back down now.

Elva finally sighed. "Alright, we'll try it, but don't come crying to me if it doesn't work as you expect."

Scarlet released the breath she hadn't realized she was holding. Elva took the now empty tray and cup to the sink.

"Lay on the bed. This will be easier if you're prone." Elva picked up her staff with the green stone on the tip from beside the rocking chair.

The old woman stretched out her staff and started to chant in the same language she'd used outside at the alpha challenge. Softly at first, but then her voice grew in momentum with every word. The purple and green swirls of magic curled around her, and Scarlet's vision went white.

She couldn't see anything, but she could feel every tendon and bone in her body moving, pulling, tearing, shifting. She screamed and closed her eyes, her body going rigid on the bed.

Then everything stilled. She floated in the whiteness, and her dad's voice echoed in her head.

"Hey there, Pipsqueak," he said.

She looked around, but couldn't see anything but white. "Dad?"

Her heart should've been pounding in her ears, or she should've been sweating or something. But all was quiet, peaceful, and content.

"It's me. I can't stay long. Your time isn't over, and you have so much left to accomplish, my girl."

"Dad," Scarlet said, a pressure building inside her.

"It's alright. I just wanted you to know that I love you. And remind you that it's alright to love someone, to be vulnerable."

Scarlet tried to scoff, but her father called her on it like he'd always done.

"I know, I know," he said with a chuckle. "You're strong, like your mother. But being vulnerable with someone you love is so worth it, Pip. Trust me. There's nothing that can compare. If you have the chance with this Growler to be happy and find the kind of love your mother and I had? Scarlet, you have to take it. Promise me you'll take it."

The pressure built, the air growing heavy and his voice fading.

"Dad? No, come back."

"Promise me."

"I promise, I promise. Just stay with me," she sobbed, the whiteness somehow still the same, even though she felt like she was spinning out of control, falling into an abyss.

"I love you, Pip."

Every bone in her body twisted, and she screamed in pain. It sliced through her, bending her in unimaginable ways. She tried to claw away from the pain, but a heavy weight settled over her.

Then the familiar blackness of sleep enveloped her.

---

Wulfric sat in the longhouse and stood at the high table in his fanciest beaded clothing. Hair combed, freshly washed, he welcomed the visiting alphas from the other tribes in the center of the room.

Scarlet still slept off the effects of her first shift. He

hadn't wanted to leave her, but there had been so many questions that morning about the ice monster.

The Elders had placed it in the lone tent under guard when he'd finally stumbled into camp with Scarlet in his arms just before dawn, the litter and others following them and shivering from the cold. They'd inspected it while he'd bathed and tried to sleep for a few hours.

It hadn't worked. His mind was furiously making plans, and he kept remembering different things to talk to different people about. So he'd gotten up, bathed, and had met with the Elders before the noon meal.

He'd spent the meal with his tribe, calming fears and telling the story of Scarlet taking down the boar and then the ice monster. They were all excited by the changes in the Luna after the mate bond had been completed. They saw it as proof of the goddess' approval.

Messengers had arrived saying that the betas would not be joining as planned because the other alphas were coming instead. They'd each been escorted to a guest tent to clean up from the journey and rest until the meeting. Now they all took their places around the firepit in the center of the room. They sat cross-legged on cushions and passed around a rolled bacca leaf, each taking a puff and adding to the smoke that rose into the hole in the ceiling.

"Welcome, brothers. I appreciate your presence today, so quickly after the full moon ceremonies," Wulfric began. Nomani and Barley sat at their normal seats at the high table, talking quietly to each other as they observed and listened.

"A lot has happened in the past few weeks in your camp, Ironpaws, and it affects all of us," the alpha of the Night-stalkers said.

Wulfric nodded. "I won't deny it. I know my messengers

relayed the events, but let me assure you, I am still solidly the alpha. The original challenge was illegal, and I quickly dispatched the challenger in an officially recognized match. Elders, do you corroborate?"

Nomani nodded, and Barley said, "Aye, alpha. The official challenge wasn't even close. Wulfric won his third challenge in the years he's been alpha."

Nomani cleared her throat. "Each of your Elders know the significance of the third challenge. When we became an Elder, we were privy to secrets of our people. One of those secrets involved an alpha who would win three challenges. When Wulfric won, the Elders here performed an ancient spell which removed the memory block from all turned Growlers."

The Duskkeeper's alpha crossed his arms. "And all hell broke loose in my tribe."

"Mine too," said the Battlefangs alpha.

The other two nodded. Wulfric puffed on the bacca and passed it as he blew smoke in the air.

"I apologize that it was a surprise. It was a surprise to me as well. My new mate and I have worked the past two days to calm our people and reassure them that we will take action."

Silentclaws, the oldest of them all, grunted. "We don't need to take action. Things are fine the way they are. We will protect our people and will live as one like we always have."

Nomani went to the door and took a basket of fresh bread from a Growler, closing it behind her. She brought it to the alphas around the fire as Wulfric addressed them.

"Are the turned not asking after their families in Busparia?" Several of them nodded, so he continued. "There are several who want to march into Busparia today and find their former families. We've all heard the rumors about Busparia. The monsters, the terror, the martial rule. If our Growler families were stuck under such harsh living conditions, wouldn't we stop at nothing to rescue them?"

Again, several nodded. Nightstalkers' alpha said, "My people have already made a plan to sneak into Busparia to find them."

"Mine swear they can sneak in under the cover of darkness, kidnap their families, and return all in the same night," Duskkeeper's alpha said, rolling his eyes.

Battlefangs' alpha chuckled and crossed his arms as he rocked side to side. "They obviously don't remember the geography of Busparia. They can't get in and out in one night."

Wulfric glanced around. Battlefangs was young and jumpy, but he and Nightstalkers were both turned Growlers. Nightstalkers had been alpha for more than twenty years though and had wisdom that Wulfric often sought when he had first learned to lead.

He took a deep breath and explained about the Dragon Claws, the ice monster, and the prophecy.

Silentclaws stroked his thick white beard. "I wonder if these Dragon Claws are the missing Growlers that have gone into Busparia over the years."

Nightstalkers nodded. "Perhaps it wasn't the goddess' will for us to stay locked in this forest after all. Perhaps it's been the kings of Busparia this whole time."

Battlefangs' eyes glowed with anticipation. "So something is controlling these other Growlers, probably the new queen of Busparia, and if we don't stop them, an ice age will freeze our balls off."

They chuckled, and Duskkeepers said, "That's true. If we do nothing, we won't survive a longer winter. A year or two of perpetual snow would ruin our livestock with no grass or hay to feed them."

Wulfric took a deep breath, passing the bacca without partaking. He'd hit his personal limit and needed to think clearly to convince them. "This is why I'm proposing a treaty with the dragon kingdom in the north."

The others stiffened, and the overlapping of murmurs rose among the alphas.

Silentclaws hit his knee with a fist. "We will not subjugate ourselves to anyone, much less some upstart *dragon*."

"I agree, a treaty isn't the wisest action," Nightstalkers said.

Wulfric held his hands out, palms up. "And what choice do we have? We can't just go into Busparia and risk our people, when it's been proven that none of those who have gone have ever returned. We need allies who can get in and out of Busparia and check on our families, who might be able to bring them into the forest where we can reconcile in a neutral place."

"Why can't we just bring them to our camps?" Battlefangs asked.

Nightstalkers swallowed a piece of bread. "Don't you remember the first time you came to camp as a Growler? Imagine how intimidating and scared they would be to walk into the den of monsters they've been told to avoid since the time they were babies."

"Be that as it may, they're not going to just help us recover our families," Duskkeepers said. "They'll want something in return."

Wulfric took a piece of steak from Nomani as he replied. "My new mate is a fount of information, as her brother is the dragon king to the north."

The other alphas all paused, every eye turning to him as

he tore into the hunk of steak. He waited them out, maintaining the upper hand.

Battlefangs eyes glowed softly. "I've heard that she's not a true Growler. What is she?"

Silentclaws snorted and took his own piece of meat. "It doesn't matter. If she's not a Growler, she can't be his mate."

Surprisingly it was Barley who came to her defense. "I can attest to the mate bond. I saw it snap into place when they completed it, and it was the same as every other fated mate I've ever seen. It was definitely not the regular chosen mate ritual."

Nomani nodded as she brought a tray of drinks. "I saw it too. The Elders were all outside the tent near our communal fire."

The door burst open, and Elva raced inside. "Alpha, quick."

All five of them jumped up, two spilling their cups in the process. Elva glanced between them, finding Wulfric. Her brow was wrinkled as she said, "The Luna. She's—she's shifted."

He strode around the fire. "What's the problem? She shifted into a Growler last night. It's early to shift back, but not unheard of."

Elva shook her head, clutching her side as shouts and howls echoed outside. "No, she's a *rabbit*."

Wulfric sucked in a breath then raced through the door. A small streak of red shot through camp toward the central bonfire pit, followed by a dozen Growlers. They raced straight for him, and he could smell the paralyzing fear wafting off her.

Behind him, Silentclaws said, "Is *that* your mate? I told you it won't work."

"Gods, she's not one of us at all," Duskkeepers whispered in awe. Scarlet heard the comments and turned to dart around the giant firepit.

In her wolf form, she resembled a large jackrabbit with powerful legs and tall ears that helped her swiftly navigate through the terrain. Of course his mate would not be a simple cottontail rabbit—she was much more than that.

Wulfric watched in admiration as she used her long legs and tall ears to speed through the camp, evading their pursuers. She was unlike any creature he had ever seen before. She looked back at him with wide eyes before tripping over her own feet and letting out an angry rabbit's scream.

Wulfric leaped after the group, shifting and tearing through his clothes as he barked. "Enough. Leave her alone."

He could feel the power of his alpha position coursing through him, but it seemed to have little effect on the Growlers who continued their relentless pursuit. Wulfric refused to give up. With all his might, he leaped over the remaining Growlers and landed in front of Scarlet, crouched low and ready to defend her.

She looked up at him with wide eyes, her small body trembling beneath him. She was a stark contrast to his own massive and muscular wolf form. But they were mates, destined to protect and care for each other no matter their differences.

As Scarlet stumbled on her big feet, Wulfric spun around to keep her protected between his legs. He felt the grazing of her soft fur against his stomach and knew that he would do everything in his power to shield her from harm, even if it meant fighting every single one of his fellow Growlers.

"I said, stand aside," he snarled at the remaining

Growlers, daring them to come any closer and harm his mate.

The pack skidded to a halt, flinging snow into their faces. "It's a rabbit. You can't expect us to not eat it," someone in the back of the pack yelled.

The alphas followed, forming a silent group of four behind them. Silentclaws crossed his arms and frowned.

"It's not an it at all. This is the Luna," Wulfric panted.

There were barks of denial and growls, but Wulfric yelled. "I said enough. She is protected and to be kept safe as my fated mate. She's a fierce warrior who can shift into a Growler *and* a rabbit. This is amazing. It's never been done before. There's never been anyone like her."

Someone snorted. "Who are you trying to convince, us or yourself?"

"She was pretty cool as a Growler, but all this *other*?"

"I don't care," Wulfric said, his lip bared. "You will respect her as you respect me. If you keep pushing, I'll ban all rabbit and deer meat in the entire camp. Now go about your business until dinner."

"This is why we sided with Brody. He rules with an iron fist," someone grumbled as the crowd dispersed back to tents. When they were gone, it was only the four alphas and the three Elders.

"This is highly unprecedented," Nightstalkers said, stroking his thick jaw.

Battlefangs rocked from foot to foot. "I want to see her Growler form. Can she shift on command yet? That is so cool."

"It's not going to work. She doesn't belong here," Silentclaws said, stroking his beard. "She'll never be accepted."

Wulfric growled. "I remember the same being said of the turned, yet we are *one* people. It's the same with my mate. We are one, joined together by the gods themselves. Where she goes, I go, and I will not tolerate disrespect like this. Am I the head alpha or not?"

Silence fell among them, and Wulfric stomped a foot, making Scarlet flinch beneath him. "I asked a question. Answer me."

Duskkeepers was the first to speak, saying nervously, "Yes, that's what we agreed to two years ago when Battlefangs got this new pup of an alpha."

"Hey," Battlefangs' alpha said, punching Duskkeepers on the shoulder.

Wulfric growled. "Do any of you challenge me as head alpha? Do any of you have any better plans to save our people?"

Silence filled the edge of the camp. Tucked under the trees, they were barely within earshot of several who lived nearest the forest. None of them replied, and one by one, each alpha placed a fist to his heart and bowed his head.

Wulfric breathed a sigh of relief, but before he could say another word, magic gathered beneath him. He couldn't see it the way she could, but the Elders jumped forward with hands outstretched.

"Back up," Nomani gasped.

# Chapter Thirty-One

Scarlet had to get out of there. Her nose twitched furiously, and she rubbed at the whiskers. The trees looked so tall and scary, and fear slithered up her spine as Wulfric's wolf form surrounded her on all sides.

She remembered this feeling from before, from when she'd first been cursed. She hated the panic, the vulnerability. She paused, thinking about her father and what he'd said as Wulfric talked to the others. Was love worth letting down her guard for Wulfric?

She trusted him with her life. Otherwise, she wouldn't have fallen asleep next to him so many times.

So why couldn't she trust him with her heart? It was fear, plain and simple. A Hunter she might be, but how did she fight herself?

Besides that, she wasn't welcomed and didn't belong. She couldn't stay, and the need to escape overshadowed the fear. Magic flooded her body, making her blood zing in her veins. Then pain tore through her, a pain she was slowly becoming all too familiar with.

She screamed, and Wulfric's concerned gaze flashed through her vision before she squeezed her eyes shut. Each word they'd spoken had driven a stake through the gut. She'd begun to think this could be a new home where she would be accepted.

But she was just kidding herself. She'd never been accepted before. Why had she thought she would be now?

She screamed as her body transformed. It was a long and painful process, and she panted through it, focused on simply breathing.

When she blinked, she saw the world through fresh eyes. She was taller, no longer so close to the ground as she'd been as a rabbit. With her red furred hindquarters and little white and red tail, there was no doubt she was a deer.

Wulfric's jaw dropped, and his eyes glowed as he licked his lips. That glint in his eye was a predatory gleam that drove her normal body wild with desire. In this form, though, she leaped into the woods, her small white and red tail swishing as she ran away from danger.

She had to escape. It was the only way she'd finally end her curses. She heard voices behind her, shouts, and then footsteps pounded on the frozen ground. She ran faster, the need to escape making her heart race.

There was no way she would last, not with already shifting to rabbit and then deer, and all too soon her energy waned. She'd escaped past the two perimeters of guards deep into the forest. She was almost as far north as where she'd killed the boar when she slowed.

Her chest ached and burned, and before she could find a hiding place, the footsteps behind her pounced. He slammed into her back, and they rolled in the snow. Ice scraped her shoulder and jaw, drawing blood. Pain tore through her, but his body laid on her back, heavy and nearly crushing her with his sheer size.

His hot breath at her ear made her shiver. "For fuck's sake, Scarlet, stop running."

Wulfric nuzzled the side of her deer's neck, and she wiggled, trying to get away yet somehow pressing closer.

"You're mine, bunny, whether you run to the ends of fucking Celawynn or not. I will hunt you down and find you, so just fucking *stop running.*"

She panted, wiggling her ass to get her feet all under her. A distinct length thrust against her, and she froze with a gasp.

"That's right, bunny. Keep wiggling that ass and find out what I'll do to you in this form."

She whimpered, her ear wiggling. Would it feel different like this? A part of her yearned to feel loved just one more time before she walked away. Logically she knew sex wasn't love, but she wanted to feel close to him. She needed him, if only for this one last thing.

He sniffed and thrust his hips, "Ah, I see you *do* want me to fuck you like this. I can smell your pussy begging for it. Say you want it."

She lifted her back hips and spread her legs slightly as she panted. "I don't beg."

He traced his cold, wet nose along her neck, and she shivered. "All you have to do is say yes, love, and I'll fill that pretty pussy with this hard cock."

"Just yes?" she asked, her jaw clenching as he ground into her, so close but not close enough.

"Yes," he said, thrusting closer and lining the tip of his dick with her opening. She held still, and he didn't move.

One breath, two, three. Finally, she rocked back, "For

fuck's sake, *yes*." The last sound was drawn out as he slowly slid inside.

He filled her, stretching her so wide she whimpered. Her legs shook, and he crooned softly.

"That's it, take this big dick like the prey you are. Submit to me."

"Yes," she screamed when he bottomed out. He was too big normally, but like this, she felt like she was being ripped in two. He eased back out, her wetness squelching as she finally took a deeper breath and relaxed.

When he thrust back in, all the air whooshed out again. Squealing as he thrust to a rhythm only he could feel, she pressed her jaw into the frozen ground. The contrast of his burning heat behind her and the cold beneath her made her rock, craving first one then the other.

Soon, her ass was rising, pushing back to meet him thrust for thrust. She couldn't take much more of this. It was too soon, too hard, too everything. She squealed again, her legs shaking as the abyss approached.

His Growler jaw opened, and he bit her neck. She shivered and came apart under him. Spasms wracked her body, and she cried as he thrust once more, his knot pressing against her opening as he released inside. He pulsed, filling her with his lava warmth as she clenched around him.

His mouth detached from her neck, and he licked the wound. The rasp of his wolf's tongue made her spasm again, and he groaned. "Gods, Scarlet, that was—surreal. Are you alright? Are you back from being feral?"

She hummed. "Yes, I'm—I'm fine now." So that's what it was like to go feral.

Her body relaxed, and the familiar flood of magic made her clench her eyes tightly. The pain wasn't as long this time, and when she opened her eyes, Wulfric knelt in his normal mostly human form with a frown. He ran his hands down her body, pausing on her skinned shoulder.

"You're hurt," he said.

She looked at it. "It's barely a scratch."

"I shouldn't have been so rough. I'm sorry."

She shrugged and sat up, the cold seeping into her bones quickly now that she was naked and her human self, antlers and all. She shivered, rubbing her arms as she looked around. "I said yes, Wulfric."

He held out a hand, and she took it, standing on wobbly legs. She was tired, but not as much as she'd thought she would be. Perhaps having sex had made it an easier transition or it had given her a jolt of energy.

"Well, we're not going to argue about it here. Let's get you back to camp and the warmth of a fire before you freeze to death."

Scarlet stepped away, wrapping her arms around her stomach, her nipples pebbling and her feet freezing on the snow. "I'm not going back to camp. You heard what they say. I'm not welcomed and never will be, not until I get the curses reversed, anyway. I had Elva do the spell, but it didn't do anything except trigger me to shift into the scared little rabbit."

She kicked at the snow, welcoming the stinging pain.

He slid his hands up and down her biceps. "Then we'll find another way, but for now, come back to camp. We can talk this through once I'm done convincing the alphas to approve the treaty."

The zing from his hands filled her, warming her chest and stomach down to her dripping pussy. She felt her resolve wavering, so she took a step back. "No, Wulfric, I can't go back to camp. I don't belong there. I'm right back where I started, and my only solution is still to make the Queen fix this."

"And what if she can't?" he asked softly as he strode toward a tree. "Follow me at least while we talk. There's a pack of spare clothes nearby."

Scarlet took a shuddering breath, following him on frozen feet. "Then she'll die, consequences be damned."

His eyes glittered gold as he glanced over at her. "That need for revenge will eat you alive, Scarlet. There's more to life than that."

She scoffed and wrapped her hands around her stomach again. "What, like being a good little mate at your beck and call in a camp full of my enemies who'll never accept me as I am?"

He frowned and stopped, wiping the tear off her cheek. She took a slow breath as she stopped too.

His hand dropped weakly to his side as he pleaded. "Scarlet, I accept you."

"You're not enough," she said. Immediately, her stomach twisted, and he reared back, his face going slack. "I mean, I need more. I need a family."

But he only clenched his jaw as he said, "Give them time to come around. You haven't even talked to any of them since shifting into the rabbit and deer. Once they understand, they'll love you just the way you are. Just give them a chance."

"No, they won't, and I can't," she said stubbornly, ignoring the stab of pain in her chest.

His hands fisted at his sides. "If you can't accept them, how will they ever accept you? You hold people at arm's length and refuse to let anyone close. Well, being tough is going to get you killed, and if it doesn't, you're going to be damn lonely and miserable."

She blinked rapidly as he stomped to a bush heavy with icicles. Her dad's voice echoed in her head, and she stood frozen to the ground until he turned and thrust a bag at her. Her hands automatically took it, opening the drawstring and wiping her cheek.

She thought through his words as she pulled on the pants and shirt. They were loose, but warm. She found a plain brown cloak too and a pair of leather bottomed socks.

Damn it, Wulfric was right. Her dad was right. This was fucking shit. She wasn't some weak woman to cry like this. She glanced at him. He stood a few paces away, staring with hard eyes as she dressed.

"If you won't come back to camp, where will you go?"

"First to my brother, then to find the Queen."

His jaw clenched, and he crossed his arms. "Of course." His voice was so bitter and disappointed, it made her stomach knot.

She sighed, pulling the cloak around her shoulders. "Damn it, Wulfric, why do you have to be so noble and good all the time? Why can't you just–"

"Be a typical bloodthirsty Growler?" he said quietly, crossing his arms.

She glared at him, but he just shook his head. "You know, Scarlet, I don't think I ever had a chance with you. We may be mates and I accept you as you are, but you'll never be able to accept me. You'll hold on to your prejudices forever, won't you?"

The last wasn't really a question, but a resigned sigh. He walked around her and shook his head. "The mate bond is finished, so neither of us will die now. You're free to run off and get yourself killed, but know this." He half faced her, finger raised to point. "If you do, I will feel it. Every pain of yours is pain for me."

She swallowed hard as he raked a hand through his hair. "I'll be arriving within a week to speak with your brother. Perhaps I'll see you then, and we can talk this out."

She couldn't speak, was frozen in place as his words sank in.

He stared into the dark forest, the snow falling on his black and gray mane of hair as he stood naked and proud. "I'd like to talk this out. I'll have no one else for as long as I live, Scarlet. You're it for me. There will be no others."

Her breath caught in her chest, but he wasn't finished as he turned to face her, his beautiful eyes glowing in the soft afternoon light.

"But if you don't want this, a mate, a life togeth-er...me...I won't force you. I may be alpha, but I'm not a monster. Decide what you want, bunny."

Then he turned and walked away. Scarlet's heart broke, but she refused to give in. There was no decision to make. She couldn't live like this. Why couldn't he see that?

She stomped north to the main road in her leather soled socks, muttering under her breath and ignoring the icy winter around her.

Her anger and rage carried her through the long trek through the frozen forest, well past nightfall. Weariness clawed at her, but she didn't stop. Birds twittered in the distance, mixing with the sounds of her footsteps crunching below. The temperature dropped steadily until she had to walk with her hands under her armpits. Around midnight, she made a pitiful campfire and shivered as she struggled to stay warm.

She'd had no problem being warm with Wulfric near. He was like a furnace. She'd brought this on herself, yet still she continued on. She woke before dawn and broke camp.

She needed to move and get her blood pumping. Every step was an ache.

But when she stood in the middle of the road, the long frost-covered dirt stretching out before her, her soul cried out in pain.

Son of a bitch, he was right. She looked up at the morning sky, the sun not quite visible with the trees. Her stomach growled in hunger for breakfast, but she'd been too cold to hunt or trap anything last night.

The road stretched before her, empty and barren like her life. The emotions within her built, and her head pounded.

She didn't want to leave him. She could live with the Growlers, form a life at his side, right?

It had been fun, fighting back-to-back and defending him against Brody. Perhaps she could still use her Hunters skills, and she'd make Grandma and Knox proud if she could help bring peace to the forest. She was shit at talking in front of a crowd, but surely she could get to know people and help. Surely they would get to know her and accept her in return.

Tears streamed down her cheeks, ashamed and afraid of rejection again. The icy fingers of fear licked up her spine. It squeezed her chest, making it hard to breathe. She ripped off her cloak and dropped it to the ground. She still couldn't fill her lungs.

Her vision started to blur, and her head swung side to side. The forest hadn't changed. The vines over the road still waved ominously. The distant squawk of the giant eagles in the north echoed off the trees.

The cold was too much. It froze her heart, her lungs, her chest. Her ears rang with panic, and she felt the magic build within her. She breathed through it, her body twisting as she ground her jaw together.

When she opened her eyes, she was smaller, sitting in a pile of clothes on the Lone Road. She shivered, feeling her already low energy draining. She tried to will a transformation, and the familiar crackle of bones sent a flash of pain through her. Faster than the last time, when she blinked, she was in deer form.

She bounded across the road and north toward Grandma's house as her strength waned. When she finally stumbled through the front door and shifted back to normal, her legs were shaking and her nose bleeding. Darkness claimed her, and the wind blew snow over her naked body.

# Chapter Thirty-Two

Wulfric shifted into Growler form and prowled the Feral Forest, making a wide circle around his camp's perimeters. He found a few youths meeting at the old abandoned ruins but didn't have the heart to confront them. He avoided them, his heart hurting too much.

She's walked away. Admittedly, she'd said from the beginning that she was going to, but he'd hoped the past few days together had shown her what could've been. When he finally went back to camp, it was well past midnight, and he tumbled into bed in a fitful sleep.

At dawn, he was back outside, checking the perimeter guards, talking to a few of the Growlers about mundane things. When it was time for breakfast, he went back to his tent to wash and change. The alphas were still here, and he had a job to do as the head alpha. Just because his mate had left didn't mean he could mope about feeling sorry for himself.

He shook his head, trying to dispel the melancholy. He'd been through this before, in a past life when he was human.

He'd live. It wouldn't be good for a while, but he'd live. As long as she didn't get herself killed, he'd be alright.

He strode through the side door of the longhouse and to his normal seat at the head of the raised table. Two alphas sat on either side of him. He grunted, and Nightstalkers leaned closer.

"Are you alright, brother?" Of all the alphas, he was closest to Nightstalkers. He'd been a mentor all those years ago, and Wulfric vaguely remembered the haunted look in the Growler's eyes when they'd first met. It had been after the death of his own Luna, and somehow—miraculously—the Growler had survived. It was why no one dared challenge him as alpha. If he was strong enough to survive losing a mate, he could survive anything.

Wulfric's chest was tight, and his throat closed. He swallowed hard, reaching for the warm spiced tea someone brought him. "I will be. She's gone ahead to her brother's to prepare for the treaty. I'll join her in a few days, once we've agreed to it and the terms."

Nightstalker frowned and leaned back. "So sure of yourself."

Wulfric shrugged. "Can you deny that it's what's best for all of us? This is the only way we'll survive a possible ice age, the only way we might be able to prevent it, the only way..."

Nightstalker's alpha raised a bushy brown eyebrow. "The only way you'll get your mate to stay by your side?"

Wulfric met his gaze and didn't back down. Finally Nightstalker sighed and rubbed his chin. "Look, I get it, I really do. But you have to convince both the turned and the natural born that this will work. You can't just approach it as though it's what's best for your mate, even though it is."

Wulfric's lips pursed, and Battlefangs wiped his mouth

on the back of his hand. "We've had reports of monsters prowling Busparia at night. Any creature—man or beast—who roams after dark is dead by morning. The creature you killed—"

"Only thanks to Scarlet's help," Wulfric interrupted.

Battlefangs nodded. "It's the same type that we've heard reports on. The threat of an ice age is a very real one, and I and my tribe will stand behind you on the treaty."

Wulfric's brows rose in surprise. He'd not expected the first to agree to be the Battlefangs clan. They were normally the attack first, ask questions later type of people.

Nightstalker's alpha slid a rolled parchment over to him. "After you and your Luna disappeared yesterday, the rest of us talked with a few of your clansmen and Elders. We drafted this working document that outlines all that we agree to thus far. It's ready for your review. Perhaps after breakfast, we can discuss it further."

Wulfric's throat clogged, and he took it as he leaned back in his thick, wooden chair. He squinted and a Growler handed him a pair of glasses. He looked up, brows raised as Todd took his plate. "Alpha," he said solemnly. Behind it, the man held all the support of the tribe. Wulfric looked across the crowded room. There were murmurs, but even the old guard dissenters appeared to be quiet this morning.

He put on the glasses and read. He paused and looked up as Todd placed a pen and inkwell on the table in front of him. When Todd walked away, Nightstalkers leaned over and said quietly, "If you're looking to replace your beta, I recommend that one. He is very knowledgeable about the ins and outs of this tribe."

Wulfric nodded and turned back to the document. He annotated, scratching out this and writing in that. When he was finished, the room was emptying of the last of the cleaning staff and the other alphas were seated at the high table next to him and the Elders.

He blinked as Todd ushered the rest of the cleaning crew out the door. On impulse, he called, "Todd, a moment, please."

The Growler stiffened, then shut the door behind the last and turned on his heel. He strode around the firepit to the raised table, stepping up to it. Wulfric met the man's gaze. "Todd of the Ironpaws tribe, your service the past few days has not gone unnoticed, but neither has your service over the past few years. You are a credit to our people. Will you accept the role of beta of the Ironpaws and sit in on this meeting?"

Todd blinked swiftly, and his gray and black chest puffed up. He opened and closed his mouth in surprise, but just cleared his throat and nodded. Fist to heart, he bowed shallowly and rounded the table to stand at Wulfric's back.

Wulfric turned to the other alphas, and they debated line by line of the document. Todd fetched new parchment, and together they drafted an agreed upon version. When all alphas and Elders signed, Wulfric rolled the document to Todd. "Have copies made as soon as possible so the other alphas can take the decree and treaty proposal to their tribes."

Todd bowed and left. Silentclaws leaned back in his chair and scowled. "Nothing in that treaty mentions your Luna, Ironpaws. What are you going to do about her?"

Wulfric growled, the hair on the back of his neck rising. "I'm going to do what I promised. I'll take the treaty to the dragons and talk to her."

Silentclaws stroked his beard. "And if she doesn't want to talk?"

Wulfric shrugged, his mouth tilting in the first smile of the day. "I have ways of persuading her."

The men chuckled, but it seemed to be what the old alpha wanted to hear. He harrumphed and nodded in approval. Nightstalkers clapped him on the shoulder as he stood. "I wish you luck, my friend. May the gods find favor with your soul."

One by one, the alphas stood and stretched. They all needed a run after the hours discussing politics. He stood to follow them, but his stomach twisted. Something was wrong.

He frowned as he stepped out the side door, the Elders following him. He analyzed the situation and searched his soul. It wasn't the tribe or the leaders' visit that was the problem.

His heart screamed that something was wrong with Scarlet. Sweat broke out on his back, and his stomach quivered. He felt like he was going to be sick. Elva sniffed beside him and frowned.

Elva patted his back. "It's the mate bond. You can feel her distress. You have to find her."

"She doesn't want me," he gritted through clenched teeth.

"Then save her and leave again. But if you let something happen to her, you'll never forgive yourself. And by the gods, you might not survive either."

Damn it, she was right. He nodded once, and she raised her voice. "Alphas, the Elders of Ironpaws thank you for this major accomplishment. However, I propose that our alpha go to the dragon's camp today to secure the treaty and information. Aye? We can send messengers with questions as needed."

The alphas glanced at each other, and Nightstalker

slowly smiled, the pain in his eyes clear as he nodded. "You have our full support, head alpha. You will do our people proud, we have no doubt."

Wulfric straightened his spine as they continued to their guest tents, his head swimming. Elva followed him, giving advice and mothering him as he stepped into his tent and stuffed a pack with extra clothes and a waterskin. Then he shoved his boots inside too, grabbed Scarlet's cloak and daggers and her pack, and walked out the tent barefoot.

The alphas stood naked around the communal fire. They nodded, and Battlefangs moved from side to side. "We'll shift and run with you for a while north. Then we'll return here before going back to our homes and advising of the changes."

Now that he'd decided to find her, his body was humming with energy. He hefted the two bags onto his back and jogged to the edge of camp. When he was out of sight, he shoved his clothes off and into the pack, shifted, and picked both up with his teeth.

Then he sprinted through the woods, following his nose and his heart to his mate, the alphas following him part way and howling encouragement in his ears.

---

It was well after dark when he arrived at the cottage. He'd almost made camp along the road, but when he'd seen her tattered clothes, he'd taken off faster than before.

He pushed open the door with his shoulder and growled. A layer of snow covered Scarlet's frozen body just inside the doorway to the cottage. He shifted, kneeling and rolling her onto her back.

Her lips blue and her fingers white, her body didn't even shiver.

"Damn it, bunny, what did you do to yourself?" he growled, scooping her up and grabbing a blanket from the chair by the banked fire. He wound it around her and laid her down in front of it.

He quickly got a fire going, then went upstairs to grab more blankets. He piled them around her, tucking them in as he kicked himself for leaving her alone.

It'd been what she wanted, but it wasn't right.

"Fucking hells, bunny, we're meant to be together. Why can't you just accept me?" His voice grew softer as he curled his body around her, his chest aching. "Love me?"

He sniffed and prayed. "Goddess, please save her."

He laid there for what felt like hours, not sleeping but just feeling her thin heartbeat beneath the palm he kept on her chest.

Dawn approached and he added more wood to the fire, keeping it blazing hot. A moan rumbled softly, and he spun on his heels, leaning over her. Her eyes fluttered, and a line formed between her eyes as she frowned.

"You?" she croaked.

His chest grew tight, and he brushed her hair out of her face. "You're alive," he breathed in relief and blinked away tears.

She groaned and nodded, licking her lips. He jumped up and ran to the kitchen for a cup of water. When he came back, she was blinking rapidly and struggling to get out of her blanket cocoon.

"Hydrate first," he murmured as he sat her up and held the cup to her lips.

When she was done, he leaned back against one chair with her between his legs. Had it been a week ago that he'd sat right here, naked and weak from his fight, and fallen in love with her?

He kissed the side of her head where her antlers grew out of her skull, and she shivered in his arms. "Thank the gods," he said, holding her tight.

"Wulfric, I—"

"Shh, it's alright. Let's get you better. Don't talk," he said, his chest growing tight. If she talked, she might push him away again. He felt her grow limp in his arms, and he froze.

Then he felt her slow and even breath, and realized she'd just fallen asleep. He bit his lip and looked around. When she woke, she might be hungry. Slowly, he eased her back down and went to the kitchen.

Hours later, he'd made a good broth for her. With his memories restored, he remembered a few recipes from the human world. He brought the bowls over and sat on the floor next to her, sipping his own as he waited for her to wake.

He didn't have to wait long. Her nose twitched as the scent of the broth reached her. Then her eyes fluttered on her rosy cheeks, the color back as she'd warmed up. Her eyes did have golden flecks in them now. Mixed with the green, it was unusual and beautiful.

"There you are," he sighed, relaxing for the first time since leaving her in the woods. Her eyes were clear with no sign of fever.

He felt her forehead anyway and smiled. "No fever. How do you feel?"

She lifted on one elbow and finally displaced the blankets. She nodded, her eyes going to the steaming bowl. She picked it up in a shaking hand and downed it so fast, he blinked in surprise. Then he chuckled and offered her the rest of his own.

She took it eagerly but sipped more slowly as he got up to refill her own bowl. When he turned around, she was leaning against the chair, the blanket tucked under her armpits for modesty as she drank.

He handed her the fresh bowl, then sat in the chair opposite as she ate that too. When she'd slowed to barely a bite every minute, he asked, "Are you feeling better?"

He wouldn't rest until she was whole and hearty.

She sighed and sipped the broth before answering. He thought she wasn't going to answer at all, but then she looked up at him with those captivating eyes full of such sorrow and anger.

"I'm such an ass," she said.

His lips twitched but he knew better than to let her see, so he raked a hand down his face and grunted. He wasn't about to point out that he'd been talking about her clothes in the road and finding her naked, freezing self here. If she finally wanted to talk about them, he wasn't going to stop her.

Her chin fell to her chest and her shoulders slumped.

"I was running away from whatever this is between us because I'm scared. I'm scared of being hurt, of being abandoned like my parents did when they died. And being scared makes me mad."

She said it with such an attitude he couldn't stop the laugh that broke out. She looked up and glared at him.

"Well, it's true. When the queen cursed me, I was a scared little rabbit, running for my life. I swore I'd never be like that again."

There was a pause in the air as she faltered and looked down at the broth. "But here I am, running scared again."

Wulfric shifted on the chair. "Are you scared of me? Of my tribe?" he asked, his voice soft, reminding him of when he'd been human.

She shook her head slowly. "Not when I first arrived, no. When I was in the Growlers camp, I felt...safe. It wasn't like what I expected. I haven't had a home in a very long time, but when I was in camp, and everyone was surrounding me, even with Brody and his people threatening me, I felt at home. I–I think I can make a home there, but I shifted into the rabbit and the deer again. I'm not just a Growler, and if they can't accept me—"

He leaned forward on the chair, his eyes flashing. "They'll accept you. The alphas have already told me as much. You just surprised us all, and they needed a little bit to get used to the idea of you."

Her chin quivered, and the pressure on Wulfric's chest eased as he sank to the floor on his knees. He cupped her cheeks as she sat the bowl on the ground. When he stared into her eyes, he saw the regret.

"But I'm not going to sit idly by the fire and pop out babies," she glared.

He smiled and kissed the edges of her mouth softly. "I've wanted you from the first, and I'll accept whatever you can give me."

She pulled back, her gaze wary as she watched him. "Are you sure? I'm not an easy woman to live with. Plus, I'm a freak of nature, still double cursed, and—"

He kissed her to silence, probing her mouth open and dueling with her tongue. It was a kiss that promised hope and a future. It spoke of possibilities, and most of all trust, acceptance, and love.

When the kiss broke, he sat on the floor with her sideways on his lap. Her gold rimmed green eyes stared up at him, her lush lips swollen from his kiss.

"You're not a freak," he murmured. "You're my beautiful mate."

She arched a brow and snorted, trying to sit up. "Yeah, right. Where are my clothes?"

He tightened his arms on her, holding her in place. "Scarlet, I'm serious. When I look at you, I see the deep magic of the forest in your eyes."

She stilled in his arms and looked at him with those big doe eyes. He smiled as he realized she liked this kind of flowery language. Now that he knew, he'd use it to explain, to wrap her closer around him so she'd never want to leave again.

"Don't flatter me like your camp followers," she glared.

His grin widened, and he resettled her to straddle him on the floor. Blankets draped around them. It was an inferno, but his hands roamed her body anyway. She gasped and pressed herself closer.

"There are no others like you. You're the only one I can think about, the only one I want to spend every moment of every day with. Don't you get it?"

He tweaked her nipples, and she arched, rubbing her clit on his ever-growing cock.

"I can pick your fiery hair out of a crowd. I know those antlers will protect you and those ears make you an excellent listener. I love your heart and how you care, even when you're mad about it. You're independent, and I don't have to worry about you in a fight because you can take care of yourself."

She frowned, "And you like that?"

He chuckled and nodded. "Hells yes, I like that. I'm

obsessed with you, Scarlet, my fierce little bunny. So never call yourself a freak again, alright?"

Her eyes flashed, and she lifted slowly, then sank down on his cock. He groaned as she rubbed her breasts on his chest and whispered, "Or what? Will you spank me if I do?"

He thrust into her, and she clenched. Her fingers grabbed his shoulders as she came up onto her knees and sank back down.

He gripped her hips and thrust, setting a bruising tempo. She battled with him here too, and it made his spine tingle. They fought for dominance, he from beneath and she from the high ground.

The back and forth, the ebb and flow of it drove him mad with desire. His hands moved from her hips to her breasts and clit.

He twisted, strummed, and stroked her into a frenzy, causing her to lose her rhythm. Then he took over, thrusting his hips so hard his ass left the ground.

Too soon, she exploded around him, crying out with a shout. Eyes glowing and heavy lidded, her sheath quaking around him, he burst inside, filling her with liquid fire. He pumped, growling as her claws sank into his chest.

When she finally slumped onto his chest with a shaky sigh, he wrapped his arms around her and pulled the blankets up over them. He held her tight and thanked the gods she was alright.

# Chapter Thirty-Three

Scarlet blinked awake to a knock on the door. Wulfric grunted, and her eyes opened. Who in the devils was knocking on her grandmother's door? No one but the Robins knew it was here.

At the reminder of the Robins, she pushed Wulfric off her and sat up. She found her pack discarded by the door, and she called out, "Who's there?"

She reached inside and pulled out her red and green cloak. Feeling swiftly, she slid the daggers free and stood behind the door as the knocking stopped.

"Excuse me, is Luna Scarlet or Alpha Wulfric inside? We've come with a message from the alphas."

Wulfric sat up, crouching and standing all in one fluid movement. The ripple of his muscles still took her breath away, but he strode to the door all in his naked glory without a care in the world.

He eased the door open and peered outside, then stepped back and opened it. "What's going on?"

Scarlet grabbed a cloak from the hook by the door and tossed it around her shoulders.

Four Growlers stood in the doorway, but they weren't Dragon Claws. One put a fist to heart and bowed his head.

"Ironpaws alpha, the message." He handed Wulfric a letter, but Scarlet reached out and opened it, stepping closer to the dying firelight to read aloud.

*We thought it might be a good idea to show the ice monster to the dragon king. It might help convince him of the seriousness of the ice age and the evil one who can usher it in.*

*Take these four with you. They are all former turned, and might help convince them that we're not all monsters ourselves. They also have the list from the Ironpaws of family members, towns, and ages. The other tribes will have their lists ready within a few days as well. We will send messengers to the druid's cottage in five days. If we do not have replies or if no one is there to meet them, we'll send a contingency of soldiers to the two settlements to find you. Don't want the dragon to eat you, after all. ;)*

*Sincerely,*

*Nightstalkers*

Scarlet looked past Wulfric, who peered behind the group too. Together, they saw the litter with the ice monster wrapped tightly in frozen blankets. She sighed and waved her hand.

"Well, come in if you're cold. Wulfric made a stew. I'm going to get dressed, then we can head to Hartsgrove."

"The dragon's lair," one of the Growler's whispered.

"Shit, I'm more worried about stepping into the druid's cottage. Are you sure she's not home?"

Wulfric chuckled and waved them inside while Scarlet grabbed her pack and went to the washroom under the stairs. She tried not to eavesdrop as she dressed, but it was hard.

"Did you see her antlers?" one asked.

A slap could be heard through the door, and a pained bark echoed out. "Mind your manners. That's our Luna, you Duskkeeper."

"Enough. There will be no fighting among tribes. We need to show a united front with the dragon, and that won't happen if you disparage one another. That applies to my Luna too, am I clear?"

"Yes, alpha," rang out in unison. Scarlet tightened the drawstrings on her vest and frowned. She was now dressed except for her socks and boots.

She threw open the door and marched into the living room. They were all seated at the kitchen table, sipping directly from bowls.

She put her hands on her hips. "I'm going to the Queen of Busparia to get rid of these antlers and rabbit ears. Yes. I am a Growler," she flicked her red Growler's tail. "But I can also shift into a rabbit and deer, as you might've seen already. Do any of you have a problem with that?"

One man's jaw dropped, but the others just bowed their heads and shook them. "No, Luna."

She felt some of the fight go out of her and nodded. "Very well. My horse is in the barn. I'm going to check on her. If she's fit for travel, I'll hook her up to the litter. You can all travel as shifted if it'll keep you warmer. Wulfric, find them some extra clothes if they need it."

Wulfric nodded and put his bowl down. "Sure, but they each came with a pack already."

"That's fine then. I'll be back," she said, throwing the

red and green cloak around her shoulders and stepping out the door. She winced as she realized she still didn't have her boots on, but she wasn't going to go back in there yet. She'd made a spectacular exit and didn't want to ruin it.

She winced. Gods, that was something Eirwyn would say. She must've picked up more in the past six months than she'd thought.

She walked through the clearing, the crunch of ice and snow quickly making her feet numb. She struggled to open the door, pressing against the wind, but a big hand grabbed the edge. She didn't have to look to know it was Wulfric. He held the door open while they both slipped inside.

Light filtered through the tall windows along one wall, and Rain nickered, tossing her head over the stall's door. The smell of manure and piss made her want to gag, but Rain kicked at the door.

"I know, girl, I'm sorry I was gone so long. Are you ready for a run?" Scarlet stomped to the stall and opened it. Rain nearly bowled her over, nudging her with her big head. Scarlet laughed and rubbed her jaw and neck, reaching for the bridle on the wall. "I'm so sorry, girl. Let's get you out of here, yes?"

Wulfric held something out. "For gods' sake, Scarlet, put on your boots before you lose some toes."

He reached for the bridle, but she jerked away from him. He grabbed the brush instead. "Never mind, I'll brush her first."

She tightened her boots and went to the far corner's tack room. She lit the lantern but ultimately found a bag of dried apples. When she stepped back out, the door to the barn was open and Wulfric was leading Rain out by the bridle.

Her brows rose. "She likes you."

He smiled. "Don't sound so surprised, love. I'm great with animals. It's people who have a problem with us."

Scarlet shook her head. He was so much more than the monster she'd thought. She cleared her throat and fed Rain an apple as she nodded to the cottage.

"Do you think the others will be alright going into Hartsgrove?"

He nodded as they walked to the litter. "I do. Two of them are betas, one from Duskkeepers and one from Night-stalkers. The other two are mine, and they've always longed for Busparia. I talked to them a little, and they're the most keen to ask about their families. All of them were from villages near the forest."

She frowned and nodded. Now that it was time for the mission, she didn't want to delay. She hooked up the litter to Rain, who was more than ready to run.

"I wonder if a monster like this is responsible for the attacks in Busparia, instead of the Dragon Claws," she said.

He shrugged as he slowly looked back and forth through the trees, alert to the danger that was the Feral Forest even in the protective bubble around the cottage. "Does the dragon have mages who can identify the thing? The Elders just called it an ice monster."

She scoffed. "Does he have mages? What king doesn't have mages these days?"

He arched a brow but didn't respond, so she let it go. Still, it did make her worry about what else was out there. They remained on high alert as they set out for Hartsgrove. It was a grueling day. She strapped a pack to each of the Growlers' backs, and they ran next to her on Rain. They reached the river, just a stream at this point in the forest, and made camp for the night.

Knox had set up a protective bubble at that exact spot

for stops just like this one. The Growlers tried to outdo each other in hunting dinner, and they feasted on pheasant, squirrel, lynx, and boar. She snuggled into Wulfric's arms while the other four Growlers all piled together on the other side of the fire.

The next morning, they set out at dawn at a steady pace. They fought assassin vines and ran from spiders, but it was all expected. One of the Growlers cried about the spiders, and the rest of them laughed about it after the fact, ribbing him.

When they stopped for a quick drink before they got too far into giant eagle territory, she got off Rain to use the bathroom. The others guarded the horse and litter while eating jerky as she stepped out of sight in the woods. Wulfric was too deep in conversation about war stories to follow her, thank the gods.

She'd just pulled her pants up when a sound to her right made her pause. Wulfric and the others were still to her left on the trail, just out of sight. She slipped around the trees to her right, daggers out as she stalked silently to the sound. The aura shone behind a tree, and she moved to flank it.

A figure stepped out from behind a tree with hands up, a bow in one. She rocked on the balls of her feet, but didn't let down her guard. She could feel Wulfric's presence moving closer.

"Striker," she said softly.

"Huntress," he said with a nod. "Do you need help with the Growlers?"

She straightened and arched a brow. "Seriously? You've been trailing us for a quarter of an hour. Does it look like I need help?"

He shrugged, lowering his arms. "What was I supposed to think?"

She pursed her lips and spun her dagger in one hand. His eyes watched it warily, but he didn't move. She smiled softly, feeling the familiar pleasure of seeing someone realize how deadly she was.

"I'm fine. I'm escorting him to meet with the Feral King to broker a treaty. What news of Busparia?"

The man's brows rose, the white scar on the side rising with it. "Busparia's winter has gotten worse, but I'm sure you can tell. It's worse here in the forest too."

She tossed the dagger and caught it easily. "The Feral King is in Hartsgrove?"

He nodded, so she continued. "Take a message to the dwarves for me. Ask if they've figured out how to make the pocket mirrors work yet. They've had months, and the Growler will need to communicate with his tribe. The mirrors would be ideal. If they work, bring them to me at Hartsgrove within three days."

"Aye, Huntress. As you wish." He turned, but paused with a frown. "Are you sure—"

"Yes," she said, daggers now held easily at her sides in each hand. She arched a brow. "You can stop in Vidrland and have the Guild Master meet me in Hartsgrove too."

He sighed and nodded, then disappeared into the trees. She didn't bother watching him leave. They were all trained to be shadows in any environment.

She walked back toward the trail and came out in front of Wulfric. He tugged his shirt down over his head before meeting her gaze.

"Who was that?" he asked.

She shrugged. "Another Hunter."

He tensed, so she continued. "He's going to deliver some messages while we go talk to Knox. We should be there in a few hours, if you're ready."

He grunted and followed her as she mounted Rain. He'd probably overheard the entire conversation.

The trail took a circular path around the spider den and the flytraps, and soon they came to the eagle's nest. She looked into the trees above with a frown.

"Something wrong, bunny?" Wulfric asked into the stillness.

Her stomach knotted. "We need to make it past the eagles, then we'll reach the wall."

He opened his mouth to retort, but the screech of an angry bird echoed in the frozen winter land. An icicle fell from a tree and crashed to the ground next to them, spooking the horse.

She murmured to Rain even as she tugged the horse to go faster. "Come on, we have to hurry. We can't beat them all. Growlers, run!"

"Beat them—" Wulfric panted as his claws and jaw elongated. He roared as the first eagle dove at them. The Growlers ran ahead, leaping and snapping their jaws at it. Wulfric crouched and jumped, and Scarlet held tightly to the reins as the horse lengthened her stride.

Another screech and the flap of wings sent frigid air beating down on her. She ducked and tugged Rain to the left of the trail. The giant eagle was bigger than Rain, and Scarlet breathed a sigh of relief that it wouldn't be able to cart her away on its own.

She raced parallel to the path, Wulfric's snarls behind them combined with the barks and snarls of the Growlers ahead of them echoed in her ears. Her heart beat louder and louder until it drowned out the sounds of the eagles themselves. A glimpse of the helrose wall ahead gave her hope.

She yelled, "Look for the gap in the wall!"

An eagle grabbed one of the Growlers in its large talons, but it twisted and swiped and bit. The eagle dropped it when it was barely three feet off the ground, and he hit the ground hard. He rolled and stumbled to his feet, joining Wulfric behind them.

She tugged on the horse's reins harder and swiped with her dagger as another eagle reached for her. The eagle's claw dug into her shoulder, and she screamed in pain as it pulled her from the saddle. Her bones cracked, and she swiped up with her dagger, stabbing it in the tendon.

It screeched and dropped her, but she was already changing, magic enveloping her like a cocoon. Swift in deer form, she shot past the leading Growlers to the helrose wall and searched for the opening. Rain and the others followed her on thundering hooves, the litter bouncing wildly. When she found the tunnel's entrance, she skidded to a halt. The three front guard Growlers flanked her, but she didn't fear them.

Rain didn't stop, turning automatically and racing inside along the passage to safety. Scarlet glanced back, two eagles still circling the trees to her left as Wulfric watched the back of the injured and limping Growler.

Magic swirled as she watched him jump over the Growler's back, the other Growlers beside her racing back down the path to help their alpha. She needed to help too. A snap of bones and blinding pain, then she panted and took off running with a snarl. Big red paws covered the ground quickly for a Growler, and her gaze sharpened on the battle.

Wulfric swiped a great paw at the eagle that held him in its claws, and one of the Growlers leaped onto its back. It spun, throwing the Growler to the ground. It landed with a thud and a sharp whine of pain and laid still. Another

Growler surrounded it, standing guard while the eagle circled with a loud screech. The fourth Growler escorted the injured one to the gap in the helrose wall.

Wulfric didn't stop, but turned his head and bit into the bird's leg. Even from there, Scarlet heard the crunch of bone breaking, and the scream of the eagle as it let go.

Wulfric fell, twisting in the air from a higher angle than the other Growlers who'd fallen. Her heart raced and magic swirled with her fear, but she fought it. Before he could hit the ground, the other eagle caught him.

Scarlet's heart raced faster, and a red haze settled over her eyes. She would not let him go. He was hers, and she would fight for him as she'd vowed. She jumped onto a tree and used it to launch herself higher and higher as Wulfric clawed, bit, and scratched at the attacker.

Scarlet pushed off the closest tree and landed on the eagle's back, her fangs plunging into its neck. The taste of feathers made her gag, but she didn't let go. Her claws dug into the back of the giant eagle as it screeched and twisted in pain.

*Scarlet, jump now.*

The roar in her head surprised her enough that she jumped. She barely saw Wulfric tumbling through the tree-tops before she crashed into them. Pine filled her nostrils. Bark scratched her Growler fur. She slammed into a branch, then all went black.

# Chapter Thirty-Four

Scarlet's shoulder hurt as she came awake. Soft hands and the familiar scent of herbs kept her relaxed.

"There, there, you're alright now, child," Grandma said softly. "Wake up now. I want to know *everything*."

Scarlet wiped her eyes with her free hand, pushing her wet hair out of her face. Grandma gently rubbed another bloody spot from her face, and Scarlet turned her head away with a groan. "Leave me alone. I hurt everywhere."

"Oh stop your grumbling and get up. You have a big goose egg on your head and your shoulder is pretty mangled, but I have a potion and a hot bath waiting for you."

The last she said in a sing-song voice, and Scarlet's eyes opened as she looked around. She was in her room at grove Manor, and a steaming copper tub sat in front of the roaring fire. The servants must've just left, yet she didn't see Wulfric.

She frowned and asked, "Where's Wulfric? The Growler?"

Grandma pulled on her good hand, and Scarlet rolled to her side, holding her shoulder and arm tight to her body. The pulsing pain was familiar, and she knew it was dislocated. She sat on the edge of the bed, breathing deeply as she waited for the nausea to wane.

The door opened softly but she didn't turn around. A soft warmth spread through her body as shuffling steps came closer.

"Ah, there you are. I had wondered how long it'd take you to get up all those stairs," Grandma said.

"Don't sass me, girl. I'm exactly where I'm supposed to be at the exact time I'm supposed to be here," said the soft, raspy voice.

Scarlet's eyes tightened as she heard the woman draw closer. "Lailant?" she gasped through the pain twisting her shoulder and stomach.

A soft hand settled on her shoulder, and the warmth spread from there. "Aye, bite down on this, as it's going to hurt more before it gets better."

Scarlet opened her eyes, saw the old woman holding a hairbrush, and opened her mouth. She bit on the carved handle, and the woman's hand tightened on her shoulder. Her nails bit in as if there was no shirt or vest to protect her.

The pressure increased in waves, and she whimpered. The warmth that had felt so good just moments before turned to racing fire in her veins, and she screamed. Her body shook and she jerked back, but Grandma held her in place on the other side. The woman put all her weight onto Scarlet's shoulder and it popped, sending pain exploding up the side of her neck to her head.

The waves of fire settled from a hurricane to a gentle trickle, and Scarlet took a shuddering breath. The pain in her head remained a steady beat but she blinked as the women's hands let her go. Bright spots made her vision swim, and then a vial was thrust into her good hand.

"Here, drink quickly now," Grandma said softly. Scarlet's hand shook as she drank, and Grandma wiped the dribble off her chin and took the empty vial.

"There, now you can remove those stinky clothes and take a nice, hot bath. Won't that feel good?"

Scarlet groaned, and the medicine woman shuffled to the settee beside the window to sit. "Talk while you bathe. What's happened? Olive told me of her vision, but did it come true?"

Grandma hovered as Scarlet unlaced her vest, helping her remove it without needing to lift her shoulder. The slightest movement to remove her shirt made her stomach lurch but the pain was a manageable dull ache now. Grandma unlaced her boots while she sat breathing through it.

When she was finally sinking into the hot water of the tub, Grandma grabbed a pitcher and gently poured the water over the back of her head. Scarlet sighed and tipped her head back, drawing her knees to her chest. Her bad arm tucked to her side, she hugged her knee with the other and told them a quick summary of the past few days. Gods, had it really been less than a week that she'd known him?

"I assume Grandma told you that I went with the Growler to his tribe to ask the Elders for help reversing the curse. Their spell didn't work, but after completing the mate bond on the night of the full moon, I woke up partially shifted into a Growler."

Grandma sighed in relief and scrubbed soap into her hair. "So you went through with it. Thank the gods."

"Yes, I did. No point in refusing when refusal would

mean death." The soothing fingers along her scalp, especially at the base of her antlers, made her entire body relax.

"But you're not just a Growler, are you?" Lailant asked. "You still have antlers and ears and that nose—"

"Right," she swallowed hard as Grandma poured water over her head. "I ran with the pack that night, killed a boar and an ice monster, then woke up the next day right back to what you see now."

"An ice monster, you say?" Lailant asked, her eyes growing narrow as she stared across the room tapping her chin.

"Yes, we brought it with us. The Growlers couldn't identify it, but maybe someone here can," Scarlet said.

Grandma set the pitcher down and grunted as she stood. "That's good. Lailant and I will go look at it shortly. Something tells me you didn't take it well when you realized the antlers were back. What did you do?" Grandma asked as she walked to the settee and sat beside Lailant.

Scarlet took the cake of soap in her good hand and said, "That was when I asked the Elders to do the spell and try to reverse it. It didn't work, but made me shift into first a rabbit and then a deer."

Lailant chuckled. "I bet that was a sight to see, a rabbit and deer in the middle of a Growler camp."

Scarlet glared and rinsed the soap off. "Don't laugh. I was more terrified than I'd ever been in my whole life."

Lailant's brows lifted but it was Grandma who asked, "Even more than when you were first cursed?"

Scarlet frowned as she held her bad shoulder close and stepped out of the tub, drying off with one hand. "No, I suppose that was worse. After all Wulfric was still there, and I knew he'd keep me safe from the other Growlers. Of course, it took him long enough to do it, but still…"

She pulled fresh clothes from her dresser, and Grandma helped her put the shirt on without moving her shoulder too much. The women remained silent while she dressed, and Scarlet thought back to those first shifts. She'd been so scared, but somehow had known Wulfric was close and would help.

She trusted him, wanted him nearby in a fight. Her throat tightened in surprise. For the first time since losing her dad, she didn't mind traveling with a partner.

When she was dressed, she turned to the settee and frowned. "Grandma?"

Olive sat crying silently, Lailant's arm around her shoulders. She waved a hand. "Oh, I'm fine. I'm sorry, child, I'm just so happy."

Scarlet's brows rose as she strode closer and dropped onto the couch on the other side of Grandma. She patted her knee with her good hand, unable to put her own arm around her as it was her bad arm.

"Why?"

Grandma's green eyes shone with tears as she turned and cupped Scarlet's cheeks in her hands. "Oh my darling child, don't you know what this means? You can shift into a Growler, rabbit, and deer, right?"

Scarlet nodded, but Grandma didn't let go of her face.

"It means that you're a full druid now," Grandma said, tears filling her eyes and spilling down her cheeks.

Scarlet's eyes widened, and her chest grew tight as it swelled. She'd been so mad as a child when she couldn't do any of the druid things her grandma and mother had tried to teach her to do. None of the magic had worked for her. Then when her mother had died, she'd turned to her dad and learned everything she could about being a Ranger.

He'd taken her on missions, taught her how to hunt, live

off the land, and follow orders on missions. But the Rangers had only welcomed her because of him. They'd always been wary around her, whispering behind her back about being a druid. She'd gone to the Hunters after his death, trying to find her place. But she'd never quite fit in.

And now, after all the pain and sacrifices and heartache, she was a druid?

"This doesn't make any sense. How can I be a druid now?"

Grandma sobbed, and Scarlet drew her awkwardly to her shoulder. She met Lailant's smiling eyes over Olive's back.

"Either the mate bond magic, the Growler spell, or both unlocked a piece of yourself that had been lying dormant all this time," Lailant said matter-of-factly. "You're no longer more connected to man, but are more connected to nature now."

Grandma cried, "It's as the dream said. I was so afraid to hope, but it's true. You've always been one of us, but now you'll be able to come to the annual meetings and actually feel the goddess at the pilgrimage, maybe even hear her, and—"

"For gods sake, Olive, don't overwhelm the girl," Lailant said, pushing to her feet. "I'm going to leave you two to talk and go check on that Growler of yours. I need to see how much he remembers and see what this prophecy business is all about."

The door clicked closed behind the medicine woman as Scarlet held Olive, her throat still too choked on emotion to speak. Her body hummed with nervous energy. She had so many questions, but the most pressing thing making her antsy was the need to tell Wulfric.

She wanted to run down the stairs and tell her she really

was a druid now. Finally, she belonged somewhere. She frowned, unsure of how he'd react. Would he be excited or would he remind her that he wanted her to go back to the Growlers with him when all of this was over?

Grandma leaned back and wiped her cheeks. "I'm sorry, child, it's just... your mother would be so proud of the woman you've become. She already was, I'm sure, but do you know what I was thinking the whole time you were telling us what happened the past few days?"

Scarlet shook her head, still unable to speak.

"I was thinking... you seem so much more settled now. Less angry at the world. Less jumpy, like you're content to be where you are. I haven't seen you like that since she died."

Scarlet sat back on the settee and blinked. Grandma looked so much like her mother, like herself even. It was why Scarlet spent so little time on her appearance or looking in a mirror, why she didn't bother with makeup or fancy hairstyles like Eirwyn or the other nobles or women in the villages.

Grandma cupped her cheek and smiled. "I think being mated suits you, child, and *that*? That's what your mother always hoped for. That you'd find someone to love and be loved unconditionally in return. You did it. You found someone to share your life with the way she did with your father. You opened yourself up to him, and I—I'm just so happy."

Grandma stood, wiping her cheek again. "Here, let me bind your arm until the healing potion finishes." She grabbed the gauze from the vanity, and Scarlet scooted forward on the edge of the seat to let her work.

Was this really what her mother—of course it's what she would've wanted. Scarlet remembered the way her parents had looked at each other. It was the same disgusting way Knox and Eirwyn looked at each other, like they were the only two people in a room.

Her chest grew tight, but thankfully Grandma didn't press her on it. She cleared her throat. "I—uh, I need to check on Wulfric. Make sure Knox hasn't killed him."

Grandma chuckled and nodded. "I'm sure we would've heard things breaking by now if he had, but very well."

Scarlet slipped her feet into a different pair of boots that didn't lace up, Grandma pulling the sides up over her calves with a grunt. Then they both turned to the door to go downstairs. She had so much to talk to him about, and she wasn't sure what he would say.

# Chapter Thirty-Five

The pull on his shoulders and hips hurt with every step. Wulfric's eyes fluttered open, each breath harder than the last. He was in a tunnel of some sort with his hands and feet tied to a long pole, two big men carrying his swinging body between them. The scent in the tunnel of roses was cloyingly sweet, and he looked around in panic.

The other Growlers were in the back of a cart with a large net on it, and a giant gargoyle singlehandedly dragged the cart through the tunnel.

"Where's Scarlet?" he grunted.

One of the men's steps faltered, but neither of them responded. Wulfric turned to the gargoyle.

"Damn it, don't leave her there. The eagles will come back. Go get her. The dragon—"

As he spoke, they'd broken through the tunnel and marched him up a wide driveway to the front door of a giant mansion. His voice broke at both the sight of the giant building and the door swinging open.

"She'll be fine," the gargoyle said softly but deeply.

Wulfric opened his mouth to reply, but another giant of a man strode down the steps, equally as big as the gargoyle. The brass buttons on his green shirt gleamed and his brown pants were starched crisp in the weak winter sun. But his boots were scuffed and muddy, in contrast with the fine material of a noble.

Wulfric turned his attention to the newcomer, unable to see his head with the angle of the sun. "Do you have Scarlet? These jackasses left her back there. Send them to get her, for gods' sake—"

"We have Scarlet."

The man's deep voice echoed in Wulfric's soul and made him blink. But then his fear for his mate pushed him to struggle at his bonds. "Where is she? Is she hurt? Is she safe? Fuck, let me out."

"Not yet," the man said as he waved a hand. The men set his back onto the ground so his bonds no longer pulled. Even as he struggled, he could feel his wounds stitching themselves closed. The net over the cart moved as the others came awake.

"First, tell me what you're doing here, Growler."

Wulfric ground his teeth together. "I'm here to broker a treaty with the dragon, but if you don't let me out of this, it'll mean war."

The man laughed, and a puff of green smoke sank to the ground as he stepped out from the direct line of the sun. Wulfric took in his stubby horns, the green scales on the side of his head, the knot of brown hair at the top, all things he'd initially not noticed from the angle on the ground.

"Don't you think there's enough war going on in this godforsaken land?"

"You're the dragon, Scarlet's brother." Wulfric eyed the

beast. They both had freckles all over, but this man's were more scaly than true soft freckles like his mate's.

The man bowed slightly. "Knoxious Clawson, king of the Feral Forest, at your service. Now, tell me the truth. What's a band of Growlers doing with my sister?"

"I'm telling you, I'm here with Scarlet. I would never harm her," Wulfric growled, struggling anew at his bonds. "Ask the druid woman. She knows. Let me go. Where is she? Scarlet!"

He roared the last word and took a deep breath to yell again. But the dragon was faster, swiftly cutting his ropes and grabbing him by the throat. Pressed into the dirt, Wulfric stilled, his hands on the dragon's arm.

He could fight, but this was Scarlet's brother. She wouldn't be pleased if he was harmed.

"Shut up, you'll wake my mate," the man growled.

"Then tell me where *my* mate is, and let me see that she's safe," Wulfric's claws lengthened on the dragon's arm.

Their eyes met, and Wulfric's burned as he held the stare. Finally, the dragon frowned and backed away, dropping his hands and rubbing one on the back of his neck.

"Hells, explain yourself. What do you mean mate?" the dragon asked, the gargoyle standing behind him with arms crossed.

Wulfric stood slowly, naked and proud with claws held at the ready at his side. "I mean what I said. Scarlet is my fated mate. She's in the castle. I can feel her, but I can't tell if she's injured from our fight with the eagles."

He paused as the dragon stared at him, green smoke sinking from his nose.

Wulfric's chest was tight, and finally he said softly, "Please."

The dragon king blinked and took a deep breath before waving the two men away. "That'll be all. Thank you."

"Wait," Wulfric said as they started to walk away. "She shifted to fight the eagles. That means her cape, her daggers —they're still out there. Can you fetch them?" At his words, the gargoyle walked around them toward the cart.

One of the men who had held him captive straightened and murmured, "We're not fetching shit for the likes of you."

The gargoyle waved to the cart. "For fuck's sake, her cloak and daggers are in the cart with the other Growlers."

The dragon clapped a hand on Wulfric's injured shoulder, making him wince, and met the two men's gazes. "That was very thoughtful of you, Growler. It would mean a lot to the Huntress to have her cloak and weapons safely back beside her."

"The Huntress," the other one whispered in awe.

Knox let go of Wulfric's shoulder and dismissed the two men. "That'll be all. Thank you for your assistance. Oh, and just so we're clear, the Growlers will be treated as our guests as long as they behave accordingly. We don't speak to guests in such a disrespectful ways, understood?"

The two men shuffled on their feet, eyes cast down as they nodded. "Aye, your highness." Finally, they left and Wulfric could breathe a little easier.

"Did you mean it?" he asked as they walked away.

Knox's dark gaze met his, the intensity of it sending a shiver down Wulfric's spine. "Until Scarlet says otherwise, you and your men are under our protection."

Wulfric gripped Knox's offered hand tightly, relieved by the dragon's show of trust. Knox matched his strength before releasing their handshake before they could start a pissing contest on grip strength. As they approached the cart where the trapped Growlers were tied up, one of them snapped his jaw aggressively at the gargoyle guard.

Wulfric quickly intervened. "Enough! You heard what our host said—we are guests here."

The Growler whined, "Then why are we tied up like prisoners?"

Knox smirked slightly before replying, "Well, if you'd wait a moment, Ashur will remove the net."

He wanted to trust the dragon and believe that they would be treated fairly, but deep down he knew there was more to this situation than meets the eye. He silently vowed to tread carefully in this unfamiliar territory.

Ashur removed the net while the dragon said, "If you'll all follow me inside, we'll tend to your injuries and provide food and clothing. Then I'll take you to Scarlet."

"No, Scarlet first. I—"

The dragon stopped on the first step to the entrance and turned to stare down at him. "You can still be prisoners, if you like. That I'm letting a pack of Growlers into my home where my wife and hatchling are in residence speaks for my optimism. Don't push me."

Wulfric searched his face and realization dawned. "Scarlet is near your mate, and you will protect your mate."

"And my sister, if need be. Though she's rarely needed my protection, if ever," he said wryly.

Wulfric grinned. "Yes, that sounds like Scarlet."

The front door opened to reveal a spectral man with a heavy frown, his clothes fine but outdated. "Who is this?"

"Leopol, this Growler claims to be Scarlet's mate."

"Wulfric, head alpha of the Growlers," Wulfric bowed. He fucking bowed to a ghost. Some of his human memories must be stronger than others, because he didn't even hesitate.

The ghost's frown eased though as amusement sparkled in his eyes. "Indeed. Well, come inside. Would you like to wash in the—"

"Kitchens," the dragon said. "They're not allowed upstairs. Not until I sort out what in the hells is going on."

Leopol snorted. "Fair enough. Since I'm sure Knox won't let you out of his sight, he can take you to the servant's bathing chamber while I fetch clothes that might fit."

"We have packs with clothes. And Scarlet's horse, Rain! There's an ice monster on the litter. I do not recommend touching it," Wulfric said as they turned down a hallway. The spectral man's brow raised, and he floated to the front door.

"Indeed? I shall investigate."

They walked through the castle to the kitchens, Wulfric's head turning swiftly to take it all in. If this was what Scarlet was used to, he'd never be accepted. Why would she choose to give up all this finery to live in tents in the forest?

But her Grandma's cottage... now that was something they could live in easily. An excellent compromise. It would just take convincing the Growler tribe to change their nomadic way of life, but he didn't think that'd be a problem for many. They always grumble so much when they have to pack up with the changing season.

Knox led them into a small room off the kitchens, a servant woman with feathers for hair following them. The dragon sat in a chair in the corner while the woman poured a bucket of water into a sunken stone pool. When she left, Wulfric stepped down into it, hissing at the lukewarm water.

"Don't worry. They're heating more water as we speak."

The other Growlers followed him, one grumbling, "This is where the dragon boils us alive and eats our bones and all."

Another elbowed him, making him fall into water. The others snorted, trying to cut off their laughs, but the dragon just let his head back and roared. Wulfric stilled at the sound, then realized it was a laugh and relaxed. The others sank into the water. It was plenty big for the five of them, but just barely.

"I'm not going to eat you, alive or dead, bones or anything else. Thanks, but no thanks. Are you here to eat any of us?"

The dragon tilted his head and waited, hands at ease in his lap. His posture on the chair was deceptively relaxed. Wulfric didn't buy it for a moment.

"Of course not. We're here to negotiate a peace treaty like I told that gargoyle out front," Wulfric retorted.

The dragon smiled and nodded as more servants came in with more warm water. "Well, let's discuss then. No time like the present. I suggest you start at the beginning. Who are you? Why are you here? What makes you think Scarlet is your mate? And what's this about a treaty?"

Wulfric glared and splashed water on his legs and arms before grabbing a cake of soap on the ledge. "I don't *think* she is. I know she is. We completed the mate bond on the night of the full moon."

Knox's eyes narrowed, but before he could say anything, another servant brought a bucket of steaming water and poured it over Wulfric's head, making him hiss.

A snort of laughter from the corner made him glare through the dripping water. "You look like a drowned rat," said the dragon.

"I feel like one," he grumbled, scrubbing furiously.

Memories of baths similar to this one made him frown. Had he and his wife lived in the tavern or above the shop?

He hadn't had a chance to ask other turned Growlers if all their memories had returned or if some parts were still hazy. Another bucket of water poured over him, and he closed his eyes as the heat began to soak into his sore muscles. The healing process was almost complete, thank the gods.

"Grandma said to expect a visitor, but I wasn't expecting a Growler," the dragon said as Leopol led a servant in with their packs and another with stacks of clothes.

Leopol waved to the neatly folded pile as it was set on a chair. "You may wear your own clothes, of course, but I brought these just in case. They should fit, but let me know if they're not comfortable."

"Are they his?" Wulfric nodded to the dragon, who smirked.

"Doubtful," said Knox.

"No," Leopol said. "They belong to Knox's second in command. The gargoyle from outside? They're his, from before he was cursed. They're clean, if dusty."

"Six months ago when Scarlet was cursed? He was cursed too?"

Knox crossed his arms and ankles and leaned back in the seat. "Hundreds of people were cursed, but she was the only one who got a double portion. But that's a story for after you explain yourself."

Wulfric stood and toweled off, not turning his back on the dragon or the ghost. "When you came to get the druid at the cottage, I was there."

Wulfric nodded as he tugged on the pants that were laid out for him. They were a little loose, but that was preferable to too tight.

The dragon ran a hand over the back of his neck. "I see we have much to talk about. Your men can eat in the kitchens when they're done here. Would you join me in my office?"

# Chapter Thirty-Six

The dragon led him to an office library and waved to a chair in front of a large oak desk. "Have a seat. Leopol will bring something to eat soon. What led you to the cottage?"

He told the dragon about the illegal alpha challenge, his injury, and how it led him to the druid's cottage.

"The druid wasn't there, but Scarlet arrived and patched me up before I bled out."

The dragon's brows rose. "That's surprising. She'd as soon gut you as fix you."

He smiled and leaned back in the chair, spreading his legs and trying to get comfortable. "Aye, she's a gem, isn't she? But my natural healing wasn't working as fast as it needed to, so she stitched me up, put on salve, made some type of disgusting potion and forced it down my throat." His voice trailed off but his smile remained.

Knox scowled. "That doesn't sound like Scarlet."

Wulfric's smile widened. "Well, at first, she almost ended me with her daggers even though I was barely conscious."

Knox relaxed and chuckled. "Ah, that sounds more like her."

Wulfric explained about the druid arriving, the glockenberry, and the bond that kept him and Scarlet together for days.

Knox frowned and rubbed the back of his neck. "Grandma was meddling again."

Wulfric just nodded and opened his mouth to continue the story when a knock interrupted.

An old woman poked her head around the corner, and his brows rose. Knox stood, his eyes wide. "Lailant, is Scarlet going to be alright?"

The woman came into the room, leaning heavily on a gnarled walking staff. "Of course she'll be fine. Are you questioning my healing abilities?"

Knox rubbed his forehead. "Of course not. I apologize. It's been an exhausting week."

She chuckled as she sank into the chair by the fire. "Just wait until the egg hatches. Then you'll reach new levels of exhaustion that you didn't even know existed."

Knox groaned, but the woman's eyes flashed white It was so quick, Wulfric blinked, not even sure what he'd seen had been real or just a flash of the light.

Her eyes narrowed. "Do you recognize me?"

He shook his head and frowned. How would he know her when he'd been a Growler for ten years?

Her eyes flashed white again, then returned to a normal brown. "Ah, so your memories haven't returned yet?"

His brows rose. "I—ah, yes?"

She tilted her head. "Is that a question?"

He shook his head. "I was just telling Knox about how I met Scarlet and took her to the Growler camp. If I continue my story, I'll answer your question as part of it."

She waved her hand and settled back on the chair. "Very well."

Knox's lips twitched at the imperious note of authority in the woman's voice, but Wulfric chuckled and continued with the story. He took them through the events at the Growler camp and the meeting with the other alphas, Scarlet's shifts, and even their fight when she left and how he found her in the cottage.

"Then my men showed up with the ice monster so you'd see the severity of the situation and why I'm here to broker a treaty between the Growlers and your kingdom."

Knox pulled out a piece of paper and pen. He dipped the tip into the ink pot and scribbled while the old medicine woman scratched at her knee.

"So most of your memories are back, but not quite all of them. Well, I guess I'll keep waiting for the right time," she said, standing and shuffling to the door again.

Knox didn't look up as she left. "The kingdom that I rule with my queen is organized in such a way that requires a vote to agree to a treaty. You and I can work on the details of the document, but ultimately the people and the Confederation will need to approve it."

Wulfric frowned and glanced out the window behind Knox. "If the reaction of the two men who brought me in here is any sign, I'm not sure your people will approve a treaty."

Knox looked up at him then went back to writing. "Perhaps not, but given enough time to prove positive relationships, we can change stereotypes and make it happen."

Wulfric's hands clenched on his thighs. "I'm not sure how much time we have, but I did bring a rough draft of the treaty signed by all the alphas. It's in my pack."

The door burst open, banging against the wall. Wulfric

jumped and shifted on the balls of his feet to put his back to the bookcase to his right. He kept Knox on one side and faced the threat. The only threat was to his heart though, because Scarlet stood in the doorway looking like an avenging goddess.

Hair still wet but piled into a messy bun on her head, bandage held her left arm tight to her body, but she looked ready to fight. She took his breath away. Wulfric strode to her and ran his hands over the side of her face and down her uninjured arm.

"Are you alright?" he whispered, checking her for more injuries.

Olive said behind her, "She'll be fine. She's healing much faster than normal, which I can only attribute to her new abilities. Well done, Growler."

Wulfric moved them out of the doorway, pulling Scarlet into his arms. She sagged against his chest, and he ran his hands up and down her back, soaking in how perfectly they fit together. Knox's gaze made the hair on the back of his neck stand on end, but he couldn't look away from Scarlet.

The druid winked at him then went across the room to the other chair by the fireplace, greeting the medicine woman as she sat. A servant came through the door rolling a cart full of sandwiches and tea.

Scarlet pushed his shoulder with her free hand, and he winced as she glared. "Have you been fighting my brother? Are you alright? Did the eagles hurt you? What about the other Growlers?"

He took her free hand in his, his other settling on her lower back as he led her further into the room. "Everyone's fine and healing. Your brother is more bark and no bite—"

"Hey," Knox said.

Scarlet glared at him and lifted a finger. "Don't you go

complaining about that. If you were more like me, they'd all be dead already. I'm glad you're a talk first, action second kind of man because heavens knows how much trouble I get into by acting first."

Wulfric chuckled and drew her to the couch in front of the fire. "Calm down, bunny. We're all fine, see? Just a few more hours, and we'll all be healed. Those claws were massive and hurt like hell, but I'm almost back to normal."

They sat, and he pulled her into the crook of his arm, wrapping it around her back. She shifted imperceptibly closer as Knox pulled one of the chairs in front of his desk closer to their group.

"The Growler was beside himself with worry for you, Red," Knox smirked.

Scarlet glared, "Don't call me that, and when are you going to do something about those eagles? Why are they still hanging around? I haven't had this much trouble with them in months."

Knox closed his eyes, and Wulfric suddenly saw the dark smudges under his eyes.

"I know," Knox said. "The colder weather has made them more desperate for food and warmth."

The tight material of the blue shirt stretched over his back as he settled deeper into the couch. Wulfric's hand settled on the back of it, his fingers playing with the wisps of hair falling out of the bun on the top of her head. She placed her head on his shoulder and sighed, the angle knocking his hand away. He slid it down her bandaged shoulder, gently holding her.

"Why don't you feed and shelter them, then?" Wulfric asked, eyes meeting Knox's without shame. If the man had a problem with him holding his sister, well, he better get used to it because Wulfric wasn't going to stop.

All three of the others looked at him with surprised expressions, and he squirmed.

"What?" he asked.

Knox stroked his chin. "Maybe... Eirwyn has had people raising baby eagles to domesticate them from a young age, but perhaps it's not too late to train the older ones."

The druid looked at Knox with a smile. "See? He's a keeper. If Growlers can be tamed, then so can the eagles."

Wulfric stiffened. "I wouldn't say tamed exactly—"

Scarlet laughed, and the knot in his stomach dissolved at the sound. She rarely laughed, and it was like sunshine after a rainstorm. It lit him from inside, spreading warmth wherever it touched.

Knox grinned and said, "Now, about this treaty..."

Hours later, after a fight with Knox about Wulfric being allowed upstairs, Scarlet led him to her room. When the door finally closed behind her, she leaned against it. He didn't take his eyes off her, smelling the apprehension on her as they'd gotten closer to the room.

"What is it?" he asked, taking her hands in his. "Are you tired? Hurting?"

She shook her head and stood straighter. "Help me take this bandage off. I feel fine now, and it's too confining."

He nodded, and found the edge. Slowly, he began to unwrap her like a present. "Are you sure that's all? You seem nervous."

She looked to the side, avoiding his gaze. "So, um, Grandma said that either the mate bond or the Elder's spell made me into a full druid now. I'll need to train with them, go to the annual meetings, and other druid things that I'm sure I don't remember."

Wulfric's hands paused and he looked at her. "How do you feel about that?"

She looked at him, her gaze guarded. "How do *you* feel about that? I mean, the Growlers have been afraid of the druids for years."

Wulfric kept unwrapping her bandages. "I'm not afraid of you, Scarlet. I'm proud of you. You're an amazing fighter, fierce and determined. You're going to make a great druid, just like you'll make a great Growler."

Her breath hitched and her eyes widened. "You—still want me to go back to the tribe with you?"

He arched a brow and tossed the bandages aside. "As if it's even a question. Of course I do. I want to be where you are. Think they'll let me tag along to those druid meetings? Because I'm not so keen on being apart from you."

She blinked, then snorted and walked around him toward the settee. "Now don't go thinking this means I agree to live with the Growlers. But I'm glad you're alright with me being a druid. Now come help me take these boots off. I'm tired."

He prowled to her, the scent of her desire and relief flooding his senses. "Well, if it'll get you naked in that big bed, consider me at your service, my lady."

She chuckled, and the sound sent a shiver up his spine. He wanted her to always be happy and relaxed, and he'd do everything in his power to make it so, even tag along to mysterious druid gatherings.

# Chapter Thirty-Seven

Wulfric lay on the soft sheets of the oversized bed and cradled his head with his hands. The deep green of the bedding complimented the gold and red trim, the red damask walls, and ivory furniture. The plush green carpet reminded him of the softest grass. He'd run his toes through it for several minutes when Scarlet had led him up to her room two days ago after the grueling interview with Knox.

The way she'd argued with Knox over him not being allowed upstairs had been adorable, and they'd fucked for hours last night in this enormous bed. More memories of his past had teased him in the early morning light of dawn, and he'd slipped downstairs to shift and run a path along the helrose hedge that encircled the castle.

They'd spent the past two days talking alternately with Knox, Olive, Ashur, and Leopol, who knew a surprising amount of details about the Growlers. They'd worked out the details of the treaty, but Knox kept running upstairs with the latest draft to show to his wife, whom Wulfric still had not met. Yesterday they'd finally settled on a version that suited them all. Tonight, he and Knox would propose the treaty to the Confederation leaders at a fancy dinner tonight. Tomorrow he'd send two Growler messengers with an update.

While waiting for the dinner—and to get Scarlet's mind off of it—they had talked more with Olive, who had tried to get him to call her Grandma. They'd discussed the prophecy and the events surrounding Scarlet's mother's death.

Between remembering her mother's death and the upcoming meeting with the confederation, Scarlet had been on edge all day. He'd tried to distract her with more fucking, but she was still too jittery. He'd woken up from a post-sex nap to find her pacing a path on the floor.

She turned once more in front of the fireplace, and he sighed, "I don't see that we have a choice, bunny."

She waved her arms to the side. "I know, but it's fucked up, and Knox knows it. Neither of them have ever asked me to attend a formal dinner before. There's so many rules and—"

"Etiquette be damned," Wulfric said, sitting up on the bed and swinging his legs to the side. Bare feet sank into the carpet as he walked to her side and took her hands in his.

"We're going to eat some good food and have a nice, long discussion with the Confederation. This is what we need to do to get the treaty approved before it can be presented to the people, remember?"

She looked up at him with those big green and gold doe eyes and frowned. "But—"

He kissed her, sweeping his tongue along the seam of her mouth before hers came out to play. They dueled lazily until he felt her relax in his arms. When he broke the kiss, he gathered her tighter and ran his hands along her back, careful not to stab himself on her horns.

"It's alright, bunny. I'll be right beside you. You don't have to say anything, but if you want to, just whisper it to me, and I'll be your voice, alright?"

She sighed and nodded against his chest. After too few moments, she pulled away and scowled at the clothes the maid had left on the settee.

"I don't know what they were thinking. A fucking dress?"

He chuckled and nuzzled her ear. "Think of it like this, bunny. If we sneak away from dinner as soon as possible, the dress will provide easier access for playing with dessert."

She looked up at him with a sly grin. "Am I dessert, wolfie?"

He wiggled his eyebrows. "You know it, bunny."

She laughed, and it made some of the stress over the night ease. It didn't escape his notice that she'd laughed more while they were here the past two days than in the week prior. It made him want more of that for her.

They helped each other put on the fancy clothes, and he peppered kisses after every item was added and every button slipped into place. Her cheeks were flushed and her eyes sparkling when they were finally ready. She'd been very vocal about not wearing the dress and not going to the dinner, but Knox had worn her down on both.

It had been helpful for him to see how her brother handled her. But now that she was in front of him in a dress that draped her body like silk, his mouth went dry and his tongue thickened. She'd adamantly refused to wear a corset, so it was a different style than the servants he'd seen wear. But this dress suited her.

The silk was high necked and laced up the front like her vest. The green silk draped from her hips, making them look fuller. She met his eyes in the mirror and reached for the hem. The movement made her breasts sway, and he suddenly wanted to lick every inch. She bared a leg and slid a dagger into her stocking, tying the garter over it snugly.

"Do you need help with the other one, bunny?" His voice was a deep rumble, and he knelt at her feet.

Her eyes darkened as she licked her lips. He slid his hands up her other leg, the silk catching on his rough skin. He strapped her dagger to her thigh, tying the garter like she'd done with the previous one.

"Th—thanks," she said softly.

He smiled up at her. "Oh, I'm not done yet, bunny. I'll never be done with you."

Then he pushed her skirt into her hand and said, "Hold it tight now."

He felt her suck in a breath as he slid her drawers to the side. He groaned at the sight of dusky pink flesh framed by a riot of flaming curls, and his thumb grazed the nub of her clit. She swayed, then sat heavily on the settee.

He pushed her legs wider and licked up her slit until she bucked, then he swirled his tongue around the center of her pleasure. Her hand cradled the back of his head and pressed him closer, and he slid his thumb inside her dripping pussy.

He continued to tease and stimulate it, circling and tugging until she was panting and grunting with need. Low, guttural moans echoed in the room as she pressed her hips against him in perfect rhythm with his movements.

"Wulfric, please," she begged, pulling him closer. He chuckled in response, sitting up and freeing his throbbing cock from the confines of his pants.

"Again, bunny. Beg for me," he purred as he traced her

slit with his dick. She thrust her hips, and he teased her entrance.

"Damn it, Wulfric, if you don't—ah!"

He speared her to the hilt, and he gloried in her eyes rolling. He slid out, and thrust again, going deeper, trying to fill every crack and crevice within her. He was on a mission to imprint himself so deeply into her psyche that she'd crave nothing but him for all time. Every thrust, every moan grew more desperate for them both until he was slamming into her with a fierceness that would make any Growler proud.

Her hands fluttered on his arms then his biceps, her mouth open and panting as she peaked.

"Fuck, fuck, fuck—oh!" Her eyes rolled again, and his own fluttered as she clamped down on his dick like a vise. She cried out as she milked him, her hands shifting into claws and puncturing his shirt. Her eyes glowed golden as she came, and he roared as wave after wave of her orgasm tightened around him.

His balls drew tight, and he felt his knot pressing against her entrance. Just the pressure of her pushing against it sent him over the edge. He groaned and bent over her as he thrust once, twice more. Heat flooded from him into her, filling her as they both spasmed. Time stopped. There was nothing but the rush in his ears of his release and her whimpers.

When the world stopped spinning, he leaned back and brushed the hair from her face, tucking a strand behind her little rabbit's ear. He kissed her nose and she mewled, finally calm and with a smile on her face.

Until the dinner bell echoed through the halls. She tensed, and he groaned.

"Fuck, Scarlet, don't flex or we'll fuck through dinner."

She grinned and squeezed him again. "Now there's the perfect excuse to skip this awful dinner."

He chuckled and pulled out, grabbing a handkerchief and cleaning her until she took it from him. It was one of the many things he loved about her. She wasn't delicate and could take him, rough edges and all. Sometimes she'd let him take care of her, and sometimes she had no patience for him. It was adorable.

Wulfric tucked himself into his pants, his new boots pinching his feet. The need to hold her pressed on him, and he turned to her. "Scarlet—"

A knock interrupted him, and Scarlet fiddled with her hem, shaking the skirt out.

"Come in," she called absently.

A servant came in to style her hair, and Wulfric sighed, turning on his heel and walking to the adjoining sitting room to wait. The way the servant kept looking at him, he knew he made them uncomfortable. They hadn't warmed up a lot, although one of the Growlers had made friends in the kitchen.

Like always, his mind turned to Scarlet. How could he provide for her, convince her to come back to the tribe and live with him for good. They hadn't really discussed it since he'd found her at the cottage, but he knew she was still wary and nervous. He wanted to hold her and make her see that if they were together, it would be alright. Love would see them through a lot.

He loved her. Of course, he fucking loved her. She was his mate. She had to choose him, didn't she?

Although... he'd heard of other mates completing the process and then living separately. Some even claimed to be enemies, which he couldn't imagine. Scarlet was everything.

None of it would matter if he didn't secure this treaty

though. If Knox's people approved it, he could build her a home where she'd smile and laugh at the end of a long mission as a Hunter. Maybe he could build all the Growlers homes so they'd be solidified as one people. It was something Knox had said yesterday that had made him think about it.

If they had family left in Busparia, those family members would want homes like those they were used to. They'd not want tents or a nomadic lifestyle. The Growlers were going to have to adapt, but hopefully without losing their lifestyles and traditions. It'd be complicated to navigate, and he hoped Scarlet would help him with it.

Her hand on his back brought him to the present, and he smiled down at her.

"Are you alright?" she asked softly, her hair now braided in tiny braids and piled into some complicated bun between her antlers.

He nodded and winced. "Yes, there's just a lot riding on this treaty. Everyone's counting on me."

Her jaw tilted, and she got that stubborn glint in her eye. "So let's go make it happen." And with that, she spun on her heel—still her normal well-worn but polished boots—and strode to the door, her skirts tangling around her ankles.

She cursed as she stumbled, and he prowled after her. By the time she settled her skirts, he held the door open and offered his arm.

"My lady," he growled with a bow.

She flushed and tucked her hand into the crook of his elbow. "Don't be ridiculous, Wulfric."

He smiled but didn't reply as they walked slowly down the hallway to the stairs.

They reached the parlor without incident and stopped

in the open doorway. A dozen other fancily dressed men and women stood around the room, conversing quietly. Then two of them stepped away from a couch, and his breath caught.

A black-haired beauty with ruby red lips sat with queenly grace, her red and blue dress flattering her curves. Her light blue eyes swung to his, and her jaw dropped. They were almost white, they were so bright. His head flashed, and he reached for his temple.

*A disheveled little girl stood in the stables, sniffling as she brushed some lord's horse behind the tavern. The cook had come to fetch him after her bathroom break to say some brat was hiding, and sure enough, here she was.*

*But as he stepped closer and lifted the lantern, her light blue eyes flashed and the light of the lantern swayed with her magic. She sniffed and frowned, backing into the corner.*

*"You're not going to make me go back, are you?" Her voice was small, but her diction perfect for an aristocrat.*

*He sat down the lantern outside the stall and draped his arms over the stall door, crossing at the elbows and leaning his chin on his arms.*

*"Well, that depends on who you are, what you want, and what you're avoiding."*

*She sniffed again, hiding behind the mare. He sighed, "Come on then, I don't have all day. Customers are bound to get into a scuffle this time of night. Isn't it past your bedtime, little girl?"*

*She came around the mare with arms waving, but the horse didn't seem to mind. Light flickered off the ceiling as she spoke. "If my bed was safe, I'd be there, now wouldn't I?"*

*She burrowed deeper against the stable wall, shadows nearly swallowing her. He wanted to beat up whoever threatened her, but if he did that for every lost soul who came to the tavern, he'd be away from the tavern all day, everyday.*

*He leaned back and picked up the lantern before opening the stall door just enough for her to come through. "Well then, I guess you'll be staying until it's safe. Come on now. I've got a nice bowl of venison and potatoes inside with fresh bread. Are you hungry?"*

*Her feet scuffled on the ground, then she came into the light, a brow raised suspiciously. "I—I didn't bring any coin."*

*He shrugged. "You can work for it."*

*Her brows rose, and judging by the fine stitching on her dress, it might've been the first time anyone suggested such a thing to her.*

*"How? I'm not trained for anything."*

*He shrugged. "You can wipe down the tables when customers leave, maybe help Madge in the kitchen."*

*She sniffed and took another step forward. "That... that doesn't sound too bad."*

*He turned and walked slowly out of the stables, hearing the tap of her little steps following behind.*

A hand on his sleeve made him blink and look down.

"Wulfric, what is it? You look like you're in pain," Scarlet asked.

Brow furrowed, he glanced back to the black-haired woman who now stood, speaking quietly with Knox. The dragon bent his head to her deferentially then frowned and looked up at Wulfric. He stiffened and faked a smile to those around him before walking with the black-haired woman toward Wulfric and Scarlet.

Someone tried to enter the room behind them, so Scarlet tugged him toward the gigantic windows in the corner. It was quieter and away from the other groups of people, but he felt cornered.

His mind was racing with conflicting emotions as he watched Knox and the woman approach. He wasn't ready to confront his past, but it was about to collide with his present no matter what he wanted. His breath grew shallow, his chest tight.

Knox turned to Scarlet and said, "You look fetching, Red. Who knew you'd wear a dress so well?"

Scarlet punched him on the shoulder, and he laughed as he grabbed her hand. "Come on, sister. Ashur has been asking after you all night. Wulfric, this is my wife, mate, and queen, Eirwyn. Eirwyn, the Growler Alpha."

Scarlet's eyes narrowed. "You've kept Eirwyn resting for days, refusing to even introduce her to Wulfric, but now you're leaving them alone to talk? What's going on?"

Knox tugged her away toward the towering gargoyle across the room, saying, "You're too suspicious, Red."

"Don't call me that."

The look Knox shot him over her shoulder told him to proceed with caution as he distracted her. When Scarlet reached the gargoyle, Knox turned so he could keep watch over his mate, his wife.

Wulfric pulled his gaze away from his own mate to the petite woman in front of him. "You—you've grown up," he said, his voice gravelly.

She smiled, that same mischievous sparkle returning to her eyes. "That's what happens when ten years passes. We thought you were dead, Warren."

*Warren.* His previous name for a previous life. Such a simple thing to have forgotten, yet it was like a weight lifted from his shoulders. He swallowed hard.

"I'm Wulfric now. Warren is long gone, dead like you said. When I became a Growler, I lost all memories, my... humanity. I've only regained them recently, and some seem to still be missing."

"What's missing?" she asked, head tilting to the side.

He pursed his lips and arched a brow. "If I knew what they were, they wouldn't be missing."

She laughed and the lights near them danced along the

wall. It was a familiar sound and sight that reminded him of his former home. His chest tightened.

"Too true." She turned as if pulled by a sixth sense and frowned at Knox. Then she nodded and turned back to him.

"We have little time and this isn't the place to discuss it, but I must know. What do you remember of your daughter?"

He blinked, his head aching as he searched his memories. "She... died in the fever that took my wife."

Eirwyn's eyes saddened as she shook her head. "No, Wulfric. She didn't die. She's still alive. Don't you remember us in the tavern all those years ago? Do you truly not remember?"

He blinked and images swam in his mind, his head pounding with each flash of memory. The funeral pyres. A little hand holding his as they walked through the grave-yard. A brown haired girl who frowned too much and worked too hard.

The girl at ten when she'd stopped asking him to lace her shoes. The girl at fourteen when she'd grown too cynical about men. The girl at fifteen when he'd led little Eirwyn into the kitchens of the tavern, and he'd desperately hoped the companionship would help his daughter to open her brittle heart.

It'd helped, for a while. "The six months before I left," he said hoarsely. "You made Trix smile more in those six months than she had in the six years before that."

Eirwyn wiped a tear from her cheek and nodded. "Oh Wulfric, we have so much to talk about, but this isn't the time of the place."

The butler, Hobbs, announced dinner, and Knox led Scarlet back to him. Scarlet frowned and Knox glared at

Wulfric for making his wife cry. But his entire world shifted around the idea that he still had a *daughter*. He still had a daughter.

"She's alive?" His chest ached, and he wanted to roar at all the missed years.

Eirwyn smiled and nodded as Knox led her into dinner. Where was she now? Was she happily married and running the tavern still? Had she found joy and laughter or had his death led her to be even more bitter than she had been growing up?

He needed to make this treaty work even more than before. If his daughter was still in Busparia, he had to get to her, save her. He finally understood the need that drove Brody to attack him.

Scarlet waited with him, smiling and nodding as everyone filed past them.

"Wulfric, what the fuck's wrong?" Scarlet asked when they were alone.

He shook his head and swallowed hard. "I—I'm not sure if anything's wrong exactly. Everything might finally be turning up right. I have to make this treaty work." As if in a daze, he followed, dragging Scarlet by the hand behind him.

## Chapter Thirty-Eight

Scarlet sat between Knox and Wulfric at the table eating her soup. Something had happened when Wulfric had talked with Eirwyn. She'd thought about speaking to him about it, but he was busy smiling and talking with the couple beside him.

He was in his element. It should have been impossible, a Growler, a monster at a dinner party. But he was a predator on a mission to force every single person near him to surrender. Was there anything he wasn't good at? She seriously doubted it.

Knox turned to her and smiled. "Are you making it, Red?"

Her nose wriggled at the dreaded nickname. "I'm fine. Thanks for sitting me next to you. You know I'm no good at these social situations."

He shrugged. "I wouldn't say that. I'd say you're just very selective in social situations."

The servants brought the next course, and Wulfric engaged the couple across the table from them. They'd been prominent nobles back in Busparia but had spent the past six months trying to build a road to the gem mines in the north. She'd expected them to give up well before now like the pampered nobles they were, but they were still pushing strong.

A quarter way down the table, voices rose higher.

"I'm not so sure a treaty benefits us at all," said one of the Robins on the Confederation Council.

Ashur crossed his arms and leaned back to glare across the table. "I disagree. They're a ready army should we need them. You've heard the stories as well as I have."

The Robin glared back. "Exactly. It's not safe. Besides, what use have we of an army when the Robins are still ready to meet whatever need our king declares?"

The other conversations around the table faltered until Eirwyn at the end of the table cleared her throat. "An excellent point, gentlemen. Perhaps—since you obviously do not wish to wait until tomorrow to talk politics—we can discuss it right here, right now. Wulfric? An introduction, please."

Wulfric stiffened beside her, and Scarlet put her hand on his thigh under the table. He gripped her hand tightly but smiled down the table. "Very well, princess—"

"Queen," Knox said quietly.

Wulfric paused and nodded, "Pardon, my queen. Many have heard stories of Growlers as mindless beasts who hunt, fuck, and kill indiscriminately."

Several of the ladies gasped at the crude language, but Wulfric ignored them as he smiled and let his face shift into the Growler. The seams of his shirt at his neck tore, and he reversed the magic back to his normal self.

"Growlers are much more, as you can see. I'm sitting here eating and drinking. I'm not tamed, but neither am I a monster. In fact, I was born in Busparia right on the edge of the Feral Forest. I grew up listening to those same stories of Growlers."

"Then where do the stories come from?" someone asked.

Wulfric explained. "Excellent question. Three hundred years ago, the Growlers were all natural born but dying off. Very few pregnancies led many to fear that the entire race would go extinct. The goddess decided to spare the Growlers and taught them how to weave a spell to turn humans into Growlers. That's what I am, a turned Growler."

A woman gasped. "What's to stop the Growlers from turning every human into a beast?"

Wulfric frowned. "No, being turned is always a choice, and some choose not to accept the chance at a second life. The goddess made sure the Growlers took the ability seriously and would not abuse it. It works best when a human body is near death."

"So you'll attack, then as we're bleeding out, turn us?"

Scarlet's teeth ground together, and Wulfric stiffened. But it was Knox who interrupted.

"For gods' sake, let the man explain his purpose here before you go jumping to the worst possible conclusions. You did the same thing when you first saw me as a dragon, remember? I thought we'd grown past this."

Murmurs along the table made Scarlet squirm, but Knox turned to Wulfric. "Please, Growler, continue. Is that what happened to you? Were you near death?"

Wulfric paused, a flash of sorrow and pain on his face. He didn't hide it, and the sight made the murmurs stop. "Yes, the Elders approached as I lay dying on the Southern Road, injured in the war. The army had transported the injured home, but several of those who were too close to death were simply... left to die."

A woman gasped, and Wulfric cleared his throat. "I thought my family was all dead, so I had nothing else to lose. I accepted the Elders' offer of a new life, and when the spell was done, all my memories of my life in Busparia were gone too."

"No memories?"

"Ah, I wouldn't mind forgetting myself."

"You said you were born in Busparia. How do you know if your memories are gone?"

Wulfric chuckled, and she squeezed his hand at the sound. "The prophecy I mentioned? When dragons ride once more, Growlers will regain what they've lost. Only when the dragons, Growlers, and druids unite will they be able to defeat the evil one and stop the next ice age."

Knox cleared his throat. "You've felt the winter lingering, haven't you? Growing colder? When Wulfric and Scarlet arrived three days ago, they brought an ice creature they'd defeated."

Leopol stepped from behind Knox and said, "The creature is a Memphit, a skeletal ice daemon spawn."

At the word daemon, several chairs raked the stone floor as men jumped up. One woman fainted in her seat. Scarlet's lip twitched as Ashur rolled his eyes down the table. She'd always liked the man, even before he'd turned into a gargoyle.

"Enough," Knox bellowed. Everyone froze as a haze of green smoke sank from his nose, and he waved it away. "Sit down and listen. Please."

Leopol cleared his throat and gripped the lapels of his jacket. "As I was saying, the memphit is small but powerful enough to create a blizzard. They don't travel alone either, but in packs of a dozen."

The whispers around the table grew louder, and Leopol put his hand on Knox's shoulder.

Knox rapped on the table, and all eyes turned to him. "Someone has to be controlling the memphits, or at the very least, releasing them into our world. They don't belong here."

Wulfric coughed, and Knox's gaze swiveled to him. Wulfric said quietly, "The prophecy mentioned an evil one who would bring the next ice age."

Scarlet tightened her grip on his hand. They'd talked about this with Knox and Grandma for the past two days, researching books in the library with Leopol and trying to find everything they could about the evil one and daemons. They each had theories, but this was the one that made the most sense.

Knox looked around the table once more, meeting each person's gaze. "We have a plan to root out the evil one and stop the ice age, but it will require us to work with the Growlers. We need their help to protect the forest and investigate Busparia, which seems to be the center of the cold according to recent reports."

Eirwyn cleared her throat and all eyes swung to her end of the table. "Right, so this is what the Growler alpha Wulfric, Knox, Scarlet, and I have been discussing thus far."

Eirwyn threw light magic to the ceiling, casting shadows of figures running through the forest as she explained.

"The turned Growlers are going to be the most easily integrated into our society, especially now that their memories are back. Remember, some of them might even be your missing family members who went off to war and never returned."

A murmur of whispers echoed in the room as the servants removed the now cold food and served the next course. Eirwyn continued.

"The Growlers can root out other memphits in the forest and provide wider protection. They can work with the Robins, but we'll start with low doses. We'll introduce a few Growlers at a time to Vidrland, but if there are objections in town, then we'll start here at Hartsgrove."

The light and shadows danced on the ceiling, showing wolves chasing a monster and making it burst into a shower of light.

"While the Growlers help the Robins protect the forest, Scarlet will lead the Hunters into Busparia to ferret out exactly what's going on there. You've heard the reports from the other Hunters. Monsters roam at night. Anyone out after dark is never heard from again. Is this because there are more memphits or something else, something more, something bigger?"

The lights on the ceiling showed a shadow attacking a village, and the villagers bursting into light. One man cleared his throat and braved a question.

"But there's no need for a treaty with the Growlers. They can help ferret out the daemons, but so can the Robins. It's what they're trained for. We don't need the Growlers."

Scarlet's chest itched, and she cleared her throat. All eyes swiveled to her, and she froze. Wulfric squeezed her hand, and she looked up at him. She leaned closer to his ear and whispered, "Dragon Claws."

He nodded and sat up straight, turning to the table. "The druid Olive can attest to this story, but as you all know, Scarlet's mother was killed by Growlers thirty years ago."

Several people nodded around the table, but Wulfric's

thumb stroked the back of her hand, distracting her from their eyes.

"What you might not know is that they weren't just turned or natural born Growlers. There is a secret division of the Hunters known as the Dragon Claws."

Whispers flew across the table, and Scarlet saw Ashur frown and nod, saying to the man next to him, "I've heard of them."

Wulfric said, "If asked a few weeks ago, Scarlet would've said they were a myth. But she asked the Elders of my tribe about it, and between them and Olive's own account, we now believe the Dragon Claws were the ones who killed her mother."

"For what purpose?" someone asked.

Knox shook his head. "We don't know."

Ashur rubbed his chin. "But we do know the purpose of the Dragon Claws. They were always rumored to be the king's personal mercenaries, an elite hidden force who originally belonged to the Hunters but were no longer."

Scarlet looked at Ashur and nodded. "But when the Hunters began to offer their services for a fee to anyone who could pay, the kings of Busparia kept the Dragon Claws for their own political machinations."

Her face flamed and her throat closed again. Wulfric squeezed her hand twice, and she took a deep breath.

Eirwyn's shadows shifted to six Growlers wearing Buspartan army clothing, the medallion on their cloaks clear in the light magic. Scarlet had drawn them a picture, and it had even been in one obscure book Leopol had found in the library.

"So someone—most likely the king—had Scarlet's mother killed. Olive the druid has confirmed that there have always been sporadic attacks against the druids, which is why there are only three of them left," Knox said.

Wulfric's voice grew louder. "This is why the treaty is necessary. Who better to sniff out an elite band of Growlers than other Growlers? We can find them and the daemons, if you'll help us."

"Help how? What exactly is in this treaty, then?" someone grumbled.

Eirwyn's light magic shifted. "I'm so glad you asked. Growlers, both turned and natural born, will maintain sovereignty over themselves, but the Feral Forest will officially be split into a northern and southern kingdom. They will keep their hierarchy of five tribes each with an alpha and three Elders to settle disputes within their sub-territories, but will officially recognize an alpha king. Wulfric, do I understand that you already fill that role?"

"Yes, your highness. Even though we don't officially recognize my position as higher than any other alpha, I do settle disputes between the tribes. The biggest difference with the treaty is that Growlers would officially be welcomed into the northern kingdom."

Eirwyn nodded. "Correct, and if we recognize the Growlers as a kingdom, Glathen and Busparia will soon follow. If Growlers wish to settle in our new towns in the Feral Forest, they will fall under the same laws as everyone else. If they wish to swear fealty to the dragon king and renounce their citizenship as a Growler, then they will be allowed to vote as a full citizen."

"Wait, if they have five alphas, who says the other four tribes will even abide by the treaty?" someone asked.

Wulfric nodded. "That's a good point, but I met with the other four, and we're all in agreement. I speak for all of them, but I have also provided signed documentation to the king and queen to prove it. You're welcome to send delegates to each of the tribes and ask the other alphas themselves, though."

Several shifted uncomfortably in their seats but all avoided making eye contact with him. It made Scarlet angry, and the hair on the back of her neck stood up.

"I was there, in the Growler camp. He is the alpha and does have authority to make the treaty. Shove your questions of his integrity and honor up your ass. No one disparages my mate and gets away with it."

The room went silent as all eyes fell on her. The heat of anger froze in her veins, and she felt her flushed cheeks grow cold. Wulfric squeezed her hand twice, and she remembered to breathe.

Then he pulled her hand from under the table and kissed her palm. "Ah, bunny, I adore when you get all fiery and defensive. Say more nice things about me."

Ashur chuckled, and some others at the table smiled. She scowled at Wulfric, "Don't push it, wolfie."

That brought on more chuckles. Wulfric grinned wide, his golden eyes glowing with predatory desire. At whispering behind her, she turned to see Leopol talking quietly to Knox, who frowned and nodded.

When he looked back at the table, he nodded to Eirwyn. "Continue, love. And for gods' sake, everyone eat before they take the course away again."

The discussion grew more political and less antagonistic after that, and soon dessert was finished. Eirwyn and Knox led them back into the parlor, but none of them could escape the night yet. As soon as Wulfric and Scarlet settled into the same corner as earlier, Leopol came through the door and walked directly to them.

"The dwarves have arrived and wish to see you," he said.

Wulfric was being waved over by Ashur, so Scarlet shooed him over. "Go, be sociable. Remember your humanity while I go deal with the dwarves."

Wulfric paused. "Are they safe? Friend or foe?"

She rolled her eyes and stepped back through the door as she said over her shoulder, "Friends. No foe would dare enter the dragon's lair."

# Chapter Thirty-Nine

She followed Leopol down the hall to Knox's office, her stomach twisting with possibilities. They hadn't sent the messenger back to her with the mirrors, but had come themselves.

Inside stood John, Knox's dwarven friend from Vicrland, and his brother Kris from the northern mines.

"Gentlemen," she said as she entered.

Their bushy white brows rose as they took in her dress. She winced and shook out the skirts. "Not a word about this. What's the news?"

Kris pulled the mirrors from his bag on the table, and she stepped closer. "Yes, well, this magic mirror was trickier than normal."

"It's definitely not any of the normal technology the Buspartans have produced in the past few hundred years," John said.

"But we've figured out how it works. Seems to be an ancient magic, possibly from the Mer-kingdom, but we deciphered it alright."

"Deciphered—you mean it works?" she demanded.

Kris nodded, opened one of them, and handed it to her. "Aye, we made some modifications. See the seven buttons on the side? Push the second one."

She pushed the tiny knob, and the mirror shimmered with magic before it revealed one of their brothers in their northern home.

"Oi, it works over long distances!" the brother said.

"Pay up. Five gold. I told you it'd work," said another from behind him.

The men bickered as another took the mirror and held it too close to his face, showing his nose hairs.

"Huntress, is that you?"

She grinned. "Yes, it's me. I'm here with Kris and John."

The man in the mirror said, "I want to call this thing talkies. What do you think?"

She chuckled, "Talkies is fine."

The mirror's image jiggled as it was ripped from the dwarf's hand, and another one said, "Hey, you didn't even tell her my idea about commies. It's a much better name."

"Too late. Snooze you lose," sang the other. A growl, a yell, and the pocket mirror's image bounced as they argued.

Kris scowled and pointed to the side of the round pocket mirror as he said, "Push the button again to end the image and sound."

She waved, even though none of them were paying them any attention. "Bye, boys." Then she pushed the button before asking, "Do we know the effective range is for communication?"

Kris shook his head. "No, but your messenger said it needs to reach the Southern Road? We'll need someone to take these there and test them."

She nodded, turning the things over in her palm as Kris

explained how each button was tied to a different mirror. "Once we figured out how the magic worked, we could reproduce it fairly quickly. The rune on the bottom prevents anyone else from duplicating it or prying into the magic, of course. But this will help not just the Feral Forest but the entire continent communicate much faster. Can you imagine? There could be communication shops in every town. If help were needed, it could be sent right away instead of days or weeks later once word had traveled on foot."

Kris finally took a breath, and she grinned. She knew he'd keep talking if no one stopped him, so she said to John, "And what about you? I didn't expect you to arrive yourself, with all you have to manage Vidrland."

John wrinkled his thick nose and hunched his shoulders. "Yes, well, about the reports in Busparia..."

"Yes?" she asked.

He pulled out a larger hand-held mirror with a long handle. It was the size of Wulfric's giant hand, with similar runes on the edges as the pocket sized ones. He pressed a few of the ruins, and magic shimmered as he talked.

"I've been cataloging all the mirrors in Busparia in my spare time."

Kris snorted. "Who has spare time these days?"

John shrugged. "It helps me fall asleep. Anyway, this doesn't have any sound, but do you see what I see?"

Scarlet stepped closer and narrowed her eyes. The image was murky, but she saw a shimmering yellow gown on the floor of a library. The woman was bent over, her lips moving as Scarlet watched her profile.

A pack of forks and spoons pushed a book off the second to bottom shelf, and the woman sat back on her haunches and clapped, a beaming smile on her face.

Scarlet gasped, "The queen."

"Aye," John said. "But something's not quite right. See how she's almost coaxing the silverware to open the book and flip the pages?"

"Where is this?" Scarlet demanded. Anger raced through her. The woman looked unchanged, happy and smiling in the library. It wasn't fair, when Scarlet's own world had been irrevocably changed six months ago. Her stomach tightened, and dinner threatened to come back up.

"Demerel in Busparia. The Winter Palace," John said quietly. "When we reverse engineered the king's spy mirrors, we began to find the patterns and sequences to the runes and magic. Each mirror has its own signature, so to speak. It's taken months to go through, but the signatures just keep going. This is the only mirror left in the Winter Palace, though."

Scarlet frowned, her brain whirling. The latest reports had the queen in the capital. What was she doing back in Demerel?

John touched some runes on the side, and the image wavered, fading to black before revealing a town square.

"This is a village ten miles outside the capital on the Newing River. We've watched it at various times and have seen the monsters that keep the curfew. This isn't the only village like this, but the one most preyed upon."

"Probably because of its proximity to the army base," Kris scowled.

"You think they really are monsters?" she asked, watching as shadows raced down the dark street. It was too dark to truly see what they were, but they didn't move like Growlers.

John stroked his white beard. "Daemons, most likely. Leopol showed us the one you defeated, and what we've

seen in the mirrors are very similar in structure and movement, but not the abilities."

"What do you mean?" she asked, her heart racing as she
watched the shadowy creature.

"Not all of them can make a whirlwind of ice. Some
burn down buildings and others simply suck the living into a
pit of darkness."

She frowned, her mind racing through the books that
they'd poured over the past few days. She turned and found
the stack on a side table.

As she flipped through it, she said, "That does sound
like the daemons in this book Leopol found. Look here."

She held it out, and John took it, nodding as she turned
to the window. They talked quietly to each other as she
walked away.

She could barely see the stars, it was so dark outside, the
sliver of the new moon not yet risen. The Hunters—once
armed with enough knowledge about the daemons—could
probably handle them. They'd be able to track them down
and eliminate them.

"Have you seen any other monsters in Busparia?
Growlers perhaps?" She turned to face them.

John's hand froze on the book, and they looked at her
with eyes wide.

"Any that wear Buspartan clothing and a medallion on
their cloak?" she pressed, not giving them a chance to
respond.

John and Kris looked at each other, then John picked up
the mirror and pushed more runes on the side. The image
flickered to a dark room lit by a roaring fire below the
image. Three cots lined the left wall and three the right,
each with neatly tucked corners and nary a thread out of

place. The entire room looked cleaner than any she'd ever seen.

Just then the door in the image swung open and in strode two Growlers. They ducked under the doorway as they entered, and she saw their shifted jaws moving as they spoke.

"Still no sound," John said. "We're working on it, but they are definitely in Busparia. We weren't sure what they were doing there last month when we first saw them, but based on what Leopol told us while we were waiting for your dinner to end..."

He trailed off, but Scarlet didn't need him to finish. The medallions on their cloaks were bright as day.

"Where is this?" she asked, licking her dry lips as her hands shook.

John looked in the mirror and squinted. "According to our data, in the castle keep at the capital, but not in the castle itself. One of the external buildings."

Scarlet shook her head and turned to pace from the windows to the fireplace. Her skirts swirled and then caught, and she hiked them up so she could stride. She'd need to ask Eirwyn about the layout of the castle at the capital, as Scarlet had never been there.

The Dragon Claws were real. Perhaps they were even the ones who'd murdered her mother thirty years ago, although they hadn't looked that old. Perhaps they'd have answers on why the king had sought to kill the druids. Hells, she'd be happy with confirming who had ordered it done because surely the former king had been just a child then. His father, the old king who'd died in the forest?

She spun on her heel, her mind thinking through every possibility and planning her next steps. It would take time for Wulfric to pick the Growlers most likely to succeed against them. Perhaps they could make a joint mission with Growlers and Hunters.

But the queen was closer. Demerel was just outside the Feral Forest. It was the epicenter of the curse, and where her life had been changed six months ago.

Her hands shook as turned around and blinked in surprise. Wulfric walked toward her from just a few feet away. She'd been so lost in thought, she'd missed Knox, Eirwyn, Wulfric, Ashur, and Leopol coming into the room. Her gaze met Wulfric's concerned one as he took her hands in his, holding them tight to his chest.

His smooth caress made her shaking ease.

"What is it?" he asked, a worried line between his eyes.

She licked her lips, her eyes wide and heart racing. "Tomorrow morning, we ride for Demerel."

Tomorrow night, she'd have her curse reversed or the queen's head on a pike.

# Chapter Forty

"Are you sure this is going to work?" Wulfric asked, staring at the thick line of trees at the end of the Lone Road. His eyes burned from lack of sleep. He'd sent two Growlers to the druid's cottage to meet with the Nightstalkers' messengers in case they didn't return by the deadline. He'd hoped to distract her with several orgasms to get her to calm down enough to sleep last night. But by the time she'd written letters to different Hunters and he'd finished with the Growlers, it'd been well-past midnight. They'd both fallen into bed with a groan, and she'd insisted they leave before dawn.

Light just starting to come up, but a thick tower of trees formed a wall in front of them. The Lone Road appeared to continue on the other side.

Scarlet pulled out a cylindrical whistle with holes on one side and arched a brow. "How do you think the Hunters get in and out of the forest to spy on Busparia?"

She blew into the end and several notes flowed together. Wulfric's ear twitched in recognition of three different birds of the forest. How one instrument could overlap three sounds, he had no idea.

But before she put the whistle down, the trees on the road moved toward them. The dirt of the road rippled as the roots moved with them, allowing a space just wide enough for them to ride through one horse at a time.

He followed her, his stomach in knots at the thought of facing his old life. Scarlet had been so focused on getting to Demerel and the queen that he hadn't had a chance to tell her he'd lived there once upon a time.

Shoulders tense, he turned the horse Knox had loaned him on the Lone Road. The winter palace was visible, but where he'd expected to see the town, there was simply a pile of rubble and ash.

"The town is gone," he said into the stillness. No birds sang on this side of the forest. There was no sign of life at all. No rodents rustling the grass because there was no grass. Nothing but dirt turned black as if by a fire.

Scarlet nodded slightly ahead of him, but didn't turn to face him. Her gaze remained on the castle.

"When the queen's curse exploded, the spell settled over everything. Like a bomb going off, it destroyed everything."

"Except the castle," he said.

She nodded, but didn't continue. They reached the outskirts of the town. Piles of ashes and broken timbers were all that was left of the cottages. He swallowed as they turned onto the major thoroughfare, and he spied his parents' shop.

He pulled the horse to a stop and swung down.

"What are you doing?" Scarlet asked, finally turning to him.

He didn't answer. Memories of running through the shop while his pa argued with a customer flooded him. His ma insisting on him learning his sums so he could help. He looked down the street to where the tavern had stood, where he'd stared out the window at the beautiful brunette girl in pigtail braids.

His eyes stung as he remembered when they'd finally ran into each other—literally—at the market. He glanced back to the shop, not wanting Scarlet to see whatever might show on his face.

"I just need a moment," he said softly, staring at the rubble of his former life.

"Do you want me to stay? If not, I'm going to scope out the castle."

He nodded, still not turning to look at her. "That's fine. You can see if the gates are open or if we need to find another way in."

"Alright, but yell if you see anything suspicious."

"You do the same," he murmured, but she probably didn't hear him. She'd already turned her horse and continued on the road.

He pressed his hands to his eyes and ground his teeth. Within a few deep breaths, he had himself under control and dropped his hands. A flash of light caught on the edge of his vision, and he glanced over.

His heart twisted painfully as he took a few steps forward, and he strode the few steps, kicking a pile of ash and broken lumber to reveal the shop's sign. Half gone, but the faded green letters & SON were still visible.

His family legacy, fading away with each passing day. He had dreamed of passing on the business to his own son, but fate had cruelly denied him that chance. His daughter was all that remained, a reminder of the love he had lost when Mara succumbed to the fever. Once this trip to the Winter Palace was done, they'd return to Hartsgrove and finish getting the treaty approved by the people. When the Feral Forest was secure, he could go into Busparia with other Growlers and Hunters and find his daughter.

A shrill shriek pierced the air, and he spun to the road. A thick, ominous cloud engulfed one side of the walls, casting a dark shadow over the destruction. Broken stones and crumbled bricks littered the ground, a stark contrast to the grandeur that once stood there.

He jumped on the horse and raced to the cloud.

The shriek wasn't Scarlet, but he knew. Where there was trouble, she'd be there.

It took too many precious minutes to reach the castle's wall, the stone blackened but strong and solid. He raced along the edge of it and rounded the corner to see the black cloud coalescing into a darker figure.

A monstrous creature, its form rippling with foreboding black shadows, towered above them like a dark tornado. It loomed at least the size of a horse, dwarfing Scarlet and her steed in comparison. With one hand gripping the reins and the other brandishing a dagger, she faced the looming beast with unwavering determination. Her face was etched with grim resolve, unflinching in the face of fear as she prepared to do battle. He was proud of her for controlling her shift and not succumbing to the rabbit or deer.

Then the black clad figure grabbed her hand and yanked her off the horse. The dagger did nothing as if simply flying through air. But the unexpected movement made Scarlet cry out as she jerked her hand away and went flying.

The dagger clattered to the dirt, and she shifted in midair to a little red rabbit. Her clothes fell to the ground, and she burrowed inside them to hide from the shadow creature. It floated to her pile of clothes, and Wulfric roared.

The creature turned to him, and he didn't even think. He shifted, his clothes bursting as he launched himself at the villain. The shadows wrapped around him, and the air grew thin. The shadows began to choke him, and he clawed and swiped.

The thing held him above the ground with a hand on his back leg. A hand... The thing was mostly shadows, but there was something solid within it. Wulfric closed his eyes as it swung him around, pushing past the dizziness and focusing on feeling the body.

He took a deep, slow, tight breath. White spots pushed on the edge of his vision. *There.* He found the creature's body and dug his claws in. The shrill shriek reverberated through him, making his teeth chatter. With jaws open wide, he ripped into flesh that tasted of death and decay.

He tore it away as that piercing shriek filled the air. His head vibrated from the sound as he took another bite and dug his claws mercilessly into the black void. He couldn't see anything through the blackness, couldn't feel the ground. But he had to find the weak spots, the jugular, the primary arteries...

He tore bite after bite, never letting go with his left hand so he could maintain a tight grasp on the elusive shadow thing's body. The screaming turned to moaning, and then he felt the body rip into two pieces in his mouth.

The shadows burst around him, and he drew a deep breath as he dropped the few feet to the ground. He shook his head to clear the dizziness and turned to where Scarlet had huddled next to the wall.

Instead of a scared little bunny, a beautiful red wolf stood with hackles raised, ready to pounce. When she finally saw him through the dissipating shadows, her fur smoothed and she sniffed the air.

"Wulfric? Are you alright? Is it gone?"

He grinned wide and bounded to her side. She took a step back, then they circled each other. Why was he always so sex focused after a fight? Damn, her scent was even better like this. He sniffed under her neck, and he wanted to howl that she let him that close to one of her most vulnerable places. Growlers were fiercely territorial over their weak spots.

Her wet nose nuzzled behind his ear, then over his back. He licked her side down to her haunches. A cold nudge at his crotch made him yip, and he turned to see her licking around his hidden cock.

Hidden no longer, his body knew his mate was here, sniffing for more. He chuckled as she dipped her head again, licking around his shaft as it grew and made itself known.

"Watch it, bunny, or I'll mount you right here, right now."

Her eyes flashed golden green and met his, the spark of mischief clear even in this form.

"So? My heart is still racing from that—that thing, wolfie. Maybe I need a good fuck to get my head back in the game and away from the shitty way I shifted and hid."

The sparkle dimmed as she grew serious. He licked her cheek and nuzzled under her ear.

"You did what you had to survive, love. It's nothing to be ashamed of. You were just waiting for me to show up."

"Psh, I don't need you to fight my battles for me." Her words echoed in his head as she turned away with head high. He barked and nipped her tail, making her snarl and turn back to him.

"I know, bunny, but we're a team. We're stronger together, remember? Not just because we were mated, either. Side by side is how we're going to see this through, alright?"

He stared at her, unblinking, and waited as she thought through it. Then she shivered and dipped her head low, a natural sign of submission among Growlers.

He nuzzled her head, nudging it higher so they were equal. He didn't want her submission unless she was underneath him. His shoulder nudged hers as he tried to draw closer, the scent of her arousal and excitement making him lick his lips.

Then she whimpered. "Wulfric, please."

He growled, and she dipped her head again and licked between his legs. With a groan, he closed his eyes, not because of the darkness but because she was the light. She'd brought so many changes into his life, joy and life and light primary among them.

She tried to suck his cock, but Growlers didn't do that. Too many teeth scraped down his shaft, and he jerked back with a hiss. He met her eyes, and they were alight with that mischievous streak once more. Laughter echoed, and the joy spread through him unable to be contained.

He pounced, and they rolled in the dirt, the laughter drowning out the memories of the shadow monster. She landed beneath him with all four legs flat on the ground. She pressed up and back with her back legs, and he eased off her. She looked over her shoulder and wiggled that ass, lifting her tail and arching her thick red brow.

"Well? What are you waiting for?"

He grinned and licked another vulnerable spot, making her freeze her wiggling and moan. Then he mounted her and rocked forward until his dick found its way home.

She panted as Wulfric filled her completely, the stretching burning so good. He paused barely a moment to let her savor the feeling before he was thrusting in and out at a pounding pace.

Her eyes went wide, and she used her forearms to push back into him, trying to drive him deeper and deeper with each thrust.

"How do you like that, bunny?"

She moaned, and her eyes fluttered. They were barely in the shadows next to the castle wall, out in the open of what used to be the town, fucking for anyone who could see. Not that there was anyone outside the castle, but the thought of others watching made her pussy drip and pulse.

"Fuck yes, just like that, wolfie."

"You like being my bitch? Taking that big dick as I pound into you like an animal?"

She gave the low keening cry of a wolf as her pussy clenched. *Yes, yes, yes.*

"Fuck, yes," he hissed in her mind as he thrust deep.

"You like it too, wolfie. Is my pussy tighter as a Growler? Think I could take you as a fucking rabbit?"

He growled, and the thrusting grew erratic. She pushed back against him, trying to take it deeper than ever before. The knot at the base grew bigger, and she knew he was close.

Fuck, so was she. Too soon, she was chasing that orgasmic high and ready to fling herself off the edge of oblivion.

He thrust harder, the knot stretching her entrance wider. The wetness helped, but she still craved that burn and stretch. Some animalistic glutton for punishment pushed her on, and she pressed back harder.

The knot pushed in, making her scream and clench with release. He roared, still thrusting, but now unable to withdraw. Each time his knot tried to leave, it made her convulse harder, triggering her orgasm to keep going. Her vision went red. Her body quaked, and still he thrust, reaching the entrance to her womb and making her scream.

He tensed and thrust deeper, holding himself still as he swelled. She shook uncontrollably as his gushing heat flooded her. Pulse after pulse, it stretched so much it hurt. But the orgasm overshadowed the pain, and she clenched on him with every pulse.

Her back legs couldn't hold herself up anymore, and she collapsed onto her stomach, all four paws tucked under her. Wulfric followed her down as he licked behind her ear and crooned in her head.

"Fucking hells, love, that was—that was something else."

She chuckled, her eyes fluttering closed. "Best fuck ever?"

He chuckled, the vibrations making her clench around him. "Definitely. I've heard knot sex is other worldly, but didn't believe it."

He settled his paws on either side of her, his back legs wide as his entire body sheltered hers.

"Unfortunately, I've also heard the knot takes a long time to go down."

"So we're stuck like this?"

"Yes. Sorry, bunny, I know you wanted to get into the castle as quickly as possible."

She yawned and wiggled, feeling the delicious stretch of him still within her. It's fine. The castle's not going anywhere. "Besides, I could use a nap."

He huffed a laugh and licked her Growler jaw. "Sleep then, and I'll keep watch."

When Scarlet opened her eyes, she was back in human form, naked but with her cloak covering her as the sun approached the tree line. She stretched and rubbed the sleep from her eyes, but didn't see Wulfric or the horses. The tracks in the dirt led around the wall, so maybe he was scavenging for food, finding a safe place for the horses, or searching for the best way inside.

She beat the dust and ash out of her clothes, then slipped them back on. When Wulfric still hadn't returned, she followed his tracks to the side servant's entrance, losing them on the cobbled courtyard. She searched with her heightened senses, but couldn't hear or see anything outside the massive castle keep.

The stone seemed to stretch endlessly as she circled the castle. Each step made her tension rise, gnawing her insides like a ravenous beast. If she were Wulfric, where would she be? The servant's entrance door stood open, and her stomach growled.

She sighed in relief. Yes, of course he would try to find food. All men were led by their stomachs or dicks, after all.

She pulled out one of her daggers and pushed the door open with a creak. She winced at the sound, but nothing stirred. A thick layer of dust coated every surface. Dishes still sat in the sink, maggots long gone but their carcasses still scattered around. She stepped inside, searching for signs of life, tracks in the dust, or any aura or sound.

No sign of Wulfric or that he'd been here. A gnawing fear demanded she search every room downstairs before tracking the upper floor to find him. She felt tied to him by the magic of their mate bond. It spurred her inside the eerily still room.

419

A quick search showed the pantry well past the rotten phase. She guessed maybe two or three months, which didn't make sense. The curse blast had been six months ago, and if the queen was still in residence, there should be food aplenty. Servants too, for that matter.

She searched the larder, the cellar, and the icebox, but there was nothing worth eating. She pulled out a piece of dried jerky from her pocket and ate it as she walked on silent feet to the servant's stairs. She opened the door and listened, stretched her senses but felt no one near.

She let the door swing shut and went to the next door.

A shiver raced down her spine as the memory of the last time she was here filled her mind. The clanging metal of battle in the courtyard. The magical smoke and fire on the roof as the king and Knox had battled. Following the injured king and queen upstairs to their rooms…

She shook her head and pushed open the door to the short hallway. A murmur came from the other side, and she crouched as she swallowed the last bite of her jerky. She peered inside through the small circular window in the door.

The ceiling was painted with a scene of the gods and goddesses eating at a feast. Tapestries hung on the opposite wall, a thin layer of dust barely muting the vibrant colors of the battle scene. Golden drapes hung along the windows, pulled back with red silk. Although the sun would set soon, the room was lit by magical sconces on the walls, casting deliberately glows on the scene on the ceiling.

Gilt trimmed chairs with red upholstered cushions had been pushed along one side of the dining table, leaving the closest side free of chairs. The long, wooden dining table was littered with vials, potions, magical burners, herbs, jars, and piles of ingredients. Much of it was covered in dust too, but a flurry of activity at the far end of the room caught her by surprise.

A yellow and red skirt writhed on the floor. Clearly the queen was kneeling on the floor, but Scarlet found it odd that the queen would wear the same dress from the spy image in the mirror. As she stared, she thought it might have even been the same dress from that fateful day six months ago.

A fiery fury surged through Scarlet like lightning in her veins pulsing with each breath. She fought to control the burning rage within, knowing that she couldn't simply charge in and end the queen's life, no matter how her hands ached to do just that. Countless people relied on keeping the queen alive to undo the curses.

Scarlet pushed the emotions aside and slowly pushed the door open. The hinges were silent, thank the gods, and she slipped inside the room on quiet feet. She hugged the wall until she reached the buffet table and listened.

"Ah, just like that. Thank you so much, Gus. That's bloody brilliant. Now if Jaq can just put the spoonful of wormwood dust in… yes, I know it stinks and you don't want it to dirty your beautiful shine, but you're doing such a great job. I couldn't have managed it better myself, trust me. You boys don't even miss a speck!"

Scarlet frowned and peered through the window. There were other people in the room? She couldn't sense them or see any auras, but she needed to know how many before she launched an attack.

The queen leaned back on her haunches and clapped.

"Well done! I knew you could do it!" She looked to the side and her gaze collided with Scarlet's. Her jaw dropped, and she scrambled to her feet.

Scarlet felt ice slither through her body, pushing aside

the red hot emotions as her daggers hung limply in her hands. She remained frozen in place as the queen rushed forward, trying to process what she saw.

"Oh gods, praise be Borga, you're here. How did you get past the shadow monster? Oh thank the heavens. Finally, someone to talk to, someone to help! You don't know how lonely the past few months have been without..."

The queen frowned and stopped a few feet away, a wrinkle in her forehead making her so much more relatable. Bella had scowled and cursed at rowdy patrons to keep them in line at the tavern, but now, standing in front of Scarlet with a defeated look on her face, she seemed more like the tired and worn-out tavern owner at the end of a long night than an evil queen who summons monsters.

"You... you were there. When he died," the queen said, her eyes flashing and her fists clenching at her sides.

Scarlet held her daggers at the ready by her side, but she wasn't sure what to expect. It sure hadn't been this, though.

The queen was a ghost. Nearly translucent, but exactly like Leopol.

Fuck.

# Chapter Forty-One

"You cost me everything!" The ghost roared through the dining room, making the windows shake.

Scarlet swung her blades to hug her wrists, cradling the handle between a finger and thumb. The sleek metal of the blades gleamed against her tanned skin as she held up her hands, palms out. "Now wait a minute, I wasn't responsible for the king's death."

"You might as well have been! You heard him that day. If you'd just killed Eirwyn like he'd ordered, none of this would've happened."

Scarlet's mind raced with possibilities. She needed to find a way to reason with Bella before things escalated further. She couldn't let her hurt Wulfric or anyone else, if they were able to bring her back to Knox and Eirwyn.

But how could she reason with someone who was already dead?

Scarlet waved her hands wide and kept her voice even, trying to de-escalate the situation while convincing the woman to come with her. "Fucking hells, Bella, do you even hear yourself right now? This was Eirwyn we're talking about. She was your friend! She was always at your tavern, helping serve people and cleaning up."

Bella cupped her round cheeks, her face crumbling as tears burst from her eyes. "I know!" She wailed as the tears fell, "My head knows that! It's illogical to be so mad and to have wished she would've just died."

Scarlet scoffed. "But your head was turned by the king's manipulating ways. He twisted you so much that you're still siding with him, six months later!"

Bella's hands fell limply to her sides, but the tears kept falling silently. "Has it been that long? I—I hadn't realized."

The weight of Bella's struggles seemed to press down on her, making her appear smaller and more fragile than Scarlet had ever seen her. A wave of compassion washed over Scarlet, mingling with a fierce protectiveness. She longed to wrap Bella in her arms, to shield her from the cruelties of the world that had beaten her down.

Bella rubbed her forehead and sighed. Then her big brown eyes welled with more tears. "By the light, I'm sorry. What's your name again? I—my head's a mess right now, sorry."

Scarlet knew how difficult it was to become a different being than before, to lose some of her humanity and be made fun of for it. How had Bella managed becoming a ghost in this big castle alone? How long had she been this way?

Scarlet lowered her daggers. "I'm Scarlet, head Hunter of the Feral Forest. Look, I know you're upset right now. It must be difficult being a ghost."

Bella swiped at her tears. "You have no idea how difficult."

Scarlet's eyes narrowed, and she waved to her head. "I

can imagine. Do you see these horns? These ears? This nose? You're not the only one who's been changed. There are many others, possibly even thousands, like us. Why don't you come with me? We'll work together to reverse the curse and regain some sense of normalcy."

Bella's tears ran faster and she gripped her yellow skirt tightly. It shimmered in the fading light as she shook her head. "No, I'm sorry, I can't."

Scarlet's jaw clenched, a hot flush rising up her neck as frustration mounted. "What do you mean, you can't?"

Bella wiped furiously at her cheek. "I mean just that. I don't know how to reverse the curse. I've tried every day. You'll never know what I had to do to reverse it, but—"

"What *you* had to do? Do you know what *I've* had to endure?" Her voice rose, and she stepped forward. "These horns grew to fourteen points and a spread so wide, it hurt to walk and stay upright for more than an hour. It took weeks to build the muscles in my neck and shoulders so I could even walk around the village."

Scarlet felt her anger rising, hot and fierce in her chest. She carefully put her daggers in their sheaths, struggling to control the surge of emotions threatening to overwhelm her. Bella twisted her skirt and shifted back and forth on her feet, frown growing deeper.

"And the pain," Scarlet continued, her voice cracking as she paced to the end of the dining table and back to the door. "Gods, the pain. Every time they grew, it felt like my skull was being split open. I'd wake up screaming, my pillow soaked with blood."

"Oh you poor thing," Bella murmured softly. Scarlet didn't stop pacing, just raised her hand and pointed at the ghost.

"You have no idea what it's been like," Scarlet spat, her

eyes flashing dangerously. "The stares, the whispers, the fear in people's eyes when they look at me. Do you know what it's like to be treated like a monster in your own village?"

Bella bit her lip and then said, "And I'm sorry for that, I am—"

"You're sorry?" Scarlet roared, her hands going wide. "You're sorry! Well, sorry doesn't fix the fucking problem, does it? You're going to reverse this or so help me gods, you'll die trying."

Bella laughed, "Die? Oh that's funny, considering I'm already a ghost."

Scarlet snapped. She lunged at Bella, dagger swiping up. It was like cutting through smoke, and wholly ineffective. The only thing it served was to make Bella panic. She threw up her hands, and the chairs in the dining room morphed.

Their legs grew longer, and the arm rests popped off to form arms with heavy wooden fists. They marched on Scarlet, and she slid along the dining room wall back toward the kitchen door. The buffet table drawers flew open and forks and spoons flew out, landing on the chairs and standing upright.

Scarlet had never felt a sense of menace coming from silverware before, yet she backed up, her breath catching in her throat. The empty jars and bowls on the table shivered and wobbled toward her. Even the buffet table shook in warning. Scarlet's heart raced as she backed toward the door.

Bella shook her head, "Oh gods, I'm sorry, so sorry." Tears streaming down her face, she turned and fled through the door on the opposite side of the room.

The chairs and silverware lunged toward Scarlet, and she slammed her shoulder against the kitchen door, but it wouldn't budge. Frustrated, she peered behind her into the small window. A row of stools barricaded the entrance, each one with several sharp knives standing upright on them.

With a low growl, Scarlet turned her back on the door and faced the more immediate threat of the chairs, forks, and spoons. She lunged forward and grabbed hold of the closest chair, lifting it and hurling it to the side. The wooden chair shattered on impact, sending shards flying in all directions.

But there were more marching toward her. With a flurry of movement, Scarlet dodged a flying fork aimed at her head and grabbed another chair. She swung it with all her might at the oncoming chair army. More stools and chairs broke in half, the sound of splintering wood filling the air.

Still they kept coming, relentless in their attack. The chairs bumped into each other but the forks and spoons flew through the air. She reached for another chair, but when she turned away from the door, it opened a crack, allowing the stools to push inside.

Trapped between the chairs and the stools, she leaped onto the seat of one, kicking the utensils as a barrage of knives flew towards her. She used part of a chair to block as many as she could, but the knicks and slashes—tiny though they were—hurt like hell.

Dodging and weaving on the backs of chairs, Scarlet picked up one and hurled it towards the door, shattering stools and several of the attacking utensils. But more were coming, closing in on her. She desperately wished Wulfric was here with her. Fighting with him side-by-side was so much better than doing this alone.

Scarlet took a deep breath and lashed out at everything in her path, determined to break free from this deadly trap and find him. She gritted her teeth and reached for the nearest animated chair. The buffet table drawers flew open and napkins swirled through the air straight at her. They wrapped around her arms, hands, legs, and neck.

Clawing at the one on her neck, her vision turning splotchy as it choked her. Her nails shifted into Growler claws, and finally she began to shred the fiendish napkins.

Her reflexes sharpened with the partial shift, and she caught the next fork as it sailed toward her. She threw it at the wall, pinning a napkin. One down, and a hundred to go. Hopefully the chairs and stools lasted long enough to be used against the army of silverware. With every movement, she prayed to the gods that Wulfric wasn't facing a similar fight.

---

Bella fled up the stairs, her feet not touching the ground although she still ran like she had a body. Try as she might, she just did not like floating or going through walls. She stumbled on a landing and collapsed to the floor, drawing her knees up and wrapping her arms around them.

She swiped at her cheeks, her chest tight as anger and grief swirled within her, threatening to burst. Her magic was so volatile the past few months of being trapped here. And it wasn't Scarlet's fault, she knew that. She may not have a brain or a body, but she wasn't stupid.

It was the mirror's fault. But everything in the past six months? The pain of the two servants who had been left behind in the castle? The trans-mutated cat-table and the horse-pitchfork?

Those were all her fault. She rocked on the marble floor, holding her knees. She'd made so many mistakes in the past year, starting with trusting Gastone after years of warnings from Eirwyn. Eirwyn had been her friend, regardless of how many awful chores Bella had given her in those early years. Not for the first time, she wondered if Eirwyn had escaped the curse blast.

That stupid curse blast. Light faded through window as the sun set. She couldn't see out from this angle on the floor, but there was nothing to see. Nothing but rubble lay between the castle and the forest now, just a desolate, lonely place where she'd been alone for months.

So alone except for the shadow monster that kept her trapped here. How had Scarlet gotten through it?

Poor Scarlet, battling her chair army. If she could just control her emotions, maybe her magic would be easier to control too.

A clattering behind her made her glance at the stairs down to the lower level. A fork and spoon jumped up each stair.

"Gus, Jaq, you didn't have to follow me," she said softly, picking them up and crossing her legs to hold them on her lap.

That in itself didn't make sense. She was a spirit, incorporeal. But somehow she could interact with those things she'd animated. Nothing else, though. She couldn't even pick up books in the library unless she animated them, and that risked changing the contents of the books themselves. If she did that, the information inside would be useless, so she'd long since stopped trying.

She slipped into her room and ran to the pot by the window where the rose lay in full bloom. There wasn't much time left, especially now the servants were gone. She'd had to animate the dresser and break the window just to let water in so it wouldn't die faster.

But every day, she felt her spirit growing more chaotic and volatile. Her emotions were growing out of control and her magic was unpredictable—which was why Gus and Jaq's animation change seemed to be permanent. They even had personalities and a semi-language of clicks and tings. They clicked at her from her lap, and she pulled them out with a frown.

"Yes, I know, but she's a Hunter. Surely she can handle a few chairs. She'll be alright."

The metal tongues of the fork clinked together, and she sighed. "Fine, I'll go stop the spell."

With one last look at her rose, she turned and went down the stairs. It should be fine now. She felt much more in control. Perhaps she just needed more conversation. Perhaps she'd just been so long with no outside interaction that she was out of practice.

Yes, she just needed to remember her humanity and act like the queen she was now.

She passed the library on the way to the dining room, but saw a light glowing from inside. She frowned and stepped inside.

A hairy man stood flipping through the books she'd been studying in one corner of the room. She walked around him, keeping him at a distance but drawing inexplicably closer. Her movement must have alerted him to her presence, because he looked up.

Golden eyes, heavy brows, firm jaw, crooked nose. Wolf ears poked through his black and silvery mane. The way he hunched his shoulders and held the book, holding it close and tilting his head just so...

She blinked as the book dropped from his hands, and he turned to face her fully. The light from the lantern caught his features, and she gasped.

Magic flared around her, and bookshelves rattled on the

wall. Books flew off the shelves. Shelves flew off the cases, and cases flew off the wall, crashing everywhere.

The man jumped back, but she started screaming. "You're dead! You're dead! You left me and died. Ten hellish years of running that godforsaken tavern by myself because you left."

Another bookcase slammed down, barely missing him. He stumbled on the step to the circular staircase, his eyes wide and glowing.

"Trix? You—you're here?"

"Oh gods," she cried, tears burning down her cheeks yet again. His voice was like a stab through the heart. How many times had she thought she'd heard it in her dreams? How many times had she asked herself, "*What would Da do in this situation?*" Only to be reminded that she was so utterly alone.

A book flew at his head, and she fisted her hands as she tried to control the magic. He dodged it and stepped over the scattering of papers and books toward her.

Her heart raced as she panicked. No, she couldn't use magic on the books. The words would get mixed up, and all that knowledge would be lost forever. Just like Da was.

Her hands flew up, magic flaring out as she struggled to contain it. She cried out, staring at him and the destruction swirling around her favorite room. She had to leave. It was the only way to protect the books. And her father.

She turned on her heel and fled back into the hallway and up the stairs.

# Chapter Forty-Two

Wulfric lunged to the door, yelling, "No, wait!"

She was here! His precious daughter was alive and here and—and dead.

He howled in anguish, but the hair on the back of his neck pricked in warning. He turned to see the two stuffed lynx's on either side of the stairs begin to prowl toward him. Their eyes didn't blink, taxidermized but magically animated as they were.

He tried to ignore them, turning back to the door to chase after her. One cat jumped forward to block the door, and the other flanked his back. His hands shifted into claws, and he barreled into the one in the doorway. Swiping left and right, he felt the lynx's own claws dig into his forearms as it lunged for his neck.

The lynx behind him jumped on his back, knocking him to the side. The first one bit his shoulder instead, but the teeth stabbed deep into his flesh, and he howled in anger.

His claws became razor sharp, mercilessly tearing into the creature in front of him. With a single arm, he lifted the flailing beast and tossed it aside. He tried desperately to dislodge the one clinging to his shoulder. Reaching behind with his other arm, he snatched the second one by its neck and held both up high. They clawed and scratched at his arms, but he paid them no mind as he made his way through the hallway, searching for his beloved Trix. His stomach churned at the sight that greeted him instead.

Where mounted animal heads had formerly lined the walls, they now rattled against the wallpaper as they tried to pull away. A few had already made it to the ground where they waddled on their marble base toward him. Teeth flashed and snarls clearly showed their intent to attack him. But there was utter silence coming from their eerily open mouths. Their movements were jerky and uncoordinated, a result of being separated from their bodies and attached to these macabre displays. No legs or bodies, just mounted heads, except the seven foot tall bear that now lumbered awkwardly down the hallway.

Wulfric cursed, and the lynx in his hands redoubled their efforts. One particular swipe of the claw drew enough blood to sting, and he hissed as he threw it at the bear.

Shifting for the second time that day, he tore the one remaining lynx in half. It snarled and tried to crawl toward him on two legs. The creepy little fucker didn't know when to quit.

The bear fought with the other lynx as it dug its claws in, trying to get off the enormous beast. A flash of light across the hall showed an office, dusty and decaying. With a quick glance at the bear, he knocked the closest of the mounted animal heads into the office. He shifted back, grabbing the two halves of the lynx and throwing them into the office too. He turned back to face the rest of the animated animals.

The other lynx launched off the bear and tackled him mid-air. Claws dug into his softer human flesh, and he roared as pain blinded him. His face stung and he felt the warm wet of blood pour down his cheek as he shifted and tore at the last lynx. Pain pulsed from his head, his shoulder, his torso, but he was relentless. He had to survive and find his daughter and his mate.

Finally, he tossed the shredded, limp lynx into the office with the others. They were crawling closer to the door, so he slammed it shut behind him and turned to face the bear.

It kicked a deer head as it stepped closer, and the antlers embedded in the wall. The glassy eyes were unblinking, and Wulfric waited in front of the door, swaying from blood loss.

"Come on, you hairy fucker," he muttered.

The dead beast lurched the last few steps and lifted a paw to swipe. Behind him, he turned the knob on the door and rushed around the bear. He hooked his leg around the ankle of the bear and pushed hard in the back. It stumbled through the door, and he shoved again, sending it sprawling over the animal pieces. Then he slammed the door once more.

A pair of metal knights bracketed the door, and he took the lance from one, slipping it through the door handle. The animals hit the door, but at least he didn't have to deal with screaming and roaring.

He sank against the door and wiped his brow, the sting of blood in his eyes burning as he blinked and turned to a noise down the hall.

Scarlet stumbled out of a door halfway down, her face contorted in pain and shock. When she saw him, she gasped and limped forward, her eyes roving over his face with clear worry. He raced to her, his legs shaky as he gathered her into the safety of his embrace. His entire body melted to feel her safe and sound in his arms. Not even the banging behind the library door made him tense because he knew— together—they could face anything.

"I never should've left you to put the horses up. Gods, love, are you alright?" His voice was choked with emotion, and he tightened his arms around her.

She ran her hands over his neck and upper back. "I thought... I feared..." she whispered, her voice breaking.

He pulled back and cupped her face, his thumb brushing away a smear of dirt mixed with blood on her cheek. "I know. Me too."

Their lips crashed together, desperate and hungry. The kiss tasted of salt and copper, fear and relief intermingling. His hands roamed her body, checking for injuries, needing to feel her alive and whole beneath his touch.

He took a deep breath, inhaling the scent of dirt and earth, pine and lemongrass. The longer he held her, the more his body throbbed with the heat of desire. The post-battle need to fuck left him hard, but he needed to just hold her more than he needed to fuck her.

The banging behind the library door made her pull back and inspect his body. Her little hands ran up his back and gingerly traced over scratches to test the extent of his injuries. "Well, you'll live, but it'll be damned uncomfortable while you heal. I guess you ran into the queen too, huh?"

He stood there, letting her hands soothe his aching heart as it broke into a thousand pieces. The ghost woman—his daughter was *the queen*? "The—she's the queen?"

Scarlet looked at him like he was crazy, and maybe he was. "Who else would she be?"

Wulfric opened his mouth to reply but nothing came out. He closed his mouth and his eyes, then finally choked out, "My daughter."

Scarlet's hands froze on his stomach, and her nose twitched as she looked up at him. Her cheeks flushed as she shook her head. "What? I thought she died as a child."

He took a shuddering breath. "I did too. All my memories of her ended as a young child when I got them back. Eirwyn said she was alive, but I never thought—I didn't realize she was—"

"The evil queen who cursed us all?" Scarlet said, her tone hard as she clenched her jaw.

His stomach dropped to hear the bitterness and anger in her voice. She hadn't moved on from the need for revenge, but he needed her to understand. Desperately, he reached for her hands, silently begging her to let go of her stubbornness. "She's not evil, Scarlet."

She wrenched her hands out of his and stepped back down the hall to her torn clothes. "She married an evil king who taught her all kinds of magic. It twisted her, Wulfric. She's not the same little tavern owner as before."

She jerked on her pants and shirt, the tatters barely clinging to her body as he too found his pants.

His brows rose as he jerked them up over his hips. "You knew her before?"

Scarlet nodded and pulled her shirt on. "Of course. Hunters are notorious for hanging out in taverns and gathering information on their targets. And that tavern was the best in Demerel."

A flare of pride made his chest swell, and he grinned. "That was my tavern. Well, my wife's. We ran it together until she passed. Then I ran it with Trix's help."

"Don't call me that," came a voice from the stairs.

He turned at the voice, and Scarlet stepped beside him, taking his hand. He linked their fingers and drew comfort from his mate as he faced his past head on. His daughter descended the wide marble stairs, still translucent and not quite see-through.

On one hand, he was proud of how she carried herself with grace and poise, yet on the other hand, it served as a reminder of the separation between them - both in their social status and in their physical existence. The fact that he was alive and she was merely a ghost weighed heavily on his heart.

With her chin tilted up, she sniffed haughtily. "I am Queen Bella of Busparia. Trix died with you, Da."

The last she said as a whisper, stopping three steps from the ground as the knights beside the stairs saluted. He wanted to go to her, hold her and reassure them both that they were alive. But she wasn't, and it was all his fault.

He swallowed hard and nodded once. "Very well. Bella," he said reverently.

Bella took a deep breath, her nostrils flaring wide. "I apologize for the emotional outbursts earlier. I didn't mean for those things to come alive and attack either of you. I—I'm not myself these days and wasn't expecting visitors."

Scarlet snorted behind him. "No kidding."

Wulfric took a hesitant step toward his daughter. "I'm sorry I wasn't here. I'm sorry I didn't return like I promised I would."

Bella glanced away and somehow grew even paler. "It was war. I knew the likelihood of you keeping that promise."

"Still, I'm sorry I left you to run the tavern for ten years." His voice was a gentle whisper, tinged with huskiness and raw emotion. He held his breath, afraid to make any sudden movements that could trigger another outburst.

The tension in the air was palpable, like a tightly coiled spring ready to snap at any moment. Each word he spoke felt like walking on thin ice, hoping not to break through and cause even more chaos.

Her chin wobbled, then firmed as her eyes flashed. "I'm very angry about that. Why did you stay away? Is it because you're a Growler now?"

He nodded. "Mostly, yes. When I was turned, I lost all memories of my prior life. Then when the memories started to return in the past few weeks, I thought you'd died in the fevers with your mother."

The knights standing sentry along the side of the staircase landing shook along with her hands, and she fisted her skirts. The knights stopped moving as she heaved in several long, deep breaths.

"You knew I was alive when you left. Why would you agree to become a Growler? Did they trick you?" Her hands went wide as she stepped down another step on the stairs.

He held up a hand to stop her. "No, it was no trick. I lay dying on the Southern Road, and they offered me a chance at a new life."

"I see," she said softly, the banging behind the library door drawing her eyes. She waved a hand and the banging stopped, then she turned back to face him. "I can't imagine what you went through, but I know some of that feeling."

"Feeling?" As he looked into her tear-filled eyes, he could see the weight of adulthood bearing down on her young shoulders, burdening her with emotions beyond her years. He longed to take away her hurt, but knew there was little he could do to ease it.

She smiled but there was no mirth in it. "The feeling of emptiness, sorrow, and pain. The kind where it hurts so much you'll do anything to make it stop. Your brain knows the solution is a bad idea, but your body won't let you say no. So you take the offered solution...and it changes everything."

Her voice trailed off on the end, and his chest ached at the devastation he saw written on her face. She met his gaze, her own steady.

"Would you do it again? If you had to do it over, would you make the same choice again?"

He swallowed, unable to speak as he nodded. His eyes stung, whether from tears or blood, he didn't know.

She sighed and closed her eyes, a silent tear streaking down her cheek. "Me too. Borga protect me, but I would do it all again too."

Scarlet slammed her hands onto her hips. "You'd curse us all again? You still don't understand what you've done, do you?"

Wulfric pulled Scarlet into his arms, but she pushed him off and stomped down the hall to where her cloak lay crumpled on the floor. She jerked and shook it out, muttering to herself.

Bella stepped closer, wringing her hands on her skirts. "I don't understand what's going on in the world, but I know how it impacted those in the castle. I didn't do it on purpose. Surely she knows that?"

Wulfric shrugged and looked at Scarlet as she put the cloak around her shoulders to cover the tattered clothing and bared skin. Her ears twitched, and he knew she was listening. "I think she's starting to understand that, yes. But we do need you to come with us to fix the curse."

The knights on the landing at the base of the stairs rattled, and Bella stepped down another step as her eyes flashed. "I don't have to listen to you, Da. I'm the Queen and quite grown up now, or did you forget?"

The gnawing pain in the pit of his stomach twisted as he

nodded, stepping forward until he was only a few feet from the stairs. "Actually, I did forget. When the Growlers turned me, I was delirious with blood loss. My mind had already twisted things, and I thought you were dead. All I knew was the pain of death and losing you and your mother."

"But you didn't lose me. I'm right here. I'm alive," Bella cried, the knights snapping to attention and turning to face them.

He shook his head, and Scarlet's hand settled in the small of his back. He reached back for her hand, needing her strength to get through this. Yet, despite her presence, the weight of his failures pressed heavily on him. As he gazed at Bella's ghostly form, conflicted emotions ripped through him. He should have been there to protect her from harm, to stop the king and prevent her death. Wulfric needed more than just Scarlet's hand to face the truth of his actions. He pulled her into his arms and held her.

Scarlet snorted and held him tight. "But you're not here. You're a ghost, Bella."

Bella's eyes flashed and the knights formed a line in front of the stairs, standing in a battle ready stance.

Wulfric squeezed Scarlet tighter and admitted his truth. "It's my fault, Bella. I should've been here to stop whatever hurt you, stop the king, stop your death."

Bella's lip quivered and the knights froze. Then her jaw tilted, and she glanced at Scarlet, then back to him.

"There was no stopping it. But the thing is... I'm not dead," she said flatly, her gaze turning to Scarlet as her lips pinched. "Come see for yourselves, and I'll explain. Scarlet knows the way, if you get lost in this big castle." The last was sarcastic and Scarlet flinched in his arms as Bella climbed the stairs.

Scarlet groaned as the knights blocking the stairs went

back to their flanking positions. "Damn it, I was hoping to avoid that room."

"What room?" He kissed the side of her head and then breathed in her scent, trying to resettle his nerves and mentally prepare for whatever awaited upstairs.

"The room where the king died, the epicenter of the curses." Scarlet shook in his arms, and he buried his nose in the crook of her neck. He didn't want to let her go, needed her by his side to get through this. But he didn't want to cause his mate pain either.

He sighed and pulled back, holding her gently by the arms. "Do you want to stay down here, bunny? I'll follow her."

She scoffed and tugged him by the waist to the stairs. "You won't make it up the stairs by yourself, weak as you are. You're healing, but you're not there yet. No, I'll go. I'm not some simpering miss. I'll face it no matter how much it twists me up inside."

A thrill of relief went through him, grateful that he didn't have to do this alone. He'd left her outside the castle earlier, and it had been a disaster. If only they had stayed together, maybe they wouldn't be so badly injured now.

He held onto her tightly, his grip on her shoulder almost desperate. As they climbed the stairs side by side, she fell silent and he wiped the blood from his eyes. It was in moments like these, with her by his side, that he felt truly alive again. The mate bond between them seemed to strengthen with each step they took together, providing a glimmer of hope in the midst of chaos.

# Chapter Forty-Three

Bella stood at the window and waited, listening to the shuffle of feet along the hallway. After so many months of stillness, she tracked them easily. She turned when they stepped inside the room.

Her gaze paused on her father, but settled on Scarlet to see what reaction the room would have on her. To the Hunter's credit, her face paled but she simply canvassed the space silently. Her gaze stopped on where Gastone had died, and she plastered herself against her dad's side.

"Do you remember that day?" Bella asked, the pressure on her chest making it tight. "I try not to. I mean, you saw what happened below when I get upset and emotional." She sighed and smoothed her skirts to stop the shaking.

Scarlet swallowed. "I remember being cursed, yes."

Bella's eyes were fixated on the dark scorch mark on the floor, her hands clenching and unclenching her skirts as she spoke in a detached tone. "After Gastone cast that curse and you turned into a rabbit, the two Robins burst in. One claimed he was going to arrest Gastone, but then the other slit his throat without hesitation. Gastone threw a fireball at the assassin before succumbing to his injury. I became so angry, I wrapped the bedsheets around the assassin so tight that he burst into pieces. Body parts went everywhere."

Scarlet and her father held each other, but neither said a word.

The image of that gruesome scene was now burned into Bella's mind, and she let out a hollow chuckle. "I must have truly horrified the remaining Robin, because he ran out of here as soon as you transformed and hopped away."

Her father and Scarlet clung to each other, silent in their shock and grief. Bella could only give a bitter laugh. "And then there was the magic mirror on my vanity desk. It had whispered to Gastone all his life, and when I came to the castle it started whispering to me too. I didn't realize it was manipulating my thoughts and actions...even influencing what books I read..."

As she glanced over at the now empty vanity that Ignot and Sharlo had cleaned out months ago, Bella felt a tightness in her chest from the weight of those memories. But she couldn't allow herself to succumb to those emotions now; she needed to finish telling them everything about that fateful day.

"Anyway, Gastone died, and the mirror told me to rip out his heart and make a potion, so I did." She was proud of her voice for not wavering, but she didn't stop to remember, too afraid of the emotions that would be unleashed.

"You ripped out his heart?" Da asked.

Bella nodded and stared at the vanity, wiped clean of all materials yet still covered in a thick layer of dust. "I did," she whispered. She was still horrified and so afraid of what her father would say about her actions. Inside she was terrified of the darkness within her that could commit such an act and freely admit that if she could go back, she'd do it all over again anyway. Haunted by memories of her heinous deed, the guilt of her actions and fear of what he would say consumed her.

Scarlet hummed. "That was pretty badass of you."

Bella gave a surprised laugh. "I assure you it wasn't, but thank you?" She wasn't sure what to do in this social situation and winced when it came out as a question.

Scarlet just grinned and said, "You're welcome."

Da's shoulders relaxed at Scarlet's smile, and he dropped one arm from Scarlet to stay side-by-side. "Did you drink it? The heart potion?"

Bella tensed and turned to face the vanity, unable to look at him to see if he was disappointed in her or not. "I did. The potion hurt more than the pain of losing Gastone actually. It changed me into a unique creature. The mirror said it was because my human body couldn't handle the absorbed magic of the drakin king, so it had to morph into a drakin."

Silence met her pronouncement, and she glanced at them. Scarlet was frowning, and Da stared at Scarlet, taking his cues from her. Bella was frustrated by that because her father had never had a problem voicing his own opinion when she was growing up.

"You became a drakin? I haven't heard of that happening before," Scarlet said.

Bella shrugged and hugged her stomach, turmoil over her father's inaction making her want to vomit. "It shouldn't be possible at all, yet it happened. When my body began to change, I saw the mirror and my reflection. I—I became very angry and threw the mirror to the ground. It shattered, but I slipped and hit my head on the corner of the vanity."

Breathing too fast, she shivered along with the vanity

itself. Still, she forced herself to be still and control her emotions and magic. Finally, she said, "My body and spirit separated at the blow. My body fell to the ground, but I held onto the vanity. When my head stopped spinning, my body was groaning and pulling itself to its feet. You see, when the mirror broke, it released the man who'd been trapped within it for gods know how long."

She turned and glared at them as her hands fisted at her sides and her shoulders hunched. "He stole my body. He left me here and tied my spirit to that blasted rose." She pointed at the rose in the pot under the broken window, barely visible through the darkness that was quickly descending outside.

Da rubbed his chin in a gesture so familiar, it made Bella ache. "So if that rose lives, you live? You're not quite dead yet?"

She nodded, tears pricking her eyes. "He said when it dies, my spirit will go to the hells for judgment. So no, I'm not dead yet. My body lives. My soul lives. The rose lives. We just all live apart."

He swallowed hard, his face open and slack in surprise. Scarlet scowled up at her father as he took Scarlet's hands in his. "So we can fix it, right? We can get your body back and transfer your soul from the rose to it?"

Scarlet scowled and reared back from him. "Are you crazy? That's not possible by anyone but nekromancers, and that's been banned for hundreds of years."

Her father walked toward her, his eyes bright with hope. "But it's worth looking into, right? I might be able to fix it."

Scarlet walked closer too, grabbing her father by the arm and turning him away from the window to face her. "What we need is to fix the curses, remember? There are so many people relying on her to undo this nightmare."

Bella turned away from them, unable to see how at ease they were in each other's presence, with each other's touch. They were clearly lovers, and she didn't fault her father for finding a companion. But the ache of loneliness grew larger within her heart the more she was around them together.

She stepped to the window to stare into the darkness, unable to look at them when she admitted just how incapable of fixing it she was. "I've spent the past few months trying to reverse the curse I unknowingly released when I drank that blasted forbidden potion. Blood magic and nekromancy was banned for a reason, you know. I'm trying to fix what I messed up before the rose dies, but it's been difficult these past few weeks since the others died..."

Her voice died in her throat as she noticed a sudden movement in the courtyard below. A deep purple portal materialized, surrounded by blinding white light. Her heart pounded as a boot emerged from the swirling hole, followed by a figure cloaked in a long coat and waistcoat.

Bella's hands trembled as she pressed them against the shattered window, causing the curtains and furniture to shake. It couldn't be her...but it was. The man who'd stolen her body, the wizard she had feared for so long had suddenly appeared. Had speaking of him made him appear? Why was he suddenly here for the first time in all these months since the curse? Why—

She jerked, her hands fisting on the windowsill. "How did you get past the shadow monster outside?" she asked suddenly.

Da paused in his whispering with Scarlet, his voice rising as he said, "The one outside the castle walls? We killed it."

Oh no, the magic mirror's shadow babysitter had been killed. That must be why he'd shown up. The last time she'd tried to escape with Ignot holding the rose, that thing had stopped them, nearly killing the old man in the process. She'd known then it's purpose to keep her securely behind the walls.

Just when she'd thought she could escape with her father and find the resources needed to fix the curses and reunite with her body, the mirror showed up. Fear gripped Bella's heart in a vice as she realized nowhere was safe from the mirror's power.

But she could keep Da and Scarlet away from him. He looked so confident as he strode into the castle in her body, and if he was powerful enough to create a portal like that, then he'd destroy them easily. Her heart raced and her hand shook as she touched the budding yellow rose. She had to face the mirror, but first she had to distract her father and his companion.

She took a shuddering breath and turned to face them, shoulders back with determination. "I will reverse the curse, Scarlet, but I need help. It's hard to practice spells, gather ingredients, and all the other prep work when I'm incorporeal and can't pick things up."

Gus and Jaq poked her from where they sat in her pocket, and she patted them gently. She didn't have time to explain them to Scarlet and Da.

"So you'll come with us into the Feral Forest?" Da asked, his brown frowning with worry as he stepped closer to her.

She tried to walk past her father and Scarlet, but Da stepped in front of her, his hands raised. They passed right through her arms, making her wince at the icy feeling that shot through her. He stepped back with a frown, his hands falling limply by his sides. She winced at the pained look on his face and walked deeper into the room. He turned his back on the window, and she hoped he hadn't seen the wizard downstairs.

She pursed her lips and glanced around the room, her mind planning the next steps. "I will, but I need to gather some books that I don't want to leave behind. Night is falling, so we can head out in the morning, if that's alright with you both?"

Scarlet glanced out the window at the fading light. "That's a good idea."

Bella breathed a sigh of relief, but her shoulders were still stiff with tension. "Scarlet, you probably want to tell Da your version of what happened that day, so I'll leave you to it. There's also a clean cloth here to wipe away the blood."

"Thank you," Da said, reaching for the cloth and turning to his companion to dab at her cheek.

The tender move sent a pang of jealousy through her, and she stepped faster toward the door to the hall, waving to the opposite wall. "There are clean but dusty clothes in the wardrobe, Scarlet. Feel free to help yourself."

"Oh, I could never—"

Bella glanced over her shoulder, remembering the Hunter from those nights in the tavern. "If you'd prefer pants, the king's chamber is across the hall. I'm not sure if any of his clothes will fit either of you, but you're welcome to look."

She reached the door and held her hands to her stomach, fear making her hands shake as she thought of meeting the mirror below. "The water closet is through that door as well, but there's no water up here to help you wash from the battles and your journey. Since the servants died, it's been incredibly difficult to get water up here to the rose. If you'll excuse me, I'll go bag up those books. I'll see you both in the morning?"

Scarlet's eyes narrowed and she opened her mouth to say something, but Da gripped her chin gently and turned her head to the side for easier access. He wiped in soft, light circles down her neck, and Scarlet's eyes fluttered closed and she hummed.

Bella animated the door with a spell and shut it behind her. She still had so much left to explain, but there was no time. She had to face a wizard.

# Chapter Forty-Four

Wulfric rubbed his chin with the cloth as Scarlet walked further into the room. Her steps left prints in the thick layer of dust on the bare marble floors. Near the broken window by the rose, the dust wasn't so thick due to rain. The walls were bare, the lighter color revealing where paintings and tapestries had once stood.

Wulfric only assumed that the servants had scrubbed this room from top to bottom after the bloody mess. Scarlet opened and closed the vanity drawers, revealing jeweled combs and perfume bottles with delicate designs.

Scarlet shut the last drawer and stretched her neck. "Did you hear her? She said there were servants here. They probably got stuck after the curse spread. I can't imagine what they went through or how they died. Do you think she killed them?"

Wulfric scowled and tossed the cloth next to the pitcher by the rose. "No, she didn't kill them. That's my daughter you're talking about."

Scarlet rubbed her temples. "Oh gods, your daughter is

the queen. She's alive, and she hates me, and—oh gods, how old *are* you?"

Wulfric rolled his eyes and stepped behind her, rubbing her shoulders in a massage that had her melting in his hands. "I'm forty-seven. How old are you?"

"Thirty-five. I've been going into taverns first with my dad as a Ranger and then with the Hunters, but I don't remember you at the tavern here in Demerel."

He kissed the side of her neck and moved his hands down her spine. "I don't remember you either. Perhaps the goddess kept us apart until we were ready for each other."

Scarlet snorted. "The gods were smart then, if they kept me from raising your daughter. I'm not so sure about being a mother."

Wulfric paused. "If we're mates, you're practically her stepmother already."

Scarlet whirled out of his arms, her hands going wide. "I can't be the evil queen's stepmother!"

Wulfric's hands fisted, and he snatched the cloth from the vanity. Angrily, he wiped his face and ground out, "For the last time, she's not an evil queen. She's just misunderstood."

Scarlet slammed her hands on her hips. "Don't underestimate her, wolfie. I don't remember all of that day, but I do remember the flying flesh and bones when the bed exploded and the Robin died."

He prowled to the window and stared into the night. His chest ached with pent up emotions, and his head was beginning to pound with the effort to process so much information. "So that really happened?"

Scarlet nodded, and walked toward him, leaning on the damask covered wall to face him. "Yes," she said softly. "It was awful. I still have nightmares about it."

He scrubbed hard on his jaw, wincing as he reopened a barely scabbing scratch. "When I left, she was barely fifteen. She was mature for her age, probably from reading so much in her spare time, and I was afraid of leaving such an innocent girl in charge of the tavern. But she'd been tossing out drunks for years. I thought she'd be able to handle it."

Reaching down for the cloth, he blotted his face and shook his head. He was a fool. He never should've put her in that position. But when the draft came, he had no other option. The weight of responsibility sat heavy on his shoulders as he tried to wipe away the guilt and shame that threatened to consume him.

"So you never thought she'd so coldly kill someone by wrapping them in blankets and wringing them like a wet dish towel?" Scarlet asked, her brow arched and tone wry.

Wulfric dropped the small cloth onto the floor as if burned. "She was emotional and over-wrought. Let's say, for example, someone killed your grandma right in front of you like the Robin did to the king. How would you react?"

Scarlet fingered the sheath for her dagger as her eyes flashed. "Don't you talk to me like that, wolfie. You're not going to goad me into—"

He raked a hand through the dried blood stiffening his hair. "Into what? Seeing her as human? Seeing that she can make mistakes like any of us? You heard her. She's been working to fix the curse all this time."

Scarlet pointed a finger at him and stepped closer. "And you heard her too. The servants that were left here all died. Don't be fooled, Wulfric. It doesn't matter if she's your daughter or not. Be cautious."

He reared back as if slapped. She was his daughter, and it didn't matter to her? Gods, she was so cold-hearted. His stomach twisted.

"Oh because keeping people at arm's length has served you so well thus far, has it." It wasn't a question. His jaw clenched as he side-stepped her and prowled to the heavy oak bed frame. He wanted to shred it, tear *anything* apart.

No mattress remained. Whatever servants had been here had cleaned the room as best they could.

"Hey, I do what I have to survive."

He spun on his heels, his hands wide. "No, you do what you must to protect yourself. But if you don't learn to trust people, especially those who love you, then you're no better than Brody or Gastone or any of the other selfish bastards who—"

She gasped, and her daggers flashed. "Don't you dare call me selfish. I'm the one who woke up alone earlier. Where were you? You left me outside the castle walls."

The air rushed out of his lungs, and he held his head in his hands as he groaned. His chest tightened and his claws retracted.

"Fuck, that's all I'm good for, isn't it? I'm a leaver. I left you alone outside while I found a safe spot for the horses. I left Trix—no, Bella—at the tavern while I went to war and became a Growler."

Silence met his harsh words, but he just panted and pressed the heel of his palms to his eyes. He turned away from her, his shoulders hunched.

"It's all my fault," he said softly. "If I hadn't left, she would've been safe and would've grown into a different woman. If I hadn't put the energy into the world by saying she was dead, maybe she wouldn't be a spirit now."

"What, like you could've protected her from a mad wizard?"

He dropped his hands and cried out, his heart breaking.

"Yes! I'm her *father*. It's my *job* to protect her, and I failed. If I'd been here, maybe I could've kept her safe."

*Thunk.*

He looked up. A dagger quivered in the wooden bedpost, and Scarlet stalked toward it as she talked. "Damn it, Wulfric, you can't keep everyone safe. It's not your job. We have to be allowed to make our own decisions. That's just part of life. Learning from our mistakes and growing into better people. What happened to Bella, what she did… it's not your fault."

He breathed deeply, his chest rattling. "Don't be dense, of course it is."

She yanked the dagger out and held it up, tip pointed at him, her green gold eyes glittering in the soft light of dusk. "What happens if I choose not to live with the Growlers, huh? What if I keep being a Hunter and you go back to your tribe? What if I choose to live apart?"

His stomach twisted, and he choked on bile. "You—"

A scream reverberated through the castle, making the walls shake. His hands trembled as claws grew, and the scent of fear filled the air.

"Bella," Scarlet whispered. His heart in his throat, he lunged for the door, shifting mid-step.

---

Bella flew down the stairs, the knights rattling and stepping behind her as she raced through the hallway, following the glowing light to the ballroom. Lists of spells flew through her mind of possible ways to defeat him, but the problem was none of the books in the library covered Nekrosan magic in detail. She was just blindly praying to the gods at this point.

The animals still on the walls shook as she neared, and she focused on her magic and emotions. She slowed to a halt outside the ballroom doors, controlling her vibrating body with deep, even breaths. The magic threatened to burst, but she *had* to control it. It was the only weapon she could use against the wizard, weak and untrained though it was against him.

She'd long ago had the servants keep all the doors open, not liking the feeling of going through them as a ghost because it was too cold. She took a deep breath and stepped through the doors, the army of knights clanking loudly behind her as she looked around.

A layer of dust filled the empty room, but the magically lit chandeliers still glowed overhead. Cobwebs filled the corners and some of the lights, casting strange shadows on the tiled marble floor. Golden pillars were evenly spaced around the room, some forming doorways to other rooms.

Across the ballroom, the man in the mirror walked away from the open terrace doors. She swallowed and looked up and down. *Her* body was hideous. Scales covered her hands and face. Tiny horns stuck through her brown hair. Pulled into a low ponytail, the end hung over the shoulder on her deep blue finely embroidered dinner jacket.

Horror filled her to see her body this way, so foreign to what she'd been before. Her stomach clenched, threatening to be violently ill as she watched her own body move without her control, inhabited by this vile creature.

The smile was toothy and cruel when the man said, "Ah, there you are." Even her voice was lower than it should've been, hoarse and scratchy.

She shivered and fisted her skirts to hide the reaction. Questions filled her mind, and she tilted her chin up. "Are you here to kill me, then?"

The mirror—she couldn't keep calling it her body, that was ridiculous—chuckled. "Unfortunately I can't kill you outright. But I'm curious. How did you defeat the shadow daemon outside the castle walls?"

She'd had lots of practice schooling her features with Gastone and customers, so she didn't even flinch at the question. She'd known the shadows appeared when they shouldn't have, but a daemon? They were the stuff of nightmares, the things parents warned their children of when they wanted obedience. That thing that had kept Ignot and Sharlo in here with her had been a daemon?

She blinked and countered, "Why do you want to know?"

He glared. "It was *my* shadow daemon. Do you know how much energy and magic it takes to summon just one of those slimy things? Ugh." He shivered and strode closer to the mantle. The portrait of Gastone sat above it, covered in dust. He flicked a wrist, and the portrait slashed as if from invisible claws.

"No matter. I have a new plan," he said, turning to her, removing a bracelet, and tossing it to the ground. A small portal opened on the floor, growing out from the bracelet.

He knelt, leaned inside, and pulled a large mirror through, laying it face up on the ground before doing some complicated hand movement. The portal closed with a flash of purple light, leaving the bracelet behind. He grabbed it and put it on his wrist.

"What do you mean, a new plan?" Her voice wavered, but she didn't move or back down. Dread filled her stomach, making her want to vomit.

He turned to the mirror, not looking up as he answered. "Since you got rid of my babysitter, I'll just have to confine you to something else so you won't cause trouble."

"What trouble can I cause when I'm trapped here by a plant?" Her voice rose with incredulity. Panic crept up her spine, making her fingers and toes tingle at the idea of what he meant.

He chuckled. "I didn't think you could cause trouble like this, but then my shadow was dispatched. So into the mirror you go."

She imagined her reflection staring back at her for eternity, slowly going mad as the world moved on without her. Bella's mind raced, searching for a way out. There had to be something she could use against him, some weakness she could exploit. Her gaze darted around the room, looking for anything that might help.

He pushed a sequence of runes on the sides of the mirror, and she jerked back at a sound behind her. She twisted her hands, and the knights stepped in front of her, making a circular line of defense around her as she shook her head.

"Into the mirror like you? No," she said, her stomach twisting and the wall of windows rattling. She couldn't be trapped in a mirror. She'd felt trapped at the tavern and then this damn castle, but a mirror? It was too small. It would choke her, smother her. She grasped her throat, feeling the air cut off as she thought more about it. Her vision blurred, but the clank of a knight behind her brought her back to the moment.

She clenched her fists, anger burning away the fear. Who did this creep think he was? She'd been through too much, fought too hard to let some wizard tear her life apart.

He smiled but didn't look up from the preparations. "Oh yes. Sadly, you won't be trapped inside for hundreds of years like I was."

"Hundreds of years? Who are you? Why are you doing

this?" she demanded, her voice trembling with fear and anger.

"Just a disgruntled wizard tired of his lot in life who made a deal with the devil himself," he replied casually.

She gasped, falling into a knight behind her. It didn't budge, and she stood upright, stepping toward the man in the mirror.

"Are you mad? No one but the god Asmo wins in those deals. Everyone knows that, both from the old religions and the new," she whispered furiously.

He threw his head back and let out a maniacal laugh that sent chills down her spine, reminding her of Gastone's mad cackling on that fateful day. A wave of coldness spread through her body from her chest like tendrils of ice.

"Are you worried about me, little girl?" he sneered. The condescending nickname only fueled her rage. "Don't worry, I'll be just fine. Especially once phase two of my plan for world domination is set into motion."

His condescending words made her mad. Only Da had ever called her that. This wizard had no right to just dismiss her so easily. The windows rattled violently as her fists clenched at her sides.

"Too weak for world domination, eh?" She taunted him, channeling all her pent-up fury into the words. "Trapped in a mirror for hundreds of years because you couldn't escape?"

His shoulders tensed and he glared up at her with a venomous look. "Don't push me, woman. You'll still be bound to the rose and suffer for just a few more months. When it dies, you can happily go to hells and say hello to my master for me. Once he joins me in Busparia, we'll go from ruling the continent to the world to the heavens themselves."

A smug smirk spread across his face as he resumed his preparations, completely unfazed by her taunts. But she refused to back down, determined to break free from this twisted fate.

Her body vibrated in fear and anger. How dare he plan to spread his misery to the rest of the world. The windows shook, the knights rattling. If he trapped her, she'd never be able to fix the curse she'd caused. If he succeeded, he'd destroy the world, perhaps even the gods themselves. If Asmo truly was working with him, that is.

The knights shook as she animated them. It was clunky and awkward, so she pushed her spirit into one of the empty metal suits of armor and broke into a run. Still the wizard didn't look up from muttering and tinkering with the runes as part of the mirror's edges began to glow.

She screamed and dove at him, the tackle a maneuver Da had taught her years ago. She aimed low, and the knight knocked him to the ground. The knight broke into pieces, and she came to her knees, her dress twisting. She threw the knight's helmet at him, but he batted it away like a fly.

He stood and laughed, brushing off dust on his sleeve. "Did you really think it'd be that easy? Oh, you precious little girl."

Bella screamed again and threw more pieces of armor. When she ran out of parts, she pulled the curtains down from the windows with a wave of her hand. She flung them to the wizard, but he waved a finger and they turned to ash before they reached him.

The walls shook with her rage. The chandeliers swung wide. The gilded life-sized portrait of Gastone fell to the marble floor with a crash. The rest of the knights marched upon the wizard, who now crouched beside the mirror once more.

The lights on the edge of the mirror swirled, and he looked up as the knights neared. His brows rose in surprise —*her* brows, in the body that he stole. One knight lifted his foot to step on the mirror, but the wizard pushed his hands outward. A gust of wind shot from him, throwing them back where they skidded on the floor, toppling one over the other.

"Bella!" A deep voice cried from upstairs, and her stomach dropped. No, they couldn't come down here. They'd only get hurt.

A vibration on her thigh gave her pause. She reached into her pocket and pulled out Jaq and Gus. She threw them as hard as she could, then pushed magic into the action.

Gus flipped end over end, the arched handle of the spoon hitting the soft spot where the wizard's thigh and hip met before falling to the ground. Jaq's fork tongues embedded into his thigh, and the wizard howled in pain. He grabbed the fork, yanked it out, and threw it across the room toward the knights.

Eyes blazing with fury, the wizard stepped on Gus and bent awkwardly to push one last pulsing rune on the edge of the mirror. Magic swirled, and the wizard stepped back, flipped the bracelet, and stepped through the portal with one boot.

He looked at her, ears and nose smoking, and said, "Tell Asmo I'm waiting."

Then he stepped the rest of the way in and closed the portal in a flash of purple, the bracelet disappearing with him.

Bella closed her eyes against the flash, but her feet slid on the floor. Her heart still racing in anger, a swirl of smoke circled above the mirror. Pulled inexplicably toward it, she windmilled her arms then leaned her body against an invisible wind storm.

A flash of movement to her right drew her gaze, and she yelled, "No, don't come inside! It—it's sucking me in!"

Wulfric and Scarlet skidded to a halt on the floor just inside the door. Scarlet almost fell over the pile of knights, but Wulfric pulled her back with an arm around the waist.

Bella looked back at the mirror, her eyes widening as the tornado had grown as wide as the mirror. It whipped around, and she tried to grab onto anything. She threw magic at the sconces, the chandeliers even. While they vibrated, they didn't move.

She screamed, tears rolling down her cheeks as the tornado sent her airborne, flinging her around the room.

# Chapter Forty-Five

Scarlet could barely hear past the rush of wind as she finally untangled herself from the knights on the floor. After a quick glance to assess the situation, she formed a plan.

It wasn't perfect, and part of her wondered if it wouldn't be better to fail. If they failed, Bella would be sucked into the mirror. Then Scarlet couldn't kill her like she'd sworn to do, and Wulfric couldn't stop her like she knew he would.

Her heart wasn't in killing her anymore though. There was so much more involved now than just her desire for revenge. She'd said Bella being his daughter didn't matter, but it did. She wasn't so heartless as to wish him more pain. She'd seen how much he struggled with memories of losing his wife.

As the wind howled around them, she desperately pointed to the ornate chandelier above. "We have to break that chandelier and shatter it against the mirror! It's our only chance to break this spell."

She crouched, ready to leap over the knights, but

Wulfric grabbed her arm with a trembling hand. "Wait! If we believe what she said earlier, that mirror will suck us in too. I won't let us be trapped in there while our friends fight on. We have to stay together and fight side-by-side."

She could see the fear in his face as the wind blew stronger. She gripped his hand and squeezed, drawing comfort from his presence. "We don't stand a chance side-by-side. We have to fight with our strengths. It's the only way that stands a chance of getting all three of us out of here."

Wulfric searched her eyes and looked around the room. His hand gripped her arm harder when he saw Bella fly through the air, a scream echoing in the room. He nodded in determination and shouted back, "I'll jump over these knights and try to smash the mirror with my own hands!"

With a swift kiss on Wulfric's cheek, she leaped over the scrambling knights and shifted into her wolf form to claw her way to the wall. She prayed that they would both come out of this alive and unscathed.

When she reached the wall, a quick glance over her shoulder showed Wulfric fully shifted, his claws scraping against the tiles with a piercing sound that made her heart ache.

She took a deep breath. She'd wanted to reverse her curses or kill the queen. She'd finally gotten some alone time with her enemy only to realize she wasn't the enemy at all. Eirwyn had been right, and Scarlet had been too pigheaded and stubborn to see it.

But she couldn't just sit aside and let her be trapped or killed in a mirror. It wouldn't solve any of her problems. They still needed answers, and Bella was her last hope for reversing the curse. If they could get her body back, maybe she could figure out the reversal.

Scarlet stepped along the wall, one paw feeling the material to the gold trimmed baluster. She smiled, finding where the plaster changed to painted wood. The wind tugged at her fur, growing stronger as the tornado swirled.

She felt the thick edge of wood trim that wrapped around the three sides where it jutted out from the wall. She concentrated, her lip sweating as she shifted her back legs into the deer and her hands into human. She jumped, going higher than she could've as a human, and grabbed the next trim piece a few feet up. They were just too tall for her to reach comfortably, but she'd scaled smoother walls before. She closed her eyes and shifted the rest of her body to human so she could climb.

She looked at the ceiling, planning her route to the big chandelier. She didn't dare look behind her, afraid that she'd see Bella already sucked in and Wulfric close behind. She refused to believe that was their fate. This was a moment for trust and focus.

She pushed herself, her muscles screaming as the gilded wood slipped beneath her fingertips. She hung by one hand, then quickly grabbed the edge with the other.

The ceiling had several beams going up to it from the balusters toward a central point in the middle where the biggest chandelier swung in the wind. In between the beams were paintings of gods, goddesses, dragons, trolls, and sirens, along with famous battles from the nation's history. Their faces leered down at her, daring her to let go and be swept into the maelstrom.

The wooden beams above had been painted gold too and several smaller chandeliers swung from each. She wasn't close enough to stab at the wood trim with her daggers, but maybe...

Her hand slipped as her muscles seized. She pursed her

lips and shoved away from the wall, her back legs partially shifting to a deer. The added muscles sent her further than she thought she could go, but she barely landed on the closest of the smaller chandeliers.

The glass clattered together, and several pieces fell to the ground only to be sucked into the whirling vortex below. She paused, taking in the scene. Wulfric was still crawling low toward the mirror, the wind pushing him almost flat against the floor. His skin pulled in the too-strong wind, and fear raced up her spine. Her nose twitched, but she refused to give in to the shift into a rabbit, the need to hide.

Bella was halfway down the tornado, spinning around and around as she screamed. The windows shattered and glass joined the tornado. The chandelier's chain jerked, and Scarlet looked up.

The chain had cracked on one side. She looked at the next light fixture and rocked her body. She had to build up momentum or she'd never make it.

Another jerk, and she held her breath as she pushed off it toward the next, flying as it crashed below. She fell lower, but grabbed the bottom of the chandelier and climbed atop it.

The chain jerked, and she began the process again, rocking back and forth only twice before launching. Twice more she jumped, each time her muscles screaming in protest. Each jump became more difficult as her energy waned, but then she was just one jump away from the biggest chandelier.

The chain jerked and she looked up as she swung back and forth. The distance was farther and the momentum wasn't enough. She scrambled up the light, glass scraping and burning until she reached the chain.

Her hand wrapped around it as it swung away from the

big chandelier and the one beneath her snapped and dropped. The wind caught it halfway down and added it to the tornado, but Scarlet clung to the chain. With a grunt of effort, she stretched up and kicked her feet harder as she swung back to the big chandelier.

With a deep breath, she let go. Feet first, she tangled with the lowest glass. Her hands grabbed wildly, the glass burning her palms. There wasn't a moment to lose as she scrambled up the sides.

This chain was thicker than the others, and though it rocked and swung with her weight, it didn't immediately begin to snap. She grabbed her dagger and drove it between the chain links to pry the metal apart.

## Chapter Forty-Six

Wulfric clawed his way to the mirror, but he couldn't see. Wind roared in his ears and battered his body, stinging his eyes and pressing him to the cold floor. By feel alone, his claws closed on the mirror's edge. With three claws digging into the marble, he felt along the edges of the mirror.

A bite of heat shot up his arm, and he jerked his hand away with a howl of pain. He lifted it to slam down a fist, but the wind almost twisted his arm in the socket.

Pain made him howl, and desperation drove him feral. All he could think was the need to destroy the mirror before it was too late. If they were sucked into the mirror, all would be lost. Snarling, he hurled himself at the shimmering surface, ignoring the searing agony that shot through his body with each movement. His claws scrabbled frantically against the glass, leaving deep gouges but failing to shatter it completely.

Bella screamed, but he couldn't make out the words as he summoned all his strength to rain blows onto the gilded frame.

He paid her no heed, consumed by primal instinct. The mirror's surface rippled ominously, tendrils of darkness seeping out and grasping at their ankles. Wulfric redoubled his efforts, his powerful muscles straining as he slammed his bulk against the frame again and again.

Just as he felt his strength beginning to fail, a resounding crack split the air. Hairline fissures spiderwebbed across the glass.

*Wulfric! Move! It's about to come down!*

Scarlet's voice in his mind made his jaw vibrate, and he slammed his fist down onto the mirror's edge once more. Then he retracted his claws.

The wind flung him up and away in a wide arc around the room, and his stomach flipped. He kept his eyes closed and his body loose, and prayed to the goddess for safety for his mate and his daughter.

———————

Bella screamed, helpless to do anything as debris swirled around her. Her body shuddered with each chandelier that went through her incorporeal body. The pieces of glass— still magically lit up—sliced her like hot knives.

Scarlet swung from the ceiling, and Da clawed his way to the mirror. And still she screamed. All the heartache and anguish she'd felt these past few weeks, months, years... it all released in a bellow of rage. The walls shook, and the knights were sucked into the vortex with a clatter of metal.

From the corner of her eye, she saw Scarlet reach the central chandelier. There were so many things she wished she could've done differently. From her treatment of Scarlet when Gastone died to taking that blasted potion made of his heart, she wished she could change the past and make all this go away.

She prayed to Borga, Fysica, to all the old gods and new. All except Asmo. Her rage narrowed to a point. He was the root of all of this. The wizard had said as much. She just needed to survive this and destroy the wizard before he could deal more destruction with Asmo.

Surely the gods would hear her pleas. Surely they'd wish to know what Asmo had planned. Her screams turned to prayers shouted so loud the walls cracked.

Then the central chandelier fell straight down to the mirror below, so heavy the tornado didn't make it move at all. She twisted in the air, her heart racing in worry as she tried to find her father. The wind ripped Da from the edge of the mirror, tossing him straight at her.

He flew toward her, his face determined as he bellowed. She couldn't hear him over the rush of wind, but he held out his arms as he neared. She knew she was crying, knew he would just go through her, but she held her arms wide.

He passed through her, and her throat seized on a sob. She just wanted to be held, to have someone tell her it was all going to be alright, even though her head told her it wasn't. She wanted to work side by side with someone, *anyone*, to fix this mess so she wouldn't feel so desperately alone.

The chandelier crashed into the mirror, shattering it and the spell, the wind stopping abruptly. The frame lodged into the marble, and it remained mostly upright in the middle of the ballroom. Da slammed into the floor, but Bella floated as if on a gentle breeze.

Scarlet swung along a different beam on the smaller chandeliers until she reached the wall, then scrambled down. Bella pushed down her resentment. She'd never be as competent as Scarlet at anything but pouring a beer and creating a chair army to throw out a drunkard.

When the dust settled, Scarlet ran over to her father and gently turned him onto his side. Long, cylindrical pieces of glass were lodged into his fur all over, but the deepest one made Bella grow cold. Over an inch of it was stuck in his side, and he didn't wake when Scarlet shook his shoulder.

Dread and fear choked her, but she couldn't let her father die. She'd been trained by the priests and then Lailant as a healer. Maybe she was good for something other than serving beer. She rushed through the doorway of the ballroom.

----

"Damn it, wolfie, don't you dare die on me," Scarlet murmured, her hands shaking from emotion and exhaustion. She couldn't bear the thought of losing him, not after everything they had been through.

*Please*, she thought. *Please don't leave me.*

"I take it back. I said I might not want to live with the Growlers, but there's no other choice, really. Where you go, I go, remember?" She gasped, her voice shaking with fear and desperation. A surge of panic flowed through her at the thought of losing him, of not being with him every day for the rest of their lives.

She ran her hands through his hair, feeling the knot on his head. His arm was twisted awkwardly behind him, and she moved it, feeling the grinding of his broken bones. Thank the gods he wasn't awake for it to feel the pain. There were dozens of cuts, some deep and some shallow, but all bleeding. A pool formed underneath him, and her nose twitched at the coppery scent, making her panic multiply.

"No, stay with me, Wulfric. I'm here, see? I'm here, and I'm not going anywhere. You said you wouldn't leave again, remember? If you die, then you'll be leaving me. You swore you wouldn't lie again, and you said you wouldn't leave."

Her hands settled on his chest, and she froze. He didn't move. She leaned forward, pressing her ear to his chest and closing her eyes. Silently, she prayed and pleaded as the blood spread beneath him. It seeped into her pants, but still she waited, afraid to hope.

*There!* Her eyes flew open. The heartbeat was faint, but still his chest didn't rise. She leaned back and beat on his chest.

"Fuck, you better wake up, Wulfric. Breathe, damn it, *breathe!*" She screamed in his face, her hands sore from climbing and scraped up, pain lancing her with each furious blow.

She lifted both her hands, holding them in one fist to come down with all her weight, but an icy chill made her pause. Her eyes widened as his chest moved the smallest amount. Her hands dropped, settling on the soft fur.

"Fuck yes!" she hissed, a small amount of relief making her take a shuddering breath. The icy chill grew stronger, and Scarlet looked up.

Bella ran through the ballroom toward them. The worry on Bella's face reminded her so much of Wulfric, Scarlet felt tears prick her eyes.

"Here," Bella said, thrusting a small pouch out.

It fell to the dirty broken marble, and the strings waved in the air like hands when it... stood up? The strings opened the top of the pouch, and a potion rolled toward them, followed by a jar and some gauze bandages and wraps.

Then the strings dusted the ends together like hands saying there, my job is done.

The bag walked—the two corners acting as feet—toward the door, but Bella paid it no mind. "Take it. It's a healing potion. Lailant approved too. I've had it in my things that were moved from the tavern when I married, so I know it hasn't been tampered with."

Scarlet blinked. She hadn't even thought about that, but she was desperate to save him. His chest rose, but much too shallowly. She couldn't lose him, not when they'd just found each other. She—dear gods, she *loved* him.

She loved him like her parents had loved each other. Wholly, unconditionally, without boundaries. It consumed her, this need to live and work beside him, the need to love him all day and night. They were a team, somehow fated by the gods themselves.

"Pop the cork and pour it down his throat. Gently, don't choke him," Bella coaxed.

Scarlet's movements were jerky, but she pushed his chin down and slowly poured the liquid inside. She closed his mouth, and saw magic glow down his throat and spread through his torso. His chest rose deeper than before. She held a hand on him, feeling pieces of glass and slowly picking each one out as she came to it.

"Thank you for removing the glass," Bella said softly.

"It's not the first time I've patched him up."

"How long have you been together? How did you meet?" Bella asked, sinking to the floor and wrapping her arms around her legs.

As she worked, Scarlet told her how they'd met and everything that led them to this point. Wulfric didn't move when she took out the biggest piece and blood gushed from the open wound. The glow in his torso spread to the hole, blazing brighter before fading away.

Bella hissed. "I didn't pack a needle to sew that up."

Scarlet shook her head. "He won't need it sewn. He'll self-heal once it's wrapped." She reached for the gauze and unrolled it.

"I—I didn't know Growlers could do that, but it makes sense. And to think, he's been alive this whole time, and I didn't know. How different things might've turned out if I'd known..." Bella's voice trailed off as Scarlet worked.

She monitored Wulfric's chest and breathed easier to see him grow stronger.

"What happened here? Why was a mirror trying to suck you in?" She waved a hand to the destruction all around them.

Bella sat back on her haunches. "The wizard showed up and wanted to trap me in the mirror instead of waiting for me to die with the rose. He said the mirror would keep me from making trouble."

Bella's voice shook, but Scarlet couldn't tell if it was anger or fear. Scarlet's own hands had steadied the more she worked on the task. The silence settled between them, a gentle breeze from outside the broken windows lifting the hairs off the nape.

Finally, Scarlet sighed and wiped her forehead with the back of her bloodied hand, all the glass she could see or feel removed from his body. If she was going to make a real life with Wulfric, that meant making her peace with his daughter.

"I'm sorry I snapped at you earlier," Scarlet said, not making eye contact with Bella.

There was a heavy pause, then Bella replied, "It's alright. I don't blame you at all. For snapping or for any of the rest of it. It's my fault. Mine and Gastone's and the wizard's..."

Bella tensed and looked around. "The wizard set the mirror trap. He might come back, if he can sense it broke like he sensed the shadow daemon's death. You need to leave."

Scarlet nodded, not moving from Wulfric's side. "We have two horses somewhere, but you know he's not going to just leave you here."

Bella frowned and looked down at her father. The longing on her face twisted Scarlet's stomach and made her ache for her own father.

Scarlet's voice was small, barely a whisper. "If I had a chance to spend more time with my Pa, I would take it, no questions asked."

Bella bit her lip and nodded. "I know, but I'm tied to the rose. I haven't been able to leave the castle walls because of it and the shadow monster."

Scarlet waved a hand. "We already dealt with that thing, and the rose is in a pot, isn't it? Easy enough to take with us."

For the first time, Bella's eyes brightened in hope and slowly, she nodded.

"I need to pack some books too," Bella said as she stood and brushed out her skirts, her body almost vibrating at the idea of leaving.

"You go, and I'll watch him. And Bella? Yell if the wizard comes back. You knew he'd returned earlier, didn't you."

It wasn't a question. Scarlet had seen the way she'd tensed at the window, the way she'd dismissed them. She'd originally thought Bella had just needed some time away from telling the story and reliving the memories, but instead, she'd opted to try fighting the wizard on her own.

Bella nodded, glancing away from guilt. "Yes, I knew, just like I knew he'd hurt you both. He can't kill me outright, not in this form. But he can you two, and I wouldn't risk that."

Scarlet felt a knot in her stomach ease as Bella walked through the door. Perhaps the queen wasn't so evil after all.

# Chapter Forty-Seven

Wulfric groaned and blinked, pain shooting through his body with every breath. He was getting too old to wake up with so much pain all the time.

"Shh, don't move yet. You're still healing," Trix said. No, she was Bella now.

He looked up, not moving his head. Bella sat beside him on the floor of the ballroom, her knees drawn up to her chest and her arms around her knees. She'd sat like that when she was a girl, listening to her mother read stories before the fever took her.

"Scarlet?" His voice was hoarse, and he licked his lips. Bella animated a flask and it floated in front of his face. He gave a brief nod and lifted his head as it slowly poured water. Barely enough to wet his tongue, he swallowed and opened his mouth again.

As he drank, Bella said, "She went to find the horses. She should be back any minute now."

He let his head drop to the ground and closed his eyes. "Thank you," he murmured.

"You're welcome, Da."

His eyes flew open to meet hers. She sighed, "We still have so much to discuss, but you are and forever will be my Da."

Tears welled in his eyes, and he blinked rapidly. He'd not lost her, not completely. If her story was true—and it was too fantastical not to be—then they might be able to recover her body. She could have a life again, and he could be the father he should've been. Present and supportive instead of missing for ten long years.

She grinned—looking so much like her mother—and waved her hand. "Oh, none of that, now. Tell me about Scarlet. She told me some of how you've traveled together the past two weeks, but not all of it. You seem close, which is a dichotomy. A Growler and a Hunter."

He smiled at her accepting tone. "I love her. She's my fated mate."

Bella blinked and rested her cheek on her knee. "I thought I loved Gastone when I married him."

He stretched, feeling the pinch of pain in his side and around his body. "I can't believe you're old enough to be married."

She shrugged, her eyes turning sad as she looked out the open, broken windows. It was dark now, and a faint breeze blew in. The sound of hooves echoed below, but neither of them moved yet.

Bella sighed. "Marriage wasn't what I expected, that's for sure. I—I destroyed the tavern, the shop, the whole town, really. I'm sorry, Da."

"No, I'm the one who's sorry, Bella. I should've been here." The name still felt strange on his tongue, but he couldn't deny her this one request after denying her existence for ten long years. They were each different people

477

now. Hells they weren't even on the same plane of existence, but that didn't make them any less of a family. She'd always be his daughter.

She looked over to the door as Scarlet came inside. "It's water under the bridge now, Da. I'm glad you're alive though, that I'm not so alone anymore."

He reached for her hand, but pulled away before she saw the movement. He wanted to hold her. Until she got her body back, that would be impossible. She scrambled to her feet as Scarlet came into the room carrying a saddle bag.

Scarlet's voice echoed in the cavernous room. "I made a litter, but it'll be difficult to get him down the stairs. I strapped your book bag and the rose to my horse. You can ride her if you'd like."

"Thank you," Bella said. "He's awake now, but I don't recommend moving him for another few hours. It's the middle of the night too, and we are going into the Feral Forest." Bella shivered, and Wulfric smiled, remembering how terrified she was of the forest as a child.

"But what about the wizard?" Scarlet opened the saddle bag as she walked closer.

Bella shook out her skirts. "I know, but if we move him too soon, it could do more damage. I only have the smaller healing potion left, and it's not enough to get even to the forest, much less wherever we're going."

"Very well," Scarlet said, pulling her new pocket mirror from the saddle bag. She pushed a button and it lit up from within. She'd been so excited to show him the invention in Hartsgrove, but he wasn't sure how it worked. Explaining it had paled compared to her need to get to the queen.

Bella, his *daughter*, was the fucking queen. His body went from cold to hot, and his mind wandered to what she'd said about the wizard. If they could defeat the wizard and get her body back, then somehow restore her to the throne... perhaps then she'd forgive him for leaving ten years ago. Perhaps then he could make his absence up to her.

The murmur of voices was faint, and Wulfric closed his eyes and willed his body to heal. He must've dozed because a deep thud hit the terrace outside the ballroom, jerking him awake. He groaned as pain ripped through him, his whole body resisting the movement.

He blinked, glancing around and tensing. "The wizard?"

Bella jumped to her feet and paled, her hand going to her stomach as she took a step back from the broken windows. "No, not the wizard."

Wulfric tipped his head and saw a swirl of green smoke. Then Knox stepped through it, his eyes sharp as he took in the state of the room. He said nothing of the horse standing in the ballroom or the chandelier embedded in the marble floor.

Instead, he strode purposely toward them, eyes raking over Wulfric, Scarlet, and then pausing on Bella. His steps slowed to a stop.

Bella's hands shook and her mouth opened and closed. "You—I—I thought you were dead."

He shook his head. "No, Eirwyn and I are both very much alive. Are you?"

Bella snorted and her hand dropped to her side. "That's to be debated. There's an evil wizard taking up residence in my body at the moment." She indicated herself with a wave of her hand. "This is what's left of me."

Knox's lips pursed as he nodded sagely. "Well, Eirwyn will be glad to hear you're not completely dead. She's been anxious about you."

Bella's shoulders slumped and her eyes teared up. The

debris around her on the floor shook slightly as she breathed deeply to get her emotions under control. Wulfric's fingers twitched to hold her.

Scarlet interjected. "The wizard was here and tried to trap Bella in a mirror. We need to get out of here before he realizes she's not trapped, but Wulfric's still healing. Did Grandma send a healing potion? Can you fly him to Hartsgrove? I'll bring the horses and Bella."

Knox nodded and handed Scarlet a small pouch. She took it and came closer, her eyes widening when she saw him looking up at her. She dropped to her knees, her hand hovering above him as she whispered, "Wulfric." It was a sigh, a prayer of thanksgiving.

He smiled weakly and said, "Bunny."

She wiped the corner of her eye furiously and cleared her throat. Opening the pouch, she said matter-of-factly, "I told you my plan was the only one that might work, didn't I? And we're all going to be fine."

He snorted, wincing as the movement sent pain through him. "Aye, I'm happy to not be trapped, but damn if this doesn't hurt."

She gently lifted his head as she popped the cork on the vial. "Well, take this. You better survive the journey back to Hartsgrove. If anything happens to you…"

She trailed off as he drank the spicy mixture. His throat burned and his eyes watered as he swallowed.

"There, you'll be good as new by the time I get there."

He choked out, "All of us should go with Knox. I don't want to leave you."

Her eyes watered, and she dropped the empty vial to cup his cheek. "I know you don't. But this is the only way that will work. Knox can't carry us all, and we need to get out of here as fast as possible."

"How long does that potion take? I want to get home," Knox said, stepping closer.

Bella cleared her throat. "A healing potion of that power should take about ten to fifteen minutes and last maybe an hour."

Wulfric grinned. "You always were so good at healing. Lailant always said so."

Bella blushed, and Scarlet brushed the hair out of his eyes. She stood up with a sigh, saying, "Right, well that'll give us time to get the litter upstairs and load him on it. I made it out of two lances and a sheet, so it should hold while you fly..."

Knox followed her out of the ballroom, their steps echoing in the quiet, empty castle as their voices faded. The once lively and bustling castle now felt quiet and empty, a stark reminder of the chaos that had unfolded. He couldn't shake the guilt and worry for his daughter gnawing at his heart as he was gently placed onto the litter, every movement causing searing pain. His shoulder felt like it was still out of socket, and his side hurt worse than any of his alpha challenges.

Wulfric's vision swam and his stomach rebelled as Knox and Scarlet hauled him slowly to the terrace. Bella hovered, and the way she helplessly wrung her hands made his heart ache. He couldn't ignore the fact that he was now at the mercy of a wizard who had caused so much harm to those he loved. And worst of all, he couldn't even hold Bella in his arms to comfort her. He kept his gaze locked on her translucent form to distract himself from the nausea.

Knox rippled as he grew, transforming into his dragon self. Bella jumped out of the way with a gasp. He would have to find a way to confront the wizard and protect his family once he was healed.

But for now, all he could do was watch as Bella struggled with her own inner turmoil. She may not have a physical body, but her emotions were still evident on her face—fear, sadness, and a haunting memory replaying in her mind. Wulfric reached out to try and calm her, but she was too far away, and translucent besides.

Determined to help, he said softly, "Bella, it's alright. He's not going to hurt you." She looked just like she had after her mother died, scared and afraid. He couldn't smell her emotions, probably due to her not having a body, but he could see it on her face.

He waved his hand, making her look at him. She took a deep breath, her eyes watering. "I know that. Scarlet explained earlier that he's Eirwyn's mate and one true love. But I keep seeing that fight on the roof between the dragon and Gastone. It's on repeat in my mind."

All events that occurred because of the fucking wizard. As she looked at him with tears in her eyes, he knew that their fight was far from over.

Wulfric held his side, pressing against the bandaged wound. "I'm sorry, little girl. I should've been here. You never should've been in that position."

Bella stiffened and shook her head. The self-recrimination on her face made her look like him, not her mother. "Like I said. It's all water under the bridge now. We can't change the past, no matter how much we wish otherwise."

Wulfric reached for her, saying, "Maybe we can change the future though. I'd like to be a part of your present and your future. I'm not leaving you again, little girl."

Bella chuckled and shook her head. "You have to survive the journey into the woods first, old man. Now close your eyes and be still or I might accidentally turn you into a couch."

He grinned and watched her with pride as her fingers flew. She whispered a spell, and the litter lifted into the air. Wulfric closed his eyes against the nausea and pain, the dizziness not stopping even as he was set on the back of the dragon between the wings.

Scarlet wove the tassels from the curtains around him and Knox, lashing them together. "You better not drop him, Knox, or I'll never forgive you."

The scent of Scarlet and the feel of her gentle touch made his nausea dissipate, and he breathed deeply. Here was another woman he never wanted to leave or disappoint. She'd saved them all today, with her plan with the chandeliers.

The dragon snorted, green smoke billowing. Wulfric looked up at the stars above, constant and clear. It'd been a long time since he'd seen stars like this. The trees in the forest hid so much.

Scarlet ignored Knox and grabbed Wulfric's hand where it lay strapped to the litter. "And you, wolfie. You better be fully healed by the time I get there tomorrow."

He tightened his grip on her hand, reluctant to let go. The soft pressure of her touch against his bruised and battered skin brought a sense of calm to his racing thoughts. Time spent in bed just holding her, basking in the warmth of their love, was all he craved in this moment. Holding her hand was a simple yet powerful display of affection that he desperately needed.

With her by his side, he knew he could overcome any challenge that came his way, but he still didn't know if she loved him too, if she wanted to live with him as a Growler Luna... or if she wanted to continue living as a Hunter. He was loath to let her go, because every time they separated, it seemed like something bad happened.

"I'll do my best to heal, but my entire world is going to be on two horses in the woods. I'm not going to sleep a wink from worry."

She scoffed. "I was born in those woods. We'll be fine. It won't be the first time I've ridden through the woods with royalty, but at least we won't have Growlers nipping our heels this time."

He arched a brow, and she grinned. "A story for another time. I still have the talkie, and Knox has one at Hartsgrove. I'll call if I get in any major trouble, alright? I'll see you tomorrow, wolfie."

He wanted to tell her how much he loved her. It was on the tip of his tongue. He opened his mouth, but she kissed him instead. It was soft, sweet, and over way too soon. She pulled back, shadows hiding her expression but not her smirking lips.

She stepped toward the ballroom door, and the dragon launched into the air. Wulfric's stomach swirled and dipped with every beat of the wings.

Fuck, he had to focus on not throwing up and making a fool of himself on Scarlet's brother.

# Chapter Forty-Eight

Scarlet and Bella's ride to Hartsgrove was mostly uneventful. Bella had gotten to know the Hunter better over the past two days. In this form, she hadn't needed sleep, so she'd stared into the fire while Scarlet had slept. She'd finally left the castle, but what waited for her at the dragon's lair? She'd been so incredibly alone these past few months.

Her pocket jiggled, and she took out Gus and Jaq. She'd cleaned them as best she could in a stream, bending them back to mostly normal with the help of magic. They hopped around the firepit, chattering in that strange language.

Bella listened with half an ear, but then the fire flared with magic. The utensils hopped back to her, hiding behind her skirts as images flickered in the smoke.

She gasped, her hands covering her mouth. The stories from school told of messages from the gods in smoke, but she'd never met anyone who had experienced it. She gave a silent prayer of thanks to the gods for revealing this to her, then leaned forward to watch.

A giant brown dragon battled several smaller ones, circling a castle surrounded by trees. A woman ran out the front doors, her hands raised as a spear shot down the large dragon. The ground shook, but the image in the flames spun to the side of the building.

Another dragon, this one white and silver, snapped at a smaller one. The rider on its back jerked on the reins, and the smaller dragon screamed. The rider was thrown through a ground-floor window, crashing into the glass. The dragon roared and magic swirled as he shifted into a half-human version.

Bella's stomach twisted. He looked similar to her body now, the one the wizard had stolen. On two legs, he tucked his wings around his shoulders like a cape and stalked after the little man, stepping with his clawed feet over the broken glass. His head remained draconic and reminded her of Eirwyn's mate, Knox. Dragon scales covered him from the tip of his horns, of which there were several, to his toes.

He disappeared into the building, and the smoke image followed them.

It was a sitting room, standard of any noble household. A few chairs around a fireplace, a few couches, a writing desk tucked along a wall. Nothing drew her eye more than the dragon. His black gaze swung around the room.

A burst of light from the opposite side of the room hit the wall beside the dragon. He flinched out of the way and swung to face the man. She couldn't hear anything, but magic flew back and forth. The dragon jerked from a hit, then threw another ball of white. It splintered the chair, and the man behind it jumped toward the dragon.

The smoke swirled, and Bella leaned forward, gripping her skirts tightly. When it cleared, the dragon was bleeding with each step down a narrow stone staircase. He slammed into a door, and it swung open into darkness.

The dragon held up a glowing hand, the magic flickering. He shook his hand, then it glowed brighter.

Bella's spine straightened. Gastone had done that, when he'd pushed himself so far and depleted his internal magic reserves. Then he'd died. She held her hand to her mouth as the white dragon stumbled into a dark cave. Stalactites and stalagmites filled it, and he fell into one, crushing it to pieces.

The dragon straightened and kept walking, shifting into his full dragon form with a flare of magic. He reached the center of the room and fell on a pile of junk. His eyes slowly closed and smoke curled from his nostrils. His wings tucked around him, and his mouth moved. Magic swirled around him, the colors wrapping around him like a blanket.

The image faded once more, leaving her staring into the fire like nothing had happened. Normally, she would inspect the fire to see if she could identify the magic that had caused it, see if she could reverse engineer the spell or replicate it.

But her mind remained on the silver and white dragon. When he'd closed his eyes, her stomach had twisted. Her body had revolted, and she'd felt sick. It'd reminded her so much of how she'd felt when Gastone had died.

Who was he? And why had she needed to see this? Was it the work of the wizard? She bit her lip and smoothed her skirts nervously, obsessing over the details until the sky started to lighten.

Scarlet woke, and they broke camp shortly after. Her father's mate wasn't a morning person, but Bella was fine with that. Her mind replayed scenes from the dragon's fight until Scarlet drew them to a halt.

A gargoyle sat leaning against a tree, whittling a piece of wood with a knife. He looked up as they approached on the horses. Scarlet tipped her chin at him and leaned on the pommel.

"What are you doing here?" she asked. Her posture remained relaxed, so Bella assumed he was a friend and not foe.

The stone giant lumbered to his feet, putting the knife and carving away in a pocket. "Your Growler wouldn't rest until Knox promised to send me to help. I'm to escort you to safety."

Scarlet snorted, and the gargoyle raised a stone brow. "I know, I told Knox it was ridiculous. But your Growler can be as stubborn as you when pressed."

Scarlet laughed and nodded. Bella knew her father could be very obstinate. She'd argued with him a lot over the years. The man turned his stony gaze on her, and Bella lifted her chin, not looking away.

"You must be the queen. You might not recognize me like this, but I was in the room with Scarlet when the king died and you..." he trailed off, somehow growing paler than the gray stone he'd been before.

Scarlet shifted on the saddle and looked at Bella. "When you killed the Robin by wringing him like a wet towel in the sheets."

Bella flinched and looked away, stroking the horse's side. She couldn't feel it, and her hand could go through the coarse hide if she didn't concentrate. She pursed her lips and took a deep breath. "I—I'm sorry about that. I was very upset and not myself. Was he—a good man?"

The gargoyle nodded solemnly. "Yes, a bit zealous, but he was a good man."

Bella's shoulders slumped. "I'm sorry," she said softly.

She'd said it so much over the past few months, first to the servants, then just in general to the universe, the gods, whoever would listen. Tears stung her eyes, and she wiped at them furiously as she glanced at the canopy overhead. "I assume you turned into a gargoyle because of the curse?"

She saw him nod out of the corner of her eye, and she sighed, her head bowing until her chin nearly touched her chest. "I'm sorry for that too."

The silence stretched a moment, then Scarlet said, "Well, enough of that. We still need to get to the castle and see how Wulfric's healed. Bella, this is Ashur. Ashur, Queen Bella."

The gargoyle bowed, but Bella jerked back in the saddle, her hand raising. "Oh no, please don't. I don't deserve that. I deserve to be thrown in the dungeon forever for what I've done."

Ashur shrugged. "I won't deny that."

Scarlet snorted. "As someone who's been thrown into the dungeon before, I will argue against that. She's a bit emotional, but she's a decent fighter when she can control her magic."

Bella's eyebrows shot up in surprise, her eyes widening at Scarlet's unexpected defense. She couldn't believe that the usually cold and distant Hunter had stuck up for her. Despite their rocky start, perhaps traveling together had helped to soften her up. Or perhaps it was because the Hunter was her father's companion.

"Thank you," Bella said quietly. "And for what it's worth, Gastone never should've throne you or any of the others into the dungeon. I didn't know about the arrests until after his death."

Scarlet waved a hand and nodded. "See? I told you she wasn't too bad. Like we haven't all made mistakes before?

Besides, it'll be harder for her to find a cure from the dungeon, I imagine."

Bella wasn't sure who she was trying to convince, the gargoyle or herself. Either way, she hoped to avoid the dungeon and wasn't sure that her father would be able to keep her out of it.

Ashur shrugged again and turned toward the trees, his voice easily carrying. "So I've been told." He paused and looked over his shoulder, catching Bella unaware and trapping her in his gaze.

"For what it's worth, Will was determined to kill the king. We all weren't so sure that would solve the problem, but he was like a man possessed about it. I don't blame you for his death. We all knew that it was a suicide mission."

Then he led the way through the trees. Scarlet nudged Bella to follow him, and her mind wandered to the man she'd killed. She still saw his face, that whole room and the events there, every night when she tried to sleep. It was why she'd realized she didn't need to sleep at all in this form.

The saddle vibrated, making the horse prance and throw its head side to side. Blast, her memories and emotions were like a tidal wave in her gut. She tried to take deep, even breaths and control her magic. Perhaps if she thought of something else. In her mind's eye, she saw the silver dragon stumbling into the cave once more, and the saddlebags settled.

A screech drew her gaze, and she jerked on the horse. She had animated the saddle so she could actually stay on the thing, but she still almost fell off at that sound.

"What was that?" she asked, fear making her voice wobble.

Scarlet and Ashur said, "Eagles." They both glanced up, scanning the area.

Ashur's wings flared, his eyes not leaving the canopy above. "When we get within sight, I'll distract them while you make a run for it."

"What about you?" Bella asked. A large shadow fell on them, and Bella looked up. Her eyes widened at the size. When they'd said eagles, she wasn't thinking the size of a horse.

"I'm made of stone. Their claws can't hurt me, and I'm too heavy for them to lift."

The fierce cries of the giant eagles pierced the air, a combination of screeches and roars that sound like thunder clashing with lightning. Scarlet swore and grabbed the reins in her hand, kicking her horse into a faster pace and dragging Bella's mount with her. Bella's heart leapt as she looked at her rose bumping in the saddle bag. A petal floated free and her heart dropped with it. Ashur might be made of stone, and she might be incorporeal, but the rose wasn't. Neither was Scarlet.

The trees began to thin and an eagle swooped down. The flapping of their massive wings created a deafening hurricane like whoosh. Bella ducked, her arms protecting the potted rose as Scarlet jerked on the reins. The horses whinnied in freight, tossing their heads as they careened sideways, just out of reach of the eagle's lethal claws.

Ashur launched himself over them, tackling the eagle to the ground. Ice and snow billowed from the impact, and the ground shook, making Bella grip the pot tighter. She looked back as he punched it in the beak.

It fell limply, convulsing. Scarlet turned their horses, and Bella looked forward, squeezing the pot. They approached a wall of thorns and roses, and her heart pounded faster than the horses hooves. Her magic vibrated and broke free, latching onto the helrose hedge. It grew, thorns reaching higher into the sky to stab at the eagle above. Through her beating heart and terror of the rose being trampled underneath the hooves, she focused on the wall. The pot acted as a focus item, she gripped it so hard, and she actually maintained some semblance of control over her magic despite her terror. They raced along the edge of the wall, large shadows swooping until they turned sharply into a tunnel through the wall.

The sounds of battle faded as they slowed to a walk, and her magic dimmed. Bella's heart slowed as the horses calmed.

Ashur nodded and explained how the king and queen—Knox and Eirwyn—were working to solve the eagle problem. He talked quite a lot about it, the adrenaline from battle lowering his formerly stoic expression. Bella stopped listening as they exited the tunnel. Her jaw dropped, and she floated off the horse in surprise. It was the castle from the fire magic last night!

Anticipation hung in the air like a heavy fog that obscured the truth and hinted at secrets yet to be revealed. Her gaze swung to where the large brown dragon had fallen. A boulder sat in the middle of a tight circle of trees, barely visible through the grove's thickness. A tree grew out of the top of the boulder, barely a sapling.

Scarlet said, "The tree was the first magic I tried to reverse the curse."

Guilt made her wince as she replied, "The one in the center?"

Scarlet nodded. "It used to produce golden apples that had incredible magical powers. It grew in the middle of the ballroom for the past few hundred years, until it was destroyed."

Dread made her gulp, but still Bella asked, "How was it destroyed?"

Scarlet's hands tightened on the reins. "Gastone cast a spell to animate a dragon skeleton, which attacked Knox and Eirwyn. The tree was destroyed in the battle, but they've replanted it. The gardener said the roots have taken but with the winter, it's not produced any fruit. No fruit, no golden magical apples that might reverse the curse…"

Bella absorbed this new information, her mind already churning with possibilities and plans and hope. With all the resources available to her in this magical castle, perhaps she could finally correct the mistake that had tormented her for so long. The tree might be the key, if she could ferret out the secrets of this place.

She looked up, scanning the towering castle. It was easily taller than the Winter Palace in Demerel that she'd finally escaped from. Gray stone with white mortar and dotted with narrow stained-glass windows towered over them. The room where the dragon fought in her vision must be on the other side.

Bella grabbed the pommel of the saddle, anchoring herself back to sit as Scarlet halted the horses at the wide front steps. A servant took their horses' reins, but didn't even give Bella a second glance.

Bella frowned, surprised to not have a comment about a ghost. Scarlet took the pot with her rose and walked to the front stairs, taking them two at a time. Bella followed, her stomach in knots. There were *people* in there. People who might help, but also people who might hate her for what she'd done.

Her feet dragged, and the door to the manor swung open. Bella stopped on the top step and sucked in a breath. A petite black-haired woman stepped into the light, her face practically glowing. Her signature blue and red dress was in a new style than what Bella was familiar with, but the fabric and cut fit her to perfection, highlighting her new curves. Bella's chest ached at the sight of her friend so healthy and happy.

Eirwyn's flushed face beamed at them. "You made it! I knew you would. Where's—oh."

Scarlet stepped through the door, and Bella met Eirwyn's gaze for the first time since that fateful day. Her eyes widened, but the pity in her face made Bella tip her chin up and curtsy.

"Oh Bella," Eirwyn breathed, reaching with arms out for a hug. Eirwyn's arms went through her, and she stepped back with a gasp, tears pooling in her eyes.

Bella's smile was sad as she shook her head and wiped her tears. "I can't," Bella said. "As you can see, I'm a ghost. I —I hope you've been well?"

She couldn't quite bring herself to ask all the million questions she wanted to ask. Eirwyn had stood by her side for ten years when she'd tried to run the tavern. She'd helped sell her grandparents' shop when the tavern's home-made brew became more profitable. Eirwyn had helped her prosecute several bad people who had frequented the tavern too, all without revealing that Bella had been the one who'd overheard all the confessions and illegal deals.

She'd been so alone for six months, but here was her dearest friend in the world, ready to pick up their friendship where they'd left off.

Eirwyn stepped back, her nose red as tears ran down her own cheeks. "I've been fine, better than you, it looks like. You're a ghost! Wulfric said, but I didn't believe—and he's back! Your father is alive! Bella—"

Bella laughed and wiped her cheek. "Perhaps we can

chat like old times? If you'll welcome me. I'll understand if you don't want to." Bella tucked a piece of hair behind her ear. She wasn't sure how much Da had explained about what had happened.

"Of course you're welcome here. I'm so glad to see you. Come inside, please. Wait until you see the library. Oh you'll love it so much! But I'm going to wait until *after* we talk to show it to you. You'll be too distracted otherwise." Eirwyn waved a hand down the hall but turned to the right. Bella followed her with Scarlet behind them.

She stopped in the doorway of the drawing room and held her hand to her stomach. It twisted and lurched. She could almost see a hazy version of the dragon in the floor to ceiling window. She blinked, and the image dissipated. She glanced to the left of the room where the man had hidden behind a chair in her vision.

While the room had been rearranged and redecorated with more modern fabrics, several of the pieces still looked the same. This was where the dragon had died. Both of them. Nothing good could come from this place.

Except, she was already dead. And it was the only place she might be able to work on the curses.

"A library, you say?" Bella asked. New books meant new spellbooks to explore. Perhaps one of them would know how to reunite her body and spirit.

Eirwyn laughed, the sound light and airy and filling Bella with comfort. "A one track mind. Still the same as always at least. I'm glad some things never change."

Scarlet took the potted rose to the very window the silver dragon had stepped through. Scarlet placed it on a small table and strode back to the door. "I'll leave you two to talk. I need to check on Wulfric."

Bella sank onto a couch, wondering if the silver dragon's

495

battle was one from the past or something that would be in the future? Was it something she could help prevent? She shook her head and focused on her friend. "He's fine? Da?"

Eirwyn nodded. "Yes, once we sent Ashur to help, he's been resting and healing. Slept for almost a full twenty-four hours after the druid and the old medicine woman worked on him."

Bella jumped up. "They're both here? Maybe they can help break the spell. Or at least help me get my body back."

Eirwyn reached for her hand, but it went through air. "Relax, they're in the garden arguing. You do not want to get between them when they're like that. Sit and tell me everything that's happened in the past six months. I've missed you."

Bella sat back down, her chest tight with emotion at the warm welcome. She hadn't ruined her one friend or turned her against her. Thank the gods, there was still hope.

# Chapter Forty-Nine

Scarlet glanced down the hallway as Leopol came down the stairs.

"Wulfric?" she asked.

He pointed up. "I put him in your room. He's fine. No need to worry. I'm just off to ask the cook to make him another beefsteak now."

Scarlet grinned and raced past him up the stairs, but Knox came down from the west tower where he'd probably been visiting his egg. She paused on the landing to ask, "Any movement?"

Knox shook his head. "No, but Lailant and Grandma say it's to be expected. It's just as well that we need to wait, since I have my hands full trying to convince the Feral Forest people to approve the treaty with the Growlers."

"Still giving you problems?"

He shrugged and glanced out the window, searching the skies for eagles. "No more than expected. Change takes time. I suspect it'll be a few months for the nation to approve it, but hopefully by the time we go into Glathen to finally get that economic treaty in place, both halves of the Feral Forest will present a united front."

Scarlet played with her dagger hilts and hummed. "Growlers and dragons going on a diplomatic mission into Glathen? You'd better take as many Robins and Hunters as possible too. They can be tricky."

Knox sighed and raked a hand over the scales on his head. "That's what everyone keeps telling me. I really do not want Eirwyn to go, but she's still insisting she'll be the best chance we have of convincing them to recognize us as a nation."

Scarlet turned to the steps that would take her up to Wulfric. "Well, she's usually right, so you might as well listen to her."

Knox groaned and continued down the stairs. "Don't say that too loud, or it'll go to her head. Oh and Scarlet, the Hunter's Guild Master is here. He said you asked to see him?"

Scarlet paused with her foot on stair. "Ah yes, so I did. We need to discuss how the Hunters, Robins, and Growlers can work together. Tell him I'll meet with him later."

Knox called out, "I'm proud of you, sis, for working with all of these people. I know it's not easy or what you want, but I appreciate it. Sometimes all this responsibility gets a bit much to handle by myself."

She looked back at him and smiled. "It's alright, I'll always have your back, little brother. But if you don't mind, all the responsibility can fuck off for a few hours. I need to see my mate."

Knox's laughter followed her up the stairs, but her mind had already turned toward seeing Wulfric. Her chest was tight with anticipation and nerves. She'd been separated from him for less than two days, but it was too much. She'd not told him how much she loved him or that she'd decided to stay with him when this was all over.

When she pushed the door to her room open, Wulfric sat up on the bed. Shaggy black and silver hair, big wolf ears and nose, the heat in her chest spread at the unfamiliar sight of him so domesticated, reading and—

She paused, then stumbled on a rug in shock. He wore *glasses* and held a book in one hand, the other tucked up behind his head. That bicep made her mouth water. His expression when he looked up and smiled at her? Her core clenched, and she shut the door behind her quickly.

"You wear *glasses*?" Her voice was high in incredulity.

He chuckled and put the book down beside him on the bed. "The better to see you with, my dear."

She shook her head and sat on the settee to pull off her boots. She didn't want any barriers between them. "There are so many things I don't know about you," she muttered.

He threw back the coverlet and patted the bed. "Come closer, and I'll tell you all you want to know."

The confession she'd practice during the past two days of riding fled right out of her mind. She just lived in the moment and met his golden, glowing eyes. She laughed and shook her head. "First, are you healed? How are your wounds?"

He swung his feet to the side of the bed and began to unwrap his bandages. "I'm fine. I was waiting on you to take these off. I know how you love to play doctor."

She smirked as her boot dropped to the floor with a thump.

"I want to talk about something before you come over to play though," he said softly, his eyes calculating.

She tugged off her other boot and grunted, "Talk away." Now that she faced him, she couldn't quite bring herself to say those three simple words. Her parents had bandied them about over and over. Why was it so hard?

He swallowed hard and winced as he unwrapped another layer. "There may be a lot we don't know about each other yet, but there's only one thing I need to know about you," he said before taking a deep breath.

Her spine tingled. This sounded serious. She frowned as her other boot hit the floor. She sat up and met his gaze. His eyes glowed golden in the soft light through the window.

"Do you love me? Can you love me, a monster, a beast, a Growler?"

Scarlet sat back on the settee, drumming her fingers on her leg. So it was going to be that kind of talk then. Well, it was a good thing she'd already made up her mind. She pulled her dagger from her sheath and picked at her nails. "Well, there's a problem with your logic there, wolfie. You see, you're not a monster or a beast."

She looked at him from beneath her lashes. He blinked. "I'm not?"

She shook her head and looked into his eyes. Tossing the blade and catching it without looking, she said, "No, you're not. You're my mate, Wulfric, and there's no getting out of that or escaping it. I'm not about to walk away from you."

"What are you saying?" he demanded, setting the last of the gauze aside, his jaw clenching.

"I'm saying, I'm in it until the end. You almost *died*, Wulfric. Bella's a spirit, Leopol's a ghost. We're all going to die someday, and it got me thinking." She paused, rubbing at the sore spot where her antlers grew from her head. It didn't hurt nearly as much as it did before she'd met him.

She sighed and sat forward on the settee, settling her elbows on her knees and looking into his eyes across the room. She just had to spit it out. "If at the end of my hopefully long life I could've spent even one more day with you, would I do it? Hells yes, I would. I'd be a fool not to spend every day possible with you. And Grandma didn't raise a fool, regardless what she says otherwise."

Wulfric chuckled, and she stood, stepping toward him. He held his hand out, palm facing her. "Wait, does this mean you're still going to obsess over ending the curse?"

She frowned, reaching for the ties on her vest. She unlaced them as she asked, "What do you mean?"

He raked a hand down his haggard face, still too pale from healing. "We may be fated mates, but I fell in love with *you*, Scarlet. Not because it was destiny or the gods manipulating us, but because you're fucking amazing. Antlers, rabbit shifting, and all."

Her heart raced, and her nose twitched. "You love me?" She'd hoped, had been fairly sure, but to hear it said aloud. Her throat closed, and she swallowed hard.

His brows wrinkled, and he put the glasses on the side table, rubbing his eyes with a sigh. "Of course I fucking love you. Who wouldn't?"

She rolled her eyes. "Just about everyone else, dipshit. I'm a freak of nature."

He growled and pointed. "There. That right there is the problem. Will there ever be a time you can love yourself the way I love you?" He laid back against the bed, closing his eyes.

She frowned and tossed the blade again.

He sighed. "What happens if Bella can't reverse the curse? Yes, she'll have more resources here, more books to research and find a solution. But if you stay like this, will you be happy? Or will you always be chasing a way to change back into what you were before?"

She caught the blade and held it. Her breathing stopped

too, her stomach twisting. Could she live with herself like this? Eirwyn had asked her that same question, but so much had changed since then.

It wasn't just about her though. "I'm not making it up when I say literally everyone thinks I'm a freak. You haven't seen them, but they avoid me, walk on the other side of the street."

"But my tribe didn't act like that, did they?"

She swallowed hard and lowered her hand. Why was she fighting this? It was like she was grasping at straws, trying to find reasons to stay apart when that wasn't what she wanted at all.

Still she powered ahead. "It's not the same as living there. I don't know if your tribe will accept me like this."

"You know they will. You're a warrior, and they respect that. It's more about who you are than what you are. Now stop avoiding the question. Can you accept yourself like this?" His gaze bored into her soul, and she couldn't escape any longer.

Her chest felt too tight, and she paced to the fireplace. She spun with hands wide, one still holding the dagger. "I can if you can," she finally said, her jaw tilting up in defiance.

Wulfric arched a brow and sat up once more. "What the hells have I been saying? Are you not listening? Gods."

He grumbled as he slowly swung his feet over the side of the bed. He crooked his fingers and said, "Come here, bunny. I'm still too weak to chase after you right now."

She sighed and pulled her vest off, tossing it and her dagger onto the settee as she walked past. She stood between his knees, and he put his hands on her hips.

He looked up, his golden eyes glowing and so full of emotion. "I love you, antlers, whiskers, tail and all."

He kissed her forehead and traced her antlers with his fingertips. "I love your bunny side, how soft and cuddly you are, how you need my protection sometimes, even though you'll deny it with every breath."

He kissed her bunny nose, then rose and kissed the base of her antlers. "I love your antlers, the beautiful doe who doesn't know whether to run or freeze in terror. I love how you stare down danger but use your amazing brain to know when it's smart to retreat."

Her chest swelled hearing the acceptance she craved. He kissed her cheeks, and her breath hitched.

"And I love the Growler side of you that you try to hide. I love the fierceness of your protection, your determination to do what's right, even if you don't want to, like saving a pathetic creature like me. Saving Bella when you could've killed her."

Scarlet snorted. "I can't kill a spirit."

He wiped the tear from her cheek and leaned back. "Hey, I wouldn't put it past you. You're a badass, the strongest and best Hunter in the land. If anyone could kill a spirit, it'd be you."

She smiled and shook her head as he kissed her cheek. "You're so good to me."

"Then stay with me," he said softly. "I'll be the best mate in the world. I'll protect you with all my breath for all my days. We can work side by side to protect the Growlers, or we can roam as Hunters together."

She paused, her hands settling on his shoulders. Something shifted within her chest, a knot dissipating that she didn't even know had been there. The trapped feeling eased and her brows rose in surprise.

"You'd do that? Give up the alpha position you deserve, the one you earned?"

He shrugged. "In a heartbeat, if that's what you wish. What matters to me is that we're together through it all, every day and night. Flying away on your brother's back was torture because it separated me from you. I never want to be apart from you again. We can rule an alpha tribe or be Hunters together or just live like hermits in the woods. As long as we're together."

She threw her arms around his neck and her body shook. He clutched her to his chest, and she buried her face in his neck, her body relaxing for the first time since she'd sent him with Knox. She couldn't let him go. Never again.

She squeezed her arms tighter and snorted into his ear. "If I'll have you? Well, that depends, doesn't it. Will you put up with me not knowing which type of animal I am at any time? I may go from scared to mad in the blink of an eye. I may scream or try to fight you."

"Ah, the spice of life. I'm looking forward to it, love," he said with a chuckle.

She leaned back and glared. "I'm serious. There's no one else like me, and I don't know if this will ever feel normal. Life with me will never be peaceful, Wulfric. Is that something you can do day in and day out?"

He leaned back and laughed. She frowned and put her hands on his hips, but he just pulled her closer, lifting them both until she was sitting on his lap sideways on the bed. He stroked her cheek and shushed her with a chuckle.

"Hush, I'm not laughing at you. I'm laughing because my life has never been predictable or calm. I went from the shop to the tavern to the army to the Growlers. I'm always managing people, solving disputes, and fixing problems. If you come at me swinging, well, that's a problem I can solve. Life with you won't be peaceful, but it will be an adventure. What do you say? Will you marry me?"

She leaned back, her eyes clear for the first time. She'd not felt like this in so long, well before the curses changed her life. It was as if the weight of the world had lifted from her shoulders. He brushed his thumb over her cheek as she smiled.

"That's dumb. We're already mated."

He shrugged. "Let me retain some of my humanity. I want to marry you, build a house and a community and a home for our babies."

She rolled her eyes and smiled. "Fine, we'll get married. But no darning socks."

He chuckled. "Deal."

"Now will you kiss me already?" She leaned forward as he chuckled.

The future was still unknown, but for the first time in months, she didn't feel the pressing need to go find a cure for her curses. And for the first time in years, she felt blissfully happy. Like Grandma had said, she was settled because she was finally accepted exactly as she was. She was *home*, exactly where she belonged—fighting the world by his side.

She could be a handful, but he was the indomitable Growler who refused to give up on her. Together, they'd faced challenges unlike any she'd experienced before. And if they faced the world side-by-side, she knew their love would be stronger than any magic an evil wizard might throw at them.

It was the last thought in her head before their lips met, sweeping her into animalistic pleasure to make her heart race.

# Epilogue

Hanzel vibrated with energy as he glared at the Dragon Claws squad in front of him. "What do you mean, the mirror was shattered by a chandelier? You're saying there's no one trapped inside it?"

The squad leader, a burly werewolf twice his own monstrous size, nodded with a snort. "Aye, your highness. Not in that one or any other mirrors in the Winter Palace."

Hanzel gripped the edge of the office desk so hard the wood splintered. The sneaky bitch had defeated his shadow monster and escaped his mirror trap. But how?

"We did see signs of others, your highness. Growler paws, boots, and bare feet. There appeared to be three of them."

Breath heaving, smoke curled from his nose. Of course, she'd had help. There was no way that weak wench had escaped on her own. He straightened, his hands clutching each other behind his back. "Ah, I see. And were you able to track them?"

The Dragon Claws leader shook his head. "Only to the

edge of the Feral Forest, your highness. We thought you'd want to know before we push inside and track them further."

More smoke curled as he sneered. "Oh you *thought*, did you? I don't pay you to *think*. I pay you to get the bloody job done. Get your asses back out there and bring me her accomplices, dead or alive. I'd prefer to talk and see what she's planning, but dead will work too."

The Dragon Claws snapped to attention then filed out of the luxurious room. Hanzel spun on his heel and stared out the large windows over the city below. He'd been in residence for barely a few months, but he was consolidating his power nicely. There would be no mistakes this time. He *would* bring his god to Celawynn and take over the world.

"Your highness, if I may give the latest report on the army?" A deep voice asked from the doorway.

Hanzel turned, watching the general of the Busparian army stride inside on long legs. The drakin's white hair revealed his age, but his body was in its prime, fit and lean yet packed with enough muscle to keep all his soldiers well in line. The man paused in front of the desk and saluted, then began to rattle off a report on supplies, ammunition, and even morale of the troops being back home.

Hanzel didn't care, and let it go in one ear and out the other, all the while plotting his next move.

## Next in the Royal Oath Series

vinci-books.com/OathofRedemption

**She was cursed to the grave. He's bound to a soul that isn't his.**

To break the curse and reclaim her stolen body, Bella must join forces with a spirit dragon and confront the god of death, before the final petal falls.

Turn the page for a free preview...

# Oath of Redemption: Chapter One

*Seven Months Ago...*

Leopol's spirit stirred, a wisp of consciousness coalescing amidst the rubble of what was once the grand ballroom. Dust hung like a shroud over the remnants of opulence, the air thick with the scent of charred wood and magic turned sour. His form flickered, translucent and unstable, as if he were but a breath away from being whisked into oblivion.

Again.

This feeling, the reforming—it was familiar and yet not.

The skeletal dragon, a monstrous relic that brought faint memories, lay in a pile of bones in the jagged opening where a wall had collapsed. Beyond it lay the forest where Knox had ridden away, Eirwyn cradled in his arms. Leopol's gaze, however, was drawn downward, to the fractured mirror that lay prostrate at his feet.

A sense of urgency gripped him as he hovered closer, the broken glass reflecting his spectral visage in disjointed fragments. This form... he remembered this form but not from his time on Celawyn—from his time *before*.

His head pulsed as he tried to remember more of the before, more of his time with the dragons here. The gaps in his knowledge grated on his nerves, making his headache worsen. How could a spirit have a headache if he didn't have a body? It defied logic.

The golden apple tree stood nearby, once vibrant and heavy with fruit, trembling under an unseen assault, almost in time with the pulsing in his mind. With each pulse of nekros magic that seeped from the mirror's cracks, the tree's leaves curled inward, turning to ash upon their branches, weeping golden tears that evaporated before they could touch the earth.

Nekrotic was wrong, soul sucking, opposite of his own. It—like all magic—could be used for good or harm, but this reeked of darkness, evil, and something more. Something familiar.

As Leopol's eyes locked with his own shattered reflection, the mirror became a gateway to the past. Memories surged forth like floodwaters breaching a dam—images of an ancient library, a place of infinite knowledge where he had been in this humanoid form but also more than a mere wraith, where he had served a purpose greater than himself. Illustros, the celestial god resplendent with light and wisdom, flashed through his mind as he walked beside Leopol through the rows of shelves. A woman smiled at him proudly from the other side of the all-father god—a goddess in her own right, and her features so reminiscent of those that stared at him from the broken mirror.

Yet her name was out of reach, beyond the memory. All that remained was the feeling she'd instilled within him, even all those years ago before he had come to this realm.

The memory shifted. Another mirror materialized within his recollections, this one whole and gleaming in another part of Hartsgrove Castle, in another time. A wizard stood before it, a figure both formidable and familiar, weaving spells that echoed through the ages. And there he was, not as the apparition he was now, but majestic and powerful—a dragon whose scales shimmered with the very essence of magic.

Yet the clarity was fleeting. As the dark magic faded from the mirror and the apple tree in the center of the broken ballroom withered, doubt clouded his newfound awareness, leaving him adrift in a sea of fragmented truths. He sensed a connection to Knox, a thread woven between them by the enigmatic tapestry of lost magic. But the certainty of kinship eluded him, leaving only questions in its wake. Knox was his cousin, but also... not.

Leopol lingered in the shattered ballroom, a spirit haunted by echoes of what once was, determined to reclaim the scattered pieces of his existence. Knox and Eirwyn had said he was a ghost, which meant he was dead.

But he wasn't, not really. He couldn't be dead when he'd never really been alive. Ghosts were untethered, but he *knew* this place.

The truth of that was the most real thing he knew. Of all the scattered memories, visions, and dreams that had haunted him the past few days since awakening in this corporeal form, he knew two things to be true. He'd never really been alive, and he still had a body somewhere.

Magic hummed through this castle, calling to him to search every nook and cranny, read every book and spell, find the construct of his body that the gods had given him.

Leopol felt something tugging at the edges of his spectral form—a subtle vibration that spoke of hidden pathways and forgotten connections. Each shard of the broken mirror reflected not just his translucent image, but glimpses of landscapes and moments that seemed both familiar and alien.

One fragment showed a stone archway carved with intricate runes, another a spiral staircase descending into darkness, and a third a library shelf lined with scrolls that seemed to breathe with their own strange life. The magic coursing through Hartsgrove Castle was not merely ambient; it was sentient, deliberate, watching him with an intelligence that felt almost... calculating.

His ethereal hand hovered over the largest mirror fragment. As his translucent fingers neared the surface, the glass began to ripple like liquid mercury, its reflection shifting like a living entity. The magic within the castle walls seemed to pulse with an ancient rhythm, drawing Leopol closer to the mystery that lay just beyond his spectral perception.

A whisper, soft as a breeze yet sharp as a blade, cut through the stillness. *Not yet*, it seemed to say, the words forming not in sound but in the very essence of the magical currents surrounding him, running through him.

That voice was familiar, like a homecoming in its own right. A whisper of wind carried fragments of an ancient dialect, words that seemed to pulse with forgotten power, the translation just beyond his reach.

The mirror fragment trembled, its surface now a kaleidoscope of shifting images—glimpses of battles long forgotten, arcane rituals performed in chambers hidden from mortal eyes, and fleeting shadows of figures whose identities remained tantalizingly out of reach.

Something ancient moved just beyond his perception, a presence that felt simultaneously familiar and alien.

A sudden tremor rippled through the ballroom—not of physical movement, but of magical resonance. The broken mirror pulsed with a dim golden light, its fractured surface reflecting nothing and everything at once. Leopol felt the magic surge around him, a living thing that breathed and shifted with its own consciousness.

Threads of golden magic—gossamer-thin yet strong as steel—began to weave around his translucent form, pulling, probing, searching. Something was coming. If only he could remember, could recognize it...

The withered golden apple tree's remaining branches creaked, responding to the energy that pulsed through the castle's stone foundations. Its branches now brittle as old bones, a single golden leaf detached, spinning through the air in defiance of natural laws.

Leopol drifted closer to the tree, his ethereal form wavering like smoke caught in an imperceptible current, like the exhaled breath of some forgotten hope of the world.

Another memory flickered—broken images of arcane rituals, of power exchanges that transcended mortal understanding.

Each breath of magic seemed to pulse with recognition, as if the very stones of Hartsgrove Castle remembered him and urged him to remember in return. Leopol extended a translucent hand toward the withered golden apple tree, feeling the residual energy that still trembled within its dying branches.

It quivered, its leaves releasing a final, desperate breath of magic that intertwined with the emerging energy. Threads of golden magic swirled around him, filling him with light, hope, a vibration of knowing something important...

He blinked slowly, feeling through the magic, following the threads back to the source. The magic filled his soul, knitting his memories back together, the magic transferring out of the dying tree and into him.

A sudden tremor rippled through the ballroom floor, causing fragments of the broken mirror to shift and realign momentarily. His eyes widened where he stood next to the tree. In that fractured reflection, Leopol glimpsed movement—something darker than his own spectral form, something that did not belong. The shadows seemed to breathe with a malevolent intelligence, watching, waiting.

The nekros magic that had been seeping from the mirror's cracks began to coalesce, forming tendrils that reached out like seeking fingers. They probed the edges of Leopol's ethereal form, and he threw his hands up, the golden tendrils of magic forming a shield.

The tendrils recoiled, hissing like serpents burned by sunlight. Something ancient and malevolent pushed against the golden shield, probing for weakness. Leopol felt the magic surge through him—not just defensive, but sentient, almost hungry.

His spectral form flickered, solidifying momentarily as the nekrotic energy tested his ethereal boundaries. The shadows that breathed at the edge of his perception seemed to pulse with recognition, as if they knew something about him that he had not yet remembered.

A piece of memory surged forward—a ritual binding conducted in a chamber within this castle where time warped and contorted. The golden magic within him vibrated in sync with this hazy recollection, blending with the image he had seen in the shattered mirror earlier. This fusion produced harmonic vibrations of truth within him. It triggered the fragments of the broken mirror to emit an unearthly resonance, as though they too recalled the traumatic event.

The shadows retreated, but not in defeat. Their withdrawal felt calculated, like a predator biding its time before the next attack. Leopol understood–or rather, felt–that something was gathering strength, preparing for a more calculated assault.

He had to be ready. Somehow, he was the best hope of defeating it.

The golden magic within him pulsed, like a living thing that remembered pathways and connections long forgotten. He remembered the first time this magic had flown through his dragon body, bringing him to so-called life after the–the memory failed him.

The magic tugged at him, urging movement, exploration instead of introspection. Each fragment of the broken mirror now seemed to vibrate with potential–portals waiting to be understood, memories waiting to be unlocked.

A distant rumble echoed through the castle's stone corridors, like the deep growl of some ancient, awakening beast. The last of the shadows disappeared–and with it, the images in the broken pieces of glass. For the first time since awakening, Leopol was truly alone.

## Oath of Redemption: Chapter Two

*Present Day...*

Bella followed Eirwyn into the sunroom, fingers flicking as she concentrated on holding the spell to animate the potted rose. The golden sunlight that bathed the space brought no warmth to her translucent skin. The rose petals brushed her cheek, though she couldn't feel them—only the memory of touch remained.

She hadn't held anything physical in seven months. Not since the wizard stole her body, tethering her soul to this single fragile rose. If it died, she died. Simple as that. It was her curse, her punishment, her prison.

Eirwyn's voice broke through her thoughts. "Isn't it wonderful, Bella? To have you here—it's like the old days, reborn from ashes."

Bella nodded, the corners of her mouth twitching upward. "We never just sat in a sunroom in a castle, Eirwyn. The good old days involved the tavern, spilled ale, stinky peasants, and your light shows entertaining the masses. Not this..."

"Peacefulness?" Eirwyn smirked, waving to a table by the window. "It doesn't seem real to me either, and I grew up in the palaces! Here, put your rose here before you tire out your magic carrying it around."

Bella floated toward her and assessed the room, thinking about their shared history.

She'd been catching up with Eirwyn all day as if no time had passed between them. As if Eirwyn's brother, Gastone, hadn't created a rift between them when he'd married Bella. As if Bella herself hadn't set aside their friendship for her new husband in her quest for knowledge. As if Eirwyn's mate, Knox, hadn't battled Gastone on the castle roof, triggering the events that led to Gastone's death and Bella's widespread curse on the land.

Eirwyn didn't seem to care how many mistakes Bella had made. She'd been welcomed with open arms by both Eirwyn and her mate, Knox, both of whom were apparently ruling the Feral Forest as king and queen.

It didn't surprise Bella, though. Eirwyn was born to rule; the princess never should have sought refuge in Bella's tavern as a child. But her father and Lailant had insisted that Eirwyn's presence was not going to bring about their ruin, so Bella had taken the little girl under her tutelage. It had been the last request he'd made before being called to war, leaving her to manage the tavern.

Now they were both all grown up, both queens, even though Bella hadn't had a chance to rule and prove herself. That was why she was here, after all, to fix the curse and make it up to her people.

The sunroom was beautiful, quiet, untouched. And maybe, just maybe, it could serve as a sanctuary to begin her work undoing the damage she'd caused—a place to weave magic and unlock secrets from nature's depths.

"Are you sure this space isn't already in use?" she asked.

Eirwyn laughed. "Hardly. It's a glorified sitting room. Empty and waiting for you."

Bella stepped further in, scanning shelves and tables, her mind already spinning with ideas. It was a suitable location for her to set up a makeshift laboratory. She would need to get supplies and ingredients, but that was a challenge she was ready to face. Her years of training and experience had prepared her for this moment.

"I have some old shelves in the storage room that we can use," Eirwyn offered, eager and helpful as always. Her friend knew Bella would want books everywhere. "And I can start gathering some herbs from the inside garden for you. Unfortunately, the long winter has kept us from spring planting."

Eirwyn had explained her concerns about the lack of food being planted for the growing nation of forest people, but there was little they could do to make the lingering winter end and force spring to arrive.

Bella smiled gratefully at Eirwyn's offer. Having a friend like her was truly a blessing Bella didn't deserve. "Very well, if you're sure I won't be intruding here."

"Never an intrusion," Eirwyn said, running her finger over the top of the central table near the chaise to inspect the layer of dust. She held up her finger. "See? No one uses this room. But with the garden doors, it's easy access for when the garden does start producing."

Bella carefully used her magic to set the budding rose down on a small table behind the glass double doors that led outside. Eirwyn was right, the furniture in this room was slightly dusty from disuse.

The glass door flew open with a gust of wind, banging into the table.

"Eirwyn, where is the—?"

The movement startled her and her hand jolted, the pot slipping—shattering on the floor.

"No!" Her cry echoed, vibrating the walls. The earth shook, soil scattered, and petals fluttered.

Bella dropped to her knees, hands trembling above the broken rose. Her entire being ached, torn as though she'd been physically struck. Her soul strained to reach the damaged tether.

The once-beautiful flower now lay ruined, mirroring the state of her life. Clusters of soil clung to the twisted roots, and the vibrant orange rose drooped with the weight of its own petals. Some lay fluttering on the ground around it, while others still clung to the stem, barely holding on.

"I'm so sorry," the man said, stepping forward. "Are we turning this into a conservatory now? I wasn't aware we were adding new gardeners before the eastern wing was finished."

Bella's head snapped up. His calm voice rubbed like sandpaper against an open wound.

"It's not just a plant," she snapped. The furniture behind her shuddered an inch across the floor.

Eirwyn raised her hands, her eyes wide. "Bella—"

The man lifted a brow, the bright light masking his features. "My apologies. Shall I call it a specific type of rose? Are you the new gardener, then?"

Magic crackled in the air, pulsing in time with her rage. "I don't know what type of rose it is. All I know is it's the tether to my soul."

The man stiffened. "Tether? Wait, let's talk this through rationally—"

"Rationally?" Her hands clenched into fists. "You nearly killed me, and you want calm discussion?"

Before he could answer, her father Wulfric entered the room. "What's with all the rattling and yelling? Who's upsetting my daughter?"

Wulfric's wolf-like features—ears, nose, tail—hadn't changed the comfort she found in her father's presence. But he couldn't touch her, hold her like he used to when they'd lost her mother.

He prowled toward her, his frown of concern making her feel like at least one person in the land still had her best interests at heart. It made her feel less alone after half a year of being so lonely in this form.

"Just a klutz who's going to get me killed," Bella cried, blinking furiously to keep the tears at bay. Logically, she knew she was overreacting, but she struggled to hold in her emotions.

Her father's eyes softened, and the tears grew bigger.

The man in the doorway to the garden tugged on his jacket. "Wait, who said anything about killing—"

"I did, you idiot! The evil wizard took possession of my body and tethered my soul to that rose. It dies, I die. Understand now?" The air crackled around her, charged with the force of her indignation.

Wulfric crouched to inspect the rose while Bella bit her lip, unsure if she should cry or scream.

The man's gaze returned to her. "Daughter? Then you must be—"

"Bellatrix," Eirwyn said. "Queen of Busparia. Lord Leopol, meet my dear friend Bella. Bella, this is Leopol, our royal advisor and right-hand man."

The tension in the room shifted, becoming something more profound, a recognition of invisible threads that knew something she didn't. The man rubbed a ring on his finger

JANE POLLER

and stepped forward, bending into a deep bow. "Your Majesty, forgive me."

Guilt raced up her spine, and she twisted her hands in her skirt with a loud sigh as she waved her hand. "Oh, none of that majesty business. I haven't done anything to earn that title. Until I fix this curse on the people, just call me Bella."

She had a mission to accomplish before her soul descended into the underworld for judgment—before the last petal on the rose fell, that is. She was in a race against time and didn't have, well, time for titles of grandeur like your majesty.

---

The moment her pot shattered, something inside Leopol twisted, freezing him to the moment while he analyzed and assessed.

He hadn't felt anything in months. But the crack of the pot, her broken cry—and the powerful tether of golden magic linking her to the flower—it all sent a pulse through him.

Leopol's chest tightened as the gravity of his carelessness settled upon him like chains. He watched, horrified, as Eirwyn cradled the fragile rose in her hands, her fingers working with delicate urgency. Leopol whispered a simple spell, much easier to do now than when he'd first woken up seven months ago.

A yellow-orange smoke-like line of magic flowed from Bella to the rose. The air hung heavy with tension, and within it floated an unspoken truth that Leopol could no longer ignore—the rose was more than just a plant; it was an anchor to Bella's very soul.

522

Tears clung to her lashes, and he walked toward her, his feet not making a sound in this form. There was something about her that drew him inexplicably closer.

"I'm so sorry, Your Majesty. I didn't mean to hurt you or your tether," he said softly, reaching for her hand and bowing, an outdated habit that he'd been unable to break these past few months. It'd always brought a stab of pain, a reminder that he was no longer who he once was.

He froze as his hand contacted hers.

Contact.

The touch sang through him, burning into his core. A connection he hadn't known he craved until now. For the first time in months, his soul ached for something other than his own body and memories. A shadow phantom feeling of his draconic form hit him like a punch to the gut, heat and desire flooding his psyche. Even in that draconic physical form, he hadn't ached like this. Emotion, heat, and desire threatened to overwhelm him.

He breathed deeply, slowly, trying to maintain control as his spirit vibrated with *something* he didn't know how to identify.

He frowned, eager to puzzle out this feeling and why she triggered it. She was in spirit form, like him, but it couldn't just be that.

She turned sharply, her hazel eyes widening as she met his gaze, her fingers gripping his tightly in shock. Her lips were full and curved in a perfect bow, inviting and tempting even as they parted in surprise. Her gasp was like music to his ears, echoing in his mind as he drank in her beauty.

Their magic swirled around them, crackling with recognition.

Her oval face was filled with surprise and her wide hazel eyes sparkled with wonder. Her skin was smooth and glowing, highlighting her high cheekbones, delicate features, and the light dusting of bronzed freckles across her nose.

Her lips parted, light from the window falling on her pert little nose, the light seeming to gather around them as their magic danced, testing each other on a plane most people couldn't see.

The shaking fingers of her other hand reached up as if in slow motion, settling on his chest.

"You're a ghost like me," she whispered, awed.

Leopol swallowed. "Not a ghost. Not exactly."

Their fingers remained locked, and he covered her other hand on his chest, just over where his heart had been. Light glowed faintly from her rose, the golden tether pulsing between them as her magic flared.

Her hand trembled. "I didn't know... I thought I was alone."

"You're not," Leopol said, fiercely. She wasn't a ghost or alone.

He knew she was a spirit; if she was a ghost, she wouldn't be tied to the rose. He didn't know why they were both in the same place at the same time. But they were together now, bound by more than accident and more than magic.

The pieces of her story, her soul, the sorrow in her gaze—they drew him in, and he would not let her go. Lightning shot through him with a rush of heat, magic, and belonging.

His hand shook, and when his thumb caressed the back of her hand, her breath hitched. The castle, his body, his memories, the curses, the war—all of it faded beneath the sheer force of this moment, this touch, this woman.

*Mate.*

The word slammed into him, unbidden and undeniable.

Nonsensical. Mates were for the living. Not for him. Not for a spirit construct like him or a spirit tied to a rose like her.

Yet he couldn't deny how his lips tingled with a desire to feel the softness of hers against his own. Imagining the warmth and plumpness of her lips under his, he lifted her fingers and kissed the soft skin of her knuckles. Magic and need flared between them, flowing through them, swirling together for one brief, intense moment that should've brought him to his knees.

Bella gasped, swaying closer as their magic swirled around them faintly. "What—what is that?"

Eirwyn hmmed where she knelt. "Interesting."

"Very," Wulfric said, but Leopol couldn't look away from Bella to see what they were talking about.

Bella had no such problem. Blinking swiftly, she looked down at their hands but didn't step away from him. Her eyes widened as she gasped again, and he nearly groaned at the way her mouth bowed up.

"What is that?"

At her words, he finally glanced down to see the rose flickering on the floor, its petals glowing faintly. A tether of golden energy pulsed between her and the flower.

His jaw clenched as memories of spells and books swam in his mind, as if touching her had released some of what had been withheld from him. Some of the puzzle pieces of who he was slipped into place, forming a hazy picture.

He blinked, focusing on her, always her. "You're tied to the rose, you said?"

She swallowed hard and nodded. "If it dies, I die. But it's never pulsed before. I've never been able to see the threads of magic before..."

A sharp possessive fury burned through him at the thought of her dying for real. Unacceptable.

His hands curled into fists. He didn't know her, had no claim on her. But every instinct in his soul rebelled at the idea of her slipping away.

The fates had bound them together. He would not even let death tear them apart. If he admitted it now, though, it'd scare her away. She appeared human, fragile, delicate, graceful, and beautiful.

Bella stepped away, crouching to inspect the rose. As she released him, some of the brightness of the magic swirling around them faded.

He tugged on the hem of his blue dinner jacket and stepped back, using magic to close the glass doors as softly as he could.

"Wait, why is it no longer glowing? It looked like it was getting healthier, didn't it? Or was that just a wish?" Bella asked, questions flying. She was clearly intelligent, inquisitive, everything he'd hoped for in a mate.

He had a hard time reconciling her with what he knew of her.

This was the evil queen Scarlet had been so angry with. Wulfric's daughter and Eirwyn's friend, a former tavern owner who had kept her safe from the evil king Gastone. The same king who had married Bella before sending Scarlet to kill Eirwyn.

The same king who had wrought nekrosan magic through the mirror, animating the skeletal dragon to attack Knox and Eirwyn when they'd reached Hartsgrove, wakening Leopol from wherever his spirit had been slumbering.

The same queen who—when the king had died—had

made an illegal blood magic potion from his heart, releasing a curse and wiping out an entire city on the edge of the forest.

No wonder he'd felt such power. The tendrils of his magic probed the edges of hers, almost like a taste on his tongue. She didn't feel like a nekromancer. She was an enigma, an anomaly that he wasn't sure he'd ever come across in however many hundreds of years he'd been on this world.

"No, I saw it too, although I didn't see any magic threads. Just the faintly glowing rose as it seemed to perk up," Eirwyn said.

"Right, well, looks like we need a better solution for the rose. I'll hunt down a better pot," Wulfric said, standing.

Leopol stepped forward, almost in a clumsy lurch, eager to impress his mate. "I can fix it. Here," he said, waving his hands and kneeling. With a frown of concentration, he wove the threads of magic and knit the pot back together, the seams glowing.

"How are you doing that?" Bella asked, but Leopol ignored her as he fixed her pot, weaving in a protection spell while he was at it, carving the runes into the pot itself like a hot brand.

"Leopol is the strongest, most knowledgeable sorcerer I've ever met," Eirwyn said softly. Bella gasped, and Eirwyn continued as if she'd spoken. "Exactly. Even among all the years of formal schooling and the best tutors the kingdom could buy, Leopol out magics them all. He just can't touch anything living."

Bella seemed to vibrate, the furniture in the room shaking along with her. "Just like me," she whispered.

At that moment, he breathed a sigh of relief. "There, all

fixed. It should withstand being dropped now. Wulfric, would you care to test it before one of you re-plants the rose?"

Wulfric picked up the plain brown pot and dropped it. It bounced, so he picked it up and stood, dropping it from higher, then again with as much force as he could muster. Still, it held up, and Leopol breathed a sigh of relief as he stood.

Eirwyn beamed up at Leopol as she gathered up the plant. "Excellent, I know that was weighing on your mind, Bella. Thank you, Leopol."

Wulfric helped Eirwyn plant the rose, but Bella stood and launched herself into Leopol's arms. He gasped, gathering her tight against his body in his first hug since waking. It felt... like coming home.

The moment her arms wrapped around him, Leopol's breath caught in his throat. Her ethereal form pressed against him, cool and light as mist, yet with a surprising solidity he hadn't expected. His hands instinctively splayed across her back, fingers tracing the delicate lines of her spirit-form.

"Thank you," Bella whispered, her voice trembling. "For saving the pot and helping me protect the rose. Thank you for... understanding."

Wulfric cleared his throat. "I see you two are... becoming acquainted."

Bella pulled back, her translucent cheeks flushing a soft golden hue even though she didn't drop her hands from around his neck. Leopol noticed how the magic threads between her and the rose pulsed differently now—stronger, more vibrant.

"I apologize," she mumbled. "I'm not usually so... physical."

Leopol wanted to reassure her. "No need. It was pleasant."

Her cheeks turned pink, even under the translucence of her spirit form. "I just—I haven't been able to touch anyone in months."

Leopol's fingers hovered on her waist, uncertain. "Neither have I."

Wulfric cleared his throat, watching them with a mixture of curiosity and something deeper—a protective father's careful observation. "Perhaps we should discuss how you two seem to interact when neither of you can typically touch physical objects."

Eirwyn's eyes sparkled with intrigue. "Exactly. Something's different here. The rose perked up when you touched—both times, actually."

Bella dropped her arms and stepped back, turning to the potted rose now in Wulfric's hands. He set it on a small, low table next to a settee in the middle of the room—still where it could get light from the tall, glass windows, but not where it could be knocked over by someone opening the garden door.

Eirwyn's knowing smile suggested there was more happening than a simple embrace, her eyes darting between Bella and Leopol. Something unspoken passed between them—a recognition of the magical connection that had just sparked to life.

Bella stepped toward her rose and tapped her chin as the magic swirling around it faded. Still strong, but it no longer pulsed. She muttered under her breath, and Leopol watched, waiting to see what her brilliant mind would deduce.

"Leopol has been searching for answers about his own

condition for months," Eirwyn interjected. "Perhaps you two might find more together than apart."

Leopol nodded in a soft bow, murmuring, "It'd be my pleasure."

Bella blushed again, and Eirwyn chuckled. "I'll leave you to discuss the details then, so I can get ready for the council dinner tonight."

Leopol knew this was a bigger meeting than the normal monthly meetings with the council. The new leaders in the Feral Forest—Robins, druids, and elected villagers who reported to Knox and Eirwyn—would want to know about the battle at the Winter Palace. Scarlet and Wulfric were supposed to report tonight on what had happened, but he wondered if Bella would attend.

After all, spirits didn't need to eat dinner.

Eirwyn smiled and reached for Bella's hand before she remembered they couldn't touch. She cleared her throat and said, "Bella, I'm so glad you're here. I know this is a chaotic time for you, but I want you to think of this castle as your home, and Leopol knows every inch of this place better than anyone. I've assigned you to the Rose Room, obviously. Leopol, can you escort her there when you're done showing her around the sunroom?"

Leopol nodded, his gaze connecting with Bella's once more.

"Wulfric, come with me, please."

"But—"

Eirwyn paused in the doorway and gave the Growler a heavy look. "We need to prepare what you're going to report tonight."

He just sighed and narrowed his eyes on Leopol. Leopol lifted his chin and held the man's gaze. Finally, he just snorted and followed Eirwyn toward the door.

Eirwyn chuckled, her footsteps fading as she smiled. "I'll see you both at dinner, then."

Then he was left alone with the only other spirit he'd ever met. His mate.

# Oath of Redemption: Chapter Three

"Come, sit and talk with me," Leopol said, settling on the velvet settee, his voice sending a shiver down Bella's spine. "Tell me your story so I might know how to best help you."

"Why would you help me?" Her voice was a whisper, and her eyes narrowed, studying Leopol with a mixture of suspicion and intrigue. She'd never met anyone like him, much less another spirit. Her fingers traced the edge of her golden gown—a nervous gesture that betrayed her carefully constructed composure.

She couldn't help but stare at him, this spirit who had so thoroughly captured her attention since he'd walked through the door like he owned the place.

The man was almost as tall and muscular as her father, Wulfric. Indeed, they both had hair that was too long by society's standards. Leopol's hair was tousled, as if he had been running his hands through it in frustration and fell just above his ears. Her fingers tingled to brush it out of his eyes.

Her fingers tingled. She hadn't felt anything in months,

nothing but grief and heartache and anger. But he made her feel so much more.

Leopol matched her calculating gaze, ever watchful with those brilliant blue eyes that were so bright, they could be ice or gemstone. Colors were muted in this form, and she could almost see through him. But those eyes were as vivid as if she were still living.

"Let's call it mutual curiosity. I've searched every grimoire, every ancient text and spell book in this castle. I know things about magical curses that most scholars would kill to understand, and your magic is... unique. I'd like to get to know you."

Her hazel eyes narrowed, her foot tapping where she stood. "You mean to study me."

He arched a brow. "Study, examine, inspect, probe—call it what you will, but I promise not to harm you. It's just, I've not been able to...touch...anyone else since I woke like this last year. Yet somehow, I can touch you..."

His words drifted into the space between them, teasing them both with the promise of more touching, more exploring. The tension and magic flared along with his eyes. She was as attracted to him as he was to her. She felt it as surely as she could see their magic swirling in the air earlier while they were touching. That alone led to so many questions, and curiosity—the need to know everything so that she could best help save others—had always been her downfall.

She licked her lips. "And what makes you think your knowledge applies to my particular curse?"

Her heart seemed to race as his gaze dipped down to her lips, a phantom fluttering feeling in her stomach at his smile reminding her of the first crush of her youth.

The sharp angles of his face, the prominent jawline and cheekbones that hinted at a life of intensity and purpose, it all painted a heart-stopping package that made her lick her lips in surprise and anticipation. She hadn't expected to meet someone who made her entire body sit up and take notice. Not even Gastone had done that; she'd been more attracted to his power and what he could offer her than the actual man himself.

"We won't know if we don't try, now will we? Aren't you just a little bit curious? What do you have to lose?"

Her eyes shuttered at his words, and she finally sank onto the settee, frowning slightly.

"Everything," she whispered, her voice catching. "I have everything to lose."

"You saw a sampling of what magic I could wield earlier. I can teach you to protect yourself too, even in this form. Tell me your story. Let me help," he whispered, his fingers along the back of the couch playing with her hair.

Normally, she was very protective of her space, but when he was near, when he touched her, it was as if her soul settled into a soft hum of peace.

Leopol's clothes were outdated but of fine quality. She hated judging people by their clothing, but she'd learned a lot by doing so during the decade she'd managed the tavern. Despite the fatigue on his face, determination shone through, giving him an air of strength and resilience. This man was no ordinary noble, to still be hanging around as a spirit.

Ghosts were rare, the things of myths and story books. Spirits even more so. She'd done enough research after her own incident that left her in this damn incorporeal form. She knew she wasn't a ghost, but people just saw a semi-transparent being and lumped them all together.

For him to be a spirit, he had to have been powerful or experienced a powerful death to be here like this.

She took a deep breath and leaned her head back further into his touch even as she decided to test him. She closed her eyes and tried to feel the magic around her.

"The magic you used earlier. What was it, and how did you do it?"

"Synthara for the protective barrier around it and vitas to preserve the flower itself, using ancient runes to bind it all together into a permanently enchanted object. As a dragon, my magic is inherent, and something I just feel. I don't need spells, although they certainly help."

Her eyes widened. "You're a dragon?"

He ran a hand over the back of his neck and smiled sheepishly as he turned and placed his hand along the back of the couch. His eyes turned guarded, though, and she wondered what he was hiding. "Yes, Knox and I are both full-blooded dragons. From what Eirwyn tells me, we might be the only two dragons left on the continent, if not the entire world."

Bella's mouth opened and closed, then she turned away from him to process. Eventually she said, "That sounds lonely."

He nodded, tilting his body to face her, his other hand resting on the velvet between them. He ran his fingers over it, and Bella wondered if he could actually feel it. "Not as lonely as being a spirit."

They shared a commiserating smile before she continued, touching the velvet fabric near his hand. She couldn't feel it. She missed such simple things in life.

"I used to think it would be amazing to be born with magic instead of learning it. I was never happy with what I had and always wanted to learn more. Since becoming a ghost, my magic has gone all wrong."

Leopol's chuckle filled the room like a gentle melody,

revealing straight white teeth and deep dimples. His transparent form seemed to glimmer and sparkle in response to his joy, making him look even more ethereal.

As Bella looked at Leopol's mischievous, smiling face, she couldn't help but reach out and lightly touch his arm. His skin felt cool to the touch but also oddly comforting, like soft silk against her fingertips. A warm sensation spread from her hand throughout her whole body, causing her stomach to flutter with excitement.

"You're a spirit, not a ghost, but let me guess. The more emotional you are, the harder it is to control?" His grin was like the first sip of a sweet and potent potion, filling her with a heady and electrifying rush. She could quickly become addicted to him.

Her eyes widened in surprise, and she leaned forward. "Yes! How did you know?"

He settled his hand along the back of the couch as he talked. "When I first arrived, my father taught me to channel magic through meditation and breathing exercises. But when I woke up like this, I found my emotions all over the place. It was like I was a youngling learning to fly all over again, and my innate magic fluctuated with my emotions."

It was a weird way to talk about being born, but she sighed, letting the thought go as her shoulders slumped against the settee.

"That's exactly how I feel about it. It's more difficult to learn how to control this magic inside of me than it was when I first learned spells as a child."

Humans weren't typically born with innate magic. Those who were often became healers like her mother. Drakin, shifters, and others had magic, but humans? Not so much.

One of his brows dipped in confusion. "But when you were emotional earlier, you seemed to have a decent control on it. None of the tables flipped over or anything."

Bella chuckled and leaned her head back on the couch. His hand brushed her neck, but she didn't pull away. It was like her body craved his touch, after almost a year without touching anyone. She'd come a long way from waiting tables and being sick and tired of people touching her without her permission.

"If that's the measure of having control, then yes, I'd say I'm learning slowly but surely. Doesn't change the fact that if I could go back, I'd do it all differently."

"What kind of magic do you wield as a human? I've studied for months about the curse on the people, but I still haven't figured out the mechanics of it." He paused, tilting his head. "Is that what you would do differently? The curse on them?"

She nodded as she thought, frowning. His spell on the pot and rose had been more complex than a simple binding; she could sense that when he'd done it. She sat up, and his hand dropped away. With eyes closed, she felt the magic fade, grow more muted somehow.

She sat back, his hand brushing against her shoulder, and the magic flared.

Why could she sense his magic? It would need more experimentation, but the strength of magic when they touched was—abnormal. What did it mean?

If she wanted to find out, if she wanted to experiment on this bond and the magic between them as much as he did, then she would have to trust him, at least a little.

"The curse is just one of the things I'd change."

Her mind drifted to all the mistakes she'd made. Each memory felt like a blow to her being, leaving bruises that would never fully heal. Her thoughts became tangled like a thorny vine, each misstep and regret looping together until it formed a dense and impenetrable barrier in her mind.

"What do you mean?" The smoothness of his voice was calming, and she opened up to him like a blossoming rose.

She rubbed her forehead and closed her eyes. "What do you know of my story? What has Eirwyn told you?"

The silence stretched, and the faint echo of birds chirping outside drew her eyes to the window.

She was going to be upfront and honest about her mistakes. If he was to be an ally—and she desperately wanted an ally who knew what she was going through—then she wanted to have everything laid out in the open.

"Not much. They've been preoccupied with the drag-onling egg's delivery and before that, the restoration of the castle. I've attended all the monthly council dinners, and there are a lot of complaints about you. But there's two sides to every story. Tell me everything," he said, his fingers winding into her hair.

She laughed, a brittle sound. "Everything is a very long story. And trust does not come easily to those who have been betrayed as thoroughly as I have."

It was because of her trust in Gastone that she hesitated to trust Leopol now. Logically, she knew it. Eirwyn trusted him, so she should too.

He laid a hand on hers, and she froze before her eyes swung to his. The electric shock of being able to touch someone confirmed that he was integral to her survival. The magic that she could somehow see now—but only when they were touching—showed the rose pulsing with strength and magic and vitas.

"Tell me anyway," he growled low and deep. Her eyes widened at his words. Something in his tone—a blend of command and compassion and raw need—drew her forward. Finally, she nodded.

"My entire existence is bound to this flower," she continued, her voice raw with a vulnerability she didn't intend to reveal. "One wrong move, one miscalculation, and I could vanish forever. Forgive me if I'm not eager to trust another magical being with my fate. I'm more nervous than I care to admit that you wove magic anywhere near it, much less such powerful magic."

"I'll never hurt you, Bellakari. I swear it on the gods," Leopol said. The fervency in his words made her turn to him.

His gray-blue eyes pierced into her soul as he listened unlike any man ever had before, not even Gastone. None of the men who had frequented the tavern had ever sat with such an enraptured, intense expression as he listened and asked clarifying, insightful questions about her story.

His stare was like a caress, and her spine straightened under his scrutiny. With such a deep and soothing voice, he calmed some of the chaos that has consumed Bella's mind, and she paused, taking a deep breath to control her rioting emotions.

Half of her was distracted by him, but the other half was cataloging all the questions and experiments she wanted to complete with him, with their combined magic, and more.

Bella's breath hitched as memories clawed their way to the surface—a torrent of anguish and longing that pushed away her fascination with Leopol. She looked away, her gaze finding the sunlit plant lifeline standing proudly on the small table in front of her.

"Magic... has always been a double-edged sword for me," she started, her voice quivering like the delicate petals

539

of her counterpart. "When my husband was murdered, a voice urged me to rip out his heart and make a potion from it. And yes, I know that nekrotic blood spells and potions are forbidden. But grief drowned out my consciousness, rationality...humanity. It was almost like I was in a trance as I drank it."

He sucked in a breath. "It sounds very traumatic."

"Oh, it was. It transformed my body into a drakin of some sort. The spell twisted my body so much—there was so much pain—and somehow I cursed thousands of innocents, knocked my spirit out of my body, and found myself tethered to this rose, which grew from Gastone's ashes."

The walls of the chamber pulsed with her anguish, slight tremors that sent whispers through the tapestries. Leopol, ever attentive, caressed the back of her neck, offering comfort without being pushy. She wanted to turn away from him; she didn't need him. But oh, it was so good to finally have someone to talk to, someone who understood, someone to touch. She couldn't bring herself to push him away like she'd done with all the men before.

"That's a lot of pain and change all at once. Overwhelming," he said.

Bella choked out, her laugh as bitter as wormwood. "Every day, I am reminded of my failure, of my need to fix it before it's too late. I've worked tirelessly ever since to find a spell or potion or combination that will separate the living from the non-living objects they've been cursed to become."

"What have you done so far to find a solution?" he asked.

The storm of regret lashed out from her core, and Leopol's hand fell from her neck as she sat up straighter on the couch. Without his touch to anchor her, the emotions swept through her like a malevolent tornado. Her body itched, and she wanted to scratch under her skin.

Experience had taught her to jump up and move. She paced around the table toward the windows as the room shuddered more violently, a mirror to Bella's inner turmoil.

"I started experimenting on the plants around the castle that had merged with objects, but the plants all died. I thought I'd gained progress, and a servant tried one of my potions on a kitten—it didn't end well."

"The kitten or the servant?"

Bella snorted, her magic flaring at the memory and the glass doors rattling open. "Both. All the kittens died, one by one. Then both the servants that had been trapped with me..."

She caught her reflection in the glass of the window—a ghost of a queen, haunted by specters of her own making.

"There's no changing the past. All I can do is try to make the future better, and it's all up to me. But I only have as long as the rose lives," she said, tears streaming down her cheeks as the emotions inside her built.

Her form wavered, ethereal in the sunlight as she looked around for escape. "I–I need air, space to think... to breathe. Excuse me."

Without another word, she whirled around and fled from the room, her dress a swirl of yellow and red silk. The garden called to her, promising a reprieve from the intensity of the past. As she moved, the castle itself seemed to groan in sympathy, the stones no match for the force of her sorrow.

Grab your copy...<br>
vinci-books.com/OathofRedemption

# About the Author

Jane Poller read her way through middle school. Romance books got her through countless life changes... moves, degrees, having kids, deployments, teaching high school, international living, health coaching, running a wellness business, homeschooling, and more. She finally gave in to the characters in her head demanding their stories be told. She's an avid reader of historical romance but writes primarily fantasy romance and contemporary small-town romance. Look for the fantasy romance series on her website. The Crimson Creek series is a contemporary steamy small-town romance set in a fictional town in Texas. Speaking of, she lives in Texas with her middle school sweetheart. He's her real-life hero, Army veteran, and the inspiration for her stories. His interest in Role playing games inspired her love of fantasy romance too. Without him, the fantasy stories wouldn't exist. When she's not doing all the things, she's reading and writing. Or arguing with her characters, who refuse to do what she wants. But that's par for the course, since she's currently raising teenagers and two dogs. Those reviews really brighten her day and are much appreciated.